NG

MIDLOTHIAN LIBRARY SERVICE

Please return/renew this ... To
renew please give yo... ... y
be made in person, o... ...
www.midl...gov...

STEAMPUNK!

AN ANTHOLOGY OF FANTASTICALLY
RICH AND STRANGE STORIES

EDITED BY
KELLY LINK
&
GAVIN J. GRANT

First published 2011 by Walker Books Ltd
87 Vauxhall Walk, London SE11 5HJ

This edition published 2012

2 4 6 8 10 9 7 5 3 1

FOR URSULA

CONTENTS

INTRODUCTION

Orphans use the puppet of a dead man to take control of their lives. A girl confronts the Grand Technomancer, Most Mighty Mechanician and Highest of the High Artificier Adepts. Another girl, who might be from another universe, stuns everyone when she pulls out her handmade Reality Gun.

Welcome to fourteen steampunk visions of the past, the future, and the not quite today.

Depending on whom you believe, steampunk has been exploding into the world for the last hundred years (thank you, Monsieur Jules Verne) or maybe the last twenty-five (when the term was first used by K. W. Jeter in a letter to *Locus* magazine). We have had fabulous fun working with this baker's dozen of authors, investigating some of the more fascinating nooks and crannies of the genre.

You'll find the requisite number of gaslit alleys, intrepid urchins, steam-powered machines, and technologies that never were. Those are the basic accoutrements that no self-respecting steampunk anthology could be without, but as we assembled the book (filing down this story here, finding the right solder to put these two ideas together there), we discovered that steampunk has gone far beyond these markers. The two Philips (Reeve and Pullman, respectively) brought moving cities and armored polar bears. Alan Moore and Kevin O'Neill's *The League of Extraordinary Gentlemen* brought nineteenth-century London to a halt. Cherie Priest introduced zombies (*Boneshaker*), Gail Carriger introduced vampires (*Soulless*), and Jeff and Ann VanderMeer brought it all together in *Steampunk* and *Steampunk II*.

Makers and artists have taken the romance and adventure of steampunk and remixed, reinvented, and remade the genre from whole cloth — and, yes, brass widgets. We've spent hours wandering through the online galleries on Etsy and Flickr, marveling at the clockwork insects, corsets, art, hats, gloves, canes, modded computers, and even a steampunk house (*want!*), and we love the DIY craftiness that keeps inspiring more decadent and more useful machines and toys.

The continuing reinterpretation of the steampunk idea made us ask the writers for stories that explored and expanded their own ideas of what steampunk could be. So we have a book of mad inventors, child mechanics, mysterious murderers, revolutionary motorists, steampunk fairies, and monopoly-breaking schoolgirls, whose stories are set in Canada, New Zealand, Wales, ancient Rome, future Australia, alternate California, and even the postapocalypse — everywhere *except* Victorian London.

Kelly Link and Gavin J. Grant

Some Fortunate Future Day

{ CASSANDRA CLARE }

When I have seen by Time's fell hand defac'd
The rich-proud cost of outworn buried age;
When sometime lofty towers I see down-raz'd,
And brass eternal slave to mortal rage;
When I have seen . . . the kingdom of the shore,
And the firm soil win of the watery main,
Increasing store with loss, and loss with store;
When I have seen such interchange of state,
Or state itself confounded to decay;
Ruin hath taught me thus to ruminate —
That Time will come and take my love away. . . .

— William Shakespeare, Sonnet LXIV

Time is many things, her father told her. Time is a circle, and time is a great turning gear that cannot be stopped, and time is a river that carries away what you love.

When he said that, he looked at Rose's mother's portrait, hanging over their fireplace mantel. He had invented his time device only a few short months after she had died. It had always been one of his greatest regrets in life, though Rose sometimes wondered whether he could have invented it at all without the all-consuming power of grief to drive him. Most of his other inventions did not work nearly as well. The garden robot often digs up flowers instead of weeds. The mechanical cook can make only one kind of soup. And the talking dolls never tell Rose what she wants to hear.

"Do you think he's ever coming back?" says Ellen. She means Rose's father. She is the dark-haired talking doll, the saucy one. She likes to dance around the room, showing her ankles. She arranges the sugar cubes in the tea service to form rude words. "Perhaps he has taken to drink. I hear that is common among soldiers."

"Shush," says Cordelia. Cordelia is the gentle doll, redheaded and quiet. "Ladies should not speak of such things." She turns to Rose. "Would you like more tea?"

Rose accepts more tea, though it is now more like hot water flavored with a few leaves from the garden than real tea. She ran out of real tea months ago. There had been a time when food and tea and household goods were regularly delivered by the grocer's boy from the nearby town. It was weeks after he stopped coming that Rose got up the nerve to put on her bonnet, pick a few coins from the box on the mantel, and walk alone into town.

It was then that she realized why the grocer's boy had stopped coming.

The town was flattened. Great zigzagging cracks ran through

the streets, steam still pouring out of them. Great sinkholes had opened in the ground, houses half tipped to the side.

She wondered how she hadn't heard the destruction, though her house is more than a mile away. But then, airships flew overhead almost every night, dropping incendiaries into the nearby forest, hoping to flush out spies and deserters. Perhaps she was simply used to it.

She reached the edge of one great pit and stared down into it. She could see the top of the church spire sticking up, nearly reaching the top of the sinkhole. All around was the smell of decay. She wondered if the townsfolk had taken refuge in the church when the Wyrms came — she'd seen pictures of Wyrm fighters before, enormous, riveted copper tubes covered with incendiary bombs. She decided that her father was right. Towns were dangerous places for young ladies on their own.

"We're very happy here, aren't we?" says Cordelia in her tinny doll's voice.

"Oh, yes," says Rose, sloshing the tinted water in her cup. "Very happy."

When Rose was eight, her father bought her a white bunny rabbit as a pet. At first she took good care of it, stroking its long silky ears with her fingers, feeding it lettuce from her hands. One day while she held it in her arms like a baby, letting it nibble a carrot from her fingertips, it sank its teeth into her skin, not knowing where the carrot ended and Rose began. She screamed and dashed it to the floor. She was immediately sorry, but it was no use: the bunny was dead, and Rose was inconsolable.

That was when her father showed her the time device.

It has been almost six months since her father left and went to the war. Though she hasn't been marking the calendar, Rose can tell that she is outgrowing her dresses. They are too tight in the bosom now and too short. Not that it matters, when there is no one to see her.

She goes out to the garden in the morning to gather ingredients for the cook. The cook used to make all sorts of things, but now it is broken and it makes only soup—whatever you put in it comes out in a sort of thick gruel. The garden robot follows her—in fact, it does most of the work. It digs long, even furrows and plants the seeds; it crushes bugs and other pests. It uses its calipers to measure the vegetables and fruit for ripeness.

Sometimes, out in the garden, she sees smoke in the distance and hears zeppelins overhead. She finds other unusual things, marks of the war in the sky. Once she found a metal leg, torn off, lying among the carrots and vegetable marrows. She told the garden robot to get rid of it, and it dragged it away to the compost heap, leaving a trail of dark oil behind. Sometimes she finds dropped pamphlets, showing pictures of starving children or great metal hands crushing innocent families, but the words are in a language she doesn't understand.

This time she finds a man. The garden robot notices him first, whistling in surprise like a teakettle. She nearly screams herself, it's been so long since she saw another living creature. He looks odd to her as she draws closer. He is collapsed among the rose-bushes, one shoulder of his blue uniform—so he is on her side, not an enemy soldier—dark with blood. He is moaning, so she knows he isn't dead. The roses' thorns have scratched and torn at him, and his blood is the brightest, reddest thing she's seen in six months, much brighter than the roses.

"Bring him into the house," she says to the garden robot. It clicks and whirs around him busily, but its calipers are sharp, and when it tries to close them around the soldier's wrist, he bleeds distressingly. He cries out, without opening his eyes. His face is very young and smooth, the skin almost translucent, his hair white-blond and fair. He is wearing an airship crewman's goggles around his neck, and she wonders what battle in the sky he fell from and how far he had to fall.

Eventually she shoos the garden robot away and approaches the soldier carefully. He has an energy rifle strapped to his belt; she undoes it and gives it to the robot to dispose of. Then she sets about the task of freeing the soldier from the tangled briars. His skin is hot when she touches him, much hotter than she remembers human skin being. But maybe it's just been so long that she doesn't really recall.

She half drags, half carries the soldier up the stairs and into her father's bedroom. She hasn't been in there since he left, and despite the ministrations of the cleaning robots, the room has a dank, fusty smell. The heavy wooden furniture seems to loom over her, as if she had suddenly become very small, like Alice in the children's book. She gets him into the bed somehow and under the covers, using scissors to cut away the bloody parts of his uniform, baring his shoulder. He fights her weakly, like a kitten, as she does it, and she murmurs *hush*, and that it is for his own good.

There is a wound through the upper part of his shoulder. It is red and swollen and smells of infection. Dark-red lines radiate out from the puckered edges. Rose knows those lines mean death. She goes into her father's study and pulls down one of the boxes from the mantel. It is slippery, polished wood, and from the inside she can hear a chittering noise, as of birds.

Back upstairs the soldier is tossing in her father's bed, crying out unintelligible words. Rose wishes there were someone else with her, someone to hold him down as she opens the box and lets the mechanical leeches run over his body. The soldier screams and thrashes at them, but they cling tenaciously. They fasten on to the wound and the skin around it, their half-translucent coppery bodies swelling and darkening as one by one they fill with blood and fall to the side. When they are done, he is whimpering and clawing at himself. Rose sits down beside him on the bed and strokes his hair. "There, there," she says. "There, there."

Slowly, he calms. His eyes flutter open and then close. They are a very pale shade of blue. He is wearing copper dog tags around his neck. She lifts them and examines them carefully. His name is Jonah Lawrence, and he is a second lieutenant on the airship *Skywitch*. "Jonah," she whispers, but his eyes don't open again.

"He is going to fall in love with me," she tells Ellen and Cordelia over tea, after the soldier has fallen asleep. "I am going to nurse him back to health, and then he will love me. That is always how it happens in books."

"That is wonderful news," says Cordelia. "What does it mean?"

"Love, stupid," says Rose, annoyed. "You know what love is, don't you?"

"She doesn't know anything," says Ellen, rattling her teacup with amusement. After a pause, she says, "Neither do I. What *do* you mean?"

Rose sighs. "Love means someone wants to be with you all the time. All they want is to make you happy and give you things. And if you go away from them, they will be miserable forever and ever."

"That sounds terrible," says Cordelia. "I hope it doesn't happen."

"Don't *say* that," says Rose. "Or I will slap you."

"Do you love *us*?" Ellen asks.

The question hangs in the air, and Rose is not sure how to answer it. Finally she says, "Cordelia, you're good with your needle. Come with me. I need you to help me sew up his wound, or it won't heal."

Rose sits and watches while Cordelia's tiny hands sew up the wound in Jonah's shoulder. The sleeping potion she had given him earlier is keeping him quiet, though Ellen sits on his elbow anyway, just in case he might wake and begin to thrash about. He shows no signs of it, though. Rose begins to worry that perhaps she has given him too much and killed him. The idea is very dramatic — what a tragedy it would be, like Romeo and Juliet.

When he finally wakes, it is just them alone in the room. It is nearly dawn, and watery light drips through the windowpanes. His eyes flutter open, and Rose leans forward in her chair beside the bed, her book and lap rug sliding to the floor. "Are you awake?" she says.

He blinks at her with his clear light eyes. "Who are you?"

"I am Rose," she tells him. "I found you in my back garden. You must have fallen from your airship."

"I was shot—" He puts his hand to his shoulder and feels the stitches. He stares at her. "You did all this," he says. "You healed me?"

She nods modestly. No need to mention Ellen's and Cordelia's contributions. They are not real people, anyway.

He catches at her wrist. "Thank you," he says. His voice is hoarse and sweet. "Thank you for saving my life."

Rose is pleased. He is beginning to fall in love with her already.

After the rabbit died, Rose sobbed for hours in her room. Her father came in at last. She remembers his shadow falling across her bed as he said, "Sit up, little Rose. There's something I want to show you."

Her father was a big man, with big, capable hands, like a gardener or plowman. In one of them he was holding an object that looked like a telescope — or no, she thought as he sat down beside her, it was a watch, for it had a face, with dials, at the far end. "When your mother died," he said, "I built this. I thought I could go back. Tell her not to go out riding that day. But I have never been able to make it take me back more than a week, and by then she had been dead for years." He handed it to her. "You can go back if you like," he said gruffly. "If you turn the dials like so — and so — you can return to the time when your rabbit was still alive."

Rose was delighted. She took the device from him and turned the dials, as he had shown her, to return her to that morning. Then she snapped the device shut. For a terrifying moment it was like falling down a well, everything hurtling upward and away from her. Then she was in her room again, the white rabbit in its cage, and she was no longer holding the time device.

Delighted, she ran to the cage and opened it, lifting her rabbit out and cradling it closely against her, squeezing tighter until it went still in her arms. She loosened her grip in disbelief, but the creature was as limp as a rag. She began to sob again, but this time when her father came to see what was wrong, she didn't tell him.

He didn't remember having shown her the time device and she was too ashamed to ask for it again.

Jonah is shocked to learn that Rose is alone in the house, aside from the servant robots. He asks her endless questions: who is her father (he's never seen him, but he thinks he's heard his name before), how long ago did he leave her, when was the town destroyed, how does she eat, live, survive? She brings him soup on trays and sits with him, answering his questions, sometimes bewildered at his surprise. It is, after all, the only life she's known.

In exchange, he tells her about himself. He's only eighteen, the youngest second lieutenant in the army. He lives in the Capital, which she has always imagined as a place with beautiful soaring towers, like a castle on a hill. He tells her it's much more like everyone rushing everywhere very fast. He tells her about the library, where the shelves of books rise high into the sky, and you can reach them on floating steam-powered platforms. He tells her about the magnetized train that runs around the top level of the city, from which the clouds can be seen. He tells her about the dressmaking automatons that can sew a silk dress for a lady in less than a day and deliver it by pneumatic post. Rose tugs at the too-tight bodice of her own plain cotton childish dress, then blushes.

"I would love to go there," she says, looking at him with enormous eyes. "To the Capital."

"It's amazing what you've managed to do here, with the little you have," he says. "How lucky I was to fall from the airship so close to your doors."

"I am the lucky one," she says, but so softly that maybe he doesn't hear.

"I wish you could meet my sisters," he says. "They would be much moved by your heroism."

Rose can barely contain herself. He wants her to meet his family! His love for her must be serious indeed. She looks up so he cannot see the delight in her eyes, and she catches a glimpse of glittering eyes watching from a panel in the corner of the room. Cordelia, she thinks, or Ellen. She will have to reprimand them about their spying ways.

"You mustn't spy on Jonah," she says to Ellen. They are having soup in tiny bone teacups. "You must respect his privacy the way you respected Father's."

"But where will he live when your father comes back?" asks Cordelia. "He will have to be put in a different room."

"When we are married, we will live in the same room," Rose says grandly. "That is what married people do."

"So he will move into your room?" Ellen's face is all squashed with disbelief: she is probably thinking of Rose's tiny bed, barely big enough for one.

"Not at all," says Rose. "We won't be staying here once we're married. We shall go to the Capital and live there."

There is an appalled silence. Finally, Cordelia says, "I do not think we will like the Capital very much, Rose."

"Then you can stay here," says Rose. "Grown-up ladies don't play with dolls, anyway. And someone must watch the house until Father returns."

She means the last to cushion the blow, but the dolls don't seem comforted. Cordelia sets up a wail that pierces Rose's ears. She hears running steps in the hallway, and the door flies open: it is Jonah, dressed in her father's clothes. "Dear God," he says, "is someone being murdered in here?"

"It's just Cordelia," says Rose, and turns to both the dolls, her face white with rage. "Stop it. *Stop it.*"

They are both silent, staring at Jonah. Rose is staring, too. She hadn't realized how tall he was until now. He is so handsome, even in her father's old clothes, that it hurts her eyes. "What are those things?" he demands, pointing at Cordelia and Ellen.

"Nothing," she says hastily, standing up, thinking how childish he must think her, having tea with dolls. "Just toys my father made me."

The look on his face does not change. "Will you come walk with me in the garden, Rose?" he asks. "I think I could do with some fresh air."

She hurries to his side, not looking behind her to see if the dolls are watching.

They walk among the carefully planted flower beds, and Rose tries to explain. "It isn't their fault — they tend to get upset over the littlest things," she says.

"I've never seen anything like them," says Jonah, catching up a stone and skipping it across the surface of the pond. "Automatons with real reactions — real feelings."

"They were prototypes," said Rose. "But my father thought giving them personalities was more trouble than it was worth, so he never sold the design."

"Your father," says Jonah, shaking his head, "must be some sort of genius, Rose. What else did he invent?"

She tells him about the garden robot and the cook. He does say he had wondered why there never seemed to be anything to eat but soup. She considers telling him about the time device, but she cannot bear to tell the story of her rabbit. He would think her cruel. All the while that she talks, he nods his head, considering, amazed.

"They won't be able to believe this in the Capital," he says, and her heart soars. She had been almost sure he was planning to take her back with him when he went — now she is completely.

"And when do you think you'll be well enough to make the journey back?" she asks, eyes cast modestly to the ground.

"Tomorrow," he says. A blue jay is calling from the treetops, and he raises his head to follow the noise.

"Then I must prepare a special dinner tonight. To celebrate that you're well." She takes his hand, and he looks startled.

"That sounds very pleasant, Rose," he says, and turns so that they are walking back toward the house again. His hand slides out of hers. It doesn't seem intentional, and Rose tells herself that it means nothing. They are going away together, tomorrow. That is what matters.

When Rose returns from the walk, she finds Ellen in her room, sitting on her bed. Cordelia is on the windowsill, singing a tuneless little song. When Rose comes in, dragging an empty trunk from the attic, Ellen scrambles to sit on it, kicking her little heels against the sides. "You can't go away and leave us," she says as Rose determinedly pushes her aside and begins to pile in her clothes.

"Yes, I can," says Rose.

"No one will take care of us," says Cordelia desolately from the windowsill.

"Father will come back and take care of you."

"He isn't ever coming back," says Ellen. "He went away and died in the war, and now you're going away, too." She can't cry — she was never designed for it — but her voice sounds like weeping.

Rose snaps the trunk shut with a final sound. "Leave me alone," she says, "or I'll turn you both off. Forever."

They are silent after that.

Rose dresses with care, in one of her mother's old gowns. Lace drips from the cuffs and the hem. She goes down into the cellar and finds the last of the preserved peaches and a single bottle of wine. There is dried meat as well, and some flour and old bread. There is no use in saving these things anymore, now that she is going, so she fries vegetables from the garden with the dried meat and puts them out on the table with the fine china, the wine, and the preserves.

Jonah laughs when he comes downstairs and sees what she's done. "Well, you did the best you could," he says. "It reminds me of midnight feasts I used to have with my sisters, when we would raid the pantry at night."

Rose smiles back at him, but she is aware of the eyes watching from the shadows — small shapes that dart and flicker when she looks at them. Cordelia and Ellen. She mentally damns them both to the pit of hell and goes back to smiling at Jonah. He is all pleasantry, filling her wineglass, and then his own, and proposing a toast to their winning the war. Rose has forgotten what the war is about or who they are fighting, but she drinks the wine nonetheless: it tastes dark and bitter, like cellar dust, but she pretends to like it. She drains her glass and he fills it again, with another toast: this one, he says, is for women like her; the war would be won already if all damsels were as valiant as she. Rose discovers that even though the wine tastes bad, it fills her with a pleasant glow when she drinks it.

On the third round of toasting, with the bottle nearly empty, he stands up. "And last," he says, "a toast to some fortunate future day when, perhaps, once this war is over, we might see each other again."

Rose freezes, the glass halfway to her lips. "What did you say?"

He repeats the toast. His eyes are bright, his cheeks flushed. He looks like a recruitment poster for airship pilots: *Seeking young men, hardy, handy, and brave* . . .

"But I thought I was coming with you to the Capital," she says. "I thought you were going to bring me with you."

He looks startled. "But, Rose, the way back to the Capital is through enemy territory. It's much too dangerous—"

"You can't leave me here," she says.

"No, of course not. I had planned to alert the authorities when I returned, and they would send someone for you. I'm not callous, Rose. I understand what you did for me, but it's too dangerous—"

"Nothing is too dangerous if we're together," says Rose. She thinks she may have heard someone say this in a novel once.

"That's not true at all." Jonah seems agitated by her refusal to understand. "It will be much easier for me to maneuver without worrying about you, Rose. And you aren't trained for anything like this. It just isn't possible."

"I thought you loved me," says Rose. "I thought we were going to the Capital so we could get married."

There's a horrified silence. Then Jonah stammers out, "But, Rose, I'm already engaged. My fiancée, her name is Lily—I can show you a chromolithograph—" His hand strays to his throat, where a locket hangs on a chain. But Rose has no interest in this girl, this fiancée with a flower name like her own. She stumbles to her feet and away from him, even as he moves toward her. "I think of you as if you were my own little sister, Rose—"

She runs past him, runs up the stairs and into her father's study, slamming the door behind her. She can hear him calling out for her, but after a while, he stops calling, and there is silence. The sun has begun to set outside, and the room is filled with reddish light. She slips to the floor, her head in her hands, and begins to weep. Sobs rack her body. She is aware of the touch of hands on her hair and someone stroking her back. Ellen and Cordelia surround her, petting her as if she were a crying child. She sobs for hours, but they don't tire; it is Rose, finally, who wearies first. Her tears slow and stop, and she stares at the wall, vacantly, gazing into nothingness.

"He was supposed to fall in love with me," she says aloud. "I must have done something wrong."

"Everyone makes mistakes," says Ellen.

"It's all for the best," says Cordelia.

"I never liked him, anyway," says Ellen.

"If only I could do it again," Rose says. "I'd be different this time. More charming. I'd make him fall in love with me and forget everything else."

"It doesn't matter," says Cordelia.

Dawn is lightening the room. Rose gets to her feet and goes over to her father's desk. She rummages through the drawers until she finds what she is looking for, then returns to the window. Looking down, from here, she can see the front door, the garden, the meadow, and the forest in the distance.

The dolls clamor around her legs like children, but she ignores them. She waits. She has nothing but time. The sun is high in the sky when the front door opens and Jonah steps out. He is wearing his uniform, patched at the shoulder where she cut it away from him. He is carrying nothing in his hands, taking nothing from her house as he goes. Nothing but her heart, she thinks. He sets off down the path that leads from the front door toward the meadow and to the wider road beyond.

He stops once, a few steps from the house, and looks back and up, squinting into the sun. He raises his hand in a halfhearted wave, but Rose does not respond. This Jonah, this version of him, no longer matters. It doesn't matter where he thinks he's going. It doesn't matter that he doesn't love her. She is going to change all that.

He drops his hand and turns away, and Rose looks down at the time device. She spins the dial back. One day. Two days. Three. She hears Cordelia call out to her, but she snaps the device shut, and the doll's voice is lost in the whirlwind that picks her up and spins her round and carries her backward through time. In moments, it is over, and she is breathless, sitting once again on the windowsill. The dolls are gone, the time device no longer in her hands.

She anxiously looks out the window. Has she guessed the time right? Did she miscalculate? But no — her heart leaps up with happiness as she sees the man staggering out of the forest and dropping to his knees in the meadow. Leaving a trail of blood behind him, he begins the long and painful crawl toward her garden, where she will find him again.

The Last Ride of the Glory Girls

{ LIBBA BRAY }

I were riding with the Glory Girls, and we had an appointment with the 4:10 coming through the Kelly Pass. I fiddled with the Enigma Apparatus on my wrist, watching the seconds tick off. When the 4:10 was in sight, I'd take aim, and a cloud of blue light would come down over that iron horse. The serum would do its work, slowing time and the passengers to stillness inside the train. Then the Glory Girls'd walk across a bridge of light, climb aboard, and take whatever they wanted, same as they'd done to all them other trains—a dozen easy in the past six months.

In the distance, the white peaks of the revival tents dotted the basin like ladies' handkerchiefs hanging on the washing line. It were spring, and the Believers had come to baptize their young in the Pitch River. Way down below us, the miners were about their business; I could feel them vibrations passing from my boots up through my back teeth like the gentle rocking of a cradle. The air a-swirled with a gritty dust you could taste on the back of your tongue always.

"Almost time," Colleen said, and the red of the sky played against her hair till it look like a patch of crimson floss catching fire in an evening dust storm.

Fadwa readied her pistols. Josephine drummed her fingers on the rock. Amanda, cool as usual, offered me a pinch of chaw, which I declined.

"I sure hope you fixed that contraption for good, Watchmaker," she said.

"Yes'm," I answered, and didn't say no more.

My eyes were trained on them black wisps of steam peeking up over the hills. The 4:10, right on schedule. We hunkered down behind the rocks and waited.

How I ended up riding with the Glory Girls, the most notorious gang of all-girl outlaws, is a story on its own, I reckon. It's on account of my being with the Agency — that's the Pinkerton Detectives, Pinkertons for short. That's a story, too, but I cain't tell the one without the other, so you'll just have to pardon me for going on a bit at first. Truth is, I never set out to do neither. My life had been planned from the time I were a little one, sitting at my mam's skirts. Back then, I knew my place, and there were a real order to it all — the chores, the catechism, the spring revivals. Days, I spent milking and sewing, reading the One Bible. Evenings, we evangelized at the miners' camp, warning them about the End Times, asking if they'd join us in finding the passage to the Promised Land. Sunday mornings were spent in a high-collared dress, listening to the Right Reverend Jackson's fiery sermons.

Sunday afternoons, as an act of charity, I helped Master Crawford, the watchmaker, now that his sight had gone and faded to a thin pinpoint of light. That were my favorite time. I loved the beauty of all them parts working perfectly together, a little world that could be put to rights with the click of gears, like time itself answered to your fingers.

"There is a beauty to the way things work. Remove one part, add another, you've changed the mechanism as surely as the One God rewrites the structure of a finch over generations," Master Crawford'd told me as I helped him put the tools to the tiny parts. By the time I left the township, I knowed just about all there was to know in regards to clockworks and the like. Before what happened to John Barks, my life were as ordered as them watches. But I ain't ready to talk about John Barks yet, and anyway, you want to know how I come to be with the Pinkertons.

It were after Mam had died and Pap were lost to the Poppy that I left New Canaan and come to Speculation to seek my fortune. Weren't more'n a day into town when a pickpocket relieved me of my meager coins and left me in a quandary of a serious nature, that quandary bein' how to survive. There weren't no work for a girl like me — the mines couldn't even hire the men lining up outside the overseer's office. About the only place that would take me was the Red Cat brothel, and I hoped it wouldn't come to that. So, with my guts roiling, I stole a beedleworm dumpling off a Chinaman's cart — none too well, I might add — and found myself warming a cell beside a boy-whore whose bail were paid by a senator's aide. I knew nobody'd be coming for me, and I was right scared they'd be sending me back to the township. I just couldn't tolerate that.

Took me seven seconds to pick the lock and another forty-four to take the gate mechanism down to its bones. Couldn't do nothing about the whap to the back of my head, courtesy of the guard. Next thing I knew, I had an audience with Pinkerton chief Dexter Coolidge.

"What's your name? Lie to me and I'll have you in a sweatbox before sundown."

"Adelaide Jones, sir."

"Where are you from, Miss Jones?"

"New Canaan Township, sir."

Chief Coolidge frowned. "A Believer?"

"Was," I said.

Chief Coolidge lit a cigar and took a few puffs. "I guess you've already had your dip in the Pitch."

"Yessir. When I were thirteen."

"And you've received your vision?"

"Yessir."

"And did you see yourself here in manacles before me, Miss Jones?" He joked from behind a haze of spicy smoke.

I didn't answer that. Most people didn't understand the Believers. We kept to ourselves. My folks come to this planet as pilgrims before I were even born. It was here, the Right Reverend Jackson told us, where the One God set this whole traveling snake-oil wagon show in motion. The Garden of Eden were hidden in the mountains, the Scriptures said. If people lived right lives, followed the Ways of the One Bible, that Eden would be revealed to us when the End Times came, and those Believers would be led right into the Promised Land, while the Non-Believers would perish in an everlasting nothing. As a girl, I learnt the Ways and the Stations and all the things a goodly young woman should know, like how to make oat-blossom bread and spin thread from sweet clover. I learnt about the importance of baptism in the Pitch River, when all your sins would be removed and the One God would reveal his truth to you in a vision. But we never shared our visions with others. That were forbidden.

Chief Coolidge's sigh brought me back to my present predicament. "I must say, I've never understood why anyone would submit to such barbaric practices," he said, and it weren't snooty so much as it were curious.

"It's a free world," I said.

"Mmmm." Chief Coolidge squinched together them blue eyes and rubbed a thumb against his fat mustache while he sized me up—the moleskin pants tucked into the workman's boots, the denim shirt and the duster what used to belong to John Barks. My brown hair were plaited into long braids gone half unraveled now. There were dirt caked on my face till you couldn't hardly tell I had freckles across my nose and cheeks. Chief Coolidge shook his head, and I figured I were done for, but then he went and turned a crank on the wall and spoke into a long, fluted tube. "Mrs. Beasley. Please bring up some of that superior pheasant, roasted potatoes, and a portion of orange-blossom cake, I should think, thank you."

When the fancy silver tray come, and the heavenly Mrs. Beasley put it down beside me, I dug in without even saying grace or washing the dirt from under my fingernails.

"Miss Jones, your facility with the mechanical is quite impressive. Can you put things together as well as you take them apart?"

I told him about Master Crawford and the watches, and he give me a choice: go back to jail or come work for the Pinkertons.

I told him that didn't seem like much of a choice to me, just two different kinds of servitude. Chief Coolidge give me his first real smile. "As you said, Miss Jones: it's a free world."

The next morning, Chief Coolidge set me up in the laboratory. Every manner of device and contraption you could imagine were there. Rifles that fired pulses of light. Clockwork horses that could ride for a hundred miles full out and not get tuckered. Armored vests what would stop a bullet like it weren't no more'n a fly. Master Crawford's little watch shop paled in comparison. I'd be lying if I said the sight of all them metal parts didn't make my heartbeat flutter some.

"Gentlemen, may I introduce Miss Adelaide Jones, late of New Canaan Township? She is apprenticed to our agency in the Apparatus Division. Please see to it that she receives your utmost courtesy."

Chief Coolidge put me at a long bench piled thick with gears, rivets, tubes, and filaments. A long, fat rifle of some sort with a mess of metal innards laid out for me.

"This, Miss Jones, is Captain Smythfield's Miasmic Decider. The weapon was confiscated from a Russian agent at considerable trouble. A schematic has been provided, courtesy of our engineering department. As of yet, we've not gotten it to fire. Perhaps you will prove useful in that capacity. I'll leave you to it."

The fellas didn't take too kindly to me being there. Mam would've said I should let them win, that a woman shining her light too bright was unnatural in the eyes of the One God. Mam always kept a soft voice and her eyes downcast. Folks said she were the very picture of a Believer woman. It didn't save her from the fever none. So I kept my eyes downcast, trained right on the gun in front of me.

One of the agents, fella named Meeks, stood over me while I tried to figure out the puzzle of it. "He's testing you. That gizmo's not Russian; it's Australian. From the war. Their particle know-how is second to none. Put a piece wrong and you'll burn a man's head off or turn him to vapor. H'ain't been able to crack this one yet."

He put his hand on my shoulder. "If'n you like, I can keep you comp'ny, show you what to do." That hand gave my shoulder a too-friendly squeeze.

"If it's all the same to you, sir, I'd like to have a look at her on my own."

"Her, eh? How'd you know it's a she?"

"Just do," I said, and removed his hand. He skulked off, grumbling about what the world were coming to when the Pinkertons let a girl do a man's job. I ignored him and stared at the schematic, but I could tell it were wrong, so I put it aside. Once I sat down to a contraption, it were like I could feel them gears inside me, and I could tell which pieces didn't belong. By the end of the day, I had Captain Smythfield's Miasmic Decider ready to fire. Chief Coolidge fixed his brass goggles over his eyes and took 'er out to the firing range. She vaporized the target and blew a hole clean through the wall behind. Chief Coolidge stared at the Decider, then at me.

"Made a few changes to her, sir," I said.

"So I see, Miss Jones."

"Hope that were all right."

"Indeed it is. Gentlemen, whatever needs fixing, please deliver it to Miss Jones tomorrow morning."

I give Mr. Meeks a right nice curtsy on the way out.

For six months, I worked at that gear-strewn table. The fellas and I came to a peaceable understanding, 'cept for Mr. Meeks, who took to wearing his goggles all the time so's he didn't have to look me in the eye none. I got to know the other divisions. Most agents was field types who made sure the mines were lawful and that the miners didn't rough up the Chinamen or get too drunk and cause a ruckus. They left the brothels alone for the most part, under the idea that the whores weren't hurtin' folks none and ever'body needed a little company from time to time—usually the agents themselves. They kept a close eye on the saloons and boardinghouses, where some enterprising folks had taken to peddling the new machine-pressed Poppy, with names like Dr. Festus's All-Seeing Eye, Tincture of Light-Smoke, Mistress Violet's Glimpse into the Immortal Chasm, and Lady Laudanum's Sweet Sister. Plenty of people left the Church still searching for that first taste of eternity they got in the Pitch, and they'd chase it in the petal, even if it came out of a secret mill that might also be pressing mine dust or crimson floss. I'd had Poppy exactly twice— during my baptism and just after. I weren't eager to try it again.

Mostly, I kept myself to myself and worked hard to understand the way a Turkish Oscillating Orphanage Builder were different from an Armenian Widow Maker, though near as I could tell, they both went about the same business. In my resting hours, I worked on watches, finding comfort in the way they tidied up the world and kept it moving forward with a steady tick. I even fixed the chief's old pocket watch, which had been running three minutes slow for a year. I joked with him that he'd probably lost about four months of his life and he should put in to the Office of Restitution for it. Chief Coolidge scowled and handed me the plans for a new code breaker. He weren't big on jokes.

Then one hot summer day, the Glory Girls rode in like the Four Horsemen, robbing trains and airships. No one knew where they'd come from or how they done what they did. The witnesses couldn't remember nothing, 'cept for seeing a blue light before they'd wake some time later to find their jewels and lockboxes gone and the Glory Girls' calling card left on a table all polite and proper-like. Wanted posters hung on every post-office wall, till folks knowed the girls' names like the saints: Colleen Feeney. Josephine Folkes. Fadwa Shadid. Amanda Harper. There'd always been a troublesome balance between law and lawlessness, and the Glory Girls done tipped the scales into a pretty mess.

At a town meeting, Chief Coolidge assured everybody that the Pinkertons would put things to rights. "We are the Pinkertons, and we always catch our man."

"But Not Our Girl" was the headline of the next day's *Gazette*. The chief were in a mood then. "Without law and order, there is chaos," he bellowed to us, reminding me a portion of Reverend Jackson. He thundered that he didn't care if the miners killed one another and the Poppy turned half the planet into blithering idiots; the Pinkertons was now in the Glory Girl business. Capturing them become our sole purpose.

Chief Coolidge asked me to follow him. In the corner of a paneled library were a beautiful Victrola with a crank on the side. The chief give it a few turns, and presently, a wispy shaft of light appeared with ghostly moving pictures inside it. The chief called it a Holographic Remembrance. The pictures showed riders running alongside a great black train. I couldn't make out the riders' faces none 'cause they wore kerchiefs 'cross their mouths and goggles over their eyes, but I knew it were the Glory Girls. Oh, they were a sight to behold, with their hair flying out free and the dust rising up into a cloud, like the mist of a primeval forest. One of the girls raised her arm, and I couldn't see what happened real well, but a blue light bubble come over the train and it stopped dead on the tracks. Then the picture crackled up like old Christmas paper, and there weren't no more. Chief Coolidge turned up the gas lamps again.

"What do you make of that, Miss Jones?"

"Well, sir, I don't rightly know."

"Nor do we. No one in the divisions has seen anything like it. However, we've heard that someone who may have been Colleen Feeney was seen near the mines, inquiring after a watchmaker." He leaned both fists on his desk. "I need a woman on the inside. You could gain their trust. Alert us to their plans. It would be a chance to prove yourself, Miss Jones. But of course, it's your choice."

Your choice. It were what John Barks said to me once.

Chief Coolidge set me up in a rooming house near the mines just outside Speculation. We'd heard tell that the Glory Girls come through there every now and then for supplies. It were let known that I could be handy; I fixed the furnace at the brothel and got the clock in the town square working again after a Pinkerton done a bit of helpful sabotage on it. I went about my business, and one afternoon, there were a knock at my door and then I were looking into the sly green eyes of a girl not much older'n me from the looks of it. Her curly red hair were tied back at her neck, and she walked like a gunslinger, wary and ready. Miss Colleen Feeney had arrived.

"I hear that you're handy with watches and gears," she said, picking up my magnifying glass and giving it a look-through.

"That so?" Chief Coolidge had said the less you spoke, the better off you were. I didn't talk much anyway, so that suited me just fine.

"I've got something needs fixing."

I jerked my head at the box of parts on my desk. "Everybody's got something needs fixing."

"Well, this is something special. And I'll pay."

"If it's beedleworm dumplings and good-luck charms, I ain't interested."

She grinned and it made her face a different face altogether, like somebody who knew what it was to be happy once. "I got real money. And earbobs with emeralds the size of your fist. Or maybe you'd like some Poppy?"

"What'm I gonna do with emerald earbobs on this dirt clod?"

"Wear 'em to the next hanging," she said, and then I were the one grinning.

I packed up my kit, such as it were, and Colleen stopped to pick up some sugar and chewing tobacco at Grant's Dry Goods. She bought a bag of licorice whips and give one to all the kids in the store. On the way out, we had to pass through the revival tents. It were the one time I got a might nervous, because Becky Thread-kill took sight of me. Becky and I done all our catechisms together, and she were always the one to tell if somebody stopped paying attention or didn't finish making their absolutions. I figured her to call me out, and she didn't disappoint.

"Adelaide Jones."

"Becky Threadkill."

"It's Mrs. Dungill now. I married Abraham Dungill." She puffed herself up like we oughta be laying at her feet. I had half a mind to tell her that Sarah Simpson had been his first choice and everybody knowed it. "Over to the township, they say you got yourself in some trouble." Her smile were smug.

"That so?"

"'Tis. Heard it told you stole two bottles of whiskey from Mr. Blankenship's establishment, and you was in jail three long months for it."

I hung my head and shuffled my boots in the dirt, but mostly, I were trying to hide the smile bubbling up. Chief Coolidge done a good job getting the word out that I were a thief.

Becky Threadkill took my head hanging as confirmation of my sins. "I knowed you'd come to no good, Addie Jones. One day, you'll be pitched into the everlasting nothing."

"Well, it's good I had so much practice here first, then," I said. "You have a good day now, Mrs. Dungill."

Once we were clear, I stopped Colleen. "You heard what she said. If'n you want to find yourself another watchmaker, I'll understand."

Colleen give me an easy smile. "I think we found ourselves the right girl." She put the handkerchief over my mouth, and the ether done its work.

I woke up in an old wooden house, surrounded by four close faces.

"We're real sorry about the ether, miss. But you can't be too careful in our line of work." I recognized the speaker as Josephine Folkes. She were taller than the others and wore her hair all braided this way and that. The brand from her slave days were still on her forearm.

"Wh-what work is that?" I forced myself up on my elbows. My mouth were dry as a drought month.

Fadwa Shadid stepped out of the shadows and put her pistol to my temple. My stomach got as tight as a churchgoing woman's bootlaces then. "Not yet. First, we must determine if you are who you claim to be. We have no secrets between us," she said. Her voice made words sound like fancy writing on a lady's stationery. She wore a scarf that covered her head, and her eyes was big and ginger-cake brown.

"I'm from New Canaan. Used to be a Believer. But my mam died of the fever and my pap were out of his mind on Poppy. There weren't nothing for me there 'cept a life of looking after brats and spinning oat-blossom bread. I weren't cut out for too much woman's work," I said, and my words sounded fast to my ears. "That's all I got to say on it. So if'n you're of a mind to shoot me, I reckon you should just do it now."

Master Crawford had told me once that time weren't fixed but relative. Right then, I cottoned to what he meant, because those seconds watching Colleen Feeney's face and wondering if she'd give Fadwa the order to shoot me felt like hours. Finally, Colleen waved Fadwa back, and the cold metal left my skin.

"I like you, Addie Jones." Colleen said, grinning.

"I'm a might relieved to hear that," I said, letting out all my air.

She offered me some water. "I'm going to show you what we brought you here to fix. You can still say no. Understand, now, if you say yes, you'll be one of us. There's no going back."

"Like I said, got nothin' much to go back to, ma'am."

They led me to a barn with a small desk and a banker's lamp. Colleen pulled open a drawer and took out a velvet box. Inside were the most unusual timepiece I ever seen. The clockface were twice the size of a regular one. It were set into a silver bracelet shaped a might like a spider. Colleen showed me how it clamped on her arm. I could see a little hinge on the side of the clockface, so I knowed it opened up like a locket.

"This is the Enigma Temporal Suspension Apparatus," Colleen told me.

"What's it do?"

"What it did was suspend time. You aim the Enigma Apparatus at something, say, a train," she said, allowing a smirk. "And an energy field envelops the entire thing, slowing down time inside to a crawl. It doesn't last long, seven minutes at the outside. But it's enough for us to climb aboard and be about our business."

"What business is that?" I asked, my eyes still on the Enigma.

"Robbing trains and airships," Amanda Harper said, and spat out a plug of tobacco. She were short, with wheat-colored hair that hung straight to her middle back.

"We're reminders that people shouldn't feel too smug. That what you think you own, you don't. That life can change just like that." Fadwa snapped her fingers.

Colleen opened up the watch face. There were gears upon gears, the most intricate I ever seen, more like metal lacework than parts. They'd been pretty burned and bent up. Tiny flares of light tried to catch but died before they could spark. Right in the center were a teardrop-shaped glass vial. A blue serum dripped inside.

"Pretty, isn't she?" Colleen purred.

"How do you know it's a she?" I said, echoing Agent Meeks.

"Oh, it's a she, all right. Under all those shiny parts is a heart of caged tears."

"We didn't make this world, Addie. It don't play fair. But that don't mean we have to lie down," Josephine said.

Colleen put the Enigma Apparatus in my hands, and a rush of excitement come over me when I felt all that cold metal. "Can you fix her?" she asked.

I clicked a small piece into place. Something shifted inside me. "Ma'am, I'm sure gonna try."

Colleen clapped a hand on my shoulder — they all did — and it might as well have been a brand. I'd just become one of the Glory Girls. When night come, I rolled up a tiny note, tucked it into the beak of a mechanical pigeon, and sent it back to the chief to let him know I were in.

Master Crawford taught me about getting inside the clockworks, that you have to shut out the distractions till it's just you and the gears and you can hear the smooth click and tick, like a baby's first breath. You can give lovers their moonrises off the Argonaut Peninsula or the wonder of a seeding ship with its silos pumping steam into the clouds, bringing on rain. To me, ain't nothing more beautiful than the order of parts. It's a world you can make run right.

"There's some speculators what say time is as much an illusion as the Promised Land," Master Crawford told me once, when we was working, "and that if you want to find God, you must master time. Manipulate it. Get rid of the days and minutes, the measurements of our eventual end."

I didn't quite cotton to what Master Crawford were saying. But that weren't unusual. "Well, sir, I wouldn't let the Right Reverend Jackson hear you talk like that."

"The Right Reverend Jackson don't listen to me, so I reckon I'm safe." He winked, and in the magnifying glass, his eye was huge. "I saw it in a vision when they dipped me into the Pitch. I hadn't even whiskers and already I knew time was but another frontier to conquer. There'll come a messenger to deliver us, to impress upon us that our minds are the machines we must dismantle and rebuild in order to grasp the infinite."

"If'n you say so, sir. But I don't see what that has to do with Widow Jenkins's cuckoo clock."

He patted my shoulder like a grandpappy might. "Quite right, Miss Addie. Quite right. Now. See if you can find an instrument with the slanted tip...."

We got to working again, but Master Crawford's words had set my mind a-whirring with strange new thoughts. What if there were a way to best time, to crawl inside the ticks and tocks of it and press against it with both hands, stretching out the measures? Could you slide backward and forward, undo a day that had already been, or see what was comin' around the blind curve of the future? What if there weren't nothing ahead, nothing but a darkness as thick and forever seeming as your time under the Pitch? What if there weren't no One God at all and a body were only owing to herself, and none of it—the catechisms, the baptisms, the rules to keep you safe—none of it meant a dadburned thing? That set me a-shiver, and I made myself say my prayers of confession and absolution silently, to remind myself that there were a One God with a plan for me and the infinite, a One God who held time in His hands, and it weren't for the likes of me to know. I prayed myself into a kind of believing again and promised myself I wouldn't think more on such thoughts. Instead, I concentrated on the fit of gears. The bird pushed through the doors of the Widow Jenkins's clock and give us a cuckoo.

Master Crawford beamed. "You're a right good watchmaker, Miss Addie. Better than I were at your age. The pupil will best the master soon enough, I reckon," he said, and I felt a sense of pride, though I knew that were a sin.

The night Mam took sick, Master Crawford let me harness up his horse to ride for the doctor. Our two moons shone as bright as a bridegroom's pearled buttons. The wind come up cold, slapping my cheeks to chapped red squares by the time I reached the miners' camp. Outside the bunkhouses, the guards sat on empty ale barrels, playing cards and rolling dice. There were a doc in the camp, and I went to him, begged on my knees. I told him how we'd buried Baby Alice the week before, and now here was our mam, our rock and our refuge, burning up with the fever, her fingers already slate tipped with bad blood, and wouldn't he please, please come back with me?

He didn't even put down his whiskey. "Nothing you can do 'cept stay out of its way, young lady."

"But it's my mam!" I cried.

"I'm sorry," the doc said, and offered me a drink. In the camp, there were shouting. Somebody'd come up snake eyes.

It were Master Crawford give me the Poppy for Mam. "I was saving this for the End Times, like the Right Reverend Jackson said. But I'm an old man, and your mother needs it a sight more than I do."

I stared at the red-and-black cube in my palm. I had half a mind to swallow it down myself, live out the rest of my days on some colony in my mind. But then I were scared I'd be trapped in a forever night of nothingness, and me the only livin' thing.

I fed Mam a little to ease her passage and put the rest in my pocket. Then I lit the kerosene lamp and kept watch through the night. She never said nothing, but curled in on herself till she lay whorled against the bed linens like a fossil in the rock. I heard Master Crawford died during the winter. Died in his sleep in the pale workroom, under a blanket of down. 'Tween't the fever or his heart or his veins tightening up.

It were just that his time had run out.

Over the next few weeks, I learnt a lot about the Glory Girls. Josephine and her sister Bernadette had run away from the working fields. The overseer's bullet found Bernadette 'fore they even reached the mountains, but Josephine got away, and now she wore a thread from her sister's dress woven into her coarse braids as a reminder. She could set a broken bone as easily as she cooked a pan of corn bread, said it were about the same difference to her.

When Amanda's uncle got too friendly in the night, she found refuge doing hard labor in the shipyards. She'd spent long hours there and knew how to find the vulnerable spot in all that steel, the place where the Enigma could take hold and do its work. She were able to find timetables, too, so the girls would know which trains to hit and when.

Fadwa were a crack shot who'd honed her skills picking off the scorpions that roamed the cracked dirt outside the tents where she lived with her family in the refugee camps. The authorities took her pap to who knows where. Dysentery took the rest of her family.

That left Colleen. She'd been a debutante with fancy ball gowns, a governess, and a private coach. Her daddy were a speculator what had invented the Enigma Apparatus. He were also an anarchist, and when he tried to blow up the Parliament, that were the end of the gowns and the governess. They arrested her daddy for treason. 'Fore they could collect Colleen, she took the Enigma and fled on the next airship.

I felt a might sorry for all of them when I heard their tales. It were an awful feeling to have nobody. We had that in common, and I had a mind to come clean, tell them who I were and stop lying. But I had a job to do. At first, I done like Chief Coolidge told me, stalling on the repairs while trying to sniff out details from the Glory Girls and their next robbery. But they wasn't trusting me with that yet, and I figured it couldn't hurt to know more about the Enigma Apparatus. Besides, my pride were on the line, and I figured I'd better make good on my reputation as a girl what could fix things. Soon I were hunched over that device, from rooster crow till long after the moons scarred the skin of the sky. I'd figured out most of the gears, but them sputters of light around the serum vial vexed me.

"Simple windup won't do. Near as I can tell, she needs a jolt to get her going," I said after I'd been at her for a good three weeks with not much to show for it.

Amanda looked up from the barrel where she was washing Fadwa's long black hair. "Mercy, where would we find us somethin' like 'at?"

I thought for a bit, rubbing my thumb over the old Poppy square in my pocket. "I think a blue nettle might could do it."

"What's that?" asked Josephine.

"It's a kind of flower with a little bit of lightning inside. They grow in a orchard back to New Canaan."

"But that's on Believer land."

"Believers is all at the river for baptism time," I said. "Besides, I know where to go."

"Guess we best go picking, then." Amanda said. Giggling, she poured a bucket of cold water all over Fadwa, who pulled her gun so fast I thought I saw sparks.

John Barks's family hadn't been Believers. His mam and pap died in an airship fight off the western coast when he were fourteen. The Right Reverend Jackson and his wife took John in and started teaching him the Ways of the One Bible. You'd think that an orphan left to fend for himself on a planet where even the dust tries to choke you might have a score to settle with the One God. But not John Barks. Where most of us believed 'cause we were told to or afraid not to or just out of habit, he believed with his entire self.

"I'm a free man," he'd say. "And I'll believe what I want."

I couldn't rightly argue with that.

For two years, I'd watched John Barks grow from a sapling of a boy to a fine young man with muscles that strained the seams of the prayer shirts Mrs. Jackson sewed for him. He had a head of black hair what could rival a gentleman's boots for shine. Becky Threadkill swore he'd take her to wife, said she'd seen it in her vision under the Pitch. Half a dozen other girls swore the same till the Right Reverend were forced to spend the next Sunday cautioning against the sin of sharing your visions.

But it were me John Barks said "Mornin'" to when I went to fetch water, and me he asked to tutor him in the Scriptures. It were me he asked to tell him about being baptized in the Holy Pitch when he turned sixteen.

Every spring, the Believers of the End of Days walked the five miles to the River Pitch and set down their tents to await the baptism day. Most of us got dipped when we reached thirteen and done all our catechisms. They dressed you in the robes and slipped the tiniest petal tip of Poppy under your tongue to quiet your fear, slow your breathing, and keep you still. It stole into your bloodstream and weighted your bones like stones sewn into the lining of your skin. I remember Mam telling me not to be scared, that it were just like getting in a thick bath.

"Just lay real still, Addie-loo," she cooed, stroking the eucalyptus balm over my eyes to keep the Pitch blindness out. "When you're calm, the One God'll show you a vision, your purpose in this life."

"Yes'm."

"But first you have to face the darkness. There'll come a time when you want to fight it, but don't. Just let it cover you. It'll be over before you know it. Promise me you won't fight."

"Promise."

"That's my good girl."

The catechisms said that once you lay in the Pitch and come up again, you came up newborn, your sin purged and left behind you in the thick black tar, like an impression in the mud. That's what they said, anyway. But you never knew what would come bubbling up inside you while you was under. You had to last a full minute with the oily darkness moving over you like a coffin lid, closing out the world. Even a world as damned as this one is better than the weight of nothingness the Pitch smothers you in. All sense of time and place is lost in that river. The Believers say it give you a taste of what could become of your immortal soul if you don't turn to the One God and prepare for the End Times. When you come up outta that river, your damnation sliding down your body like a syrupy shed skin, you fall on your knees and say thanks to your Maker for that breath of hot, dusty air. It makes Believers, the Right Reverend Jackson says. No one wants to spend eternity in such a place as that.

Once you was done, the priests gave you your first real taste of Poppy to seal your covenant with the One God. Miracles and wonders played across your eyes then, reminders of His mercy and goodness. Master Crawford muttered that it weren't proof of nothing 'cept folks' willingness to be hornswaggled. But nobody paid him any mind.

I told John Barks all of this the week before his baptism while we were walking in the orchard.

"They say that when you take your first taste of Poppy, your legs go all prickle bones and your tongue numbs like a snowcake feast and stars explode behind your eyes, making new flowers against the closed dark-velvet stage curtains of your retina, letting you know the One God's show's about to get under way," John said, bustin' with excitement.

"Well, the Poppy is right strong," I said.

"And did you feel the One God sure and true then, Addie?"

"I reckon."

We'd stopped under a blue nettle tree in full bloom, the glasslike, bell-shaped blossoms pulsing with small bursts of lightning. The air was sharp. Overhead, the seeding ships pierced the dark-red cloud blanket, trying to bring on rain. John Barks's arm brushed mine and I colored. We were s'posed to keep a respectful distance, as if the One God's mam walked between us.

"What did the One God reveal to you down under the river, Adelaide Jones?" His hand had moved to my cheek. "Did you see us here by the tree?"

We weren't s'posed to tell our visions. They were for us alone. But I wanted to tell John Barks what I'd witnessed, see what he'd make of it, see if he could ease my mind some. So right there with the new light buzzing all around us, I told him what I seen under the river. When I were done, John Barks kissed me soft and sweet on the forehead.

"I don't believe that," he said. "Not for one second."

"But I seen it!"

"I think the One God leaves some things up to us to decide.

He shows us a vision, and it's your choice what to do with it."
He smiled. "I can tell you what I hope to see next week."

"What?" I said, trying hard not to cry.

"This," he whispered.

It started to rain. John Barks put his coat over us and kissed me
on the mouth this time, and oh, not even clockworks could match
up to the feeling of that kiss. It made me believe what John Barks
said, that we might could change our fates, and I forgot to be afraid.

"Yes," I said, and I kissed him back.

I thought about that day while me and the Glory Girls collected
the blue nettle, and I thought about it, too, while I extracted them
tiny beats of lightning and placed 'em inside the Enigma Apparatus.
While I watched them light strands prickle and inch toward the
serum inside the glass vial, some new hope stirred in me, too,
putting me in mind of Master Crawford's vision, the messenger
who would come and liberate us from our time-bounded minds.
Maybe the Glory Girls were the ones to set us free. And the Enigma
Apparatus were the key. Them thoughts about sliding through past
and future come prickling up again, only I didn't push 'em away so
fast this time, and the only prayer that left my lips was the word
"Please . . ." while I waited for the spark to set things in motion.

The blue nettle connected with the vial. The serum pulsed
inside its cage. The second hand on the clockface ticked. I shouted
for the girls to come out quick. Soon, they was crowded 'round me
in that workshop while we watched the Enigma Apparatus hum
with new life.

"Girls, I think we've got ourselves a timepiece again," Colleen said.

I were supposed to have a rendezvous with the chief.

I missed it.

We tested it on a mail train the next day. It were just a local, steaming across a patch of plains, but it would do for practice.

"Here goes," Colleen said, and my nerves went to rattling. She bent her arm and aimed the clockface at the train.

I've had me a few thrills in my sixteen yearn, but seeing the Enigma Apparatus do its work had to be one of the biggest. Great whips of light jump out and held that train sure as the One God's hand might. Inside, the engineer seemed like he were made of wax — he weren't moving that I could see. The Glory Girls boarded the train. There weren't but bags of letters on it, so they didn't take nothing, only changed 'round the engineer's clothes till he wore his long johns on the outside and his hat 'round backward. When the light charge stopped holding and the train lurched forward again, he looked a might confused at his state. We laughed so hard, I thought the miners would hear us down below. But the drills kept up their steady whine, oblivious. And the best part yet? Somehow in my tinkering, I'd drawn out the length to a full eight minutes. I'd made her better. I'd bested time.

The pigeon were on the windowsill of my workhouse when I get back. I unrolled the note tucked into her mouth. It were from the chief, telling me when and where to make our rendezvous, saying I'd best not miss it. I tossed the note in the stove and got to work.

By the time we hit the 6:40 the next Friday, I'd taken her to a full ten minutes.

The Right Reverend Jackson used to say there were a fine line between saint and sinner, and in the long days I spent with the Glory Girls robbing trains and falling under the spell of the Enigma

Apparatus, I guess I crossed well over it. Before long, I'd almost forgot I'd had one life as a Believer and another as a Pinkerton. I were a Glory Girl as much as any of 'em, and it felt like I'd always been one. Truth be told, them were some of the happiest times I'd had since I'd walked with John Barks. Like being part of a family it were, but with no Mam to sigh when you forgot to burp the baby and no Pap to slap you when your words was too sharp for his liking. Mornings we rode the horses fast and free over the dusty plains, letting the wind whip our hair till it rose like crimson floss. We'd try to best each other, though we all knew Josephine were the fastest rider. Still, it were fun to try, and nobody could tut-tut that we was unladylike. Fadwa worked on my marksmanship by teaching me to shoot at empty tins, and while I weren't no sharpshooter, I done all right, and by all right I mean I managed to knock off a can without shooting the horses. Josephine taught me to dress a wound with camphor to draw out the poisons. Amanda liked to sneak up on each a-one and scare the dickens out of us. Then she'd fall on the ground, laughing and pointing: "You shoulda seen your face!" and hold her sides till we couldn't do nothing but laugh, too. At night, we played poker, betting stolen brooches against a stranger's looted gold. It didn't matter nothing—if you lost a bundle, there were always another airship or train a-comin'. The poker games went fine till Amanda lost, which she usually did, bein' a terrible card player. Then she'd throw down her cards and point a finger at whoever cleaned up.

"You're cheating, Colleen Feeney!"

Colleen didn't even look up while she scooped the chips toward her lap. "That's the only way to win in this world, Mandy."

One night, Colleen and me walked to the hills overlooking

the mines and sat on the cold ground, feeling the vibrations of them great drills looking for gold and finding nothing. Stars paled behind dust clouds. We watched a seeding ship float in the sky, its sharp brass nose glinting in the gloom. "Seems like there ought to be more than this," Colleen said after a spell.

If John Barks were there, he'd say something about how beautiful it was, how special. "It ain't much of a planet," I said.

"That's not what I meant." She rolled a dirt clod down the hillside. It broke apart on the way down.

It come about by accident that first time. I'd been experimenting with the Engima all along, stretching out the time by seconds, but I couldn't break past ten minutes. It were all well and good to lock the Engima on a train and stretch the Glory Girls' time on it; what I wondered were if we, ourselves, might could move around in time like prayer beads on a string. Inside the Enigma were the Temporal Displacement Dial. I'd scooted its splintery hands 'round and 'round, taken it apart, put it back together twelve ways from Sunday. Didn't come to much. This time, I got to looking at the tiny whirling eye that joined them hands at the center. I cain't rightly say what gear it were that clicked in my head and told me I should take a thin, pulsing strand of blue nettle and settle it into that center, but that's what I done. Then I pushed that second hand faster and faster 'round that dial. With my hand tingling like a siddle-bug bite, I aimed the Enigma at myself. I felt a jolt, and then I were standing still in the shop listening to Josephine ringing the dinner bell. I knowed that couldn't be right — it were only two o'clock in the afternoon, and dinner weren't till six most days. Long shadows crept over the shop floor. Six-o'clock shadows. I'd lost four whole hours. Had I slept? I knowed I hadn't—not standing up with my boots on, anyways. A tingle twisted through my insides till I felt as alive as a blue nettle. I'd done it.

I'd unlocked time.

That night, Colleen brought out a bottle of whiskey and poured us each a tall glass. "There's a train coming soon. The four-ten through the Kelly Pass. It's the best one yet. I've seen the passenger list. It is impressive. You can be sure there'll be pearls big as fists. And rubies and diamonds, too."

Josephine let out a holler, but Amanda scowled.

"Gettin' tired of gems," she said, reaching for the bottle. "Nowhere to wear 'em. Nowhere to trade 'em in much anymore."

Colleen shrugged. "There'll be gold dust on this one."

I couldn't hold it back no more. "Maybe we're goin' about this the wrong way. Maybe we should be looking at the Enigma App . . . Appar . . . the watch as our best haul," I said. I weren't used to whiskey. It made my thoughts spin. "You ever think of using it on something other than a train?"

Amanda spat out a stream of tobacco. It stained the hay the color of a fevered man on his deathbed. "Like what?"

"Say, for going forward in time to see what you'll be eatin' next week. Or maybe for going back. Maybe to a day you'd want to do over."

"Ain't nothing I'd want to go back to," Josephine said.

"What about all them tomorrows?"

"I'll likely be dead. Or fat," Amanda said, and laughed. "Either way, I don't want to know."

The girls commenced to teasing Amanda 'bout her future as a farmer's fat wife. Maybe it were the whiskey, but I couldn't let it alone. "What I'm sayin' is that we might could use the Enigma to travel through time and see if there's anything out there besides this miserable rock — maybe even to unlock bigger secrets. Ain't that a durn sight better than a pearl?" I slammed my tankard down on the table, and the girls got right quiet then. I hadn't never been much of a talker, much less a yeller.

Colleen played with the poker chips. They made a *plinkety-plink* sound. In the dim light, she looked less like an outlaw, more like a schoolgirl. Sometimes I forgot she weren't but seventeen. "Go on, Addie."

"I done it," I said, breathing heavy. "Time travel. With the Engima. I figured it."

I had their attention then. I told 'em about my experiments, how I'd jumped ahead hours just that afternoon. "It's just a start," I cautioned. "I ain't perfected nothing yet."

Fadwa licked her fingers. "I don't understand. Why do we want this?"

"Don't you see? We wouldn't need to rob trains then. We could go anywhere we wanted," Colleen said. "Perhaps there's something better ahead, something we can have without cheating."

Colleen and me locked eyes, and I saw something in her face that put me in mind of John Barks. Hope. She put the chips back on the table. "I'm in for the ride, Watchmaker. Do the Glory Girls proud."

"Yes'm," I said, swallowing hard.

"In the meantime, we'd better get ready for the four-ten."

The next morning, Fadwa and me saddled up the horses and headed into town for supplies. It'd been a year since I'd gone off with the Glory Girls. The Believers were setting up their tents along the Pitch again. I were waiting by the horses when somebody clapped a strong hand over my mouth and jerked me around the back of the Red Cat brothel, upstairs, and into a bedroom, where I were forced into a chair. Two big goons stood by, their arms folded but ready to grab me if I so much as looked at the door. In a moment, the same door opened and the chief walked in and took a seat across from me. He'd put on weight since I'd seen him last and was sporting some right furry muttonchops. He wiped his spectacles with a handkerchief and put them back on his face. "Miss Adelaide Jones, I presume. You've been gone a very long time, Miss Jones."

"Lost track of time, sir," I said, and he didn't laugh none at my joke.

"Allow me to inform you: a year. An entire year with no contact."

My stomach churned. I wanted to yell out to Fadwa, warn her. I wanted to jump out the window onto my horse and ride like I was racing Josephine all the way back to the camp and to the Enigma Apparatus.

"Do you care to tell me how the six-forty out of Serendipity came to be robbed by the Glory Girls? Or the eleven-eleven airship from St. Ignatius?" He slammed a fist down on the table, and it rattled the floorboards. "Do you care to tell me anything at all, Miss Jones, that would keep me from clapping you in irons for the rest of your natural life?"

I picked a burr out of my pants. "You're looking well, sir. I'm right fond of the muttonchops."

The chief's face reddened. "Miss Jones, may I remind you that you are a Pinkerton agent?"

"No, sir, I ain't," I said, my dander up. "You 'n' I both know ladies don't get to be agents. We end up like Mrs. Beasley, bringing tea and asking if there'll be anything else."

The chief went to open his mouth, then he closed it again. Finally he said, "Well, then, there is this to consider, Miss Jones: there is the law. Without it, we slip into the void. You are sworn to uphold it. If you do not, I'll see you prosecuted with the others. Do you take the full import of my meaning, Miss Jones?"

I didn't answer.

"Do you?"

"Yessir. Am I free to go?"

He waved me off. But when I got up, the chief grabbed hold of my arm. "Addie, which train are they aiming for next? Please tell me."

It were the *please* almost got me.

"Fadwa's just coming out. She'll be missing me. Sir."

The chief looked a might sad then. "Tag her," he said.

The goons held me down tight, and one of 'em brought out an odd rounded gun with a needle on the tip. I struggled but it didn't make no difference. They brung that gun up against the back of my neck, and it felt like a punch going in.

"What — what'd you do to me?" I gasped, and put a hand to my neck. There weren't no blood.

"It's a sound transmission device," Chief Coolidge said. "Agent Meeks is responsible for that invention. It transmits sound to us here. We can hear everything that is said. There should be enough to hang the Glory Girls, I should think."

"That ain't fair," I said.

"Life's not fair." The chief glared. "Tell us about the train — everything we need to catch them — and you'll go free, Addie."

"And if I don't?"

"I'll take you in now and throw away the key."

It weren't a choice.

Fadwa were waiting impatiently when I come down to the hitching post after my conference with the chief.

"Where were you?" Fadwa asked.

I rubbed at the back of my neck. I wanted to cry, but it wouldn't help none. If I were a better girl, I'd've told her to run and taken my chances with the law. But I couldn't stop thinking about the Engima. I was so close. I couldn't just walk away.

"Just some old business I had to take care of," I said, and helped her load up the horses.

That night, I drank more whiskey than I should have. I would've drowned my sorrows in the Poppy, but I knew that were no good. The Glory Girls was in good spirits. Tomorrow they'd take on the 4:10 in the Kelly Pass. They made their plans then, where they'd hide out, what kind of train the 4:10 was and where it were best to board—all of it being transmitted right back to the Pinkertons. A cold trickle worked its way through my insides. It were like I looked up to find the moons and stars gone to flat pictures painted on muslin.

"You all right, Addie-loo?" Josephine squinted at me like she weren't sure if she should make me a poultice for fever.

"Yes'm. Tired," I lied.

Colleen clapped a hand on my back. "You just have the Enigma ready to greet the 4:10 tomorrow, and I'll show you a haul, Addie, that will make you forget all your troubles."

They toasted me then, but the whiskey tasted sour and my head was hurting.

When everybody else was sleeping, I took myself for a walk up into the mountains. I looked down on the revival tents, at the shadowy mystery snaking through the basin, where folks left their sins and come up with a vision. John Barks told me it were choice, but I weren't so sure.

The day they baptized John Barks were terrible hot. The sky come up a gloomy orange and stayed that way. We'd gathered at the river with the young penitents. John Barks had been scrubbed pink. His black hair shone.

"I'll take you to wife, Addie Jones. Just you see," he whispered, and went to stand with the others.

My gut hurt. I wanted to tell him not to do it, to pack up his kit and run away with me on the next airship. We could see for ourselves if there were anything 'sides rocks spinning out in that vast midnight. But I wanted him to prove me wrong, too. I needed to be sure. So I watched as the aldermen dressed him in the white robes, and Mrs. Jackson balmed up his eyes, and Reverend Jackson slipped the Poppy under his tongue. When his body went limp, the women commenced to hymn singing, and the menfolk lowered John Barks's body into the Pitch. The dark river come over him like a living thing, devouring legs, arms, chest. Finally, his face were under and I counted the seconds: One. Two. Three. Ten. Eleven. Twenty.

A hand broke the surface, followed by John Barks's tar-stained face. He gagged and gasped, fighting the Poppy in his blood. He wouldn't lie still. It were like he'd been caught in one of them ecstasies you read about in the One Bible, where saints and chosen shepherds saw things beyond dust and weak moons and miners' toothless grins. He cried, "Oh Holy! There are stars newborn and great ships with searching sails set against pink-painted ribbons of eternal clouds — oh Holy! Oh Lamb! — the electric blood of the most heavenly body, oh sweet warm breath — kiss of a girl you love! What more? What more?"

The aldermen looked to Reverend Jackson for what to do. Sometimes people got too scared and had to come up from the Pitch before their time. But nobody had ever done like John Barks. And I could see in the Reverend's face that he were frightened, like there weren't no commandment to explain this.

"Reverend?" an alderman named Wills whispered.

"The sin fights him!" Reverend Jackson shouted. "He must be held still to accept the One God's vision. Let us come to his aid!"

The women lifted their arms in fervent hymn singing, and the Reverend Jackson spoke in tongues I didn't know. I kept listening to John Barks calling out wonders, like a madman on the mountain. The men took hold of his arms and legs and held him under, waiting for him to still, to accept the darkness and the One God's grace that allows us to see what comes next. But John Barks fought with everything he had in him. I screamed out that they was a-killin' him, and Mam told me to hush-a-bye and turned my face to her breast. The song rose louder, and it were a terrible song. And when John Barks finally went quiet, it were for good. He drowned in that river, his lungs full of Pitch and his vision stilled on his tongue.

The authorities come and pronounced it an accident. They took cider from the church ladies while John Barks's body lay on the scrubby bank under a sheet, the dried Pitch on his long arms gone to peeling gray scales. "The One God moves in His own way," Reverend Jackson said, but his hands shook. The aldermen dug a grave right there in the basin and buried John Barks without so much as a wooden stake to mark it. They said later he were too old for obedience. That were the problem. Or he might've gotten too much Poppy and seen the glory of the One God too soon, before he'd made his confession. A few folks believed he were chosen to receive a vision and die for all our sins, and we should honor John Barks on the feasting day. Still others whispered that his sin must've been too great for the One God to forgive or that he weren't willing to give up his sin, and I thought about our kiss under the blue nettle tree, what we done there with the lightning pulsing around us. I wondered if I hadn't damned John Barks with that kiss, sure as if I'd poured the Pitch into his mouth myself. I don't know. I don't know, I don't know, and that not knowing haunts me still.

The first streaks of graying orange come up in the sky when I walked down from the mountains and wrote my last note to the chief. Then I set about my work. The lamp burned through the night, and by the time the two moons was as pale as a skein of ash against the hot orange glow of the day, I'd done what I aimed to do. The Enigma Apparatus was ready.

"It's time, Addie," Colleen said.

The 4:10 puffed right into line. I pressed the button on the side of the clockface, bracing myself for the recoil as the train ground to a stop, floating in a blue light cloud. Amanda let out a loud whoop. "Let's go, Glory Girls! Time's a-wastin'."

They patted my back as they went, told me I done good. I grabbed Colleen's arm.

"Addie!" she said, trying to shake me loose. "I've got to go!"

I wanted to tell her everything, but then the chief would hear and swoop in too fast. "Mayhap there's something better up ahead, in the tomorrows," I said. "Strap yourself in good."

She gave me a strange look. "You're an odd one, Addie Jones."

And then they was across the light bridge and on the train. It took a few seconds longer than I figured for them to realize there weren't nobody on the 4:10, just a bunch of sawdust dummies. Weren't no treasures, neither. No comforts to keep in a pocket or a drawer. The Pinkertons had seen to that after I'd let the chief know the plan. Even from where I was, I could see their confusion. The sound of hoofbeats told me the agents was near. They were just coming over the ridge in a cloud of dust. Colleen saw it, too. The leader of the Glory Girls looked at me through one of the train's windows. In the blue light, her face had a strange, haunting beauty to it. She'd cottoned to what'd happened and who'd done it. And I think she knew her time had run out. She nodded at me to do it. I clicked the tiny switch that bled blue nettle into the whirling eye at the center of the Temporal Displacement Dial. With my index finger, I pushed that second hand 'round and 'round, the devil racing you through the woods and gaining fast. Colleen Feeney was yelling something at the others and they strapped themselves in. The cloud over the 4:10 sparked with angry light. I can't say what the Glory Girls felt then — wonder? Amazement? Fear? I just know they never stopped looking at me. Not once. And I wondered if it would be the last time I'd see 'em or if I'd ever make it to where they was going. The cloud crackled again, and the train car disappeared in a shower of light that brought a mess of rain over the basin. The recoil on the Enigma were like a punch then. Knocked me clean out.

Chief Coolidge weren't none too happy with me when I come to. He paced the floor while I sat in the one uncomfortable chair in his office. He'd had me sit there special. "We were supposed to catch them alive, have a trial, Miss Jones! That is the way of law!"

"Something must've went wrong with that contraption, Chief. Time's a tricky proposition."

He scowled and I tried real hard not to twitch. "Yes. Well. At least we were able to salvage what was left of the Enigma Apparatus. With effort, we'll get it running again."

"That's real good news, sir."

"I would be happy to know that you were working on the Enigma project, Miss Jones. Are you quite certain you won't stay with the Agency?"

I shook my head. "My time's up, sir."

"I might be able to recognize you as a deputy agent. It isn't full, you understand, but it is something."

"I 'preciate that, sir. I do."

He saw I weren't budging. "What will you do, then?"

"Well. 'Spect I'll travel some. See what's out there."

The chief sighed, and I noticed his mustache had more gray in it these days. "Addie, do you really expect me to believe that you had nothing to do with what happened to those girls?"

I looked him right in the eyes. I'd learned to do that. "You can believe what you want, Chief."

Chief Coolidge's gaze turned hard. "It's a free world, eh?"

"You can even believe that if you like."

When they'd lowered me down, them years ago, I'd done as my mam told me. I lay real still, even though I wanted to scream out, to beg them to pull me up even if I still had all my sin attached. It were as terrifying as the grave under the river. But I were a good girl, a true Believer, and so I made my full confession in my mind, and I waited — waited for the One God to show me a small glimpse of my future.

It started as the tiniest ticking sound. It grew louder and louder, till I thought I might go mad. But that weren't as bad as what followed. My vision come up over me in a wave, and I felt the weight of it all around me.

Darkness. That were all I saw. Just a vast nothing forever and ever.

There were hands pulling me up then, singing, "Hallelujah!" and pointing to the shape of my sins in the Pitch. But I knew better. I knew they'd never left me.

I slipped into John Barks's duster and headed out into the dry, red morning. On my wrist, the Enigma Apparatus shone. The Pinkertons was fellas. They'd never thought to question a lady's jewelry. I'd given Chief Coolidge a bucket full of bolts what might make a nice hat rack, but nothing that would bend time to his will.

The storekeepers swept their front walks in hopes of a day's good business. The johns stumbled out of the Red Cat ahead of the town's judging eyes. The seeding ships was out, piercing the clouds. Farther on, the Believers packed up their tents. They was done with visions and covenants for another year.

I reached into my pocket, letting my fingers rest for just a second on that Poppy brick before finding the coin in the corner. Forward or back, forward or back. John Barks told me once I had a choice, and I guess it come down to heads or tails.

I flicked the coin with my thumb and watched it spiral into the sudden rain.

Clockwork Fagin

{ CORY DOCTOROW }

Monty Goldfarb walked into Saint Agatha's like he owned the place, a superior look on the half of his face that was still intact, a spring in his step despite his steel left leg. And it wasn't long before he *did* own the place, had taken it over by simple murder and cunning artifice. It wasn't long before he was my best friend and my master, too, and the master of all Saint Agatha's, and didn't he preside over a *golden* era in the history of that miserable place?

I've lived at Saint Agatha's for six years, since I was eleven years old, when a reciprocating gear in the Muddy York Hall of Computing took off my right arm at the elbow. My da had sent me off to Muddy York when Ma died of the consumption. He'd sold me into service of the Computers and I'd thrived in the big city, hadn't cried, not even once, not even when Master Saunders beat me for playing kick the can with the other boys when I was meant to be polishing the brass. I didn't cry when I lost my arm, nor when the barber-surgeon clamped me off and burned my stump with his medicinal tar.

I've seen every kind of boy and girl come to Saint Aggie's—swaggering, scared, tough, meek. The burned ones are often the hardest to read, inscrutable beneath their scars. Old Grinder don't care, though, not one bit. Angry or scared, burned and hobbling, or swaggering and full of beans, the first thing he does when new meat turns up on his doorstep is tenderize it a little. That means a good long session with the belt—and Grinder doesn't care where the strap lands, whole skin or fresh scars, it's all the same to him—and then a night or two down the hole, where there's no light and no warmth and nothing for company except for the big hairy Muddy York rats who'll come and nibble at whatever's left of you, if you manage to fall asleep. It's the blood, see, it draws them out.

So there we all was, that first night when Monty Goldfarb turned up, dropped off by a pair of sour-faced sisters in white capes who turned their noses up at the smell of the horse droppings as they stepped out of their coal-fired banger and handed Monty over to Grinder, who smiled and dry-washed his hairy hands and promised, "Oh, aye, Sisters, I shall look after this poor crippled birdie like he was my own get. We'll be great friends, won't we, Monty?" Monty actually laughed when Grinder said that, like he'd already winkled it out.

As soon as the boiler on the sisters' car had its head of steam up and they were clanking away, Grinder took Monty inside, leading him past the parlor where we all sat, quiet as mice, eyeless or armless, shy a leg or half a face, or even a scalp (as was little Gertie Shine-Pate, whose hair got caught in the mighty rollers of one of the pressing engines down at the logic mill in Cabbagetown).

He gave us a jaunty wave as Grinder led him away, and I'm ashamed to say that none of us had the stuff to wave back at him, or even to shout a warning. Grinder had done his work on us, too true, and turned us from kids into cowards.

Presently, we heard the whistle and slap of the strap, but instead of screams of agony, we heard howls of defiance, and, yes, even laughter!

"Is that the best you have, you greasy old sack of suet? Put some arm into it!"

And then: "Oh, deary me, you must be tiring of your work. See how the sweat runs down your face, how your tongue doth protrude from your stinking gob. Oh, please, dear master, tell me your pathetic old ticker isn't about to pack it in. I don't know what I'd do if you dropped dead here on the floor before me!"

And then: "Your chest heaves like a bellows. Is this what passes for a beating round here? Oh, when I get the strap, old man, I will show you how we beat a man in Montreal—you may count on it, my sweet."

They way he carried on, you'd think he was *enjoying* the beating, and I had a picture of him leaping to and fro, avoiding the strap with the curious skipping jump of a one-legged boy, but when Grinder led him past the parlor again, he looked half dead. The good side of his face was a pulpy mess, and his one eye was near swollen shut, and he walked with even more of a limp than he'd had coming in. But he grinned at us again and spat a tooth on the threadbare rug that we were made to sweep three times a day, a tooth that left a trail of blood behind it on the splintery floor.

We heard the thud as Monty was tossed down onto the hole's dirt floor, and then the labored breathing as Grinder locked him in, and then the singing, loud and distinct, from under the floorboards: "Come gather, ye good children, good news to you I'll tell, 'bout how the Grinder bastard will roast and rot in hell—" There was more, apparently improvised (later, I'd hear Monty improvise many and many a song, using some hymn or popular song for a tune beneath his bawdy and obscene lyrics), and we all strove to keep the smiles from our faces as Grinder stamped back into his rooms, shooting us dagger looks as he passed by the open door.

And that was the day that Monty came to Saint Agatha's Home for the Rehabilitation of Crippled Children.

I remember my first night in the hole, a time that seemed to stretch into infinity, a darkness so deep I thought that perhaps I'd gone blind. And most of all, I remember the sound of the cellar door loosening, the bar being shifted, the ancient hinges squeaking, the blinding light stabbing into me from above, and the silhouette of old Grinder, holding out one of his hairy, long-fingered hands for me to catch hold of, like an angel come to rescue me from the pits of Hades. Grinder pulled me out of the hole like a man pulling up a carrot, with a gesture practiced on many other children over the years, and I near wept from gratitude. I'd soiled my trousers, and I couldn't hardly see, nor speak from my dry throat, and every sound and sight was magnified a thousandfold, and I put my face in his greatcoat, there in the horrible smell of the man and the muscle beneath like a side of beef, and I cried like he was my old mam come to get me out of a fever bed.

I remember this, and I ain't proud of it, and I never spoke of it to any of the other Saint Aggie's children, nor did they speak of it to me. I was broken then, and I was old Grinder's boy, and when he turned me out later that day with a begging bowl, sent me down to the distillery and off to the ports to approach the navvies and the lobster backs for a ha'penny or a groat or a tuppence, I went out like a grateful doggy, and never once thought of putting any of

Grinder's money by in a secret place for my own spending.

Of course, over time I did get less doggy and more wolf about the Grinder, dreamed of tearing out his throat with my teeth, and Grinder always seemed to know when the doggy was going, because, bung, you'd be back in the hole before you had a chance to cheat old Grinder. A day or two downstairs would bring the doggy back out, especially if Grinder tenderized you some with his strap before he heaved you down the stairs. I'd seen big boys and rough girls come to Saint Aggie's as hard as boots, and they come out of Grinder's hole so good doggy that they practically licked his boots for him. Grinder understood children — I give you that. Give us a mean, hard father of a man, a man who doles out punishment and protection like old Jehovah from the sisters' hymnals, and we line up to take his orders.

But Grinder didn't understand Monty Goldfarb.

I'd just come down to lay the long tables for breakfast — it was my turn that day — when I heard Grinder shoot the lock to his door and then the sound of his calluses rasping on the polished brass knob. As his door swung open, I heard the music box playing its tune, Grinder's favorite, a Scottish hymn that the music box sung in Gaelic, its weird horse-gut voice box making the auld words even weirder, like the eldritch crooning of some crone in a street play.

Grinder's heavy tramp receded down the hall to the cellar door. The door creaked open and I felt a shiver down in my stomach, and down below that, in my stones, as I remembered my times in the pit. There was the thunder of his heavy boots on the steps, then his cruel laughter as he beheld Monty.

"Oh, my darling, is *this* how they take their punishment in Montreal? 'Tis no wonder the Frenchies lost their wars to the Upper

Canadians, with such weak little mice as you to fight for them."

They came back up the stairs: Grinder's jaunty tromp, Monty's dragging, beaten limp. Down the hall they came, and I heard poor Monty reaching out to steady himself, brushing the framed drawings of Grinder's horrible ancestors as he went, and I flinched with each squeak of a picture knocked askew, for disturbing Grinder's forebears was a beating offense at Saint Aggie's. But Grinder must have been feeling charitable, for he did not pause to whip beaten Monty that morning.

And so they came into the dining hall, and I did not raise my head but beheld them from the corners of my eyes, taking cutlery from the basket hung over the hook at my right elbow and laying it down neat and precise on the splintery tables.

Each table had three hard loaves on it, charity bread donated from Muddy York's bakeries to us poor crippled kiddies, day old and more than a day old, and as tough as stone. Before each loaf was a knife as sharp as a butcher's, and as long as a man's forearm, and the head child at each table was responsible for slicing the bread using that knife each day (children who were shy an arm or two were exempted from this duty, for which I was thankful, since the head children were always accused of favoring some child with a thicker slice, and fights were common).

Monty was leaning heavily on Grinder, his head down and his steps like those of an old, old man, first a click of his steel foot, then a dragging from his remaining leg. But as they passed the head of the farthest table, Monty sprang from Grinder's side, took up the knife, and with a sure, steady hand—a movement so spry that I knew he'd been shamming from the moment Grinder opened up the cellar door—he plunged the knife into Grinder's barrel chest, just over his heart, and shoved it home, giving it a hard twist.

He stepped back to consider his handiwork. Grinder was standing perfectly still, his face pale beneath his whiskers, and his mouth was working, and I could almost hear the words he was trying to get out, words I'd heard so many times before: *Oh, my lovely, you are a naughty one, but Grinder will beat the devil out of you, purify you with rod and fire, have no fear.*

But no sound escaped Grinder's furious lips. Monty put his hands on his hips and watched him with the critical eye of a bricklayer or a machinist surveying his work. Then, calmly, he put his good right hand on Grinder's chest, just to one side of the knife handle. He said, "Oh, no, Mr. Grindersworth, *this* is how we take our punishment in Montreal." Then he gave the smallest of pushes, and Grinder went over like a chimney that's been hit by a wrecking ball.

He turned then and regarded me full on, the good side of his face alive with mischief, the mess on the other side a wreck of burned skin. He winked his good eye at me and said, "Now, he was a proper pile of filth and muck, wasn't he? World's a better place now, I daresay." He wiped his hand on his filthy trousers—grimed with the brown dirt of the cellar—and held it out to me. "Montague Goldfarb, machinist's boy and prentice artificer, late of old Montreal. Montreal Monty, if you please," he said.

I tried to say something—anything—and realized that I'd bitten the inside of my cheek so hard I could taste the blood. I was so discombobulated that I held out my abbreviated right arm to him, hook and cutlery basket and all, something I hadn't done since I'd first lost the limb. Truth told, I was a little tender and shy about my mutilation and didn't like to think about it, and I especially couldn't bear to see whole people shying back from me as though

I were some kind of monster. But Monty just reached out, calm as you like, and took my hook with his cunning fingers — fingers so long they seemed to have an extra joint — and shook my hook as though it were a whole hand.

"Sorry, mate, I didn't catch your name."

I tried to speak again, and this time I found my voice. "Sian O'Leary," I said. "Antrim Town, then Hamilton, and then here." I wondered what else to say. "Third-grade computerman's boy, once upon a time."

"Oh, that's *fine*," he said. "Skilled tradesmen's helpers are what we want around here. You know the lads and lasses round here, Sian. Are there more like you? Children who can make things, should they be called upon?"

I nodded. It was queer to be holding this calm conversation over the cooling body of Grinder, who now smelled of the ordure his slack bowels had loosed into his fine trousers. But it was also natural, somehow, caught in the burning gaze of Monty Goldfarb, who had the attitude of a master in his shop, running the place with utter confidence.

"Capital." He nudged Grinder with his toe. "That meat'll spoil soon enough, but before he does, let's have some fun, shall we? Give us a hand." He bent and lifted Grinder under one arm. He nodded his head at the remaining arm. "Come on," he said, and I took it, and we lifted the limp corpse of Zophar Grindersworth, the Grinder of Saint Aggie's, and propped him up at the head of the middle table, knife handle protruding from his chest amid a spreading red stain over his blue brocade waistcoat. Monty shook his head. "That won't do," he said, and plucked up a tea towel from a pile by the kitchen door and tied it around Grinder's throat, like a bib, fussing with it until it more or less disguised the grisly wound. Then Monty picked up one of the loaves from the end of the table and tore a hunk off the end.

He chewed at it for a time like a cow at her cud, never taking his eyes off me. Then he swallowed and said, "Hungry work," and laughed with a spray of crumbs.

He paced the room, picking up the cutlery I'd laid down and inspecting it, gnawing thoughtfully at the loaf's end in his hand. "A pretty poor setup," he said. "But I'm sure that wicked old lizard had a pretty soft nest for himself, didn't he?"

I nodded and pointed down the hall to Grinder's door. "The key's on his belt," I said.

Monty fingered the key ring chained to Grinder's thick leather belt, then shrugged. "All one-cylinder jobs," he said, and picked a fork out of the basket that was still hanging from my hook. "Nothing to them. Faster than fussing with his belt." He walked purposefully down the hall, his metal foot thumping off the polished wood, leaving dents in it. He dropped to one knee at the lock, then put the fork under his steel foot and used it as a lever to bend back all but one of the soft pot-metal tines, so that now the fork just had one long thin spike. He slid it into the lock, felt for a moment, then gave a sharp and precise flick of his wrist and twisted the knob. The door opened smoothly at his touch. "Nothing to it," he said, and got back to his feet, dusting off his knees.

Now, I'd been in Grinder's rooms many times, when I'd brought in the boiling water for his bath, or run the rug sweeper over his thick Turkish rugs, or dusted the framed medals and certificates and the cunning machines he kept in his apartment. But this was different, because this time I was coming in with Monty, and

Monty made you ask yourself, *"Why isn't this all mine? Why shouldn't I just take it?"* And I didn't have a good answer, apart from *fear*. And fear was giving way to excitement.

Monty went straight to the humidor by Grinder's deep, plush chair and brought out a fistful of cigars. He handed one to me, and we both bit off the tips and spat them on the fine rug, then lit the cigars with the polished brass lighter in the shape of a beautiful woman that stood on the other side of the chair. Monty clamped his cheroot between his teeth and continued to paw through Grinder's sacred possessions, all the fine goods that the children of Saint Aggie's weren't even allowed to look too closely upon. Soon he was swilling Grinder's best brandy from a lead-crystal decanter, wearing Grinder's red velvet housecoat, topped with Grinder's fine beaver-skin bowler hat.

And it was thus attired that he stumped back into the dining room, where the corpse of Grinder still slumped at table's end, and took up a stance by the old ship's bell that the morning child used for calling the rest of the kids to breakfast, and he began to ring the bell like Saint Aggie's was afire, and he called out as he did so, a wordless, birdlike call, something like a rooster's crowing, such a noise as had never been heard in Saint Aggie's before.

With a clatter and a clank and a hundred muffled arguments, the children of Saint Aggie's pelted down the staircases and streamed into the kitchen, milling uncertainly, eyes popping at the sight of our latest arrival in his stolen finery, still ringing the bell, still making his crazy call, stopping now and again to swill the brandy and laugh and spray a boozy cloud before him.

Once we were all standing in our nightshirts and underclothes, every scar and stump on display, he let off his ringing and cleared his throat ostentatiously, then stepped nimbly onto one of the chairs, wobbling for an instant on his steel peg, then leaped again, like a goat leaping from rock to rock, up onto the table, sending my carefully laid cutlery clattering every which-a-way.

He cleared his throat again, and said, "Good morrow to you, good morrow, all, good morrow to the poor, crippled, abused children of Saint Aggie's. We haven't been properly introduced, so I thought it fitting that I should take a moment to greet you all and share a bit of good news with you. My name is Montreal Monty Goldfarb, machinist's boy, prentice artificer, gentleman adventurer, and liberator of the oppressed. I am late foreshortened"—he waggled his stump—"as are so many of you. And yet, and yet, I say to you, I am as good a man as I was ere I lost my limb, and I say that you are, too." There was a cautious murmur at this. It was the kind of thing the sisters said to you in the hospital, before they brought you to Saint Aggie's, the kind of pretty lies they told you about the wonderful life that awaited you with your new, crippled body, once you had been retrained and put to productive work.

"Children of Saint Aggie's, hearken to old Montreal Monty, and I will tell you of what is possible and what is necessary. First, what is necessary: to end oppression wherever we find it, to be liberators of the downtrodden and the meek. When that evil dog's pizzle flogged me and threw me in his dungeon, I knew that I'd come upon a bully, a man who poisoned the sweet air with each breath of his cursed lungs, and so I resolved to do something about it. And so I have." He clattered the table's length, to where Grinder's body slumped. Many of the children had been so fixated on the odd spectacle that Monty presented that they hadn't even noticed the extraordinary sight of our seated tormentor, apparently sleeping or unconscious. With the air of a magician, Monty bent and took the end of the tea towel and gave it a sharp yank, so that all could see the knife handle protruding from the red stain that covered Grinder's chest. We gasped, and some of the more fainthearted children shrieked, but no one ran off to get the law, and no one wept a single salty tear for our dead benefactor.

Monty held his arms over his head in a wide *V* and looked expectantly upon us. It only took a moment before someone — perhaps it was me — began to applaud, to cheer, to stomp, and then we were all at it, making such a noise as you might encounter in a tavern full of men who've just learned that their side has won a war. Monty waited for it to die down a bit, and then, with a theatrical flourish, he pushed Grinder out of his chair, letting him slide to the floor with a meaty thump, and settled himself into the chair the corpse had lately sat upon. The message was clear: I am now the master of this house.

I cleared my throat and raised my good arm. I'd had more time than the rest of the Saint Aggie's children to consider life without the terrible Grinder, and a thought had come to me. Monty nodded regally at me, and I found myself standing with every eye in the room upon me.

"Monty," I said, "on behalf of the children of Saint Aggie's, I thank you most sincerely for doing away with cruel old Grinder, but I must ask you, what shall we do *now*? With Grinder gone, the sisters will surely shut down Saint Aggie's, or perhaps send us another vile old master to beat us, and you shall go to the gallows at the King Street Gaol, and, well, it just seems like a pity that . . ." I waved my stump. "It just seems a pity, is what I'm saying."

Monty nodded again. "Sian, I thank you, for you have come

neatly to my next point. I spoke of what was needed and what was possible, and now we must discuss what is possible. I had a nice long time to meditate on this question last night as I languished in the pit below, and I think I have a plan, though I shall need your help with it if we are to pull it off."

He took up a loaf of hard bread and began to wave it like a baton as he spoke, thumping it on the table for emphasis.

"Item: I understand that the sisters provide for Saint Aggie's with such alms as are necessary to keep our lamps burning, fuel in our fireplaces, and gruel and such on the table, yes?" We nodded. "Right.

"Item: Nevertheless, Old Turd Gargler here was used to sending you poor kiddies out to beg with your wounds all on display, to bring him whatever coppers you could coax from the drunkards of Muddy York with which to feather his pretty little nest yonder. Correct?" We nodded again. "Right.

"Item: We are all of us the crippled children of Muddy York's great information-processing factories. We are artificers, machinists, engineers, cunning shapers and makers, everyone, for that is how we came to be injured. Correct? Right.

"Item: It is a murdersome pity that such as we should be turned out to beg when we have so much skill at our disposal. Between us, we could make anything, *do* anything, but our departed tormentor lacked the native wit to see this, correct? Right.

"Item: The sisters of the Simpering Order of Saint Agatha's Weeping Sores have all the cleverness of a turnip. This I saw for myself during my tenure in their hospital. Fooling them would be easier than fooling an idiot child. Correct? *Right.*"

He levered himself out of the chair and began to stalk the dining room, stumping up and down. "Someone tell me, how often do the good sisters pay us a visit?"

"Sundays," I said. "When they take us all to church."

He nodded. "And does that spoiled meat there accompany us to church?"

"No," I said. "No, he stays here. He says he 'worships in his own way.'" Truth was he was invariably too hungover to rise on a Sunday.

He nodded again. "And today is Tuesday. Which means that we have five days to do our work."

"What work, Monty?"

"Why, we are going to build a clockwork automaton based on that evil tyrant what I slew this very morning. We will build a device of surpassing and fiendish cleverness, such as will fool the nuns and the world at large into thinking that we are still being ground up like mincemeat, while we lead a life of leisure, fun, and invention, such as befits children of our mental stature and good character."

Here's the oath we swore to Monty before we went to work on the automaton:

> I, [state your full name], do hereby give my most solemn
> oath that I will never, ever betray the secrets of Saint
> Agatha's. I bind myself to the good fortune of my fellow
> inmates at this institution and vow to honor them as
> though they were my brothers and sisters, and not fight
> with them, nor spite them, nor do them down or dirty.
> I make this oath freely and gladly, and should I betray it,
> I wish that old Satan himself would rise up from the pit and
> tear out my treacherous guts and use them for bootlaces,
> that his devils would tear my betrayer's tongue from my

mouth and use it to wipe their private parts, that my lying body would be fed, inch by inch, to the hungry and terrible basilisks of the pit. So I swear, and so mote be it!

There were two older children in the house who'd worked for a tanner. Matthew was shy all the fingers on his left hand. Becka was missing an eye and her nose, which she joked was a mercy, for there is no smell more terrible than the charnel reek of the tanning works. But between them, they were quite certain that they could carefully remove, stuff, and remount Grinder's head, careful to leave the jaw in place.

As the oldest machinist at Saint Aggie's, I was conscripted to work on the torso and armature mechanisms. I played chief engineer, bossing a gang of six boys and four girls who had experience with mechanisms. We cannibalized Saint Aggie's old mechanical wash wringer, with its spindly arms and many fingers, and I was sent out several times to pawn Grinder's fine crystal and pocket watch to raise money for parts.

Monty oversaw all, but he took personal charge of Grinder's voice box, through which he would imitate old Grinder's voice when the sisters came by on Sunday. Saint Aggie's was fronted with a Dutch door, and Grinder habitually opened only the top half to jaw with the sisters. Monty said that we could prop the partial torso on a low table, to hide the fact that no legs depended from it.

"We'll tie a sick kerchief around his face and give out that he's got the flu, and that it's spread through the whole house. That'll get us all out of church, which is a tidy little jackpot in and of itself. The kerchief will disguise the fact that his lips ain't moving in time with his talking."

I shook my head at this idea. The nuns were hardly geniuses, but how long could this hold out for?

"It won't have to last more than a week — by next week, we'll have something better to show 'em."

Here's a thing: it all worked like a fine-tuned machine.

The kerchief made him look like a bank robber, and Monty painted his face to make him seem more lively, for the tanning had dried him out some (he also doused the horrible thing with liberal lashings of bay rum and greased his hair with a heavy pomade, for the tanning process had left him with a smell like an outhouse on a hot day). Monty had affixed an armature to the thing's bottom jaw — we'd had to break it to get it to open, prying it roughly with a screwdriver, cracking a tooth or two in the process, and I have nightmares to this day about the sound it made when it finally yawned open.

A child — little legless Dora, whose begging pitch included a sad little puppetry show — could work this armature by means of a squeeze bulb taken from the siphon starter on Grinder's cider-brewing tub and so make the jaw go up and down in time with speech.

The speech itself was accomplished by means of the horse-gut voice box from Grinder's music box. Monty sure-handedly affixed a long, smooth glass tube — part of the cracking apparatus that I had been sent to market to buy — to the music box's resonator. This he ran up behind our automatic Grinder. Then, crouched on the floor before the voice box, stationed next to Dora on her wheeled plank, he was able to whisper across the horse-gut strings and have them buzz out a credible version of Grinder's whiskey-roughened growl. And once he'd tuned the horse gut just so, the vocal resemblance was even more remarkable. Combined with Dora's skillful puppetry, the effect was galvanizing. It took a conscious effort to remember that this was a puppet talking to you, not a man.

The sisters turned up at the appointed hour on Sunday, only to be greeted by our clockwork Grinder, stood in the half door, face swathed in a flu mask. We'd hung quarantine bunting from the windows, crisscrossing the front of Saint Aggie's with it for good measure, and a goodly number of us kiddies were watching from the upstairs windows with our best drawn and sickly looks on our faces.

So the sisters hung back practically at the pavement and shouted, "Mr. Grindersworth!" in alarmed tones, staring with horror at the apparition in the doorway.

"Sisters, good day to you," Monty said into his horse gut while Dora worked her squeeze bulb, and the jaw went up and down behind its white cloth, and the muffled simulation of Grinder's voice emanated from the top of the glass tube, hidden behind the automaton's head so that it seemed to come from the right place. "Though not such a good day for us, I fear."

"The children are ill?"

Monty gave out a fine sham of Grinder's laugh, the one he used when dealing with proper people, with the cruelty barely plastered over. "Oh, not all of them. But we have a dozen cases. Thankfully, I appear to be immune, and oh, my, but you wouldn't believe the help these tots are in the practical nursing department. Fine kiddies, my charges, yes, indeed. But still, best to keep them away from the general public for the nonce, hey? I'm quite sure we'll have them up on their feet by next Sunday, and they'll be glad indeed of the chance to get down on their knees and thank the beneficent Lord for their good health." Monty was laying it on thick, but then so had Grinder, when it came to the sisters.

"We shall send over some help after the services," the head sister said, hands at her breast, a tear glistening in her eye at the thought of our bravery. I thought the jig was up. Of course the order would have some sisters who'd had the flu and gotten over it, rendering them immune. But Monty never worried.

"No, no," he said smoothly. I had the presence of mind to take up the cranks that operated the arms we'd constructed for him, waving them about in a negating way — this effect rather spoiled by my nervousness, so that they seemed more octopus tentacle than arm. But the sisters didn't appear to notice. "As I say, I have plenty of help here with my good children."

"A basket, then," the sister said. "Some nourishing food and fizzy drinks for the children."

Crouching low in the anteroom, we crippled children traded disbelieving looks with one another. Not only had Monty gotten rid of Grinder and gotten us out of going to church, but he'd also set things up so that the sisters of Saint Aggie's were going to bring us their best grub, for free, because we were all so poorly and ailing! It was all we could do not to cheer.

And cheer we did, later, when the sisters set ten huge hampers down on our doorstep, whence we retrieved them, finding in them a feast fit for princes: cold meat pies glistening with aspic, marrow bones still warm from the oven, suet pudding and jugs of custard with skin on top of them, huge bottles of fizzy lemonade and small beer. By the time we'd laid it out in the dining room, it seemed like we'd never be able to eat it all.

But we et every last morsel, and four of us carried Monty about on our shoulders — two carrying, two steadying the carriers — and someone found a concertina, and someone found some combs and waxed paper, and we sang until the walls shook: "The Mechanic's Folly," "A Combinatorial Explosion at the Computer Works," and then endless rounds of "For He's a Jolly Good Fellow."

Monty had promised improvements on the clockwork Grinder by the following Sunday, and he made good on it. Since we no longer had to beg all day long, we children of Saint Aggie's had time in plenty, and Monty had no shortage of skilled volunteers who wanted to work with him on Grinder II, as he called it. Grinder II sported a rather handsome large, droopy mustache, which hid the action of its lips. This mustache was glued onto the head assembly one hair at a time, a painstaking job that denuded every horsehair brush in the house, but the effect was impressive.

More impressive was the leg assembly I bossed into existence, a pair of clockwork pins that could lever Grinder from a seated position into full upright, balancing him by means of three gyros we hid in his chest cavity. Once these were wound and spun, Grinder could stand up in a very natural fashion. Once we'd rearranged the furniture to hide Dora and Monty behind a large armchair, you could stand right in the parlor and "converse" with him, and unless you were looking very hard, you'd never know but what you were talking with a mortal man, and not an automaton made of tanned flesh, steel, springs, and clay (we used rather a lot of custom-made porcelain from the prosthetic works to get his legs right — the children who were shy a leg or two knew which leg makers in town had the best wares).

And so when the sisters arrived the following Sunday, they were led right into the parlor, whose lace curtains kept the room in a semidark state, and there they parleyed with Grinder, who came to his feet when they entered and left. One of the girls was in charge of his arms, and she had practiced with them so well that she was able to move them in a very convincing fashion. Convincing enough, anyroad: the sisters left Grinder with a bag of clothes and a bag of oranges that had come off a ship that had sailed from Spanish Florida right up the St. Lawrence to the port of Montreal, and thereafter traversed by railcar to Muddy York. They had made a parcel gift of these succulent treasures to Grinder, to "help the kiddies keep away the scurvy," but Grinder always kept them for himself or flogged them to his pals for a neat penny. We wolfed the oranges right after services and then took our Sabbath free with games and more brandy from Grinder's sideboard.

And so we went, week on week, with small but impressive updates to our clockwork man: hands that could grasp and smoke a pipe, a clever mechanism that let him throw back his head and laugh, fingers that could drum on the table beside him, eyes that could follow you around a room, and eyelids that could blink, albeit slowly.

But Monty had *much* bigger plans.

"I want to bring in another fifty-six bits," he said, gesturing at the computing panel in Grinder's parlor, a paltry eight-bit works. That meant that there were eight switches with eight matching levers, connected to eight brass rods that ran down to the public computing works that ran beneath the streets of Muddy York. Grinder had used his eight bits to keep Saint Aggie's books — both the set he showed to the sisters and the one in which he kept track of what he was trousering for himself—and he'd let one "lucky" child work the great, stiff return arm that sent the instructions set on the switch back to the Hall of Computing for queuing and processing on the great frames that had cost me my good right arm. An instant later, the processed answer would be returned to the levers above the switches and to whatever interpretive mechanism you had yoked up to them (Grinder used a telegraph machine that printed the answers on a long, thin sheet of paper).

"Fifty-six bits!" I boggled at Monty. A sixty-four-bit rig wasn't unheard of, if you were a mighty shipping company or insurer. But in a private home—well, the racket of the switches would shake the foundations! Remember, dear reader, that each additional bit *doubled* the calculating faculty of the home panel. Monty was proposing to increase Saint Aggie's computational capacity by a factor more than a *quadrillionfold*! (We computermen are accustomed to dealing in these rarified numbers, but they may surprise you. Have no fear—a quadrillion is a number of such surpassing monstrosity that you must have the knack of figuring to even approach it properly.)

"Monty," I gasped, "are you planning to open a firm of accountants at Saint Aggie's?"

He laid a finger alongside of his nose. "Not all all, my old darling. I have a thought that perhaps we could build a tiny figuring engine into our Grinder's chest cavity, one that could take programs punched off of a sufficiently powerful computing frame, and that these might enable him to walk about on his own, as natural as you please, and even carry on conversations as though he were a living man. Such a creation would afford us even more freedom and security, as you must be able to see."

"But it will cost the bloody world!" I said.

"Oh, I didn't think we'd *pay* for it," he said. Once again, he laid his finger alongside his nose.

And that is how I came to find myself down our local sewer, in the dead of night, a seventeen-year-old brass jacker, bossing a gang of eight kids with ten arms, seven noses, nine hands, and eleven legs between them, working furiously and racing the dawn to fit thousands of precision brass pushrods with lightly balanced joints from the local multifarious amalgamation and amplification switch house to Saint Aggie's utility cellar. It didn't work, of course. Not that night. But at least we didn't break anything and alert the Upper Canadian Computing Authority to our mischief. Three nights later, after much fine-tuning, oiling, and desperate prayer, the panel at Saint Aggie's boasted sixty-four shining brass bits, the very height of modernity and engineering.

Monty and the children all stood before the panel, which had been burnished to a mirror shine by No-Nose Timmy, who'd done finishing work before a careless master had stumbled over him, pushing him face-first into a spinning grinding wheel. In the gaslight, we appeared to be staring at a group of mighty heroes, and when Monty turned to regard us, he had bright tears in his eyes.

"Sisters and brothers, we have done ourselves proud. A new day has dawned for Saint Aggie's and for our lives. Thank you. You have done me proud."

We shared out the last of Grinder's brandy, a thimbleful each, even for the smallest kiddies, and drank a toast to the brave and clever children of Saint Aggie's and to Montreal Monty, our savior and the founder of our feast.

Let me tell you some about life at Saint Aggie's in that golden age. Whereas before, we'd rise at seven AM for a mean breakfast — prepared by unfavored children whom Grinder punished by putting them into the kitchen at four thirty to prepare the meal — followed by a brief "sermon" roared out by Grinder, now we rose at a very civilized ten AM to eat a leisurely breakfast over the daily papers that Grinder had subscribed to. The breakfasts — all the meals and chores — were done on a rotating basis, with exemptions for children whose infirmity made performing some tasks harder than others. Though all worked — even the blind children sorted weevils and stones from the rice and beans by touch.

Whereas before, Grinder had sent us out to beg every day — excepting Sundays — debasing ourselves and putting our injuries on display for the purposes of sympathy, now we were free to laze around the house all day or work at our own fancies, painting or reading or just playing like the cherished children of rich families who didn't need to send their young ones to the city to work for the family fortune.

But most of us quickly bored of the life of Riley, and for us, there was plenty to do. The clockwork Grinder was always a distraction, especially after Monty started work on the mechanism that would accept punched-tape instructions from the computing panel.

When we weren't working on Grinder, there was other work. We former apprentices went back to our old masters — men and women who were guilty but glad enough to see us, in the main — and told them that the skilled children of Saint Aggie's were looking for piecework as part of our rehabilitation, at a competitive price.

It was hardly a lie, either: as broken tools and mechanisms came in for mending, the boys and girls taught one another their crafts and trade, and it wasn't long before a steady flow of cash came into Saint Aggie's, paying for better food, better clothes, and, soon enough, the very best artificial arms, legs, hands, and feet, the best glass eyes, the best wigs. When Gertie Shine-Pate was fitted for her first wig and saw herself in the great looking glass in Grinder's study, she burst into tears and hugged all and sundry, and thereafter, Saint Aggie's bought her three more wigs to wear as the mood struck her. She took to styling these wigs with combs and scissors, and before long she was cutting hair for all of us at Saint Aggie's. We never looked so good.

That gilded time from the end of my boyhood is like a sweet dream to me now. A sweet, lost dream.

No invention works right the first time around. The inventors' tales you read in the science penny dreadfuls, where some engineer discovers a new principle, puts it into practice, shouts, "Eureka," and sets up his own foundry? They're rubbish. Real invention is a process of repeated, crushing failure that leads, very rarely, to a success. If you want to succeed faster, there's nothing for it but to fail faster and better.

The first time Monty rolled a paper tape into a cartridge and inserted it into Grinder, we all held our breath while he fished around the arse of Grinder's trousers for the toggle that released the tension on the mainspring we wound through a keyhole in his hip. He stepped back as the soft whining of the mechanism emanated from Grinder's body, and then Grinder began, very slowly, to pace the room's length, taking three long—if jerky— steps, then turning about, and taking three steps back. Then he lifted a hand as in greeting, and his mouth stretched into a rictus that might have passed for a grin, and then, very carefully, Grinder punched himself in the face so hard that his head came free from his neck and rolled across the floor with a meaty sound (it took our resident taxidermists a full two days to repair the damage), and his body went into a horrible paroxysm like the Saint Vitus dance, until it, too, fell to the floor.

This was on Monday, and by Wednesday, we had Grinder back on his feet with his head reattached. Again, Monty depressed his toggle, and this time, Grinder made a horrendous clanking sound and pitched forward.

And so it went, day after day, each tiny improvement accompanied by abject failure, and each Sunday we struggled to put the pieces together so Grinder could pay his respects to the sisters.

Until the day came that the sisters brought round a new child to join our happy clan, and it all began to unravel.

We had been lucky in that Monty's arrival at Saint Aggie's coincided with a reformers' movement that had swept Upper Canada, a movement whose figurehead, Princess Lucy, met with every magistrate, councilman, alderman, and beadle in the colony, with the sleeves of her dresses pinned up to the stumps of her shoulders, sternly discussing the plight of the children who worked in the Information Foundries across the colonies. It didn't do no good in the long run, of course, but for the short term, word got round that the authorities would come down very hard on any master whose apprentice lost a piece of himself in the data mills. So it was some months before Saint Aggie's had any new meat arrive upon its doorstep.

The new meat in question was a weepy boy of about eleven — the same age I'd been when I arrived — and he was shy his left leg all the way up to the hip. He had a crude steel leg in its place, strapped up with a rough, badly cured cradle that must have hurt like hellfire. He also had a splintery crutch that he used to get around with, the sort of thing that the sisters of Saint Aggie's bought in huge lots from unscrupulous tradesmen who cared nothing for the people who'd come to use them.

His name was William Sansousy, a métis boy who'd come from the wild woods of Lower Canada seeking work in Muddy York, who'd found instead an implacable machine that had torn off his leg and devoured it without a second's remorse. He spoke English with a thick French accent and slipped into joual when he was overcome with sorrow.

Two sisters brought him to the door on a Friday afternoon. We knew they were coming; they'd sent around a messenger boy with a printed telegram telling Grinder to make room for one more. Monty wanted to turn his clockwork Grinder loose to walk to the door and greet them, but we all told him he'd be mad to try it: there was so much that could go wrong, and if the sisters worked out what had happened, we could finish up dangling from nooses at the King Street Gaol.

Monty relented resentfully, and instead we seated Grinder in his overstuffed chair, with Monty tucked away behind it, ready to converse with the sisters. I hid with him, ready to send Grinder to his feet and extend his cold, leathery artificial hand to the boy when the sisters turned him over.

And it went smoothly — that day. When the sisters had gone and their car had built up its head of steam and chuffed and clanked away, we emerged from our hiding place. Monty broke into slangy, rapid French, gesticulating and hopping from foot to peg leg and back again, and William's eyes grew as big as saucers as Monty explained the lay of the land to him. The *clang* when he thumped Grinder in his cast-iron chest made William leap back, and he hobbled toward the door.

"Wait, wait!" Monty called, switching to English. "Wait, will you, you idiot? This is the best day of your life, young William! But for us, you might have entered a life of miserable bondage. Instead, you will enjoy all the fruits of liberty, rewarding work, and comradeship. We take care of our own here at Saint Aggie's. You'll have top grub, a posh leg, and a beautiful crutch that's as smooth as a baby's arse and as soft as a lady's bosom. You'll have the freedom to come and go as you please, and you'll have a warm bed to sleep in every night. And best of all, you'll have us, your family here at Saint Aggie's. We take care of our own, we do."

The boy looked at us, tears streaming down his face. He made me remember what it had been like, my first day at Saint Aggie's, the cold fear coiled around your guts like rope caught in a reciprocating gear. At Saint Aggie's we put on brave faces, never cried where no one could see us, but seeing him weep made me remember all the times I'd cried, cried for my lost family who'd sold me into indenture, cried for my mangled body, my ruined life. But living without Grinder's constant terrorizing must have softened my heart. Suddenly it was all I could do to stop myself from giving the poor little mite a one-armed hug.

I didn't hug him, but Monty did, stumping over to him, and the two of them bawled like babbies. Their peg legs knocked together as they embraced like drunken sailors, seeming to cry out every tear we'd any of us ever held in. Before long, we were all crying with them, fat tears streaming down our faces, the sound like something out of the pit.

When the sobs had stopped, William looked around at us, wiped his nose, and said, "Thank you. I think I am home."

But it wasn't home for him. Poor William. We'd had children like him, in the bad old days, children who just couldn't get back up on their feet (or foot) again. Most of the time, I reckon, they were kids who couldn't make it as apprentices, neither, kids who'd spent their working lives full of such awful misery that they were *bound* to fall into a machine. And being sundered from their limbs didn't improve their outlook.

We tried everything we could think of to cheer William up. He'd worked for a watch smith, and he had a pretty good hand at disassembling and cleaning mechanisms. His stump ached him like fire, even after he'd been fitted with a better apparatus by Saint Aggie's best leg maker, and it was only when he was working with his little tweezers and brushes that he lost the grimace that twisted up his face so. Monty had him strip and clean every clockwork in the house, even the ones that were working perfectly — even the delicate works we'd carefully knocked together for the clockwork Grinder. But it wasn't enough.

In the bad old days, Grinder would have beaten the boy and sent him out to beg in the worst parts of town, hoping that he'd be run down by a cart or killed by one of the blunderbuss gangs that marauded there. When the law brought home the boy's body, old Grinder would weep crocodile tears and tug his hair at the bloody evil that men did, and then he'd go back to his rooms and play some music and drink some brandy and sleep the sleep of the unjust.

We couldn't do the same, and so we tried to bring up William's spirits instead, and when he'd had enough of it, he lit out on his own. The first we knew of it was when he didn't turn up for breakfast. This wasn't unheard of—any of the free children of Saint Aggie's was able to rise and wake whenever he chose—but William had been a regular at breakfast every day. I made my way upstairs to the dormer room, where the boys slept, to look for him and found his bed empty, his coat and his peg leg and crutch gone.

"He's gone," Monty said. "Long gone." He sighed and looked out the window. "Must be trying to get back to the Gatineau." He shook his head.

"Do you think he'll make it?" I said, knowing the answer but hoping that Monty would lie to me.

"Not a chance," Monty said. "Not him. He'll either be beaten, arrested, or worse by sundown. That lad hasn't any self-preservation instincts."

At this, the dining room fell silent and all eyes turned on Monty, and I saw in a flash what a terrible burden we all put on him: savior, father, chieftain. He twisted his face into a halfway convincing smile.

"Oh, maybe not. He might just be hiding out down the road. Tell you what. Eat up and we'll go searching for him."

I never saw a load of plates cleared faster. It was bare minutes before we were formed up in the parlor, divided into groups, and sent out into Muddy York to find William Sansousy. We turned that bad old city upside down, asking nosy questions and sticking our heads in where they didn't belong, but Monty had been doubly right the first time around.

The police found William Sansousy's body in a marshy bit of land off the Leslie Street Spit. His pockets had been slit, his pathetic paper sack of belongings torn and the clothes scattered, and his fine hand-turned leg was gone. He had been dead for hours.

The detective inspector who presented himself that afternoon at Saint Aggie's was trailed by a team of technicians who had a wire sound-recorder and a portable logic engine for inputting the data of his investigation. He seemed very proud of his machine, even though it came with three convicts from the King Street Gaol in shackles and leg irons who worked tirelessly to keep the springs wound, toiling in a lather of sweat and heaving breath, heat boiling off their shaved heads in shimmering waves.

He showed up just as the clock in the parlor chimed eight times, a bear chasing a bird around on a track as it sang the hour. We peered out the windows in the upper floors, saw the inspector, and understood just why Monty had been so morose all afternoon.

But Monty did us proud. He went to the door with his familiar swagger and swung it wide, extending his hand to the inspector.

"Montague Goldfarb at your service, Officer. Our patron has stepped away, but please, do come in."

The inspector gravely shook the proffered hand, his huge gloved mitt swallowing Monty's boyish hand. It was easy to forget that he was just a child, but the looming presence of the giant inspector reminded us all.

"Master Goldfarb," the inspector said, taking his hat off and peering through his smoked monocle at the children in the parlor. All of us sat with hands folded like we were in a pantomime about the best-behaved, most crippled, most terrified, least threatening children in all the colonies. "I'm am sorry to hear that Mr. Grindersworth is not at home to the constabulary. Have you any notion as to what temporal juncture we might expect him?" If I hadn't been concentrating on not peeing myself with terror, the inspector's pompous speech might have set me to laughing.

Monty didn't bat an eye. "Mr. Grindersworth was called away to see his brother in Sault Sainte Marie, and we expect him tomorrow. I'm his designated lieutenant, though. Perhaps I might help you?"

The inspector stroked his forked beard and gave us all another long look. "Tomorrow, hey? Well, I don't suppose that justice should wait that long. Master Goldfarb, I have grim intelligence for you, as regards one of your young compatriots, a Master—" He consulted a punched card that was held in a hopper on his clanking logic engine. "William Sansousy. He lies even now upon a slab in the city morgue. Someone of authority from this institution is required to confirm the preliminary identification. You will do, I suppose. Though your patron will have to present himself posthaste in order to sign the several official documents that necessarily accompany an event of such gravity."

We'd known as soon as the inspector turned up on Saint Aggie's doorstep that William was dead. If he was merely in trouble, it would have been a constable, dragging him by the ear. We half-children of Saint Aggie's only rated a full inspector when we were topped by some evil bastard in this evil town. But hearing the inspector say the words, puffing them through his drooping mustache, that made it real. None of us had ever cried when Saint Aggie's children were taken by the streets—at least not where the others could see it. But this time around, without Grinder to shoot us filthy daggers if we made a peep while the law was about, it opened the floodgates. Boys and girls, young and old, we cried for poor little William. He'd come to the best of all possible Saint Aggie's, but it hadn't been good enough for him. He'd wanted to go back to the parents who'd sold him into service, wanted a return to his mam's lap and bosom. Who among us didn't want that, in his secret heart?

Monty's tears were silent, and they rolled down his cheeks as he shrugged into his coat and hat and let the inspector — who was clearly embarrassed by the display — lead him out the door.

When Monty came home, he arrived at a house full of children who were ready to go mad. We'd cried ourselves hoarse, then sat about the parlor, not knowing what to do. If there had been any of old Grinder's booze still in the house, we'd have drunk it.

"What's the plan, then?" he said, coming through the door. "We've got one night until that bastard comes back. If he doesn't find Grinder, he'll go to the sisters, and it'll come down around our ears. What's more, he knows Grinder, personal, from other dead ones in years gone by, and I don't think he'll be fooled by our machine, no matter how good it goes."

"What's the plan?" I said, mouth hanging open. "Monty, the plan is that we're all going to jail, and you and I and everyone else who helped cover up the killing of Grinder will dance at rope's end!"

He gave me a considering look. "Sian, that is absolutely the worst plan I have ever heard." And then he grinned at us the way he did, and we all knew that, somehow, it would all be all right.

"Constable, come quick! He's going to kill himself!"

I practiced the line for the fiftieth time, willing my eyes to go wider, my voice to carry more alarm. Behind me, Monty scowled at my reflection in the mirror in Grinder's personal toilet, where I'd been holed up for hours.

"Verily, the stage lost a great player when that machine mangled you, Sian. You are perfect. Now, get moving before I tear your remaining arm off and beat you with it. Go!"

Phase one of the plan was easy enough: we'd smuggle our Grinder up onto the latticework of steel and scaffold where they were building the mighty Prince Edward Viaduct, at the end of Bloor Street. Monty had punched his program already: he'd pace back and forth, tugging his hair, shaking his head like a maddened man, and then, abruptly, he'd turn and fling himself bodily off the platform, plunging 130 feet into the Don River, where he would simply disintegrate into a million cogs, gears, springs, and struts, which would sink to the riverbed and begin to rust away. The coppers would recover his clothes, and those, combined with the eyewitness testimony of the constable I was responsible for bringing to the bridge, would establish in everyone's mind exactly what had happened and how: Grinder was so distraught at one more death from among his charges that he had popped his own clogs in grief. We were all of us standing ready to testify as to how poor William was Grinder's little favorite, a boy he loved like a son, and so forth. Who would suspect a bunch of helpless cripples, anyway?

That was the theory, at least. But now I was actually standing by the bridge, watching six half-children wrestle the automaton into place, striving for silence so as not to alert the guards who were charged with defending the structure they were already calling the Suicide's Magnet, and I couldn't believe that it would possibly work.

Five of the children scampered away, climbing back down the scaffolds, slipping and sliding and nearly dying more times than I could count, causing my heart to thunder in my chest so hard,

I thought I might die upon the spot. Then they were safely away, climbing back up the ravine's walls in the mud and snow, almost invisible in the dusky dawn light. Monty waved an arm at me, and I knew it was my cue and that I should be off to rouse the constabulary, but I found myself rooted to the spot.

In that moment, every doubt and fear and misery I'd ever harbored crowded back in on me. The misery of being abandoned by my family, the sorrow and loneliness I'd felt among the prentice lads, the humiliation of Grinder's savage beatings and harangues. The shame of my injury and of every time I'd groveled before a drunk or a pitying lady with my stump on display for pennies to fetch home to Grinder. What was I doing? There was no way I could possibly pull this off. I wasn't enough of a man—nor enough of a boy.

But then I thought of all those moments since the coming of Monty Goldfarb, the millionfold triumphs of ingenuity and hard work, the computing power I'd stolen out from under the nose of the calculators who had treated me as a mere work ox before my injury. I thought of the cash we'd brought in, the children who'd smiled and sung and danced on the worn floors of Saint Aggie's, and—

And I ran to the policeman, who was warming himself by doing a curious hopping dance in place, hands in his armpits. "Constable!" I piped, all sham terror that no one would have known for a sham. "Constable! Come quick! He's going to kill himself!"

The sister who came to sit up with us mourning kiddies that night was called Sister Mary Immaculata, and she was kindly, if a bit dim. I remembered her from my stay in the hospital after my maiming: a slightly vacant prune-faced woman in a wimple who'd bathed my wounds gently and given me solemn hugs when I woke screaming in the middle of the night.

She was positive that the children of Saint Aggie's were inconsolable over the suicide of our beloved patron, Zophar Grindersworth, and she doled out those same solemn cuddles to anyone foolish enough to stray near her. That none of us shed a tear was lost on her, though she did note with approval how smoothly the operation of Saint Aggie's continued without Grinder's oversight.

The next afternoon, Sister Mary Immaculata circulated among us, offering reassurance that a new master would be found for Saint Aggie's. None of us was much comforted by this: we knew the kind of man who was likely to fill such a plum vacancy.

"If only there were some way we could go on running this place on our own," I moaned under my breath, trying to concentrate on repairing the pressure gauge on a pneumatic evacuator that we'd taken in for mending.

Monty shot me a look. He had taken the sister's coming very hard. "I don't think I have it in me to kill the next one, too. Anyway, they're bound to notice if we keep on assassinating our guardians."

I snickered despite myself. Then my gloomy pall descended again. It had all been so good. How could we possibly return to the old way? But there was no way the sisters would let a bunch of crippled children govern themselves.

"What a waste," I said. "What a waste of all this potential."

"At least I'll be shut of it in two years," Monty said. "How long have you got till your eighteenth?"

My brow furrowed. I looked out the grimy workshop window at the iron gray February sky. "It's February tenth today?"

"Eleventh," he said.

I laughed, an ugly sound. "Why, Monty, my friend, today is my eighteenth birthday. I believe I have survived Saint Aggie's to graduate to bigger and better things. I have attained my majority, old son."

He held a hand out and solemnly shook my hook with it. "Happy birthday and congratulations, then, Sian. May the world treat you with all the care you deserve."

I stood, the scrape of my chair very loud and sudden. I realized I had no idea what I would do next. I had managed to completely forget that my graduation from Saint Aggie's was looming, that I would be a free man. In my mind, I'd imagined myself dwelling at Saint Aggie's forever.

Forever.

"You look like you just got hit in the head with a shovel," Monty said. "What on earth is going through that mind of yours?"

I didn't answer. I was already on my way to find Sister Immaculata. I found her in the kitchen, helping legless Dora make the toast for tea, over the fire's grate.

"Sister," I said, "a word, please?"

As she turned and followed me into the pantry off the kitchen, some of that fear I'd felt on the bridge bubbled up in me. I tamped it back down again firmly, like a piston compressing some superheated gas.

She was really just as I remembered her, and she had remembered me, too—she remembered all of us, the children she'd held in the night and then consigned to this hell upon earth, all unknowing.

"Sister Mary Immaculata, I attained my eighteenth birthday today."

She opened her mouth to congratulate me, but I held up my stump.

"I turned eighteen today, Sister. I am a man; I have attained my majority. I am at liberty and must seek my fortune in the world. I have a proposal for you, accordingly." I put everything I had into this, every dram of confidence and maturity that I'd learned since we inmates had taken over the asylum. "I was Mr. Grindersworth's lieutenant and assistant in every matter relating to the daily operation of this place. Many's the day I did every bit of work that there was to do, while Mr. Grindersworth attended to family matters. I know every inch of this place, every soul in it, and I have had the benefit of the excellent training and education that there is to have here.

"I had always thought to seek my fortune in the world as a mechanic of some kind, if any shop would have a half-made thing like me, but seeing as you find yourself at loose ends in the superintendent department, I thought I might perhaps put my plans on hold for the time being, until such time as a full search could be conducted."

"Sian," she said, her face wrinkling into a gap-toothed smile, "are you proposing that *you* might run Saint Agatha's?"

It took everything I could not to wilt under the pity and amusement in that smile. "I am, Sister. I am. I have all but run it for months now, and have every confidence in my capacity to go on doing so for so long as need be." I kept my gaze and my voice even. "I believe that the noble mission of Saint Aggie's is a truly attainable one: that it can rehabilitate such damaged things as we and prepare us for the wider world."

She shook her head. "Sian," she said softly, "Sian. I wish it could be. But there's no hope that such an appointment would be approved by the board of governors."

I nodded. "Yes, I thought so. But do the governors need to approve a *temporary* appointment? A stopgap, until a suitable person can be found?"

Her smile changed, got wider. "You have certainly come into your own shrewdness here, haven't you?

"I was taught well," I said, and smiled back.

The temporary has a way of becoming permanent. That was my bolt of inspiration, my galvanic realization. Once the sisters had something that worked, that did not call attention to itself, that took in crippled children and released whole persons some years later, they didn't need to muck about with it. As the mechanics say, "If it isn't broken, it doesn't want fixing."

I'm no mechanic, not anymore. The daily running of Saint Aggie's occupied a larger and larger slice of my time, until I found that I knew more about tending to a child's fever or soothing away a nightmare than I did about hijacking the vast computers to do our bidding.

But that's no matter, as we have any number of apprentice computermen and computerwomen turning up on our doorsteps. So long as the machineries of industry grind on, the supply will be inexhaustible.

Monty visits me from time to time, mostly to scout for talent. His shop, Goldfarb and Associates, has a roaring trade in computational novelties and service, and if anyone is bothered by the appearance of a factory filled with the halt, the lame, the blind, and the crippled, they are thankfully outnumbered by those who are delighted by the quality of the work and the good value in his schedule of pricing.

But it was indeed a golden time, that time when I was but a boy at Saint Aggie's among the boys and girls, a cog in a machine that Monty built of us, part of a great uplifting, a transformation from a hell to something like a heaven. That I am sentenced to serve in this heaven I helped to make is no great burden, I suppose.

Still, I do yearn to screw a jeweler's loupe into my eye, pick up a fine tool, and bend the sodium lamp to shine upon some cunning mechanism that wants fixing. For machines may be balky and they may destroy us with their terrible appetite for oil, blood, and flesh, but they behave according to fixed rules and can be understood by anyone with the cunning to look upon them and winkle out their secrets. Children are ever so much more complicated.

Though I believe I may be learning a little about them, too.

SEVEN
DAYS
BESET BY DEMONS

Shawn Cheng

Ah ... How clever.

What is it supposed to be?

This one tells the tale of Lancelot and Guinevere.

It is Lancelot — not Arthur — who rescues Guinevere from the Rogue Knight.

And, finally, Guinevere chooses Lancelot.

She realizes it is their Destiny.

It is True Love.

Darling, we're dreadfully late.

Oh, foo!

ENVY

WEDNESDAY

Now ...

Which one was it?

Ah, here it is.

Lancelot and Guinevere.

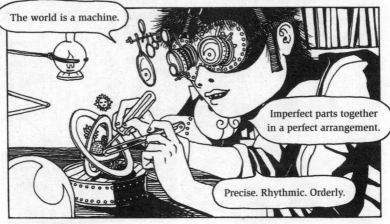

WRATH

Hand in Glove

{ YSABEAU S. WILCE }

❖ I. THE POLICE ❖

Like bees to honey, they cluster around him, Anibal Aguille y Wilkins, the golden boy of the Califa Police Department, thrice decorated, always decorative. Eyes like honey, skin as rich as molasses, a jaw square enough to serve as a cornerstone. He's a dish, is Detective Wilkins, but that is only half of his charm. More than just ornamental, he gets the job done. When he is on the dog, no criminal is safe. He's taken stealie boys and jackers, cagers and rum padders, sweeteners and dollymops. He's arrested mashers and moochers, B-boys and bully rocks. He's a real hero. Everyone adores him.

Well, not everyone. Not the shady element in Califa, who prefer their unlawful livelihoods and criminal hobbies to go unmolested. Not the families of those he has sent to the drop. They hate and fear Detective Wilkins. But the honest citizens of Califa consider him a real trump. Except for one lone constable, who thinks he is a real jackass. And whose opinion matters to this story, as we shall soon hear. Hold that thought; you'll need it later.

It's after hours at the police department's favorite saloon, the Drunken Aeronaut, and jubilation, centering on Detective Wilkins, is in full swing. The PD is celebrating a successful conviction in the detective's biggest case yet, a hard case, the worst crime that Califa has seen in a hundred years. For three months, until Detective Wilkins snared him, the Califa Squeeze had the city in an uproar. He was crafty, and busy, with a modus operandi quite chilling: he crept up on his victims—in the bath, in an alley, at breakfast, weeding the garden—and squeezed the life out of them. Then he stole their jewelry and vanished. The city is not unfamiliar with the petty thief, but normally its murderers confine themselves to those who are asking to be murdered: other criminals, dollymops, street orphans, to name but a few unfortunates.

The Califa Squeeze was a different breed of homicide, shameless and daring. He chose his victims from the ranks of the utterly blameless: a city gardener, a lawyer, a lamplighter, a nanny. Innocent folks who kept to the law and expected, therefore, to die old and happy in their beds. By itself each murder was shocking, but when it became apparent that the heinous crimes had been committed by the same maniac, the city had erupted into a frenzy of fear and shrill indignation: the Califa Squeeze must be stopped!

Well, the great Detective Wilkins stopped the Califa Squeeze. Using his wiles, and his extensive underworld contacts, with a hefty dose of charm, and then some deadly browbeating, Detective Wilkins tracked the Califa Squeeze and caught him, red-handed, with the boodle. The terror of the city turned out to be a small mumbling shambling old man known as Nutter Norm, who had been living in a crate not far from the Islais Creek Slaughterhouse. The boodle, no longer quite so shiny after spending so much time in close proximity to offal, was discovered in a sack in the crate. When arrested, Norm protested that he had found the loot, but gentle (and not gentle) pressure from the Great Detective finally persuaded the old man to confess tearfully that he was indeed the dreaded Squeeze, though he couldn't explain exactly why he had done such great crimes for such little reward.

The trial lasted barely an hour. The jury, primed by Detective Wilkins's silky-smooth testimony, delivered a verdict after only twenty minutes of deliberation: guilty on all charges. Nutter Norm will hang. The jury went home, pleased that they had done their duty. The police adjourned to the Drunken Aeronaut to celebrate their hero, who would no doubt soon be called to Saeta House to be congratulated there by the Warlady Sylvanna Abenfarax herself. Until then, they are drinking champagne, eating oysters, and boisterously toasting the man of the hour.

Remember how I said not everyone in the department loves Detective Wilkins? Well, here we come to the one who does not: Constable Aurelia Etreyo, not splendid at all, but small and round and scowly. She sits in a dark corner, chewing furiously on a cheese waffle and furiously watching the other police officers pet Detective Wilkins. If Detective Wilkins is the department pride, Constable Etreyo is the department crank. She came to the PD the youngest graduate from the police academy ever, full of fever and fire to do good, catch criminals, make the city a safer, better place. Instead, she patrols the Northern Sandbank, the coldest, foggiest, most forlorn part of the city, where nothing at all happens, because there is almost nothing there. The Sandbank encompasses a series of tall hills, too tall to build upon, intermixed with sand dunes too sandy to build upon. Only two structures stand in the Northern

Sandbank: the Califa Asylum for the Forlorn and the Nostalgically Insane and a windblown octagon-shaped house, now abandoned. The Northern Sandbank is the worst beat in the city.

Constable Etreyo's been on the job a year, and she's bitter. Constable Etreyo is an acolyte of the great forensic investigator Armand Bertillo, whose book *A Manifesto of Modern Detection* created the template for modern police work. A modern police officer, says Professor Bertillo, uses facts, not fists, to solve crimes. A modern police officer understands that crime can be measured, that criminals leave behind clues, which, when properly interpreted, make the resolution of the case obvious. Fingerprints, bloodstains, murder weapons, murder scenes, all these help the police answer the only question that truly matters in police work: who did it. The Bertillo System categorizes crimes and criminals into types that can be tracked, anticipated, and caught. It is a thoroughly modern way of solving crime, as aloof from the dark old days as day is from night.

Unfortunately for Constable Etreyo, Califa is not a modern police force. Sure, the chief of police frowns upon interrogation via thumping, and they've done away with the old dirty, overcrowded prison in favor of the clean, silent penitentiary system, but otherwise the police force remains old-fashioned. Crimes are solved with a carrot or a stick, and order is kept through intimidation and fear—all practices that Detective Wilkins has made perfect, and the reason he sits at the apex of the list of people that Etreyo hates. Etreyo's attempts to persuade her fellow officers to employ the Bertillo System have gained her only ridicule. Her attempt to get the chief of police to endorse the Bertillo System failed miserably. Banished to the worst beat in the city, Constable Etreyo has grown snappish and mean.

So, snappish and mean, she sits in a corner listening to the jolly police officers bombard the Great Detective with praise and free beer. You probably wonder why she pains herself so. If the sight of Detective Wilkins makes her so sick, why not go where he is not? Well, first, she'll be fiked if she'll quit. And she'll be fiked if she'll be driven from her dinner. Also, she can't afford to quit. She's the second of ten children, and all her paycheck goes to the support of the other nine siblings, her parents, an elderly aunt, and a blind gazehound. She can't afford to eat elsewhere; the Drunken Aeronaut gives a police discount.

So Constable Etreyo sits and stews, cheese waffle growing soggy and heavy in her stomach. Detective Wilkins is recounting for the fourth time how he leaned on Nutter Norm: "... said to him, 'Dear man, I want to help you, I really do, but I cannot,' and here I paused and offered him a cigarillo; he took it, poor soul. I said, 'I want to be your friend, but you will not let me,' and he began to cry, and I knew he'd crack, the Califa Squeeze — I'd squeezed him —"

"Not!" Constable Etreyo's shouted interruption is so loud that the other officers are startled. Detective Wilkins is astounded by the interruption. He turns his gaze toward Etreyo's dark corner, sees her there, smiles, and says genially, "Ah, Constable Etreyo, welcome. How is your waffle? A bit sandy, maybe?"

The other officers giggle, and one of them slaps Detective Wilkins on the shoulder in a friendly sort of way. This friendly slap cockeyes the detective's straw boater and earns the slapper a most unfriendly look in return.

"Better to have sand in my teeth than sand in my eyes," Etreyo says. She hadn't meant to speak. The word had just exploded out of her, but now that she's said one word, it's easy to say a whole lot more.

"I cry your pardon, what do you mean?" Detective Wilkins asks.

"I mean, you've got the wrong man."

"But, dear Constable Etreyo, Nutter Norm confessed."

"He was scared and hungry and you promised him a bacon supper."

"Who would confess to murder — four murders — for a bacon supper?" Subdetective Wynn asks scornfully. He's one of Detective Wilkins's chief cronies.

Constable Etreyo can think of several occasions in her life where she would have happily confessed to murder for one slice of bacon, much less an entire bacon supper. But none of these fat plods looks like he's ever missed a meal, so they have no idea what a driving force hunger can be.

"I never get the wrong man," Detective Wilkins says.

"You've got the wrong man now."

"The jury said not."

"The jury did not know all the facts."

Detective Wilkins says, "What do you know of the facts, you who have spent the last weeks traipsing about sand dunes, looking after the safety of cows and crazies, whereas I have examined every crime scene, interviewed every witness, recovered the stolen goods—"

"Fingerprints," Constable Etreyo says. "Fingerprints."

Her words are met with an indulgent sigh (Detective Wilkins), eye rolls, and head wagging (the other officers.) *Here goes Etreyo,* they are all thinking, *with her* science.

"Fingerprints are unique," Etreyo continues. "No two prints are the same."

"So you say," Detective Wilkins says, "but can you prove it? There are millions of people in the world. Have you looked at the fingerprints of all of those people? What is there to say that my fingerprints are not the same as, say, a hide tanner in Ticonderoga, or a fisherman in Kenai?"

More laughter. The very idea!

She's heard this argument before, and so had Professor Bertillo; of course, they haven't looked at the fingerprints of everyone in the world. But Professor Bertillo had examined the fingerprints of more than ten thousand people and found not a match among them, and that is a big enough sample to support his theory that fingerprints are unique. Not that snapperheads like Detective Wilkins or his cronies will ever be convinced.

"In this case it doesn't matter whether or not Norm's fingerprints are unique," Etreyo says. "What matters is that they were not at any of the crime scenes. There were plenty of fingerprints, but none of them was Norm's. Which means he cannot be the Califa Squeeze."

Detective Wilkins now stares at her, smile vanished. He says softly, smoke from his cigarillo fluttering as he speaks, "Someone has been detecting behind my back."

This is true. Detective Wilkins had not ordered any of the crime scenes to be dusted for fingerprints; Etreyo had visited them after Detective Wilkins's exit and had done the dusting herself. She says, "You cannot execute an innocent man! And it's a matter of public safety. The Squeeze has to be stopped."

Against Detective Wilkins's own vanity, public safety has not much of a chance. He says, "I do not like people who detect behind my back."

"And I do not like officers who squabble in public," a new voice says. Ylva Landaðon, the chief of police, has been standing at the bar for the last ten minutes, but the officers have been so absorbed in their drama that they didn't notice. Now, realizing her presence, they begin a mad scramble of doffing hats, saluting. *Fiking great,* thinks Constable Etreyo. *Records room, here I come.*

"You seem awfully certain that Norm is not the Squeeze, Constable Etreyo," Captain Landaðon says.

"I am, Captain."

"But you can't prove it."

"Nutter Norm's fingerprints were not at any of the crime scenes."

"What does that prove?" Detective Wilkins says. "Perhaps he wore gloves! Did you think of that, Constable Etreyo?"

The other officers laugh, and Etreyo feels her cheeks flush with murderous rage. She swallows hard. "If he had worn gloves, he would have left smeared marks. But I didn't find any such marks."

Detective Wilkins scoffs. "All of this is irrelevant anyway. Norm confessed."

"Ayah, he did," Captain Landaðon says. "Norm confessed, had a fair trial, and was found guilty. It is not the police's place to criticize the verdict. We uphold the law; we do not rule on it. Do you understand, Constable Etreyo? I will hear no more of these wild theories of yours. The case is closed."

Detective Wilkins and his cronies roar. They don't care if they send an innocent man to the drop. They care only for their reputations. They can laugh at her all they want; she knows she is right. But being right won't save Nutter Norm. Only proof that she is right will do that.

And, other than the fingerprints, she doesn't have any.

✦ II. THE CRIMES ✦

As you might guess from Etreyo's sudden declaration to Detective Wilkins, she's been following the case since the first murder was discovered. Unofficially, she's examined the crime scenes; unofficially, she's examined the bodies; and unofficially, she's read Detective Wilkins's reports. The man may be a snapperhead, but his reports are thorough. He doesn't follow the Bertillo protocols of measuring the crime scenes, or making sketches or photograves of evidence, nor does he dust for prints, but he looks for evidence, and he interviews witnesses. Now Etreyo feels she knows the case as well as Detective Wilkins does. Better, actually, for her understanding of the case is guided by the evidence. His is guided by his own opinions. There is no room in forensics, says Professor Bertillo, for opinion.

But she's gone over and over the case file a hundred times, and all she can do is eliminate Norm. She knows the answer to who the real killer is must be there, in the file, in the clues, somewhere, but she just can't see it. And so Norm will hang. She'd visited him in jail, a broken old man, crying for his life. He'd reminded her of her grandpa. He'd died, too, because her family couldn't afford the medicine to save him.

The case of the Califa Squeeze is a strange one. Four murders and no witnesses, this despite the fact that three of them took place in the middle of the day, with potential witnesses nearby. How could a murderer gain access to his victims and yet not be seen? In the case of the nanny, his charges were in the next room coloring when the crime happened, and they didn't hear or see a thing. In the lawyer's case, the only access to the murder room was through a door that was locked from the inside. There is no evidence that anyone had climbed in through the window.

There's no obvious motive, either. The petty nature of the items stolen would seem to preclude theft as a motive, particularly since they were all recovered. The Squeeze hadn't even tried to unload them. Detective Wilkins could find no connection between the victims, and neither could Constable Etreyo, following in his footsteps. According to the Bertillo System, there is *always* a motive. But she has no idea what it could be.

The criminal, said Professor Bertillo, cannot hide himself completely. He leaves traces of himself behind, and his fingerprints are his signature. Etreyo had dusted all the crime scenes for prints. She'd used the prints she'd covertly collected from her colleagues to eliminate their prints, and she was then left with only a few unidentified prints. The same prints keep showing up at all the crime scenes. They don't belong to any of the detectives. Etreyo knows these prints belong to the killer. But that knowledge doesn't bring her any closer to discovering who the killer is.

Constable Etreyo wishes she could consult with Sieur Bertillo himself, but he's a thousand miles away, in Bexar, and she can't afford the price of a heliogram, anyway. Cast down, she returns to the station house to file her end-of-shift report and change out of her uniform. She should just go home.

Instead, we find Etreyo back at the station, standing outside the door to the Califa City Morgue, smearing the space between her nose and her lips with lavender pomade. No matter how many times she has been on the other side of that door, she cannot get used to the smell: decaying meat, quicklime, stale blood. The pomade doesn't erase the smell completely, but it certainly does cut it some. Her nose now armored, she pushes through the heavy wooden doors into the white-tile room beyond.

It's late and the morgue is shadowy and quiet. All the marble slabs are empty. The floor, newly cleaned, is slick and wet beneath her feet. Dr. Kuddle sits at the rolltop desk at the far end of the room, eating a donut and writing out a report. Etreyo's footsteps echo alarmingly as she walks past the slab, past the zinc trough where the bodies are washed, past the scales, still faintly rimmed with red, where the organs are weighed. Now, with everything cleaned for the night, the morgue seems peaceful; hospital-like. Of course, during the busy part of the day, it most closely resembles a slaughterhouse.

"I have to finish this report," Dr. Kuddle says peevishly. "That's why I am still here so late. I thought you were at the 'Naut, blowing your mouth off."

Dr. Kuddle doesn't believe in the Bertillo System, mostly because the system calls for extremely elaborate autopsies, and Kuddle is against anything that might increase her workload. But she likes Etreyo and humors her.

"How did you hear about that?"

"I hear about everything," Kuddle says. She hardly ever leaves the morgue, but she knows everything that is going on. "Don't bait Detective Gorgeous. He's an ass. His day will come."

"He's going to be responsible for an innocent man's death."

"I doubt he'll lose any beauty sleep over it."

"It's not right."

Instead of answering her, Kuddle stands up. "Come on. I have something to show you."

"What?" Etreyo asks, following her.

"You shall see," answers Kuddle, opening the door to the freeze room. "Leave the door open behind you, will you? It's freezing in here, and I'm getting a cold, I'm sure."

The freeze room is indeed freezing, but its occupants don't mind the cold. Constable Etreyo shivers; not because of the cold but because she has a vivid imagination and can easily imagine herself lying on one of the blocks of ice, her dark skin frosted white, her flesh as hard as stone. She banishes this vision from her imagination and turns her attention to the figure that Dr. Kuddle has just unveiled.

Jacobus Hermosa, lamplighter. Throttled as he made his rounds lighting the gas lamps on Abenfarax Avenue. His partner had been working the opposite side of the street and hadn't seen a thing. Taken: one signet ring. Kuddle hadn't bothered to do an autopsy because the cause of death was so obvious: a crushed throat via manual strangulation.

"I've already looked at him. Twice," Etreyo says.

Kuddle holds up the lamp. "I was getting ready to release the body when I noticed something. Look. You can see how the killer gripped Hermosa by the neck; there's the shape of his thumb under the chin, and then the fingers, here, under the right ear. The killer used his left hand—his dominant hand, for sure, as he would hardly crush the life out of someone with his weaker hand."

"Nutter Norm is right-handed," Etreyo says. "So that proves something, I suppose, but it doesn't tell you who the killer is."

"But this will, or it will help. Look at the thumb mark. See, it's crooked, as though it has been broken and fixed, but the bone didn't set right."

Etreyo bends over the corpse. Hope is beginning to well up inside her. "That's a fantastic identifying mark. I can't believe I didn't see it before!" she says excitedly. "When I find a man with a broken thumb like that, I'll have him. And the fingerprints will prove it; they'll match some of the ones I found at the scene."

They leave Hermosa in the cold darkness. Back in the slicing room, Kuddle pours them both hot coffee. As they sip, and Etreyo contemplates the new lead, her excitement dampens. "It's a good clue, but it won't help Norm. I'm not going to find this guy before tomorrow afternoon."

"I've been thinking. The broken thumb brings to mind a recent corpse I had in here. An actor, he was, young fella. He fell during the rehearsal of that new melodrama that was going to open at the Odeon, the one about the Dainty Pirate."

"Did he fall off the stage?"

"No, out of the rigging. The scene was supposed to be on the ship, you know. Sixty feet down to the stage boards, and that was it for our young ingenue. Pity. He was pretty. He had a crooked thumb. I remember it because it was his only flaw."

"If he's dead, he could hardly be my murderer."

"Thirty years ago, I'd have said you were wrong. But I ain't seen a dead man walk in years. But it's still odd."

"Where's the corpse?"

"Well. No one claimed it, you know, and he wasn't a member of the theater company, so they wouldn't spring for a funeral. I got no budget for a potter's field; it ain't free, you know." Kuddle sounds a bit defensive. "Anyway, I sold it to a medico — dissection, I suppose."

She gets up, goes over to a filing cabinet, and yanks a drawer open. "Just for laughs, here. I read that Bertillo book you gave me, and it did seem interesting, so I started fingerprinting all the corpses that came in, to see if I ever ran across the same prints more than once." She pulls a card out of the drawer and whips it through the air toward Etreyo. "Pretty boy's prints."

Etreyo catches the card and lays it on the desk. She digs through her case and finds the cards she made of the prints she had taken from the crime scene, the prints she hasn't yet identified. And what do you fiking know?

She finds a match.

✦ III. THE INVESTIGATION ✦

The case, already strange, is now turning even stranger. Clearly the chorus boy could not be the murderer; his fatal fall happened before the murders started. But the fingerprints match. That's irrefutable. Constable Etreyo remembers, uneasily, Detective Wilkins's gibe that she could not really prove that two people did not have the same fingerprints. Maybe this was the proof. If so, then she is nowhere closer to finding the true murderer. And she has no other leads. Leave no stone unturned, Sieur Bertillo advised. So, although she knows the dead chorus boy is a dead end (literally), she decides to check him out anyway.

The patrol room is empty; the swing shift is already gone to work, and the day shift has not started to trickle in. Constable Etreyo goes to the locker room and exchanges her spiffy uniform for a threadbare sack-coat suit. On her way out of the locker room, she tucks her shield into her breast pocket and drops her pistol into her pocket. A shadow blocks her way.

"Well, now, busy bee, where dost thou wander?"

"Get out of my way," she says, angling to push by Wilkins, but he does not give way. Detective Wilkins is much taller than she is and not very sober. These two qualities make him a substantial roadblock.

"What were you doing in the morgue so late at night?"

"None of your business."

"The captain said to leave my case alone. I hope you are following her orders, dear Constable. The captain would not be pleased to hear otherwise. You think the Sandbank is bad; there is always worse."

Her answer is a sharp heel to the toe of his mirror-shine-polished black boot. While he hops in anger, she breezes by him and out the door. Recklessly, she hails a hansom cab; with the help of a friend in the records division, she'll tab the expense to Detective Gorgeous. The cabbie asks her destination, and she glances, for the first time, at the address that Dr. Kuddle gave her. And she discovers it's an address she knows well, for it is on her beat: the abandoned Octagon House. Fike. The medico has given Dr. Kuddle a shill address.

"Where to?" the cabbie asks impatiently, peering into the cab through the little window behind his seat.

It's the only lead she's got.

A good detective always checks out every lead, no matter how paltry.

"Four-fifteen Sandbank Road," she orders.

The cabbie slides his window shut, and with a jerk and jingle of tack, the cab jolts forward. Normally, the journey to her beat is a long cold one, entailing two cold horsecar rides, one to the end of the line, and then a long trudge along Sandy Road to the intersection of Sandy and Sandbank, where her patrol shack sits. Today, she rides in stylish warmth and gets there in half the time of her normal slog. Still reckless, she orders the cab to wait, and the cabbie, with a shrug that says *it's your diva*, hunches down into the shelter of his greatcoat and takes out a warming flask and a *Califa Police Gazette*. "The Squeeze to Be Squeezed," the headline says. Etreyo grimaces as she walks away.

The gaslights of the city are now far behind; the house squats in fog-swirled darkness. As she approaches, a gust of wind flaps the front gate open. She walks up the stone walkway to the chipped marble stairs. The air smells of damp salt and something else, something that buzzes and crackles in the back of her throat. The brass knocker is missing its clapper; she raps hard on the door with her knuckles, but the sound is muted by the wind and the rubbing wheeze of tree limbs. As she expects, no one answers. She peers through a side window and sees darkness.

She's not supposed to enter a building without permission from the owners, unless it's an emergency, but a police officer can always find an emergency. Silently rehearsing her excuse—*I heard a distant cry of help; I thought I smelled smoke*—she rattles the front-door knob. When that doesn't turn, she goes back to the side window, but it's stuck. She doesn't want to break the glass and alert anyone who might be inside, so she goes around back to find the coal chute. The iron door hangs ajar; it's a tight squeeze, but sometimes being small has its advantages. Detective Wilkins wouldn't fit, but then Detective Wilkins would probably just kick down the front door and be done with it. She goes feetfirst, with her pistol drawn, just in case. Five minutes later, she is standing in the kitchen, covered in coal dust.

The kitchen is empty, forlorn, no sign that anyone has cooked in it for years. The iron stove is rusted with salt moisture; the sink is slick with mold. As the name of the house suggests, the Octagon House has eight outside walls instead of four. In the center of the octagon, Etreyo finds a spiral staircase; up she goes, cautiously, gun still drawn, slowly, so as to make as little noise as possible. The shape of the house means that the rooms are oddly shaped; each floor has four square rooms and four tiny little triangular rooms, all arranged around the core staircase. The rooms are empty, with cracked floorboards and peeling walls. The house appears empty, but it doesn't *feel* empty. It looks abandoned, but it doesn't *feel* abandoned. The fog means that the night is lighter than usual, and in this light, Etreyo sees footprints on the dusty floorboards, fresh footprints. She's reached the top floor now, but there is still no sign of habitation. Perhaps they were here before and are gone now.

She's about to head back downstairs when the ceiling shakes and small bits of plaster rain down. She hears the sound of footsteps and realizes that there must be one more floor above her. Either that or someone is walking on the roof. But the stairs go no farther. She circles through the floor again, each room joining the other, until she's back where she started, and then realizes that one of the windows is actually a door leading to a staircase that coils around the house, nautilus-like. The footsteps move rapidly — two sets of them: one clompy, the other light.

She exits the door onto the outside stairway, which is rusty and rickety. With one hand she clutches the slickly wet railing. In the other she holds her pistol steady; she's never fired it in the line of duty, but she will if she has to. Fog roils around her; it's so thick now that the house seems to drift in a cloud, unmoored from the rest of the world. A tickle begins in the back of Constable Etreyo's throat, a tickle that becomes a sound, low and humming. The sound spreads from her throat up into her skull, down into her feet, tingling her blood, her bones, her nerves. The stairs rattle beneath her; above her, the fog flashes purple, once, twice. Lightning? But where's the storm? The rain? And no lightning that Etreyo has ever encountered before sounds like this: a high-pitched buzzing whine, like two saws being rubbed together. Her teeth tingle, and purple sparks arc down from above. She comes around the last edged corner of the octagon and sees an open doorway to her left. The doorway leads to a solarium: glass walls, glass ceiling, currently open to the foggy night.

In the center of the solarium, a waterfall of purple lightning pours down from a central pillar. The pillar stands on a scaffold; a table lies underneath, a human form stretched out upon it. Purple lightning dances and shimmers around the stretcher, envelops the body in eye-scorching purple fire. Etreyo thinks she has never seen anything so beautiful or awe inspiring. Or so frightening, either.

She shouts, but her words are lost in the high-pitched whine. On the other side of the roof she sees a dark figure silhouetted against the glow. She shouts at it again, and then, as she dashes forward, a strike of lightning flares off the center corona and zaps her. Stunned, she drops the pistol and feels a hand on her shoulder, pulling her back.

"Don't get so close!" a voice roars.

"Stop this right now!" she hollers back. "I order you to stop this right now!"

"I can't stop it! We're almost done!"

"Stop it now!"

"It's running down now! See!"

The lightning is indeed dimming, the purple light sputtering. The high-pitched whine lessens, and then ceases as the corona of light flickers one last time and dies. For a moment the solarium is dim, foggy, and then it floods with a bright white light. Etreyo spots her pistol lying on the floor and grabs it before turning to face the figure closest to her. "Califa Police Department. Put your hands where I can see them."

"There's no need for this, really, Officer," the woman says. She's tallish, with a narrow face and wide-set blue eyes. She is wearing one pair of spectacles; another pair perches on her head. A dirty white apron covers her clothes. But when Etreyo repeats the order, she follows it.

"You could have gotten us all killed!" The figure that Etreyo had seen on the other side of the room is now furiously advancing upon her. It takes Etreyo a minute to realize that she is seeing what she thinks she is seeing, but the light in the room is far too bright for her to be mistaken.

The chimpanzee shouts, "Who the fike are you and how dare you break into private property!" It wears a white apron over a yellow embroidered vest and a high starched collar, its shirt sleeves rolled up to display muscular dark forearms. And it is walking upright.

"I am Constable Etreyo of the CPD. And I'd like to know who you are and what you are doing."

"Show me your badge," the chimp demands.

Keeping her pistol level, Etreyo fishes out her shield and displays it. "Please tell me what is going on here."

"I am Dr. Theophrastus Ehle," the chimp says, "and this is my colleague, Dr. Adelaide Elsinore. We are in the middle of a very important experiment, which you and your blundering almost ruined."

Constable Etreyo has never heard of a chimpanzee with a doctorate, or, for that matter, a chimpanzee who can speak or walk upright. However, just because she hasn't met one before obviously does not mean that they do not exist, for here one is, standing there glaring at her.

"What is that?" Etreyo asks, pointing in the direction of the column, which in brighter light is revealed to be topped with a donut-shaped ring.

"It's a galvanic coil transformer," Dr. Elsinore says. "It concentrates galvanic current and strengthens it."

"And what exactly were you doing with it?"

"Renewing life!" Dr. Ehle says scornfully. "Or we would have been if you had not interrupted us. Now I shall have to start all over again!"

"I cry your pardon," Constable Etreyo says, "but you have to admit that your experiment did appear quite alarming. What kind of doctor are you, anyway?"

"Dr. Elsinore is a surgeon. I am a doctor of galvanic physiology."

"What does that mean?"

"Dr. Ehle studies the galvanic patterns of the body, Officer," Dr. Elsinore answers.

"I study life itself," Dr. Ehle interjects haughtily. "And you haven't yet told me what you are doing sneaking around private property."

"I knocked on the door and got no answer. And the house appeared to be abandoned," Constable Etreyo said. She speaks her rehearsed excuse, but Dr. Ehle does not look as though he believes her. "Did either of you purchase a body from the Califa City Morgue?"

"I did," Dr. Elsinore says. "And what of it? The coroner assured me that the poor soul had no family, no friends. And it's perfectly legal to purchase bodies for scientific reasons."

"And where is this body now?"

The two doctors exchange glances, and then their eyes shift toward the figure lying on the stretcher. They don't answer, but they don't have to. The answer is obvious in their glances.

"Why do you ask?" Dr. Elsinore says.

Etreyo counters the question with one of her own: "Are you familiar with the Califa Squeeze?"

Dr. Elsinore answers her. "No, I fear not, Constable Etreyo. Dr. Ehle and I only arrived in the city two weeks ago. Is that a new kind of a dance? Or a drink? We have been deep in our work and have not had much time to read the newspapers."

"Can this wait until later?" Dr. Ehle says impatiently. "I must see what I can salvage of the experiment."

"No, it cannot wait," Etreyo says.

"Can we at least close the roof? It's very cold in here." Dr. Elsinore is correct; the foggy air flowing in through the open roof is very chilly. Etreyo watches closely as the two doctors crank the roof shut. A small barrel camp stove sits near a table of jumbled scientific equipment: beakers, weights and scales, bottles of mysterious liquid. Dr. Elsinore turns a dial on the stove and heat begins to pour off of it.

"What kind of a stove is that?" Etreyo asks.

"It's an Ehle stove," Dr. Elsinore explains. "It runs on the galvanic current generated by the coil transformer. So do the lights." She indicates the white glowing globes that hang from the glass-ceiling trusses.

"How does the current get to the stove?"

"It's conducted through the air."

Etreyo has read, in one of her scientific journals, about a theory that galvanic energy could be transmitted through the air. But she had no idea such a feat has actually been achieved. In fact, as far as she knew, no one had successfully harnessed galvanic energy at all. And yet here is that giant coil. And she had seen with her own eyes the galvanic current it produced.

"Please finish with us and get out, Constable," Ehle says. "I want to get back to my work. What is this Califa Squash you were asking about?"

Constable Etreyo gives the two doctors a brief history of the Califa Squeeze. As she speaks, Dr. Elsinore grows more and more pale. Etreyo glances at Dr. Ehle, but his face remains inscrutable. Or maybe she just doesn't know how to read a chimpanzee's face. When she is done, Dr. Elsinore, now perched on the edge of a trunk, as though her knees will no longer support her, says, "Theo, I think I need a drink."

Constable Etreyo waits while Dr. Ehle brings Dr. Elsinore

a beaker full of a clear liquid that she's willing to bet is gin. Dr. Elsinore drinks it down and then says, "This is terrible news. I had no idea. This is awful, terrible, awful."

"Don't be histrionic, Adelaide," Dr. Ehle says. He takes back the beaker and shakes his head no to Dr. Elsinore's hopeful look. "They can hardly blame us."

"But who else is to blame? I knew I should have gone after it. I knew it! Oh, blasted hell!"

"Perhaps you would like to share your regrets with me," Constable Etreyo says. She has angled herself so that she is closest to the door, and both doctors are before her. Clearly they do know something about the Califa Squeeze, and in case they are in league with him, she doesn't want to give them the chance to get the jump on her.

"It's my fault. I take full responsibility," Dr. Elsinore says.

"Are you saying you committed these murders?" Constable Etreyo says, her grip tightening on her truncheon.

"No, of course she didn't. Don't be an ass, Adelaide," Dr. Ehle says. "If anyone is responsible, it is me."

"Why don't you tell me what you are talking about," Constable Etreyo says, "and I can decide for myself."

"We will do better. We will show you. Come!"

Constable Etreyo hesitates. Perhaps she ought to arrest them both, take them back to the station, where she can call on backup. But they are here, and the station house is full of eager ears, and she'd prefer to keep whatever the doctors tell her private, until she's had a chance to check out their claims. Dr. Ehle says, "We are not murderers. The exact opposite, as you will see. You may release your death grip on your billy club, Constable. You are in no danger from us."

Well, they may claim so, but many police officers have ended up dead because they believed they were in no danger, so Constable Etreyo prefers to remain on the skeptical side. "You go and I shall follow."

"As you wish."

Dr. Elsinore has already darted ahead, toward the coil transformer and the stretcher beneath it. They step over a ring of charred wood flooring, still smoking slightly. Constable Etreyo hates to get too close to the coil transformer, but she swallows her trepidation and peers over Dr. Elsinore's shoulder. A narrow figure lies on the stretcher, covered to the neck with a pink sheet. Dr. Elsinore holds a white globe in her hand, and in the dim soft light, Constable Etreyo sees the pale profile of the pretty chorus boy, who has been dead for three weeks. But Constable Etreyo has seen corpses that have been dead for three weeks, and they do not look this dewy and fresh. Their lips are not so full and red, and their cheeks are not so firm and round. Their hair does not curl so romantically over their marble-smooth foreheads.

Nor do their chests rise and fall as they breathe.

"This man is not dead," Constable Etreyo says.

"He was dead. But he is alive now," Dr. Ehle says proudly. "He has been revivified."

"How is this possible? Are you magicians?"

Dr. Ehle snorts. Dr. Elsinore shakes her head. "No, not magicians. Scientists. Theo, you should explain. You are the genius behind this."

Dr. Ehle says, "I shall try to put it in layman's terms, Officer. The spark of life, as they call it, is really just a galvanic current that runs through our body, powers our brains, our muscles, our limbs. Upon death, this spark ceases. We can no longer move, no longer think. Our flesh, without the galvanic current to keep it warm, begins to decay, to die. I have simply restored the galvanic spark. And thus he lives again."

Constable Etreyo gingerly touches the chorus boy's cheek. It feels cool, but it also feels alive. "He is the Califa Squeeze," she says.

"No, he is not." Dr. Elsinore lifts the edge of the white sheet, revealing a white muscular arm—that ends in a neat stump.

She says, "His hand is."

✣ IV. THE EVIDENCE ✣

Constable Etreyo believes in science, but if she hadn't seen the proof of Dr. Elsinore's story before her own eyes, she would not have believed it, for the story seems more like a fairy tale than science. And yet there the proof lies, breathing faintly.

The body on the cot is not the dead chorus boy. Oh, the head is, and so is the right hand, and the left leg. The torso belongs to a blacksmith from Yucaipa who had an unfortunate accident with an anvil; the left leg came from an Atacasdero cowboy who fell under his horse during a stampede. Apparently, the doctors have been traveling around Califa, collecting body parts.

Dr. Elsinore says, "We would have preferred to use an entire body, of course, and not have to mix and match like this, but it's very hard to find an entire body in suitable condition. Most young, fit people die in accidents, in a manner that renders parts of them unusable. Or they die whole, but their bodies are ravaged by disease. So I had to piece our perfect specimen together. The chorus boy provided the last bits."

"Adelaide is a genius with the needle," Dr. Ehle said. "She performed the surgery that allowed me to speak. She did a marvelous job on our boy."

"Isn't he lovely?" Dr. Elsinore makes a move to withdraw the sheet farther, and Constable Etreyo hastily stops her. Seeing a body cut up is bad enough, but seeing it stitched together, like a monstrous crazy quilt, somehow that seems much worse. She is content to use her imagination. As it is, she can now see the small black stitches around the base of the neck where the head has been attached to the trunk, and that's more than enough, thank you.

"The problem remains the blood," Dr. Ehle says musingly. "In a living being, the heart pumps the blood, and the blood circulates through the body, carrying with it oxygen and other vital nutrients. By the time I get my hands on blood, it's always sluggish and thick and will not circulate. So eventually the flesh will begin to decay, anyway, and the galvanic charge weakens down, and he will die again."

"The brain is a problem, too," Dr. Elsinore says. "The galvanic spark revivifies the body but does nothing for the brain. He is alive, but vegetative —"

"I tell you, a fresher brain will be the answer —" Dr. Ehle says.

"I don't think so, Theo. That doesn't solve —"

They sound as though they have had this argument before, and that it is a lengthy one. Etreyo interrupts, "But what about the hand, Doctor? How can it act alone?"

Dr. Ehle says, "A mistake. I always prime the body part with some galvanic current before I attach it, to ensure that the part is still fresh and works. I used too much current and gave the hand such a jolt that it became completely animated. It jumped off the table and skittered away, and though Dr. Elsinore and I tried to catch it, we failed. I thought it didn't matter; the galvanic current would wear off, and the hand would die again. I had no idea that it would prove so indomitable."

"And look what has happened," Dr. Elsinore says sorrowfully.

"Ayah, look what has happened," Constable Etreyo says grimly. "Four people dead, and an innocent man about to be hanged. And more important, the hand still out there. We have to catch it before it kills someone else. And in time to exonerate Nutter Norm."

As far as Etreyo can recall, Bertillo's System has no suggestions for catching murderous revivified hands. However, before Etreyo became a police officer, she worked two summers as a rat catcher, and it seems to her that the same principles should apply. She needs a trap and bait. The trap will be easy enough; it's the bait that proves perplexing. What would lure in a hand? Etreyo thinks back to the crimes and feels like an idiot not to have seen the connection between the jewelry before: the Squeeze only stole items it could wear. It has a taste for gimcracks. She needs bait that a vain luxury-loving hand will find irresistible. Dr. Elsinore, eager to help, provides the solution. What would prove more alluring to a hand than a lovely embroidered glove? She has just the thing tucked away in her portmanteau.

Constable Etreyo extracts from the doctors the promise that they will not leave the Octagon House until the case is closed and the hand is caught. Dr. Ehle agrees, but to her surprise, Dr. Elsinore insists on accompanying her. The cabbie still waits outside, asleep in his greatcoat; the fog is beginning to lift. Dawn is not far away. They ride back into the city and stop at the first hardware store they see, where Etreyo buys a rat trap with a voucher.

Nutter Norm had claimed he had found the bag of jewelry hidden in a duck's nest near Strawberry Pond in Abenfarax Park. The cabbie drops them off near the pond. In the early morning light, the grass is wet with dew, and the ducks are still in their nests.

The pond is not far from the end of the Q horsecar line. Another connection between the murders snaps into place, belatedly; they all occurred within a block of the Q line. The Squeeze had been commuting to its crimes.

"What if it's gone?" Dr. Elsinore asks worriedly as Etreyo tramps around the bushes, looking for a good place to put the trap. In a duck's nest, she finds a small horde of nail polish and emery boards. The Squeeze is also a shoplifter.

"It's still around," she says. "I just hope it's out getting more polish and not looking for more jewelry." She drops the glove into the trap and props the door open, then pushes the trap into the bushes.

"Perhaps the galvanic current has worn off," Dr. Elsinore says as they settle onto a park bench to wait.

"For Nutter Norm's sake, I hope not. The captain is not going to believe my report if I cannot present the hand as proof."

"But at least then we shall not have to worry about anyone else getting hurt. I will swear an affidavit," Dr. Elsinore says. "Surely the captain will not doubt me?"

Surely not. Etreyo says, "Let's wait and see."

They wait and see. Foggy dawn fades into a warm blue day. The ducks leave their nests and take to the pond, swimming and diving. A group of small schoolchildren parade by, two by two, hand in hand, and are swarmed by the ducks, looking for stale bread. The chaperones look sideways at Dr. Elsinore and Constable Etreyo sitting so aimlessly on the bench. Eventually, the schoolchildren leave and the ducks go back to the water. The trap, hidden in the bushes, remains unsprung. A red dog arrives, chases a ball into the water, and then swims frantically around, barking at the ducks, until he's whistled away. The sun is getting warm. The trap springs and they rush to it, only to find an angry squirrel catapulting around inside. They release the squirrel and reset the trap. Dr. Elsinore goes to the pond chalet snack shop and comes back with two boxes of pink popcorn and two coffees. Etreyo is sweating, and not because of the sun. It's almost noon; Norm's execution is scheduled for two PM. She checks the trap again: nothing.

A horse cop clops by and asks them why they are loitering. A flash of Etreyo's badge sends him on his way. Dr. Elsinore goes off to find a bathroom. It's almost one. The trap is still empty. Etreyo's imagination keeps sliding back to poor Nutter Norm. He's probably eating his last meal right about now; then he'll be dressed in the coarse sacking of his shroud. He never hurt anyone; his only crime was to be crazy and old. She could have saved him if she'd been smarter—

"Well, what a fine day to sit in the park."

Detective Wilkins sits down next to her. He holds two ice-cream cones. He offers her one. He smells of bay rum and roasted almonds, and the slight breeze is blowing his hair into romantic curls, gusting the edges of his cape dramatically.

"What do you want?" she demands, refusing the cone with a shake of her head.

"Just taking the air."

"I thought you'd be at the prison. That you'd want to see the fruits of your labor fulfilled."

"My job is done. I never linger when my job is done. The ice cream is dripping on my hand. I'll toss it."

She takes it. It's a pity to waste good ice cream, and besides, she's starving. She's had nothing to eat since that long-ago cheese waffle. The pink popcorn had stuck in her throat when she'd tried to eat it.

"You are not very nice to me, Constable. I only did my job."

"Tell that to Nutter Norm," Etreyo says, licking at her cone: salted caramel with orca bacon. Her favorite. She knows she should not be enjoying the ice cream while a man waits to die, but she is very hungry and the ice cream tastes very good.

"He had a miserable life. He is better off dead."

She tosses the cone away, the taste of the ice cream suddenly slick and sickening in her mouth. "That's not for you to judge —"

"Constable!" Dr. Elsinore says. She has returned and yanks excitedly on Etreyo's sleeve. "The trap has sprung."

"Trap? What trap?" Detective Wilkins asks.

She ignores him and hurriedly follows Dr. Elsinore into the bushes. It's probably just another squirrel, and in twenty minutes Nutter Norm will be dead.

But the thing in the trap is definitely not a squirrel.

The murderous hand has had a hard life since it escaped the doctors. Its nails are broken, rimmed with dirt. Its knuckles are bruised and its fingertips calloused. The wrist ends in a ragged, oozy wound. It looks more pathetic than horrifying. The hand throws itself upon the glove, clutches at it, tosses it up in the air, but, of course, one hand alone cannot put on a glove. Its anger and frustration is palpable.

"Poor thing," Dr. Elsinore says. "I think it needs medical attention."

"It killed four people," Etreyo says, gingerly hoisting the cage up. "Come on — we may still have time to save Nutter Norm."

"What the fike is that?" Once again Detective Wilkins blocks her way. But this time he's not looking at her; his attention is focused on the trap.

"The real murderer!" Etreyo says. "And I can prove it, too! Get out of my way!"

Now, though you may find it hard to believe, the physical perfection that is Detective Wilkins is not without flaw. It's a flaw that he takes pains to hide, and one that he has learned to work around. His eyesight is not very good. He can see distance fine, but up close, things tend to blur, and to bring them into focus, he must get very near indeed. He sees the cage perfectly, but the hand, now clutching at the bars of its prison, is not so distinct. He leans forward to get a better look. Etreyo pivots away from this lean, tries to go around him. Wilkins reaches for the cage; she sidesteps his grip and puts her foot down squarely on a duck that she didn't know was underfoot. The duck quacks angrily, and surprised by the sudden flutter of wings at her feet, Etreyo drops the cage.

The cage pops open, and galvanic quick, the Squeeze leaps from its prison, scuttles on fingertips, crablike, across the ground, and grabs ahold of Detective Wilkins's perfectly creased trouser leg. Detective Wilkins looks down and sees something crawling rapidly up his leg; he squints and thinks it's a squirrel, a rabid squirrel probably, for whoever heard otherwise of a squirrel attacking someone? Detective Wilkins stamps his feet and bats at the hand, trying to dislodge it. The Squeeze knows what it wants: the splendid diamond pinkie ring that Detective Wilkins wears on his left hand, and it is not going to be so easily dislodged.

"Hold still!" Etreyo shouts, tearing off her coat.

Detective Wilkins is doing the tarantella now, feet stepping mighty high, hands slapping ineffectually. The Squeeze is skittering up Detective Wilkins's splendidly embroidered weskit, heading for his snow-white cravat.

"Get it off!" Wilkins hollers. His straw skimmer falls off and he steps on it, putting his foot through the crown. Now he looks as though he's invented a new dance: the Murdering Hand Fandango. Choking back laughter, Etreyo throws all her weight against the dancing detective. He goes down like a ninepin.

"Use my cloak — it's bigger!" Dr. Elsinore cries.

Etreyo snatches Dr. Elsinore's cloak and throws it over the thrashing detective, hoping to trap the Squeeze in its folds. Detective Wilkins's screams, muffled in the heavy cloak, have become wheezes, and his thrashing is lessening. His head is tangled in the cloth; when Etreyo gets it free, she sees that the Squeeze has Detective Wilkins by the throat.

She grabs at the Squeeze, tries to pry it off, but the Squeeze has a death grip on the detective. His face has turned plum purple, and his eyes are bulging out. She dares not let go of what grip she has to reach for her pocketknife. Dimly, she hears Dr. Elsinore shouting. Dimly, she hears herself shouting. Wilkins's tongue is protruding; his face is almost blue. Desperately, she leans down and sinks her teeth into the Squeeze. She bites down as hard as she can, until her teeth grate on bone. The hand spasms and slackens its grip, and Detective Wilkins gurgles. A horrible rancid iron taste floods Etreyo's mouth, and she almost gags, but grimly she holds on. Her jaws ache and the taste is making her want to upchuck. But she holds on. The Squeeze's grip is growing weaker. With one last spasm, it lets go of Wilkins's throat. Etreyo raises up her head, tears the now limp hand out of her mouth, and throws it back into the cage. Dr. Elsinore slams the cage door shut. Someone helps Etreyo crawl off of Detective Wilkins's now limp form; dimly, she hears someone yell that he is still alive. Etreyo staggers over to the bushes, and spits and spits and spits, and rubs her lips against her sleeve until they are raw.

→ V. THE TRIAL ←

Like moths to a flame, they cluster around him, the great Detective Wilkins, his muscular throat wrapped in a silken bandage, silver sunshades hiding his bruised eyes. Just back from Saeta House, where he has received a commendation for bravery in subduing and capturing the Hand of Gory (as the press have redubbed the murderer). Not every detective is willing to revisit his own case, to admit that he might have the wrong man. Not every detective is willing to lay his life on the line to capture a murderer and save an innocent man. The station house throngs with well-wishers, and people are lined up outside to shake his hand.

What a trump!

The Hand of Gory has been booked and now resides, still in its cage, in a cell in the Califa City Jail. How a revivified hand can participate in its own defense, understand the charges against, and make a plea, well, that's not the police's problem. The lawyers will have to figure that out. The police (who love lawyers not a whit) are sure that the lawyers will find a way. Nutter Norm has been released and now resides in the Palace Hotel's best suite, courtesy of the Warlady. Doctors Elsinore and Ehle have had an audience with the Warlady, the end result being that they have been appointed to her medical staff. The Warlady is canny; she sees great potential in galvanic energy, if it is harnessed to Califa's advantage. The not-quite-so-dead chorus boy has returned to the Odeon Theater, a chorus boy no longer, but now, with much ballyhoo, recast in the lead role of the Dainty Pirate. The run is already sold out.

But where is the true hero of the hour, Constable Etreyo? She's in the station house bathroom, brushing her teeth for the hundredth time. No matter how hard she scrubs, she can't get the rancid taste of the Hand of Gory out of her mouth. As she brushes, she listens to the sounds of congratulation coming from the other room and tries not to feel bitter. Nutter Norm, standing on the scaffold with a rope around his neck, was reprieved. That's all that matters. Let Detective Wilkins have the glory. He's already been somewhat overshadowed by Doctors Ehle and Elsinore and their fantastic medical experiments, anyway. Once the revivified chorus boy makes his debut, Detective Wilkins will be forgotten.

But Etreyo does feel bitter. To the press, Detective Wilkins has credited his turnaround to the Bertillo System, the very system he had earlier ridiculed. The *CPG* has published a glowing account of his investigation, of his ferocious fight with the Hand. She has not been mentioned at all. Her report, contradicting Detective Wilkins's in almost every detail, has been ignored by Captain Landaðon.

She spits into the basin one last time; she's out of Madama Twanky's Oh-Be-Joyful Tooth Polish. She's gone through two bottles already, and yet the taste still lingers. She should have bitten Detective Wilkins instead. She bets his flesh tastes just like chicken. It's almost midnight: time for her to go on shift. She's already changed into her blue tunic with the brass buttons. She collects her truncheon and her helmet; on the way out of the locker room, she finds herself blocked in again.

"I want to thank you," Detective Wilkins says. He takes his sunshades off. The blue bruising brings out the golden glints in his eyes. "You saved my life."

"That's not what I read in the papers."

"Don't take it personally. The police must always appear as heroes; that is how we keep order. But I am grateful."

"Don't take it personally," she says. "I was after the hand."

"Happy for me, then, that you are so single-minded."

"What do you want?"

"To thank you," he says sweetly, sincerely. "And to invite you to join my team."

"Your team?" she says warily.

"Captain Landaðon has agreed that it is time for the department to modernize. To that end, I'm organizing a team to study the Bertillo System. I thought you might have some interest in joining it. Am I wrong?"

Etreyo is torn. Finally—the Bertillo System is taken seriously. But to work under Detective Wilkins! She'd almost rather continue to patrol the Northern Sandbank. Wouldn't she?

"I'll think about it," she says.

Detective Wilkins grins gorgeously. "Do that. We'll be in the ready room. Oh, and here—a little token of my esteem."

Constable Etreyo waits until he's gone before she opens the beribboned box he has given her. Nestled inside is a small cut-glass flask. She holds the bottle up and reads: *Madama Twanky's Mint-o Mouthwash: Polish Your Palate Until It Shines!*

✦ VI. THE VERDICT ✦

Constable Etreyo laughs and takes the bottle to the bathroom. The Mint-o mouthwash burns the awful taste away and makes her smile almost blinding. It would be a pity to waste that brilliant smile on the Northern Sandbanks. And anyway, doesn't Detective Wilkins always get what he wants? Who is she to stand in the way of the hero of the hour?

Etreyo puts her truncheon and helmet away, tucks the bottle of Mint-o in her locker, and walks down the hall to the ready room.

Ghost of Cwmlech Manor

{ DELIA SHERMAN }

There was a ghost at Cwmlech Manor.

Everybody knew it, although nobody had seen her, not with their own eyes, for years and years.

"Ghosts have to abide by the rules," I remember Mrs. Bando the housekeeper explaining as she poured us out a cup of tea at the manor's great oak kitchen table. She'd been parlor maid at the Manor when Mam was a kitchen maid there. Fast friends they were, and fast friends they'd stayed, even when Mam left domestic service to marry. Mrs. Bando was my godmother, and we went to her most Sunday afternoons.

I was ten or thereabouts, and I was mad for wonders. Da had told me of the new clockwork motor that was going to change everything, from the mining of coal to the herding of sheep. Above all things, I liked to hear about horseless carriages and self-powered mechanicals, but I'd settle for ghosts at a pinch.

So, "How do ghosts know the rules?" I asked. "Is there a ghost school, think you, on the other side?"

Mam laughed and said there was never such a child for asking questions that had no answer. She'd wager I'd ask the same of the ghost myself, if I saw her.

"And so I would, Mam. But first I'd ask her where she'd hid the treasure."

"And she'd likely disappear on the spot," Mrs. Bando scolded. "That knowledge is for Cwmlech ears only, look you. Not that it's needed, may the dear Lord be thanked."

Sir Owen indeed had treasure of his own, with a big house in London and any number of mechanicals and horseless carriages at his beck and call. It was generally agreed that it was no fault of his that the roof of Cwmlech Manor was all in holes and the beetle had gotten into the library paneling, but only the miserly ways of his factor, who would not part with so much as a farthing bit for the maintenance of a house his master did not care for.

Which made me think very much the less of Sir Owen Cwmlech, for Cwmlech Manor was the most beautiful house on the Welsh Borders. I loved everything about it, from its peaked slate roofs and tiny-paned windows to the peacocks caterwaul-ing in its yew trees. Best of all, I loved the story that went with it — very romantic and a girl as the hero — a rare enough thing in romantic tales, where the young girls always act like ninnies and end up dead of a broken heart, as often as not.

Mistress Angharad Cwmlech of Cwmlech Manor was not a

ninny. When she was only seventeen, the Civil War broke out, and her father and brothers, Royalists to a man, left home to join the king's army, leaving Mistress Cwmlech safe, they thought, at home. But in 1642 the Parliamentarians invaded the Borders, whereupon Mistress Cwmlech hid her jewels, as well as her father's strongbox and the family plate, dating, some of it, from the days of Edward II and very precious.

The night the Roundheads broke into the manor, they found her on the stairs, clad in her nightdress, armed with her grandfather's sword. They slew her where she stood, but not a gold coin did they find or a silver spoon, though they turned the house upside down with looking.

It was a sad homecoming her brothers had, I was thinking, to find their sister dead and in her silent grave, with the family wealth safely — and permanently — hidden away.

Her portrait hung in the great hall, over the mantel where her grandfather's swords had once hung. It must have been painted not long before her death — a portrait of a solemn young woman, her dark hair curling over her temples like a spaniel's ears and her gown like a flowered silk tea cozy, all trimmed with lace and ribbon-knots. A sapphire sparkled on her bosom, brilliants at her neck and ears, and on her finger, a great square ruby set in gold. There is pity, I always thought, that her ghost must appear barefoot and clad in her night shift instead of in that grand flowered gown.

I would have liked to see her, nightdress and all.

But I did not, and life jogged on between school and Mam's kitchen, where I learned to cook and bake, and Da's forge, where I learned the properties of metal and listened to him talk of the wonderful machines he'd invent, did he only have the gold. On

Sundays, Mrs. Bando told me stories of the parties and hunting meets of Sir Owen's youth, with dancing in the Long Gallery and dinners in the Great Hall for fifty or more.

Sometimes I thought I could hear an echo of their feet, but Mrs. Bando said it was only rats.

Still, I felt that Cwmlech Manor slept lightly, biding its time until its master returned and brought it back to life. But he did not come, and he did not come, and then, when I was fifteen, he died.

A bright autumn morning it was, warm as September often is, when Mrs. Bando knocked on the door in her apron, with her round, comfortable face all blubbered with weeping. She'd not drawn a breath before Mam had her by the fire with a cup of milky tea in her hand.

"There, then, Susan Bando," she said, brisk and kind. "Tell us what's amiss. You look as if you've seen the Cwmlech ghost."

Mrs. Bando took a gulp of tea. "In a manner of speaking, I have. The House of Cwmlech is laid in the dirt, look you. Sir Owen is dead, and his fortune all gambled away. The house in London is sold to pay his creditors and the manor's to be shut up and all the staff turned away. And what will I do for employment, at my age?" And she began to weep again while Mam patted her hand.

Me, I ran out of our house, down the lane, and across the stone bridge and spent the afternoon in the formal garden, weeping while the peacocks grieved among the pines for Cwmlech Manor, that was now dying.

As autumn wore on, I wondered more and more why Mistress Cwmlech did not appear and reveal where she'd hidden the treasure. Surely the ruinous state of the place must be as much a grief to her as to me. Was she lingering in the empty house, waiting for someone to come and hear her? Must that someone be a Cwmlech of Cwmlech Manor? Or could it be anyone with a will to see her and the wit to hear her?

Could it be me?

One Sunday after chapel, I collected crowbar, magnet, and candle, determined to settle the question. Within an hour, I stood in the Great Hall with a torn petticoat and a bruised elbow, watching the shadows tremble in the candlelight. It was November, and the house cold and damp as a slate cavern. I slunk from room to room, past sheet-shrouded tables and presses and dressers and chairs, past curtains furry with dust drawn tight across the windows. A perfect haven for ghosts it looked, and filthy to break my heart—and surely Mistress Cwmlech's as well. But though I stood on the very step where she was slain and called her name three times aloud, she did not appear to me.

I did not venture inside again, but the softer weather of spring brought me back to sit in the overgrown gardens when I could snatch an hour from my chores. There's dreams I had boiling in me, beyond the dreams of my friends, who were all for a husband and a little house and babies on the hearth. After many tears, I'd more or less accepted the hard fact that a blacksmith's daughter with no education beyond the village school could never be an engineer. So I cheered myself with my ability to play any wind instrument put into my hand, though I'd only a recorder to practice on, and it the property of the chapel.

Practice I did that summer, in the gardens of Cwmlech Manor, to set the peacocks screaming, and dreamed of somehow acquiring a mechanical that could play the piano and of performing with it before Queen Victoria herself. Such dreams, however foolish in the village, seemed perfectly reasonable at Cwmlech Manor.

Summer passed, and autumn came on, with cold rain and food to put by for winter; my practicing and my visits to Cwmlech fell away to nothing. Sixteen I was now, with my hair coiled up and skirts down to my boot tops and little time to dream. I'd enough to do getting through my chores, without fretting after what could not be or thinking about an old ghost who could not be bothered to save her own house. Mam said I was growing up. I felt that I was dying.

One bright morning in early spring, a mighty roaring and coughing in the lane shattered the calm like a mirror. Upstairs I was, sweeping, so a clear view I had, looking down from the front bedroom window, of a horseless carriage driving down by the lane.

I'd not have been more astonished to see Queen Victoria herself.

I knew all about horseless carriages, mind. The inventor of the Patent Steam Carriage was a Welshman, and all the best carriages were made in Blaenavon, down in the Valley. But a horseless carriage was costly to buy and costly to keep. Hereabouts, only Mr. Iestyn Thomas, who owned the wool mill, drove a horseless carriage.

And here was a pair of them, black smoke belching from their smokestacks: a traveling coach followed by a closed wain, heading toward Cwmlech Manor.

Without thinking whether it was a good idea or a bad one, I dropped my broom and hotfooted after, ducking through the gap in the hedge just as the traveling coach drove under the stone arch and into the weed-clogged courtyard.

Loud enough to raise the dead it was, with the peacocks

screaming and the engines clattering and the wheels of the wain crunching on the gravel drive. I slipped behind the West Wing and peered through the branches of a shaggy yew just in time to see the coach door open and a man climb out.

I was too far to see him clearly, only that he was dressed in a brown tweed suit, with a scarlet muffler wound around his neck and hanging down behind and before. He looked around the yard, the sun flashing from the lenses that covered his eyes, then raised an instrument to his lips and commenced to play.

There was no tune in it, just notes running fast as water over rocks in spring. It made my ears ache to hear it; I would have run away, except that the back of the wain opened and a ramp rolled out to the ground. And down that ramp, to my joy and delight, trundled a dozen mechanicals.

I recognized them at once from Da's journals: Porter models, designed to fetch and carry, a polished metal canister with a battery bolted on behind like a knapsack, and a ball at the top fitted with glass oculars. They ran on treads — much better than the wheels of older models, which slid on sand and stuck in the mud. Articulated arms hefted crates and boxes as though they were filled with feathers. Some had been modified with extra arms, and were those *legs* on that one there?

The notes that were not music fell silent. "Hullo," said a diffident voice. "May I help you? I am Arthur Cwmlech — Sir Arthur now, I suppose."

In my fascination I had drifted all the way from the hedge to the yard and was standing not a stone's throw from the young man with the pipe. Who was, apparently, the new Baronet of Cwmlech. And me in a dusty old apron, my hair raveling down my back, and my boots caked with mud.

If the earth had opened up and swallowed me where I stood, I would have been well content.

I curtsied, blushing hot as fire. "Tacy Gof I am, daughter of William Gof the smith. Be welcome to the home of your fathers, Sir Arthur."

He blinked. "Thank you," he said. "It's not much to look at, is it?"

To my mind, he had no right to complain of the state of the house. Thin as a rake he was, with knobby wrists and sandy hair straggling over the collar of his shirt, which would have been the better for a wash and an iron.

"Closed up too long it is, that's all," I said, with knives in, "and no one to look after it. A new roof is all it needs, and the ivy cut back, to be the most beautiful house on the Borders."

Solemn as a judge, he gave the house a second look, long and considering, then back to me. "I say, do you cook?"

It was my turn to blink. "What?"

"I need a housekeeper," he said, all business. "But she'd need to cook as well. No mechanical can produce an edible meal, and while I can subsist on sandwiches, I'd rather not."

I goggled, not knowing if he was in earnest or only teasing, or how I felt about it in either case.

"You'd be perfect," he went on. "You love the house and you know what it needs to make it fit to live in. Best of all, you're not afraid of mechanicals. At least, I don't think you are. Are you?" he ended anxiously.

I put up my chin. "A smith's daughter, me. I am familiar with mechanicals from my cradle." Only pictures, but no need to tell him that.

"Well." He smiled, and I realized he was not so much older than I. "That's settled, then."

"It is not," I protested. "I have not said I will do it, and even if I do, the choice is not mine to make."

"Whose, then?"

"My da and mam," I said. "And they will never say yes."

He thrust his pipe into his pocket, made a dive into the coach, fetched out a bowler hat, and crammed it onto his head. "Lead on."

"Where?" I asked stupidly.

"Your house, of course. I want to speak to your parents."

Mam was dead against it. Not a word did she say, but I read her thoughts clear as print in the banging of the kettle and the rattling of the crockery as she scrambled together a tea worthy to set before the new baronet. I was a girl, he was a young, unmarried man, people would talk, and likely they would have something to talk about.

"Seventeen she is, come midsummer," she said. "And not trained in running a great house. You had better send to Knighton for Mrs. Bando, who was housekeeper for Sir Owen."

Sir Arthur looked mulish. "I'm sure Mrs. Bando is an excellent housekeeper, Mrs. Gof. But can you answer for her willingness to work in a house staffed chiefly by mechanicals?"

"Mechanicals?" Mam's eyes narrowed. "My daughter, alone in that great crumbling house with a green boy and a few machines, is it? Begging your pardon, sir, if I give offense, but that is not a proper household for any woman to work in."

I was ready to sink with shame. Sir Arthur put up his chin a little. "I'm not a boy, Mrs. Gof," he said with dignity. "I'm nearly nineteen, with a degree in mechanical engineering from London Polytechnic. Still, I take your point. Tacy will live at home and come in days to cook and to supervise the mechanicals in bringing the house into better repair." He stood. "Thank you for the tea. The Welsh cakes were excellent. Now, if I may have a word with your husband?"

"More than a word it will take," Mam said, "before Mr. Gof will agree to such foolishness." But off to the forge we went nevertheless, where Sir Arthur went straight as a magnet to the steam hammer that was Da's newest invention. In next to no time, they'd taken it apart to admire, talking nineteen to the dozen.

I knew my fate was sealed.

Not that I objected, mind. Being housekeeper to Sir Arthur meant working in Cwmlech Manor, surrounded by mechanicals and horseless carriages, and money of my own—a step up, I thought, from sweeping floors under Mam's eye. Sir Arthur engaged Da, too, to help to turn the stables into a workshop and build a forge.

Before he left, Sir Arthur laid two golden coins in my palm. "You'll need to lay in provisions," he said. "See if you can procure a hen or two. I like a fresh egg for breakfast."

Next morning, Da and I packed our pony trap full of food and drink. I climbed up beside him and Mam thrust a cackling wicker cage into my hands.

"My two best hens for Sir Arthur's eggs, and see they're well housed. There's work you'll have and plenty, my little one, settling the kitchen fit to cook in. I'll just set the bread to rise and come help you."

Overnight I'd had time to recall the state of the place last time

I'd seen it. I was prepared for a shock when I opened the kitchen door. And a shock I got, though not the one I'd looked for. The floor was scrubbed, the table freshly sanded, and a fire crackled merrily on a new-swept hearth. As Da and I stood gaping upon the threshold, a silver-skinned mechanical rolled out of the pantry.

"Oh, you beauty," Da breathed.

"Isn't she?" Sir Arthur appeared, with the shadow of a sandy beard on his cheeks, grinning like an urchin. "This is the kitchen maid. I call her Betty."

There followed a highly technical discussion of Betty's inward workings and abilities and an exhibition of a clarinet-like instrument studded with silver keys, with the promise of a lesson as soon as he found the time. Then he carried Da off to look at the stable, leaving me with the instrument in my hand, bags and baskets everywhere, the hens cackling irritably, and Betty by the pantry door, still and gleaming.

Fitting the pipe between my lips, I blew softly. A bit like a recorder it was to play, with a nice, bright tone. I tried a scale in C, up and down, and then the first phrase of "The Ash Grove."

Betty whirred, swiveled her head, waved her arms aimlessly, and jerked forward. I dropped the pipe just as she was on the point of crushing the hens under her treads.

And that is how Mam found us: me with my two hands over my mouth and the pipe on the floor and Betty frozen and the hens squawking fit to cross your eyes.

Mam closed her lips like a seam, picked up the hens, and carried them outside. When she got back, there was a word or two she had to say about responsibility and God's creatures and rushing into things willy-nilly. But Mam's scolds never lasted long, and soon we were cooking companionably side by side, just as we did at home.

"And what's the use," she asked, "of that great clumsy machine by there?"

"That is the kitchen maid," I said. "Betty. There is all sorts of things she can do — once I learn how to use *that* properly." I cocked my chin at the pipe, which I'd stuck on the mantel.

"Kitchen maid, is it?" Mam spluttered — disgust or laughter, I could not tell — and fetched flour for the crust of a savory pie. When it was mixed and rolled out, she laid down the pin, wiped her hands on her apron, went to the dresser, got out one of Mrs. Bando's ample blue pinafores and a ruffled white cap. She set the cap on Betty's polished metal head and tied the pinafore around her body with the strings crossed all tidy, then gave a nod.

"Not so bad," she said. "With clothes on. But a godless monster nonetheless. A good thing Susan Bando is not here to see such a thing in her kitchen. I hope and pray, Tacy, my little one, that you will not regret this choice."

"Do you pass me those carrots, Mam," I said, "and stop your fretting."

When Da came in and saw Betty, he laughed until I thought he'd choke. Then he pulled a pipe from his own pocket and sent Betty rolling back into her pantry with an uncouth flight of notes.

"This pipe is Sir Arthur's own invention, look you," he said, proud as a cock robin. "A great advance on the old box-and-button system it is, all done with sound waves. Not easy to use, look you — all morning I've been learning to make them come and go. But clever."

I wanted a lesson right then and there, but Da said Sir Arthur would be wanting his dinner, and I must find a clean table for him to eat it on. Mam read me a lecture on keeping my eyes lowered and my tongue between my teeth, and then they were off and I was alone, with a savory pie in the oven perfuming the air, ready to begin my life as the housekeeper of Cwmlech Manor.

A ruined manor is beautiful to look at and full of mystery and dreams to wander in. But to make fit for human habitation a house where foxes have denned and mice bred their generations is another pair of shoes.

Had I a notion of being mistress of a fleet of mechanicals, with nothing to do but stand by playing a pipe while they worked, I soon learned better. First, Betty was my only helper. Second, her treads would not climb steps, so ramps must be built and winches set to hoist her from floor to floor. Third, I could not learn to command her to do any task more complicated than scrub a floor or polish a table.

Like speaking Chinese it was, with alphabet and sounds and grammar all against sense, a note for every movement, tied to the keys and not to the ear. Da, who could not tell one note from another, was handier with the pipe than I. It drove me nearly mad, with my ear telling me one thing and Sir Arthur's diagrams telling me another. And my pride in shreds to think I could not master something that should be so simple. Still, the work had to be done, and if I could not make Betty wash windows, I must do it myself, with Ianto Evans from the village to sweep the chimneys and nail new slates over the holes in the roof and mend the furniture where the damp had rotted the joints.

For the first month, Sir Arthur slept in the stable on a straw mattress. He took his noon meal there too, out of a basket. His dinners he ate in the kitchen, with a cloth on the table and good china and silver cutlery to honor his title and his position. Not that he seemed to care where he ate, nor if the plates were chipped or the forks tin, but ate what I put before him without once lifting his eyes from his book.

Fed up I was to overflowing and ready to quit, except for what Mam would say and the coins I put by each week in a box under my bed. But I stuck to it.

For whatever I might think of the baronet, I loved his house. And as I labored to clean the newest wing of the house and make it fit for human habitation, I felt it come alive again under my busy hands.

Finally, one rainy June evening when Sir Arthur came in to his dinner, I led him up the kitchen stairs and down a corridor to the morning room.

In silence he took in the oak paneling, all glowing with polish, the table laid with linen and china and silver, and a fire on the hearth to take the damp from the air. I stood behind him, with needles pricking to know what he thought, half angry already with knowing he'd say nothing. And then he turned, with a smile like a lamp and his eyes bright as peacock feathers under his thick lenses.

"It looks like home," he said. "Thank you, Tacy."

I blushed and curtsied and pulled out a chair for him to sit on, and then I served his dinner, each course on a tray, all proper as Mam had taught me. Even Sir Arthur seemed to feel the difference. If he read as he ate, he looked up as I fetched in the courses. And when I brought up a currant tart with cream to pour over, he put down his book and smiled at me.

"You've done well, Tacy, with only Betty to help you."

My pride flashed up like dry tinder. "Betty to help me, is it?" I said with heat. "It was Ianto Evans swept the chimney, look you, and I who did the rest. There's worse than useless, that old pipe is."

Sir Arthur raised his brows, the picture of astonishment. "Useless?" he said. "How useless?"

I wished my pride had held its tongue, but too late now. His right it was to ask questions, and my duty to answer them. Which I did as meek as Mam could wish, standing with my hands folded under my apron. After a while, he sent me for a pot of coffee, a notebook, and a pencil, and then again for a second cup. Before long, I was sipping at the horrid, bitter stuff, writing out music staffs and scales. Telling him about intervals I was, when he leaped up, grabbed my hand, hauled me down to the kitchen, and thrust my pipe into my hand.

"Summon Betty," he ordered.

Halting and self-conscious, I did that.

"Play 'The Ash Grove,'" he said. And I did. And Betty spun and lurched and staggered until I could not play for laughing. Sir Arthur laughed, too, and wrung my hand as though he'd pump water from my mouth, then ran off with his notebook and my pipe to the stables.

As soon as Sir Arthur had puzzled out how to make a mechanical dance to a proper tune, he took the Porters apart and set about rewiring them. That time was heaven for me, with Sir Arthur pulling me from the West Wing, where I was evicting spiders and wood pigeons and rats from the corners and walls, to play old tunes to the mechanicals.

And then, at the end of June, a cart arrived at Cwmlech Manor, with a long wooden crate in the back.

Sir Arthur organized the unloading with anxious care, he and Da tootling away unharmoniously while the mechanicals hoisted the crate and carried it into the workshop, like a funeral procession with no corpse. I'd vegetables boiling for a potch, but I pulled the pot off the stove and went to watch the unpacking.

"Go to your work, now, Tacy, my little one," Da said when he saw me. "This is none of your affair."

"If that's a new mechanical," I said, "I'd dearly love to see it."

Sir Arthur laughed. "Much better than that, Tacy. This will be the future of mechanicals. And I shall be its father."

He lifted the lid and pulled back the wood shavings. I took my breath sharp and shallow, for it might have been a dead youth lying there and not a mechanical at all. The head was the shape of a human skull, with neat ears and a slender nose and fine-cut lips and oval lids over the eyes. Face and body were covered, eerily, with close-grained leather, creamy pale as pearl.

"I bought it from a Frenchman," Sir Arthur said as he rummaged through the shavings. "It's only a toy now, a kind of supersophisticated doll that can stand and walk. When I make it speak and understand as well, it will be a humanatron, and the science of mechanicals will have entered a new phase."

Over his head, Da and I exchanged a look of understanding and laughter mixed. It had not taken us long to learn that Sir Arthur Cwmlech was like a butterfly, flitting restlessly from idea to idea. Yet in some things, you might set your watch by him. Dinner he ate at six of the clock exactly, and he always had coffee to drink afterward, never tea, and with his sweet, not after.

My seventeenth birthday came and went. Sir Arthur abandoned the Porters half-rewired to read books on sonics and the human auditory system and fill reams of foolscap with drawings and diagrams. He never set foot in the village. He never went to church nor chapel, nor did he call upon his neighbors. Da and old Dai Philips the post excepted, not a mortal man crossed the threshold of Cwmlech Manor from week's end to week's end. You may imagine my astonishment, therefore, when I heard one evening, as I carried him his coffee, a woman's voice in the morning room.

In a rage of fury she was, too, demanding he look at her. Now, a lady might have left them to fight it out in private. A servant, however, must deliver the coffee, though she'd better be quick.

When I entered, I saw Sir Arthur reading peacefully over the bones of his chop, as though there were no girl beside him, fists on hips and the insults rolling from her like water from a spout. Near my age she was and wearing nothing but a nightdress with a soft gray bed gown thrown over it. Then I saw the long dark stain under her left breast and my brain caught up with my eyes, and I knew that at last I looked upon the ghostly Mistress Angharad Cwmlech of Cwmlech Manor.

Sir Arthur roused himself from his book. "Ah, coffee!" he said. "And is that gingerbread I smell?"

Mistress Cwmlech fisted her hands in her disheveled hair and fairly howled. I dropped the tray on the table with a clatter.

Sir Arthur peered at me curiously, his spectacles glittering in the candlelight. "What's wrong? Did you see a rat? I heard them squeaking a moment ago."

"It was not a rat, Sir Arthur."

"You relieve my mind. I've nothing against rodents in their

place, but their place is not my parlor, don't you agree?"

Mistress Cwmlech made a rude gesture, surprising a snort of laughter from me so that Sir Arthur asked, a little stiffly, what ailed me.

"I beg pardon, sir," I stammered. "It's only I've remembered I left a pot on the stove —"

And I fled, followed by the ghost's bright laughter.

A gulf as wide as the Severn there is, between the wanting to see a ghost and the seeing it. But Mam always said there was no shock could not be cushioned by sweet, strong tea. In the kitchen, I poured myself a cup, added plenty of milk and sugar, and sat in Mrs. Bando's rocking chair to drink it.

Thus fortified, I hardly even started when the ghost appeared on the settle. Her arms were clasped about her knees, which were drawn up with her pointed chin resting upon them, and her dark eyes burned upon me.

"Good evening," she said.

I could see the tea towels I'd spread on the settle faintly through her skirts. "G-g-g." I took a gulp of tea to damp my mouth and tried again. "Good evening to you, miss."

"There," she said, with triumph. "I knew you could see me. Beginning to feel like a window I was, and me the toast of four counties. In my day . . ." She sighed. "Ah, but it is not my day, is it? Of your kindness, wench — what year is it?"

I pulled myself together. "1861, miss."

"1861? I had not thought it was so long. Still, I would expect a better welcome from my own descendent, look you."

Sad she sounded, and perhaps a little frightened. "The Sight is not given to everyone, miss," I said gently. "Sir Arthur is a good man, though, and very clever."

"He's too clever to believe in ghosts," she said, recovering. "There is pity he's the one Cwmlech in upward of two hundred years with a need to hear what I have to tell."

I sat upright. "The Cwmlech Treasure?"

"What know you of the Cwmlech Treasure, girl?"

"Only what legend says," I admitted. "There's romantic, miss, to defend your home with your grandfather's sword."

Mistress Angharad Cwmlech laughed, with broken glass in it. "Romantic, is it? Well, it was not romantic to live through, I will tell you so much for nothing. Not"—with a rueful glance at her bloodstained skirts—"that I did live through it."

Shamed I was, and thrown into such confusion, that I offered her a cup of tea along with my apologies. She laughed, a real laugh this time, and said her mama had been a great believer in the healing property of tea. So I told her about Mam, and she said to call her Mistress Angharad, and I was feeling quite easy with her until she demanded to be told about the mechanicals, which she called "those foul and unnatural creatures infesting my stables."

Recognizing an order, I did my best to obey. I explained about clockwork and sound waves, and then I called Betty out of her pantry. A bad idea, that. For when Betty trundled into the kitchen, Mistress Angharad vanished abruptly, reappearing some minutes later in a pale and tattered state.

"Sorry," I said, and piped Betty back to her pantry with "The Bishop of Bangor's Jig."

"Mark my words," Mistress Angharad said. "That soulless *thing* will be the ruin of the House of Cwmlech."

"If Sir Arthur cannot hear you," I said shyly. "Do you tell me where the treasure is hid, and I will pass the word on to him."

"And he would believe you, of course," she said, her scorn thick as paint. "And drop all his precious experiments and maybe knock holes in the walls besides."

I bristled. "He might, if I put it to him properly."

"Maybe," the ghost said, "and maybe not. In any case, I cannot tell you where I hid the treasure, were I ever so willing. Your ears could not hear the words."

"Show me, then."

She shrugged mistily. "There are rules and restrictions upon ghosts as there are upon young ladies of gentle birth. Given my choice, I'd be neither."

Past eleven it was, and Mam waiting for me to come in before she locked the door. I racked my tired brain. "Can you not invent a riddling rhyme, then? Leave a trail of clues?"

"No and no. Only to Sir Arthur may I reveal the hiding place —"

"And Sir Arthur doesn't believe in ghosts," I finished for her. "Or the treasure, come to that."

"I wish I need not tell him anything," she said peevishly. "Great blind old fool that he is. But tell him I must. I'll not know a moment's peace until the House of Cwmlech is safe and sound."

So began Mistress Angharad Cwmlech's ghostly siege upon the doorless tower of Sir Arthur's indifference.

There is not much a ghost can do to affect the waking world, but what she could, she did. She blew in his ear, ruffled his hair, pinched his arm, spilled his coffee, knocked his food from his plate. The result of her hauntings was no more than a wry remark about drafts or fleas or clumsiness, at which she'd howl and rail and curse like a mad thing. Sometimes it was all I could do not to laugh.

This had been going on for perhaps a month when Sir Arthur told me, after I'd brought up his coffee one chilly evening in July, with the rain coming down outside in knives and forks, that three gentlemen were coming to dine with him on Saturday.

"These gentlemen, sir," I said, mild as milk. "Will they be staying the night?"

"Yes. Is there a problem?"

Mistress Angharad, hovering by the hearth, giggled.

I put my lips together and sighed. "Perhaps you did not know, sir, there's no mattress in any bedchamber save your own, nor a whole sheet to make it up with. And while you may be happy to take mutton pie in the morning room, there's shame to serve no better to your guests, and they come all the way from London."

"Oh!" he said. "I hadn't thought. Can't have Mr. Gotobed sleeping on straw, either—he'd take offense, and that would never do. These guests are important, Tacy. What are we to do?"

I was tempted to take a page from Mistress Angharad's book just then and tell him what I thought of inviting guests without notice. But, as Mam was always telling me, he was the tenth Baronet Cwmlech and I was Tacy Gof, the smith's daughter. Friendly we might be, but it was not a friendship to survive plain speaking, however justified. "We must do what we can, Sir Arthur," I said, dry as sand. "Buy mattresses, for one thing, and cloth for curtains. Bed linen, of course, and wool coverlets that can double as blankets, and—"

"Oh, damn," Sir Arthur said with feeling. "I hadn't thought— oh, *damn*. You must buy what you see fit, of course, but please remember that I am ruined."

"Ruined?" I echoed blankly. "But the carriages and the mechanicals..."

"Are all my fortune, Tacy. With work and luck all will be restored, and you may bring Cwmlech Manor back to its full glory. But first I must secure a patent on the new pipe and find someone to manufacture it for general use."

He might have been speaking of flying to the moon, so hopeless did he sound.

"Come, now," I said. "That should be easy enough for a man clever enough to invent it in the first place. Da will help you, I'm sure. As for your guests, you may leave their entertainment in my hands."

His smile was clouded with worry, but it warmed me nonetheless. "Thank you, Tacy. I have every confidence in *you*, at least."

Which is a heady thing for a girl just past her seventeenth birthday to hear. As I cleaned the kitchen, I chattered of lists and plans to Mistress Angharad until she lost her temper.

"It is dull you are, bleating about roasts and beds like an old ewe. Have you not asked yourself who these gentlemen are and what they're after, out in the damp wilds of the Borders when the London Season is at its height? Lombard Street to a China orange, they're up to nothing good."

"All the more reason to be thinking of roasts and beds," I said shortly.

Mistress Angharad wailed to curl my toes and disappeared.

After that, I had far more important things to think about than a sulky spirit. Hercules himself could not have made Cwmlech Manor fit for company in three days' time, so I went down to Mam's and begged her help.

If Da's genius was to beat dead iron into usefulness, Mam's was to settle a house into order and beauty. She began at Cwmlech by going to Mr. Thomas at the wool mill and Mrs. Wynn the shop and charming goods from them in exchange for a letter of patronage to hang on the wall, saying that Sir Arthur of Cwmlech Manor did business here and no other place. Then she summoned all the good women of Cwmlech village, who tucked up their sleeves and descended on the Manor with mops and brooms and buckets. They worked like bees in a meadow, until the windows were all draped in good Welsh wool, and the bed linen white and fragrant with lavender, and flowers on the chests, and the wood in the dining room all rubbed soft and glowing.

On the Saturday morning, Mam came with me to the Manor to help cook and wait upon the guests.

"There is funny gentlemen they are," she said when she came from showing them to their chambers. "Rat's eyes and bull's necks, no servants, and next to no luggage. No manners, neither — not so much as a smile or thanks, only a sharp warning not to meddle with their things. Were they not Sir Arthur's guests, I would not willingly give them to eat."

Which was strong speaking for Mam. It made me think of Mistress Angharad and how I'd missed seeing her these past days, sharp tongue and all, and how I wished to hear her opinion of the men who would sleep at Cwmlech Manor this night.

So you may judge my joy when I carried Mam's leek soup in to dinner that evening, to see Mistress Angharad hovering at the sideboard, bloody and disheveled as ever.

I smiled at her; she frowned back. "Eyes open and mouth shut, girl," she ordered. "Here's mischief abroad."

Which I might have guessed for myself, so smug were the guests, like cats at a mouse hole, and so fidgety was Sir Arthur, like the mouse they watched. Two of them were large and broad, very thick in their beards and necks and narrow in their eyes; the third was thinner and clean shaven, but no more handsome for that, with his mouth as tight as a letter box and his eyes hard as ball bearings.

"A fine, large workshop, Sir Arthur," Clean-Cheeks said, picking up his spoon. "A pity nothing useful has come out of it."

One of the roughs said, "Don't forget the pipe, Mr. Gotobed."

Mr. Gotobed smiled thinly. "I do not forget the pipe, Mr. Brown."

Sir Arthur nudged his cutlery straight. "It's very nearly ready, Mr. Gotobed. Just a few details about the interface...."

"Interface?" The second rough found this funny. "Them things got no face at all, if you ask me."

And then the tureen was empty, and I must run downstairs again to fetch the fish course. When I returned with the baked grayling, Mr. Gotobed and his friends had scraped their plates clean, Sir Arthur's soup was untouched, and Mistress Angharad was scowling blackly.

"I know Cwmlech Manor is haunted," Mr. Gotobed was saying. "There is a whole chapter on the subject in *The Haunted Houses of Great Britain*. Your resident ghost is precisely why Mr. Whitney wants to buy it. He has a great affinity for the supernatural, does Mr. Whitney of Pittsburgh, America. By his own account, some of his best friends are ghosts."

"Then I'm afraid he must be disappointed," Sir Arthur said. "You will be paid in full."

Mr. Gotobed smiled. "Yes," he said. "I will. One way or another. Mr. Whitney is very excited. I believe he intends to install a swimming bath in the Great Hall."

Mistress Angharad reached for a candlestick. Another time, her look of fury when her hand passed through it might have made me laugh, but I was too furious myself for mirth. Sir Arthur's hands clenched against the table. "A year's grace is all I ask, Mr. Gotobed."

"A year! It will take that long for the patent office to read your application, and another for them to decide upon it. I'm sorry, Sir Arthur. A manor in the hand is worth any number of inventions in, er, the bush. Pay me in full on the first of September or Cwmlech Manor is mine, as per our contract. Excellent fish, by the way. Did you catch it yourself?"

How I got through the rest of the meal without cracking a plate over Mr. Gotobed's head, I do not know. Lucky that Mam was busy with her cooking. My face was a children's ABC to her, and I did not want her knowing that Sir Arthur had pledged Cwmlech Manor. She'd small patience with debtors, and she'd think him no better than his father, when the poor boy was only a lamb adrift in a world of wolves like Mr. Gotobed.

The uncomfortable dinner wore on, with only Mr. Gotobed and his roughs eating Mam's good food, and Mistress Angharad cursing impotently, and Sir Arthur growing more and more white and pinched about the nose. When I took up the cloth at last and put the decanters on the table, he stood up. "I have some rather pressing business to attend to," he said. "Enjoy your port, gentlemen."

And then he went into his bedroom across the landing and shut the door.

I wanted to knock and give him a few words of comfort. But

Mam was waiting downstairs with all the cleaning up, and I could think of no comfortable words to say.

Mam and I were to sleep at Cwmlech Manor to be handy to cook the guests' breakfast in the morning. When the kitchen was tidy, we settled by the fire to drink a cup of tea, too weary to speak. So low was I, I hardly started when Mistress Angharad said, "Tacy! I have news!" right in my ear.

Mam shivered. "There's a wicked old draft in by here."

"Worse when you're tired," I said. "Go in to bed, Mam. I'll see to locking up."

She gaped fit to split her cheeks and went off without argument for once, which was a blessing, since Mistress Angharad was already talking.

"Listening I was, as they drank Sir Arthur's port. It's all a trick, look you. The Manor is sold already, to the rich American who likes ghosts and swimming baths. And Tacy, that blackguard will wreck Sir Arthur's workshop tonight, in case he might sell his machines and pay his debt!"

I clutched my cooling tea, half sick with rage and entirely awake. "Will we tell Sir Arthur?"

"Sir Arthur!" she said with scorn. "Meek as a maiden aunt all through dinner, and off to cower in his bed as soon as the cloth was lifted. No. If anyone is to save Cwmlech Manor, it must be the two of us."

"Right." I put down my tea. "To the stable, us. And pray we're not too late."

Pausing only to light the lantern, we crept out of the kitchen and across the yard to the stable, the moon sailing high and pale in a rack of cloud above us. Within, all was black, save for the sullen glow of the forge fire. The flickering lantern drew little sparks of light from the dials and gears and polished metal of Sir Arthur's machines and tools. The air smelled like pitch and coal and machine oil.

"The dragon's lair," Mistress Angharad said, full of bravado. "Is that the virgin sacrifice?"

I followed the faint glow of her pointing finger to a table set like a bier under a bank of lights, and the figure upon it draped with an old linen sheet.

"That," I said, "is Sir Arthur's expensive French automaton. Will you look?" I picked my way carefully through the chaos of strange machines and gear-strewn tables and reached for the sheet. "Only an old mechanical it is, see?"

In truth, it looked eerie enough, bald and still and deathly pale. Mistress Angharad stroked its cheek with a misty finger. "There's beautiful it is," she said, with wonder.

I touched the key in its neck. "Still, only a mechanical doll, simpler than the simplest automaton." Without thought, almost without my will, my fingers turned the key, feeling the spring coil tight as I wound.

Mistress Angharad turned her head. "Douse the lantern," she hissed.

Heart beating like one of Da's hammers, I blew out the candle and ducked down behind the table. The door flew open with a crack of splintering wood, and Mr. Gotobed and his two thugs rushed in, waving crowbars.

I cursed my tired brain, drew my pipe from my apron pocket, and played the first tune that came to mind, which was "Rali Twm

Sion"—a good rousing tune to instruct the mechanicals to break down walls.

Someone shouted—I think it was Mr. Brown. Then the air was filled with whirring gears and thumping treads and grunts and bad language and the clang and screech of metal against metal.

"Sons of pigs!" Mistress Anghard screeched. "Break their bones like matchsticks I would, could I only touch them!"

From the corner of my eye, I saw her hovering, cloudlike, over the automaton. Then she said, "I am going to break a great rule. If it means the end of me, then I will at least have tried. Good-bye, Tacy. You have been a good friend to Cwmlech and a friend to me as well." And then she disappeared.

Though tears pricked my eyes, I went on playing "Rali Twn Sion" as though my life depended on it—until the French automaton twitched and thrashed and sat up on the table, when the pipe dropped from my hands, grown suddenly nerveless.

The mechanicals froze, of course. The French automaton, however, swung off the table and staggered toward the noise of iron crunching against polished metal. Not to be outdone by a toy, I snatched up the first heavy tool I laid my hand on and ran, yelling to tear my throat, toward a shadowy figure whose shaven cheeks showed ghostly in the gloom.

Swinging my makeshift weapon high, I hit him on the arm— as much by luck as design. He swore and dropped the bar. I was about to hit him again when Sir Arthur's lights flared into blinding life overhead, and Sir Arthur's pipe brought the mechanicals to purposeful life.

Quick as thinking, they seized Mr. Gotobed and Mr. Brown and held them while the automaton who was Mistress Angharad picked up the third thug and slammed him bodily against the wall.

Sir Arthur came running up to me, his eyes wild behind his spectacles. "Tacy! What the devil is going on here? Are you hurt?"

I hefted my weapon—a hammer it was. "Not a bit of it. But I think I may have broken Mr. Gotobed's arm. Earned it he has twice over, the mess he's made of things."

Side by side, we surveyed the workshop then. Like a battlefield it was, with oil stains in the place of blood. Not a mechanical but was dented, and more than one stood armless or headless and dull eyed, its motive force gone. Not a machine but bore smashed dials and broken levers. Most pathetic, the French automaton lay sprawled like a puppet whose strings have been cut, one arm at a strange angle and the leather torn over its shoulder to show the metal underneath.

Sir Arthur pinched the bridge of his nose. "It's ruined," he said, a mourner at a wake. "They're all ruined. And there's no money left—not enough to repair them, anyway. I'll have to sell it all as scrap, and that won't bring enough to keep Cwmlech Manor on."

It hurt my heart to hear him say so. "What about the treasure?"

He shook his head. "That's a legend, Tacy, like the ghost—just a local variant of a common folktale. No. I am my father's son, a gambler and a wastrel. Mr. Whitney will have Cwmlech Manor after all."

"Do not lose hope, Sir Arthur, my little one," I said. "Do you lock those bad men into the tack room while I make a pot of tea. And then we will talk about what to do."

When I returned with the tea tray, Mr. Gotobed and his rogues were nowhere to be seen. Two chairs had been set by the forge fire, which was blazing brightly, and the automaton back upon its table, with Sir Arthur beside it, nibbling on his thumbnail.

I poured two cups with sugar and milk, took one for myself and carried the other to him. He thanked me absently and set down his cup untasted. I breathed in the fragrant steam but found no comfort in it. Abandoning my tea, I set myself to search grimly among the tools and glass and pieces of metal on the floor. Like looking for a needle in a haystack it was, but I persisted and turned up Mistress Angharad's key at last under one of the broken machines.

"Here," I said, thrusting it into Sir Arthur's hand. "Maybe it's just run-down she is, and not ruined at all. Do you wind her and we'll find out."

Muttering something about putting a sticking plaster on a mortal wound, he inserted the key, turned it until it would turn no more, and then withdrew it.

The eyelids opened slowly and the head turned stiffly toward us. Sir Arthur whooped with joy, but my heart sank, for the eyes were only brown glass, bright and expressionless. Mistress Angharad was gone.

And then the finely carved mouth quirked up at the corners and one brown eye winked at me.

"A legend, am I?" said Mistress Angharad Cwmlech of Cwmlech Manor. "There's a fine thing to say to your great-aunt, boy, when she is on the point of pulling your chestnuts from the fire."

It would be pleasant to write that Sir Arthur took Mistress Angharad's haunting of the French automaton in his stride, or that Mistress Angharad led Sir Arthur to the treasure without delay. But that would not be truthful.

Truthfully, then. Sir Arthur was convinced that the shock

of losing Cwmlech Manor had driven him mad, and Mistress Angharad had a thing or two to say about people who were too clever to believe their own eyes. I was ready to shut them up in the workshop to debate their separate philosophies until one or the other of them ran down.

"Whist, the both of you," I said at last. "Sir Arthur, there's no harm in hearing what Mistress Angharad has to say, do you believe in ghosts or not. It can be no more a waste of time than arguing about it all night."

"I'll speak," Lady Angharad said. "If he'll listen."

Sir Arthur shrugged wearily. "I'll listen."

The Cwmlech Treasure was hidden in a priest's hole, tucked all cozy into the side of the chimney in the Long Gallery. In the reign of Harry VIII, masons had known their business, for the door fit so neatly into the stonework that we could not see it, even when Mistress Angharad traced its outline. Nor could all our prodding and pushing on the secret latch stir it so much as a hairsbreadth.

"It's rusted shut," Sir Arthur said, rubbing a stubbed finger. "The wall will have to be knocked down, I expect."

Mistress Angharad put fists on her hips. Very odd it was to see her familiar gestures performed by a doll, especially one clad in an old sheet. It had been worse, though, without the sheet. Mute and inert, an automaton is simply unclothed. When it speaks to you in a friend's voice, however, it is suddenly naked and must be covered.

"Heaven send me patience," she said now. "Here is nothing that a man with an oilcan and a chisel and a grain of sense cannot sort out."

"I'll fetch Da, then," I said. "But first, breakfast and coffee, or we'll be asleep where we stand. And Mam must be wondering what's become of me."

Indeed, Mam was in the kitchen, steeling herself to go upstairs and see whether Sir Arthur had been murdered in his bed and I stolen by Mr. Gotobed for immoral purposes. The truth, strange as it was, set her mind at ease, though she had a word to say about Mistress Angharad's bedsheet. Automaton or not, she was the daughter of a baronet, Mam said. She must come down by our house to be decently clothed — and explain things to Da while she was about it.

High morning it was before we gathered in the Long Gallery, Da with his tools, Mam with the tea tray, and Mistress Angharad in my best Sunday costume, with the triple row of braiding on the skirt, and my Sunday bonnet covering her bald head.

Da chipped and pried and oiled and coaxed the door open at last, amid a great cloud of dust that set us all coughing like geese. When it settled, we were confronted with a low opening into a darkness like the nethermost pits of Hell, which breathed forth a dank odor of ancient drains and wet stone.

Da looked at Sir Arthur, who bit his lip and looked at me.

"God's bones!" Mistress Angharad cried, and snatching up the lantern, set her foot on the steep stone stair that plunged down behind the chimney.

Sir Arthur, shamefaced, followed after, with me and Da behind him, feeling our way along the slick stone wall, taking our breath short in the musty air.

It could not have been far, but the dark made the stair lengthen until we might have been in the bowels of the earth. It ended in a stone room furnished with a narrow bed and three banded boxes, all spotted with mold and rust. Da's crowbar made short work of the locks. He lifted the lids one by one, and then we looked upon the fabled Treasure of Cwmlech.

A great deal of it there was, to be sure, but not beautiful nor rich to the eye. There were chargers and candlesticks and ewers and bowls, all gone black with tarnish. Even the gold coins in their strongbox and Mistress Angharad's jewels were dull and plain with time and dirt.

Mistress Angharad picked a ring out of the muddle and rubbed it on the skirt of my Sunday costume, revealing a flat-cut stone that winked and glowed like fire in the lantern light.

"What think you of your variant folktale now?" she asked Sir Arthur.

He laughed, free and frank. "I see I shall have to speak better of folktales in the future."

All I recall of the rest of that day was the steady stream of police and masons and men from the village come to deal with the consequences of the night's adventures. When Sir Arthur sat down to dinner in his parlor at last, Mr. Gotobed and his thugs were locked up tight as you please in the magistrate's coal cellar, and the treasure had been carried piecemeal from the priest's hole and put in the old tack room with Ianto Evans and two others to guard it. Mam cooked the dinner, and served it, too, for I was in my bed at home, asleep until old Mrs. Philips's rooster woke me next morning to walk to the Manor in the soft dawn as usual, as if my world had not been turned upside down.

First thing I saw when I came in the kitchen was Mistress Angharad, sitting on the settle in my Sunday costume.

"Good morning, Tacy," she said.

A weight dropped from me I had not known I carried. I whooped joyfully and threw my arms around her. Like hugging a dress form it was, but I did not mind.

"This is a greeting after a long parting, Tacy, my little one," she said, laughing. "Only yesterday it was you saw me."

"And did not think to see you again. Is it not a rule of ghosts, to disappear when their task on earth is done?"

The automaton's face was not expressive, and yet I would swear Mistress Angharad looked sly. "Yet here I am."

I sat back on my heels. "Is it giving eternity the slip you are, then? The truth now."

"The truth?" She shrugged stiffly. "I am as surprised as you. Perhaps there's no eternal rule about a ghost that haunts a machine. Perhaps I am outside all rules now and can make my own for a change. Perhaps"—she rose from the settle and began her favorite pacing—"I can wear what I like and go where I will. Would you like to be trained as a mechanic, Tacy, and be my lady's maid, to keep me wound and oiled?"

"If you are no longer a lady," I said, with a chill that surprised even me, "you will not need a lady's maid. I would prefer to train as an engineer, but if I must be a servant, I'd rather be a housekeeper with a great house to run than a mechanic, which is only a scullery maid with an oilcan."

A man's laugh startled us both. "Well said, Tacy," said Sir Arthur from the kitchen door, where he'd been listening. "Only I have in mind to make your mother housekeeper, if she will do it, with a gaggle of housemaids under her to keep the place tidy. You I need to design a voice for my humanatron. You will learn engineering.

Which means I must command tutors and books from London. And new tools and a new automaton from France, of course. Perhaps more than one. I suppose I must write my lawyers first and finish work on the pipe. And the foundation needs work, the masons say." He sighed. "There's so much to do, I do not know where to begin."

"Breakfast first," I said. "And then we'll talk about the rest."

There is a ghost in Cwmlech Manor.

She may be seen by anyone who writes a letter that interests her. Mr. Whitney came all the way from Pittsburgh to talk to her. He stayed a month, and Sir Arthur persuaded him to invest in the humanatron.

She travels often, accompanied by her mechanic and sometimes by me, when I can spare the time from my engineering studies and my experiments. Last summer, we went to London, and Sir Arthur presented us to Queen Victoria, who shook our hands and said she had never spoken to a ghost before, or a female engineer, and that she was delightfully amused.

Gethsemane

{ ELIZABETH KNOX }

✦ 1 ✦

A woman and a girl. A man and a boy. And witnesses, people who were interested to see them go up the mountain separately, then come down together, the boy carrying the girl's basket, and the woman's hand resting on the man's arm. As pairs they were already notable, and when they started keeping company, they presented a real puzzle to the flourishing gossips of Gethsemane.

For a start, it wasn't usual for anyone to speak to the girl in public. The stallholders in the market would never take money from her hand; she had to leave it on the counter and they'd pick it up once she'd moved on. The girl was a witch. She lived in a dark crib in an alley off Market Square and was followed everywhere by the woman, a silent, white-eyed figure.

The boy and man weren't locals. They'd arrived in the Shackle Islands on the *John Bartholomew*. Ships that came into the port of Gethsemane would usually unload quickly, then pick up a cargo of sugar. But the *John Bartholomew* stayed. She was three days in the dock, unloading a cargo of equipment for the South Pacific

Company's thermal project. Drills and gantries, steel cable and steel beams were piled up on the wharf, then carried off along the road to Mount Magdalene. The ship then anchored out in the channel, where its crew weren't at any easy leisure. They idled and fumed within sight of the port, and only the captain came and went freely. And then the boy and the man began to appear — inexplicably exempt from the rule against shore leave.

The boy was only a steward on the ship, but the *John Bartholomew*'s captain seemed to favor him, and the talk in the port was that he was some shipowner's son getting a maritime education. This, because of the captain's odd partiality and the fact he had a servant — for it was assumed that the able seaman who accompanied him every-where was his servant. The man was in late middle age, grizzled, wiry, and as weathered as any aging sailor, but there were those who said that this was only a disguise, and that he was in fact an old family retainer. He seemed too tender of the boy — tender with a familial tenderness. He was black, and the boy white, so, given the tenderness, it followed that he couldn't be simply a shipmate.

That winter everybody was busy, and the busybodies were bus-ier than ever. Rumor rose like steam from a town that seemed to be coming to the boil. The cane had been cut, and the refineries were lit up all night. In the wind that came off the sea, the town smelled of caramel. The wind blew across the bay named Broken Crown, over the port and refineries, and right into town, where it mingled with the smells of the Saturday market and the gardens, its caramel giving body to the fruit and floral scents.

Gethsemane was a city of gardens. Its topsoil was made of eons of decayed vegetation mixed into many feet of ash, making a fertile, friable soil that parted lovingly for the hoe. The locals had always talked about their soil as if it were some kind of demigod—the way people in high-latitude ports talk about the weather. The locals discussed soil, but the engineers who arrived on the *John Bartholomew* were interested only in ash—where it lay, and to what depth. To the townspeople, "ash" was potash for porcelain, or wood ash for gunpowder—utilitarian stuff—and though they worshipped their soil, they never thought about what it was made of, or the ground beneath it. Gethsemane's earthly powers, the mayor and sheriff, the owners and managers of refineries, the plantation owners with summer houses on the lower slopes of the town, all were welcoming to the engineers because they wanted to grow Gethsemane—as the town's soil grew melons. Yet, at their parties, the talk wasn't about money but progress, the fecundity of the future. They all agreed that Gethsemane was paradise on earth. Its early settlers had discovered a salubrious climate and a most welcoming native people keen to share their bounty of bush pigs and fat native birds and fruiting trees and hot springs—the earth's own ovens. The settlers dug hot-water wells for their baths and laundries. The very earth, even barren, had utility in the form of heat. Puffed up with civic pride, the city welcomed the engineers and geologists who came to learn how to tap that earth for power, how to sink bores and find steam forceful enough to drive turbines and generate electricity, so that the refineries could run day and night, and the city could sparkle, a clean, bright, South Pacific jewel.

There was another hot property of the town's wishful gossip. The thermal project's chief engineer, McCahon, proved to be a bold and ferociously forward-looking man—a real novelty in the islands, whose planter families were old and established powers. McCahon was someone on whom the island's future prosperity might depend.

Someone *new*. He was invited everywhere, scrutinized and admired, and after scarcely a fortnight it was rumored that he'd developed a fancy for the mayor's daughter, Sylvia. Then, to pour fuel on the fire of rumor, that young woman was seen, in man's attire, and a hat pulled low, ducking in at the gate to the witch's crib.

The witch, a pretty girl aged somewhere between sixteen and twenty, had set herself up nearly a year before, selling balms and love charms, and—it was rumored—abortifacients, and sleeping drafts, and potions that produced dreams vividly reminiscent of those the moneyed people of Gethsemane would share whenever they visited Southland, the nation of which the Shackle Islands were a protectorate. No one knew the witch's name, and she had a servant—a white-eyed mute—said to be a dead woman.

In the fine residences along the inner harbor, practical-minded people tried to point out errors in the logic of these rumors. Why would the mayor's daughter be looking for a love charm if she'd already caught McCahon's eye? And—in more hushed tones—how could she be looking for an abortifacient when she'd only known McCahon for a couple of weeks? And—on the subject of the little witch—how could her servant be a zombie and also have been seen coming down the mountain path leaning on the arm of the old able seaman?

A local doctor talking to a certain group of lacy matrons over iced tea said that he thought the girl's potions were probably only opium and datura and psilocybin mushrooms. She was either a skilled herbalist or a daring experimenter. The doctor said all this to dispel the nonsense of gossip. But having sown the seeds of his own temptation, he visited the witch's crib himself several nights later. He told himself that he only wanted to procure for analysis some of her home-brewed remedies, but he came away impressed in spite of himself by the girl's terrible, cold gravity, and by the figure who stood unmoving in a corner the whole time he was there—tall, skeletal, and as inanimate as a broken grandfather clock.

You ask how we know what the doctor thought. Well—he survived. He had an operation to perform in the other big settlement in the archipelago.

The circular harbors of Calvary and Gethsemane were the "shackles" of the Shackle Islands. The towns were linked by a 150-mile "chain" of low islands, planted in sugarcane, and by a road that ran through cane fields and salt marshes.

One hundred and fifty miles. In Calvary, there was time enough for an evacuation.

The doctor lived to tell his tale. And so did Alice Lewes. Alice had sailed to Southland, sent away by her father when he discovered that she'd been out at night with her wild friend, Sylvia. It was Alice and Sylvia—Sylvia in man's attire—who were seen slipping through the gate to the witch's crib. Alice had promised to keep her friend's secret and did so even though her father threatened to send her away to school. She kept her mouth shut and was packed off. She was in transit when she heard what had happened, and she understood that there was no one left who cared what she and Sylvia had done.

It was Alice who first approached the witch. She did it to tease her friend. They were in the market and spotted the haughty girl, with a basket on her arm, taking her time over each display, to the discomfort of the stallholders—a girl who went about untouched in the crowd, shadowed by her starved, still-faced servant. "Perhaps the little witch can make you a love potion, Syl," Alice said to her friend, and darted away from Sylvia's desperate batting hand. Alice didn't know that although Sylvia liked to talk about Mr. McCahon, she hadn't liked to hope.

Alice followed the witch from the market. She waited till there were fewer people about, and she could approach the witch while keeping the girl between herself and that frightening, black, white-eyed creature. "Excuse me," Alice said. "I have a friend who requires a love potion. Can you do that?"

And the witch told Alice where she lived and when they could come.

The courtyard of the witch's crib had a wicket gate, and its walls were lined with empty poultry cages made of silvered gum-tree wood. Their grid was so tight that there was very little light. If the gate hadn't creaked and given the two people in the house some warning, Alice and Sylvia might have heard the witch say to the dead woman, "Will this do? A tisane strong enough to be offensive to the palate but not to turn the stomach. That's what you said." And they might have heard the dead woman answer, "I said, 'One that tastes bad but won't make the young lady sick.'" And then heard the witch, fondly chiding, *"Mary!"*

The gate creaked. Alice clutched Sylvia's arm. Sylvia, now resolute, shook off her friend and hurried to the door. It opened onto a long room that seemed to squeeze itself down to nothing at its end, where the ceiling dropped and there was a step down into a scullery. The only window was there, at the very back, its glass coated with black mold. For a moment all that the friends could see was the witch's white apron and her pale face. Then they glimpsed the figure standing in the room's darkest corner, thin, and sinewy, and as motionless as a monument.

The witch sprang forward and pushed Alice and her friend right back out into the courtyard. She said, "I don't want your hopes contaminating this potion before it is finished." She slammed the door in their faces. They waited in the close, hot space, Alice with her skirts gathered in her gloved hands. They heard the witch whispering— spells, they supposed. A moment later she let them in again.

The kettle had been swiveled back over the coals and was steaming. There was a bowl on the hearth, beside it a small bottle, a funnel, and a rag stopper.

Alice kept her friend between herself and the white-eyed figure in the corner. She gripped the back of Sylvia's jacket.

"How does the potion work?" Sylvia asked the witch. "What must I do?"

"You must drink one-third of the potion the night before you see this man. On the morning of the day that you see him, you must comb all but a few drops of it into your hair. The remainder you must dab *here*." The witch stepped close and insinuated her hand into Sylvia's shirt to touch her cleavage. "Over your heart," the witch said. "Then you cannot cover yourself—you must let the sun shine on your hair and breasts."

Alice giggled.

"But what if he—Mr. McCahon—can't keep his appointment with my father or comes late, when the sun is down? He's up the mountain every day, where they're drilling."

"I know where he is," said the witch. "If he fails to appear before sundown, come again and I'll repeat the charm. I won't charge you for that. We can't control all circumstances."

"But will it work?"

"It will if your heart is pure."

Sylvia's face fell. Even Alice could see the obvious hitch.

"Oh," said the witch, "you mistake me. I don't mean *maidenly*. Your hopes can be wholly carnal—but you must not be simply playing."

Sylvia nodded, solemn.

Alice, made bold by the witch's forthright and doctorly manner, ventured to ask, "Is it true what they say, that your servant is"— she dropped her voice—"a zombie?"

"My slave," the witch said, her tone gloating. "While your potion cools shall I tell you her story?"

Sylvia and Alice looked around as if they had been invited to sit. But there was nothing to sit on, not even a stool. There was the low hearth and, in a corner, a single pallet bed covered in grubby blankets.

The witch went to the fire and stood with her back to it, its light striking only one blue eye. "My craft came to me," she said. "And this is how." She pointed at her slave. "This woman and my nurse were rivals for the love of a certain man. This woman procured a curse that, she was told, would strike my nurse ugly. The curse was cast, and the following Sunday, the curser was infuriated to see my nurse holding my hand as we came into church—and looking as lovely as ever." The witch raised a finger, and an assortment of brass and silver bangles slipped, chiming from her wrist to elbow. "But, a week later, my nurse discovered a tiny blue mark on her cheekbone. She washed her face, but soap wouldn't move it. She tried pinching color into that spot and felt, between her fingers, a little hard ball, like a dry pea. Week by week that pea grew, into a cherry, into a plum, into a bluish horn of flesh. She took it to a doctor, and the doctor told her it had grown into the bones of her face. And he told her that there wasn't any hope for her. My family kept her on, and she still saw to my needs, but kept her face covered. After a time the horn stopped growing and began to sink and spread, and my nurse complained of always having a terrible smell in her nose. Then she lost the sight in her left eye. After that she stayed in bed. The horn blossomed. Once, when she was sleeping, I crept into her room and uncovered it and saw a cavity, like a crater, black at its edges and hot and bloody at its center. At the end the poor woman couldn't even speak or swallow. But before she lost her voice, she taught me a powerful curse, a curse her family had kept but the knowledge of which she had always shunned, because she was a good woman. It was a curse to take a soul. Not a life; a soul.

"The night my nurse died, I used that curse on her rival. This woman"—the witch pointed at her silent slave—"this woman came to my nurse's funeral. She followed the coffin to the church-yard and stood at the graveside, smirking. But when the mourners had moved away and the sexton was filling in the grave, this woman was still there, standing, swaying. Her head was back, and she was staring up into the sun. She wouldn't stir. They had to lead her away indoors, and by that time, her eyeballs had blistered.

"I did that," the witch said. "I made her mindless and soulless and now she follows me.

"You were watching me in the market before you screwed up enough courage to make your appointment. You must have seen how she always follows after me with her hand held out. It isn't that I'm guiding her, but that I'm *all she can see*. And what she sees is my shadow. And my shadow appears to her as a black door. She wants to go through that door. For she knows she can only escape her servitude in death. And she knows that if I die first, the door vanishes, and she is left in a desert of whiteness, the whiteness that is all she can see."

The witch finished her story and turned to the hearth to pick up the bowl and blow on it. As she came closer to the fire, her shadow moved and thickened and fell across the face of her silent slave, who raised her arm and reached — like someone putting out a hand to a door handle.

The visitors gasped and clutched each other.

The girl turned back to them and smiled at their fear. She took a funnel and decanted the potion from the bowl into the bottle, then stuffed the bottle with the rag stopper. She held it out — a reddish liquid behind grubby glass. Her hand was stained with plant juices. "For your Mr. McCahon."

Sylvia closed the bottle into her fist and slipped her fist into her pants pocket, making a little boyish bulge.

"Remember," said the witch, "you must have a heart unsullied by hesitation. I may have followed my nurse around Ragged Hat—"

Ah, Alice thought, *so she comes from Calvary!*

"—learning about herbs, but I wasn't a witch till I cast that curse. It worked because I asked justly. Magic makes judgments. Remember that."

Gethsemane's harbor was roughly circular, seven miles across, and half a mile wide at its entrance. The flat land and gentle slopes of the town were all opposite the harbor mouth. The rest of the harbor was a crown of forested cliffs. If the harbor was a clockface with its entrance at twelve, and the town at six, then at four there was Mount Magdalene, taller than all the surrounding ramparts, two thousand feet high, and the reason why everyone but lay-abouts and prisoners in the thick-walled city jail got to see the sunrise. The sunrise was always late, for Gethsemane lay in the shadow of the mountain till eight in the morning in winter.

The mountain had its own climate, a climate closer to the one that Mary — the dead woman — had known when she was young. She knew the plants that grew on the mountain, their names and uses. Several times every week she and the girl would set out along the road that snaked around the harbor to the foot of the moun-tain. The road was paved with shells, and Mary used her ears to keep to it, and she wouldn't take hold of the girl till she could hear no other footfalls near them. Once she was sure that they were unobserved, Mary would reach into the shadow she could still feel even in the shade of the mountain — a kind of black warmth in the air near the girl — and she'd take hold of the girl's plait, and they'd be able to go along a little faster.

They liked best to go plant gathering on mornings when the mountain was girdled with mist — then Mary could smell the herbs they were after, their scents diffused through the damp air. She would send the girl off the path, saying, for example, that she must look for the low plant with furred silver leaves that looked a little like lambs' ears. She would hear the scoria crunching under the girl's boots and the little *snick* of the sharp knife she carried. Then the girl would return and put a plant into her hands. Mary would hold it to her face, and inhale, and remember. And some-times she might tell some of her story.

She would tell how, in the happiest part of her life, she'd lived in the highlands out of Calvary with her husband's family. She would tell how they'd first met when he'd come down to cut cane. How different he was because his people, the Maeu, had been in the islands since the dawn of time and, in the highlands, still lived in their old ways, cooking their food in the hot springs, growing fruit trees and root vegetables, and building bird traps. Mary's husband had been sent off by his village to earn money cutting cane, to return with timber and roofing iron and pots and pans. "But he also returned with me—a cane cutter. My people—my great-grans—were brought here by blackbirders. My father and brothers were working the plantations for wages, but we hadn't come far up in the world from the days when we were slaves. We were a ragged lot compared to my husband's family. But—you see—on Sundays we all wore white. I caught his eye because he liked me in white." It had been a two-pig wedding, Mary said. Her family had traveled up-country in a big cane dray. They brought liquor for the wedding—rough sugarcane rum. The air was colder in the high country, and there were streams and swamps that *steamed*. And sometimes it was windy and the steam came up off the water in sheets, and the wind tore the sheets into rags, which flew off, growing gradually transparent. "It was as if the air were full of wedding veils."

The girl folded the lambs' ears lug into newspaper and put it in her basket. Mary was swiveling her head back and forth, tilted, as if she hoped to find an angle that let her see out under the cataracts covering her irises. "That steam smelled like this mist. That's what reminded me of that time."

"There are hot springs here, too. They warm the sea in spots all around the shore."

"I know. But today the mist has a little burn in it, a little acid, don't you think?"

It was true. The girl's throat felt sore, as if she'd spent the night shouting above a crowd in a smoky room. She could see that the mist above them was darker, not white, but blued by the sky. She led Mary on and they came out of the cloud near the summit. Two thousand feet wasn't high enough for the greenery to peter out, and the top of the mountain was a grassy cone. It had been grazed, but now it was cleared of livestock for the works of the thermal project. The girl looked down into the crater at the men and their equipment and said that she'd love to take a closer look at what they were up to. "Can I leave you here, Mary?"

Mary said, "No." She didn't want to be left alone. It wasn't that she needed company. Nor was she fearful. Only, she knew that if she was left, it wouldn't be the mist nestling up to her, its scent, and her memories of her distant past, it would be the *other* thing — the church, with its disinfected walls and floors and its pews turned seat to seat to make beds. The sealed windows of the church, the airlessness; the wet cloth in her left hand, her right searching, *feeling*, passing back and forth across her daughter's lips, vainly seeking breath.

Mary said, "I'll come with you, and as we go you can tell me what you see."

The engineers had used a skid — a series of towers, a cable, and a steam-driven winch — to carry everything up the mountain: the girders of the derrick, boxes of bolts, drill shafts, cables, tins of grease, the new acorn-head drill bits. Pack mules were used to carry the explosives. What the airship tethered by four lines to the rim of the crater had been used for the girl didn't know.

Gethsemane's newspapers had reported that the airship was a zeppelin awarded in war reparations to Southland. Like the thermal project, the airship belonged to Southland's venturesome

South Pacific Company. There had been an account in the newspaper of the ship's botched first attempt at landfall in Calvary. Apparently it hit rough air on its descent and drifted east of Ragged Hat. Its skipper ordered the anchor and landing bag cast out on the boulder bank at the head of the harbor. (The landing bag was a sturdy cylindrical canvas sack, with an anchor fastened to the bottom of it. The weight of the bag helped push the anchor down into flat contact with the terrain.) The zeppelin had come in so fast that the crew didn't see that the boulders in the bank were mostly huge hunks of scoria in beds of pumice. Despite the rope webbing that reinforced its sides, when the bag hit and dragged, it split, spilling its makeshift ballast of canned food and hand tools — which were all gathered up by a group of Maeu who were fishing off the boulder bank. The zeppelin was forced to ascend again to cruising altitude and fly far west of the islands and come into Gethsemane several days later on a kinder wind.

Suspended above the crater, the airship was an astonishing thing, but the girl was young and used to novelties, and didn't feel exactly how extraordinary it was till they reached the place on the path that put it between them and the sun. She saw Mary's face when the zeppelin's shadow fell on it. The blind woman balked and recoiled from the shadow—a shadow of something where nothing should be.

The girl said quickly, "It's the airship. It's like a cloud poured into a pan and baked solid. It's wonderful, but I can't think why they need it."

A voice behind them said, "Because the geologists wanted to take a good look at the topography of the harbor. The water is very clear and there's a lot to see. And the mountain provides only a nineteen-hundred-foot elevation."

It was the chief engineer, Sylvia's Mr. McCahon. He had come up behind them on the path. He went on. "Because the harbor is a caldera, and this mountain is what is known as a resurgent dome, and each warrants a close, and a *far*, inspection."

Mary had stiffened, and in contrast, her face had grown slack. She didn't simply mask herself; she slipped away altogether, while still standing there.

"If the harbor is a crater, wouldn't soundings have told your geologists everything they need to know?" The girl looked innocently quizzical.

McCahon was surprised. He seemed to take a closer look at her, and then his eyelids flickered, as if she were too bright to look at. "Possibly," he answered. "And possibly someone in the company simply wanted an airship. Someone unused to having his plausible explanations questioned."

The girl asked whether she might be permitted to go down to the center of the crater. She explained that they were gathering herbs for medicines.

"You're the witch who makes love potions."

"You're not supposed to know that," she said, and smiled. "I make purgatives and toothache powder, too."

"As remedies for love?"

She ignored this. She said that they were after a particular plant. "But I see you're drilling where we used to find it. Might I look to see if there's any left?"

McCahon offered to take them down. But when they got to the place where the track became a scramble, he said, "Here, girlie," and put his hands around her waist to lift her down — then didn't offer any help to Mary. "Surely you don't need your servant to mind you," he said.

"She doesn't mind me; I mind her. Or I supply her with a mind. If I go too far from her, she'll turn into confetti and blow away."

Again McCahon looked at her, assessing, as though he were thinking of buying her. Then he took her hand. "Come on."

The drill wasn't in operation, and as they stepped down the track into the crater, they moved out of the wind and away from every other sound, the noise of the port, the refineries, the ocean. The air in the crater was still and hot. At the bottom the girl spun around to view the interior of the green cone. The rim of the crater framed the sky, and the zeppelin floating in the middle of the blue looked like a keyhole in a perfectly circular lock.

Of the plant she sought she saw that there was a little remaining. She crouched to pick it, and McCahon hunkered down beside her, pulling off a flower and rubbing it between his palms to release the smell. "You say it grows only in the crater?"

She nodded. She didn't open her lips because she suddenly had too much spit in her mouth.

"Is that because it's so sheltered here?"

She swallowed. "No."

She put the plant in her satchel, then pushed the growth aside to bare its roots. She burrowed, then took one of McCahon's hands and pushed his fingers into the loose soil. She watched him thinking. He frowned and delved deeper, forcing her fingers down with his, till the grit was rammed uncomfortably under her fingernails. He said, "The thermal heat is close to the surface." He let her hand go.

"The plant wasn't here till Mary's auntie brought it back from the hot springs in the highlands after Mary's wedding and planted it."

"Who is Mary?"

"My servant."

"The zombie? And how is it that you know her story?"

She didn't answer. She asked him to observe how the foliage was yellowing.

"Meaning?"

"It does that when its roots are too hot."

"And you blame our drilling?"

"No. It was yellowing before you came. It used to be healthy — says Mary."

"Mary says things?"

She didn't respond to that either, and again her silence seemed to make him fall into a temptation to educate her. "The increase in heat is a release of pressure, not a buildup. Our bores will achieve the same thing. We are not poking a stick into a beehive, as some people seem to think. We are tapping a great reserve of energy through this bore and the one over the fumarole on the south slope."

"Are you sure that's how it works?" She sounded dubious.

"There's no reason to suppose a volcano isn't like a boiler," he said.

On their way down the mountain, Mary lifted the heavy satchel from the girl's shoulder and put it over her own. She took hold of the girl's plait. They were going along like that when they caught up with Gethsemane's other mismatched couple: the wiry, black able seaman, and his young fair-haired companion.

"Ma'am," said the man respectfully to Mary. She realized that it was she he was speaking to when she felt him lift the satchel from her shoulder. "Let me carry this for you," he said. And then he slipped his arm under hers. "The path is wider here, and if you lean on me, it will give your young friend a rest from her duties."

No one but the witch ever spoke to Mary. But this man not only spoke to her; he went on to make friendly conversation. He referred to both the girl and his companion as their "young friends."

The boy and girl, left behind together, were silent at first, then began a desultory exchange of information. He told her that he was a steward on the *John Bartholomew*, which meant he served at the captain's table. "And the captain's pleasure—I spend all the livelong day polishing the white brass."

She told him that she had a little place in an alley off Market Square. "I sell charms," she said. "I'm a witch." She sounded self-conscious—her invention and sense of drama seemed to have deserted her.

"Is that so?" said the boy politely.

Mary, overhearing this, found herself smiling. It was as if someone had removed the weights hanging on her jaw.

The man and boy saw them all the way to their crib, then went off about their own business.

The sun had been shining in the courtyard, and the cages gave off a ghostly chicken-shit smell. Mary asked the girl whether she'd discovered what kind of kin they were.

"You mean those two?" The girl was surprised.

"Yes. They are kin."

"They can't be," said the girl. "The old man is black."

"Your eyes are deceiving you," Mary said. Then she continued, "I don't suppose you learned their names?"

"No. I didn't give them mine."

But of course she hadn't—not even Mary knew the girl's name.

The following Sunday, the girl said they should go to the morning service. She wanted to see how Sylvia was getting on with Mr. McCahon. "They'll both be there. Everyone will. It's Founders' Day."

"Do you expect your potion to have worked?" Mary mocked. The girl was falling for her own fictions.

"I expect Sylvia's bared breasts to have produced some result."

They washed at the pump and put on their cleanest clothes. They went out into the street, one following the sight of the cathedral's towers, the other the sound of its bells. On the steps of the cathedral, Mary sensed the people parting around them, and a babble, as of troubled waters. She understood that she'd forgotten her place and all her own promises. She seized the girl's skirt and stopped her in her tracks.

"What?" The girl was in a hurry. Then she said, "How silly of me. Of course you can't go into a church!"

Mary released her.

"Wait for me. Look, here's some shade." The girl hustled Mary into a corner and placed her hand against a stone pillar. Then she was gone.

After a moment, "Ma'am?" a voice said. A warm, worn hand took hold of hers. "Are you waiting to go in? You can sit up the back with me, if you'd like."

Mary listened. She made sure there was no one else near them. "I can't be seen in church," she confided. "I'm dead, you see."

"Ma'am?"

"You must have heard the talk about us?"

"I don't hear anything unless it's said in front of me or my young friend deigns to tell me."

"And he doesn't?"

"He's his own man." Mary heard the old man rummaging in his clothes, and she waited with a kind of cool disenchantment. He took her hand again and placed something in it. "That's a plug of chaw."

Mary put the chewing tobacco into her mouth. Her mouth grew wet and her head hummed. They stood side by side, chewing companionably.

"You're missing the service," Mary said.

"God is here, too."

Mary thought, *God isn't anywhere.*

When diphtheria had come to Mary's village, the houses closed against one another. Mary's door was shut even to the friend who had helped her with her children when her cataracts began to rob her of her sight.

The disease was well known to all cane cutters, and Mary had had it as a child. Many people in the village had. There were a number of deaths. But in Mary's house, her Maeu husband and half-Maeu children all died. They went one by one, the baby first, and quietly, then Mary's husband, who struggled fearfully and ended draped over a windowsill trying to draw breath, as if his only trouble were the stuffy room. Mary carried her six-year-old and then her ten-year-old to the church, where they lay together along two pews pressed seat to seat. They lay gasping like beached fish, then died only an hour apart, and for a long time after that, Mary sat beside them, passing her hand back and forth across their lips, hopelessly feeling for breath. Finally she lay down between them. Her world had been turned upside down, and someone had shaken it till the last things had fallen out.

Mary's friends found her and led her back to her house. They helped her bury her family. After that they'd come with food, and to sit with her, or to water and hoe her vegetable patch. Some weeks went by, and it came to Mary that there was still something she *didn't* want, a positive something. She didn't want her friends to feel that they'd failed her. So, one night, she packed a little bit of food and put on her stoutest shoes. When the village was asleep, she set out from her home. She walked for days, through cane fields and salt marshes. She went along the road north. When people passed, she turned her head away from them so that they wouldn't see that she was blind. She stepped into the dry litter at the roadside whenever a cart, or coach, or rider went by. The road went along in lazy curves, and was easy for her to follow. And Mary wasn't going anywhere, only away, far enough away that she could sit down and die where her death wouldn't trouble her friends.

On the fourth evening of her walk, Mary was at a place where the road ran east to west and the sun shone right along it. There was no shade, and the wind had dropped, and the cane had stopped its usual percussive rustling, and the air over the road began to thicken into a syrup full of flies. Mary stopped at the roadside and stood still, her body and hands and feet burning, and her head in the faintly cool halo of her hat. As she stood there, she heard horses coming toward her. She shuffled closer to the wall of cane. She knew she must look distressed. She couldn't help it — the heat had peeled her of her skin of deathly indifference and was trying to prove that she was alive under it. Mary didn't want to draw any notice, or sympathy, so she dissembled. She took off her hat, closed her cataract-covered eyes, raised her face to the sun, and fanned her face with her hat. She stood as relaxed and flat-footed as any old cane cutter woman. Between her eyelids the world was pure white, as it always was when her eyes were aimed at the sky. And then a shadow fell across her face, a shadow from where there should be nothing that could cast a shadow. Mary knew that whatever it was, it was too high.

It was the girl. She had been hot and had stood up on her saddle to try to catch any breeze coming over the top of the cane field. Her horse was ambling along, two other horses tethered to it.

The girl stopped to ask whether the cane cutter woman wanted a ride. "I don't have a saddle," she said. Then: "Are you blind? Did I frighten you?" Then: "You can't see them, but I have two more horses. They're my father's. I've stolen them. I'm going to sell them in Gethsemane and use the proceeds to establish a new life for myself."

And, at that, Mary decided to go along with the girl to see what she did, how she managed. Mary postponed her death; after all, it wasn't as if death were going anywhere.

Mary and the old man were still standing in the shade of the church portico, turning their tobacco over with their tongues, when the girl arrived. She was in a rush, and in tears.

"Honey!" The old man was concerned.

Mary didn't say anything. She was shocked. The witch never wept. Mary heard the girl say, "Please" — choking — "will you see Mary home for me? I'd be very grateful."

"Of course," the old man said. Mary heard the girl's running steps recede from them.

They waited for the service to end, and the man's "young friend" to appear, before setting out for the alley off Market Square. The man questioned the boy. "Did you see anything? Did someone speak unkindly to the girl?"

"No," the boy said. "She ran out during the service. Everyone else was attending to the guy in the pulpit."

They went along quietly, puzzling it out. And then Mary asked, in a whisper, "What was the text of the sermon?"

"It's Founders' Day, so it was the Agony in the Garden. You know, *What? Could ye not watch with me one hour?*"

Mary woke up in the middle of the night because all the cages in the courtyard were rattling, as though filled with a bunch of agitated, voiceless poultry ghosts.

The girl cried out, then came fully awake and said into the diminishing rustle of dry timber or of the air, "What was that?"

→ 2 ←

Two days after Founders' Day, the mismatched couples went up Mount Magdalene together. The boy was carrying the girl's basket, and the man was guiding the woman. The man and woman were in conversation; the boy and girl were silent.

The boy kicked a stone ahead of him, then looked unhappily after it when he finally knocked it off the path and down the slope.

The girl asked him how he got his black eye.

He fingered the cut on his eyebrow. "I got into a fight, and the sheriff decided to take exception to me and not to the other fellow. He was in a bad mood because he was having trouble with his horses — they came out of the fort all shivering and crazy."

"So it was the sheriff who gave you that?"

"Yes. And that's why I'm up here, taking the air with you." He sneered. "I'm supposed to stay out of town, and trouble. The sheriff has been drinking with my captain, who has said something indiscreet, and now the sheriff has decided he doesn't like the cut of my jib. And we have to give up our evenings ashore."

"Then it's true?" she said.

"What?" He looked at her narrowly.

She pointed at the old man. "If you're confined, so is he, because he's paid to keep an eye on you."

The boy scowled, and his jaw clenched, and he strode out and overtook the others. He got so far ahead on the path that looped up the mountain that, after a few minutes, he was nearly out of sight. They could still see him, his figure dark against the afternoon sky, his shoulders hunched and his fists thrust into the pockets of his jacket.

There came a massive thump under their feet, and the sky before the boy filled with streaks of orange. The fiery bouquet spread, turned into a fountain of fire, and dropped burning matter onto the slope below the path. There was a roar, so deep it was almost inaudible. Its tone rose and blended with a bass hiss, and then the fountain was quenched and swallowed in a cloud of steam.

The boy threw his arms over his head and tottered back along the path. Under their feet the earth seemed to sizzle, grit jiggling, like seeds popping in a hot pan. The ground was quivering.

The girl saw, far below, an articulated mass of metal slithering down the slope — a derrick, disjointed, drill shaft following, still attached to the derrick by a steel cable. She thought she could see a body on the slope.

She had once been out on the sea when a whale came up under her boat. The long sleek back had slipped out of the waves, water pouring aside from its bulk. It came up in a rolling curve, and its bifurcated blowhole opened and it took a breath, and the sound of air sucked into those vast lungs was what the girl could hear now as steam billowed from the flank of the mountain.

Mary put her mouth close to the girl's ear and yelled, "I think I can hear people crying out."

The girl listened, then she could hear it, too. She ran along the path, elbowed the boy aside, and made her way to where he had been standing. Her hair was instantly damp, and her face felt sweaty, then scalded. The steam was much farther off than she'd imagined. There was a long, creeping slick of gray mud moving down the mountain from the point where it emerged. There were smoking lumps of rock scattered below the geyser. The girl saw more bodies on the slope, and one man was staggering her way, his face and hands red and covered in blooming yellow blisters. He fell over before he reached her, tried to rise, then rolled faceup and lay still. The girl crept forward till she could see that his tongue was fat and white and that he had blood in his mouth.

She heard a faint call: "Girlie!" She cast about—but it was the old able seaman, who had joined her, who spotted McCahon.

The engineer was lying a short distance from the steaming mud river. They scrambled down to him, and without any consultation, each grabbed an arm and dragged him away from the hot ooze and around the slight shelter of a hump in the cone. The boy joined them. They gathered around McCahon, all cringing as the ruptured fumarole spat out a few more rocks, and the sound of the geyser became deeper and softer—not quieter, only somehow more steamy.

McCahon's leg was smashed, his shinbone in his blood-soaked pants leg in several pieces, like beads on a string. His palms and one side of his face were deeply grazed. But he still was conscious, even after their rough handling. "What about the others?" he said.

The old man shook his head. Then he sprang up and went back to Mary, who was gingerly trying to make her way down to them. He took her hands and led her like a beau handing his belle out onto the dance floor. He showed her where to sit and placed her hands on McCahon. She gently felt the engineer's leg.

"We'll need a stretcher," the old man said, then added, to the engineer, "I hope that, for you, this is just like an oil strike." He meant that it was a dangerous business and was asking whether this was normal.

McCahon didn't seem to hear him. He reached past Mary and took hold of the girl's hanging plait. He pulled her closer, only to gaze into her eyes.

Mary said to the girl, "You have some devil's claw in your bag. He could chew on that."

The girl fumbled her small satchel around in front of her. It was hard for her to see what she was doing with her head to one side and hair pulled tight. She found her knife and slipped it into her apron pocket. She broke eye contact with McCahon to seek out the root. She pulled off a piece and folded it into his mouth. He let go of her hair.

The old man said, "You two youngsters should run for help. Town is a distance off—but there are men in the crater and the airship. You should try both directions, to be sure."

"Yes," said Mary.

"I'll go down," the boy said. "It's farther." He jumped up and started away from them. The old man shouted his name—which was James. The boy hesitated, then gave a hasty wave and headed off.

McCahon took hold of the girl's upper arms, the blood from his grazes seeping sticky through her sleeves. She caught his gaze again. He had hazel eyes. "I can't go," she said to Mary and the old man.

"I'm afraid it has to be you, dear," the old man said. "It's at most only a ten-minute uphill scramble. And once you're there, you can leave the problem to the men. They'll know what to do."

"Girlie," said McCahon.

"I *can't* go," the girl said. "I mustn't." She began to cry.

"You must — and be quick!" Mary said.

"It's wrong!" the girl wailed. "It's wrong to leave him."

"*We're* not leaving him. It's you who has to run for help. Mary can't see, and I'm not as spry as I once was." The old man was being patient, but under it, he was exasperated.

The girl didn't hear this. She continued to moan that she couldn't go.

Mary suddenly punched her in the chest, shoved her so hard that she fell over and her arms were torn from McCahon's grip. She lay for a moment, stunned, then staggered up and ran off.

They watched her sprint down the path till she found a good place to climb and began to clamber up toward the summit.

It took more than ten minutes, though she went as straight and as fast as she could. She didn't even pause to look up. And as she got farther from it, the sound of the geyser grew less. But by then she could hear other sounds. And *feel* them. She felt like she was climbing a long, green baize-covered door, and some terrible thing was on the other side of it, knocking, pounding, straining the latch and the hinges.

As she reached the summit, something scythed past her, thrumming. It was one of the mooring lines of the zeppelin. The airship was still secure on three anchors, but it was circling the crater lip, as though a giant invisible hand had it by the end of those ropes and was lazily twirling it. The ground was trembling. Small stones shaken from the lip of the crater crumbled in a continuous flow into the thick grass inside. That grass was bristling like hair on a chilled arm.

The men around the huts and derrick were stooped and staggering and clutching their mouths. The girl hesitated at the sight of this inexplicable clumsy dancing, then set off down one of the goat tracks into the crater. She went carefully, watching her feet. She didn't look up again till the sole shouting voice below her reached a certain mad pitch.

There had been one man on the platform at the top of the derrick. As she'd started down the slope, she had registered that he was descending the ladder to see what was up with his fellow workers. She looked again when he began to shriek, "God!" He was retreating back up the ladder, howling with terror. The men were lying on the ground now, flailing open-armed as if trying to gather in the air. The retreating man reached the platform. He looked around him, desperate. He was shouting, "Oh, please, God, help me!"

The air in the crater had changed. It felt strangely feathery on the girl's feet and legs. She began to step backward up the hill. Below her the screaming man collapsed onto his knees and began to vomit. The girl saw that the air between him and her was roiling like the water in a tidal stream, where saltwater and fresh mingle but don't melt together.

The girl turned and fled up the crater wall. There came a different sort of thud in the thumps and bangs all around her.

A *twang*. From the corner of her eye, she saw a black coil of rope drop, and then the zeppelin swung over her, tilted at a crazy angle and attached by only two lines. She saw a rope ladder dangling from its control cabin, only partly unfurled. She saw white frightened faces at the open hatchway.

She charged upward, hauling herself forward on hunks of the soft grass.

Another mooring line was cut and dropped. The girl reached into her apron pocket and grabbed her knife. She yelled wordlessly at the airship, waved her knife, and rushed to the last anchor line. She didn't stop to spare a glance at the men above her, who were clambering quickly to that same last line with their own knives. She reached the anchor, grasped the taut rope, and slashed at it. She sawed furiously with one hand, holding hard with the other. The rope parted, her feet left the ground, and the jerk flung her arm down so abruptly that she stabbed herself in the leg. But she didn't let go of the rope. She dropped her knife, fastened both hands to the rope, and was swept up, spinning, and plowing through the air like a rudder through water. The soft, heavy, gaseous stuff had filled the crater and overflowed, following the airship, rolling behind it like a wave and pushing it down again, toward the slope of the mountain.

The girl heard frenzied activity above her, and things began to fall past her — a big leather bag, a telescope, books, a chair —

The rope ladder was fully extended now, and the zeppelin was so low that the ladder was dragging along the slope. It combed through the geyser at the fumaroles, caught on something for just a moment, then came away again, swinging heavily. The girl saw two figures dangling from the ladder, one apparently struggling with the other. Then the airship hitched higher, and one figure fell, plunged through the plume of steam, and disappeared.

Once the girl had left them, the old man had taken Mary's hands and laid them with his own, clasped, on McCahon's chest. They bent over McCahon, very intent, on him as well as each other. They seemed so calm. McCahon was in pain, but the pain was remote. He didn't have to be patient, because he wasn't hoping to be rescued. He only wished that the girl had stayed. He wanted to see her. To see her and what would happen. He hoped he'd still be conscious when the fireworks really got under way. And he hoped that before she was killed, girlie got to see something truly beautiful.

The old people were talking, and after a moment he began to attend.

Mary told her story. She explained how she had come to be on the road where she and the girl had met, and how she had followed the girl to Gethsemane just to see what she did. "But," Mary said, "I didn't want to survive. I only wanted a moment free of the pain. So I made a promise to it: I won't be long—I said—I won't stay in a room I can't pay for."

The old man pressed his palm against her cheek. He touched her very tenderly.

She said, "I only wanted one moment free, to climb to a high place and look back on my whole life, not just the final low place it had taken me to."

McCahon slipped away for a moment and woke when the earth tossed him, as if it meant to turn him like a pancake on a skillet. Mary was asking the old man questions. "He's your kin, isn't he, the boy?"

"Yes, my grandson, though he goes by another name. It's

understandable. He wants what he can have. And I don't feel disowned." He sounded like someone making an effort to make his peace.

A volley of stones went by, vicious and hissing, over their heads.

"God save them," Mary said — of everyone.

"Tell me about your girl."

"She's a runaway. She stole her father's horses and sold them in Gethsemane, and that's all I know. I don't even know her name."

"That's not *all* you know, though, is it?" the old man said.

Mary thought for a moment. "No. You're right. We know this, too: *What? Could ye not watch with me one hour?*"

The boy was able to reach the coastal road, where he borrowed a very nervous horse. He rode hard for town and help. He rode right into the sheriff and some deputies. The sheriff called the boy a panic monger — and a number of other things — and told his deputies to carry him off to jail.

Thirty minutes later, the mountain exploded. A great white cloud swelled up into the sky, then its soft flesh of steam burned away to show its black, ashy bones. The cloud flashed with fire and continued to grow and throw off boulder bombs and thick bolts of lightning. The ships in the harbor leaned over till their spars touched the water. Then they were torn from their moorings and overturned. The cloud toppled slowly and inclined toward the town. A white half circle raced off across the sea toward the horizon — faster than anything in nature.

The people in the airship watched the mountain fall in on itself and the sea turn into a mountain.

The zeppelin was blown away from Gethsemane on a blast of hot wind, but when the cloud collapsed, it was caught at the edge of the ash fall. The survivors waited in numb dread as ash accumulated on the airship's canopy. But the top of the canopy was thickly rubberized, strengthened for flights in European snow. The ash scoured the rubber but didn't puncture the canopy. And the weight of accumulated ash finally brought the ship down in the ocean seventy miles from Gethsemane.

Weeks later, in his hospital bed in Westport, Southland, McCahon told reporters that he owed his life to an able seaman from the *John Bartholomew*. The quick-thinking, strong old man had caught the ladder as it flashed by, fidgeting over the turf. "He grabbed the ladder in one hand, and me with the other, and told me to hold on. We were, by turns, dragged along the ground or in the air. He took off his belt and fastened me to the ladder, and then he let go."

When people heard that a girl had survived, carried off on one of the airship's mooring lines and hauled up by its crew, there were many who had hopes. Even Alice had hopes of her bold friend, Sylvia. But only one man was lucky. It turned out that the girl was his daughter, Amy.

The lucky father told people that he'd known his daughter was in Gethsemane. She had run away a year before. She had stolen his horses and sold them. He'd traced the horses, but hadn't been able to find his daughter. He didn't like to speak ill of the dead, but he had to say that Gethsemane's sheriff wasn't a very helpful man.

Why had she run away? Her mother was dying of a terrible illness. A cancer of the bones of her face. No one had expected the girl to keep watch by her mother's sickbed, but still . . .

What's that? Do I think it was a punishment? Well, sir, do you suppose God would destroy a city in order to punish one weak girl?

The doctor left town, and lived. Alice was sent away, and lived. The nine men and one girl on the airship lived—and witnessed everything. *"The light which puts out our eyes is darkness to us,"* said the skipper of the airship. But McCahon said it wasn't like that. Years later he wrote a memoir of the eruption that destroyed the beautiful town, burned and buried all its houses and gardens, and sent a giant killing wave rolling northward, swamping islands and drowning villages. He wrote, with stark honesty, that he'd willingly dig a thousand graves and fill them himself just to see something so beautiful again.

There was one other survivor.

$$\rightarrow \ 3 \ \leftarrow$$

The manager of the carnival took Amy's hand as she climbed the steps to the low door. "There you are, ma'am," he said, and went away.

The colored lights of the midway failed to illuminate the interior of the caravan. Amy left its door open. There were louvers on one window. The bed was striped with light. She said, "May I sit?"

A hand came through the grid of shadow and pointed with blunt, fused fingers at a stool tucked under a bench. She drew it out and set it down by the head of the bed. "Does the light hurt your eyes?"

There was no answer.

"The darkness must be a respite from being looked at."

The figure in the bed moved his head on the pillow and faced her. His flesh was like rough plasterwork, the scars were like trowel marks, and pigmented purple, and beige, and gray-white. His right eye-lid had fused to his brow bone, and the hairs of that eyebrow showed in places like some dry herb not fully mixed into a smooth batter.

She regarded him calmly. "The bill of fare doesn't have your picture, only your story. It says the jail had thick walls and its windows were high and small and faced away from Mount Magdalene. It relates how that jail, its walls packed in hot ash and pumice, turned into an oven. And how, when you were found, the newspapers dubbed you the Baked Man. It says that the carnival has no option to call you anything different, since you never told anyone who you were."

His mouth was like a turtle's beak, but he could make himself understood. He said, "I know you."

Amy said, "I hadn't ever thought to speak to the Baked Man, because I never realized it was you, James. Tonight I came along to the carnival with my children, and a barker on the midway was shouting out your story." She unfolded a bill of fare and smoothed it on her skirt. She read: "'The Baked Man is the only person to live through the cataclysmic eruption of Mount Magdalene, which destroyed the South Pacific town of Gethsemane. He was discovered in the town jail and it is possible he has kept his identity secret because his ordeal and disfigurement were not enough to make him stop fearing the rope. For, with no record of arrest, or witnessing officers of the law, who is to say that this pitiful figure's silence isn't evidence of the magnitude of his crime? For why else, ladies and gentlemen, would this man have remained silent for so many years?'"

Amy stopped reading and returned her gaze to the eyes in the botched face. "It says the Baked Man wouldn't even admit to his race, wouldn't say whether he was black or white. And that's when I realized it was you. You see, your grandfather told Mary your story. And McCahon was there. And, as soon as he was able, McCahon came to tell me how Mary had died, and that she hadn't died alone."

The figure in the bars of light gathered himself to speak, and Amy leaned close to hear him.

He said, "I wanted the life a pale skin could give me. I wanted to be something I wasn't, and because of that I accepted the attentions of anyone who would go along with my fiction. I was trying to steal a better place in the world. And I didn't have the patience to try to make my purchase with my good character. My grandfather was a good, civil man, and I let everybody think he was only my shipmate. I was ashamed of him. I *denied* him. And now I'm dead." The ruined eyes grew wet.

Amy tried to take his hand, but he wouldn't be comforted. After a time he managed to choke out, "If he had lived and found me, I'd have shouted out to the world, *This is my grandfather!*"

He wept for a time, and she didn't offer to comfort him again, only waited. When his sobbing had subsided, she said, "Mary used to say that she was dead, too, and she was, except in the way it mattered most. And in that way she's still not dead. And neither is your grandfather. My husband always says, 'That man saved my life.'"

"Is it a good life?"

Amy laughed. "He walks with a limp. He's still in the same line of work. He built the thermal power station in Spring Valley. He's still poking at beehives."

The man on the bed was quiet for a long time. Finally he said softly, wistfully, "The window was facing the wrong way," then, "I wish I'd seen it."

The Summer People

{ KELLY LINK }

Fran's daddy woke her up wielding a plant mister. "Fran," he said, spritzing her. "Fran, honey. Wake up for just a minute."

Fran had the flu, except it was more like the flu had Fran. In consequence of this, she'd laid out of school for three days in a row. The previous night she'd taken four NyQuil and fallen asleep on the couch, waiting for her daddy to come home, while a man on the TV pitched throwing knives. Her head felt stuffed with boiled wool and snot. Her face was wet with watered-down plant food. "Hold up," she croaked, and began to cough so hard she had to hold her sides. She sat up.

Her daddy was a dark shape in a room full of dark shapes. The bulk of him augured trouble. The sun weren't up the mountain yet, but there was a light on in the kitchen. There was a suitcase, too, beside the door, and on the table a plate with a mess of eggs. Fran reckoned she was starving.

Her daddy went on. "I'll be gone some time. A week or three. Not more. You'll take care of the summer people while I'm gone. The Robertses come up next weekend. You'll need to get their groceries tomorrow or next day. Make sure you check the expiration date on the milk when you buy it, and put fresh sheets on all of the beds. I've left the house schedule on the frigerator, and there should be enough gas in the car to make the rounds."

"Wait," Fran said. Every word hurt. "Where you going?"

He sat beside her, then pulled something out from under him, one of Fran's old toys, the monkey egg. "Now, you know I don't like these. I wish you'd put 'em away."

"There's lots of stuff I don't like," Fran said. "Where are you going?"

"Prayer meeting in Miami. Found out about it on the Internet," her daddy said. He shifted on the couch and put a hand against her forehead, so cool and soothing that she closed her eyes. "You don't feel near so hot. Joanie's giving me a ride down. You know I need to get right with God." Joanie was his sometime girlfriend.

"I know you need to stay here and look after me," Fran said. "You're my daddy."

"Now, how can I look after you if I'm not right?" he said. "You don't know the things I've done."

Fran didn't know, but she could guess. "You went out last night," she said. "You were drinking."

Her daddy spread out his hands. "I'm not talking about last night," he said. "I'm talking about a lifetime."

"That is —" Fran said, and then began to cough again. She coughed so long and so hard that she saw bright stars. Even so, despite the hurt in her ribs, and despite the truth that every time she managed to suck in a good pocket of air she coughed it all right back out again, the NyQuil made it all seem so peaceful her daddy might as well have been saying a poem. Her eyelids were closing again. Later, when she woke up, maybe he would make her breakfast.

"I left two hundred-dollar bills by the stove top," he said. "Which leaves me but fifty for gas money and prayer offerings. Never mind — the Lord will provide. Tell Andy to let you put groceries and such on the tab. Any come around, you tell 'em I'm gone on ahead. Any man tells you he knows the hour or the day, Fran, that man's a liar or a fool. All a man can do is be ready."

He patted her on the shoulder and tucked the counterpane up around her ears. When she woke up again, it was late afternoon and her daddy was long gone. Her temperature was 102.3°. All across her cheeks the plant mister had left a red raised rash.

On Friday, Fran went to school because she wasn't sure what else to do. Her temperature was down a touch, but she fell asleep in the shower and only woke up when the hot water ran out. Breakfast was spoons of peanut butter out of the jar and dry cereal. She couldn't remember the last time she'd eaten. Her cough scared off the crows when she went down to the county road to catch the school bus.

She dozed through three classes, including calculus, before having such a fit of coughing that Mr. Rumer sent her off to see the nurse.

"What I don't understand, Fran, is why you're here today," Mr. Rumer said. Which wasn't fair at all. She came to school whenever there wasn't something else she had to do, and she always made sure to turn in the makeup work.

The nurse, Fran knew, was liable to call her daddy and send her home. This would have presented a problem, but on the way to the nurse's station, Fran came upon Ophelia Merck at her locker.

Ophelia Merck had her own car, a Lexus. She and her family were summer people, except that now they lived in their house up at Horse Cove on the lake all year round. Years ago, Fran and Ophelia had spent a summer of afternoons playing with Ophelia's Barbies while Fran's father smoked out a wasps' nest, repainted cedar siding, tore down an old fence. They hadn't really spoken since then, though once or twice after the summer, Fran's father brought home paper bags full of Ophelia's hand-me-downs, some of them still with the price tags.

Fran eventually went through a growth spurt, which put a stop to that; Ophelia was still hardly a speck of a girl. And as far as Fran could figure, Ophelia was still the same in most other ways: pretty, shy, spoiled, and easy to boss around. The rumor was her family'd moved full-time from Lynchburg after a teacher caught Ophelia kissing another girl in the bathroom at a school dance. It was either that or Mr. Merck being up for malpractice, which was the other story — take your pick.

"Ophelia Merck," Fran said. "I need you to tell Nurse Tannent you're gone to give me a ride home right now."

Ophelia opened her mouth and closed it. She nodded.

Fran's temperature was back up again, at 102°. Tannent even wrote Ophelia a note to go off campus.

"I don't know where you live," Ophelia said. They were in the parking lot, Ophelia searching for her keys. Fran had a pocketful of toilet tissue for her nose, and a Coke.

"Take the county road," Fran said, "one twenty-nine." Ophelia nodded. "It's up a ways on Wild Ridge, past the hunting camps." Fran lay back against the headrest and closed her eyes. "Oh, hell. I forgot. Can you take me by the convenience first? I have to get the Robertses' house put right."

"I guess I can do that," Ophelia said.

"I wish I didn't have to ask," Fran said. She turned her head to look out the window.

At the convenience she picked up milk, eggs, whole-wheat sandwich bread, and cold cuts for the Robertses, Tylenol and more NyQuil for herself, as well as a can of frozen orange juice, microwave burritos, and Pop-tarts. "On the tab," she told Andy.

"Your pappy was creatin' and aggravatin' the other night," Andy said. He licked a finger, then flipped pages on the dirty yellow legal pad, thick with other people's debts. He found the page he wanted and stapled Fran's receipt onto it. "Way he carries on, may be best he doesn't come in here no more. Maybe you'll tell him I said so."

"I'll tell him when I see him," Fran said. "Him and Joanie went down to Florida yesterday morning. He said he needs to get right with God."

"God ain't who your pappy needs to get on the good side of," Andy said.

Fran coughed and bent over. Then she straightened right back up. "What's he done?" she said.

"Wish I could say it was nothing that can't be fixed with the application of some greaze and good manners," Andy said. "But we'll just have to see. Ryan's all riled up."

Half the time her daddy got to drinking, Andy and Andy's cousin Ryan were involved, never mind it was a dry county. Ryan kept the liquor out in the parking lot in his van for everwho wanted it and knew to ask. The good stuff came from over the county line, in Andrews. The best stuff, though, was the liquor Fran's daddy brought down and traded Andy and Ryan for every once in a while.

Everyone said Fran's daddy's brew was too good to be strictly natural. Which was true. When he wasn't getting right with God, Fran's daddy got up to all kinds of trouble. Fran's best guess was that in this particular situation he'd promised to supply something that God was not now going to let him deliver. But it weren't Fran's problem anyhow. Andy weren't ever a problem, and it was no hard thing staying out of Ryan's way, long as you did your shopping at the convenience in the daylight hours. "I'll tell him you said so."

Ophelia was looking over the list of ingredients on a candy wrapper, but Fran could tell she was interested. When they got back into the car, she said, "Just cause you're doing me a favor don't mean you need to know my business."

"OK," Ophelia said.

"OK," Fran said. "Good. Now, maybe you can take me by the Roberts place. It's over on—"

"I know where the Robertses' house is," Ophelia said. "My mom played bridge over there all last summer."

The Robertses hid their spare key under a fake rock, just like everybody else. Ophelia stood at the door like she was waiting to be invited in. "Well, come on," Fran said.

There wasn't much to be said about the Robertses' house. There was an abundance of plaid, and everywhere Toby mugs and statuettes of dogs pointing, setting, or trotting along with limp birds in their gentle mouths.

Except that up in the master bedroom, Fran waited for Ophelia to notice the painting. "Is that Mr. Roberts?" Ophelia said. She proceeded to turn an interesting shade of red.

"I guess," Fran said. "Although he's poochier around the middle nowadays. Mrs. Roberts painted it. All the paintings downstairs of bowls of fruit and trees in autumn are hers. She has a studio down the hill. It's got a refrigerator in it. Nothing in it but bottles of white wine and Betty Crocker vanilla cake icing."

"I don't think I could go to sleep with that hanging over my head," Ophelia said. Mr. Roberts grinned down at them, life-size and not embarrassed in the least.

"Maybe he sleeps in the altogether, too," Fran said. But then she began to cough so hard that she had to sit right down on the bed. A bubble of snot came right out of her nose and plopped on the carpet.

Fran made up the other rooms and did a quick vacuum downstairs while Ophelia put out fresh towels in the master bathroom and caught the spider that had made a home in the wastebasket. She carried it outside. Fran didn't quite have the breath to make fun of her for this. They went from room to room, making sure that there were working bulbs in the light fixtures and that the cable wasn't out. Every once in a while, one of Mrs. Roberts's fruit bowl paintings would set Ophelia off, giggling. She sang under her breath while they worked. They were both in choir, and Fran found herself evaluating Ophelia's voice. A soprano, warm and light at the same time, where Fran was an alto and somewhat froggy, even when she didn't have the flu.

"Stop it," she said out loud, and Ophelia turned and looked at her. "Not you," Fran said. She ran the tap water in the kitchen sink until it was clear. She coughed for a long time and spat into the drain. It was almost four o'clock. "We're done here."

"How do you feel?" Ophelia said.

"Like I been kicked all over," Fran said. She blew her nose into the sink, then washed her hands.

"I'll take you home," Ophelia said. "Is anyone there? In case you start feeling worse?"

Fran didn't bother answering, but somewhere between the school lockers and the Robertses' master bedroom, Ophelia seemed to have decided that the ice was broken. She talked about a TV show, about the party neither of them would go to on Saturday night. They weren't the kind of girls who got invited to parties, or at least Fran wasn't. She began to suspect that Ophelia had had friends once, down in Lynchburg, before she'd got caught in the bathroom with her tongue in some other girl's mouth. She had the habit of easy conversation. She complained about the calculus homework and talked about a sweater she was knitting. She mentioned a girl rock band that she thought Fran might like, even offered to burn her a CD. Several times she exclaimed as they drove up the county road.

"I never get used to it, to living up here year round," Ophelia said. "I mean, we haven't even been here a whole year, but . . . it's just so beautiful. It's like another world, you know?"

"Not really," Fran said. "Never been anywhere else."

"Oh," Ophelia said, not quite deflated by this retort. "Well, take it from me. It's freaking gorgeous here. Everything is so pretty, it makes your eyes ache. I love the morning, the way everything is all misty, like a movie with a unicorn in it. And the trees! And every time you go around a corner, there's another damn waterfall. Or a little pasture and it's all full of flowers. All the *hollers.*" Fran could hear the invisible brackets around the word. "It's like you don't know what you'll see, what's there, until suddenly you're in them. Are you applying to college anywhere next year? Everybody talks about Appalachian State, party school, yay, or else they're joining the army. But I was thinking about vet school. I don't think I can take another English class. Large animals. No little dogs or guinea pigs. Maybe I'll go out to California."

Fran said, "I'm not the kind of people who go to college."

"Oh," Ophelia said. "I know you skip class and stuff, but you're a lot smarter than me, you know? I mean, you read books. And there was that time you corrected Ms. Shumacher in physics. So I just thought..."

"Turn here," Fran said. "Careful. It's not paved."

The dirt road wound up through beds of laurel into the little meadow with the nameless creek. Fran could feel Ophelia breathe in, probably trying her hardest not to say something about how beautiful it was. And it was beautiful, Fran knew. You could hardly see the house itself, hidden like a bride behind a veil of climbing vines: virgin's bower and Japanese honeysuckle, masses of William Baffin and Cherokee roses overgrowing the porch and running up over the sagging roof. Bumblebees, their legs armored in gold, threaded through the meadow grass, almost too weighed down with pollen to fly.

"Needs a new roof," Fran said. "My great-granddaddy ordered it out of the Sears catalog. Men brought it up the side of the mountain in pieces, and all the Cherokee who hadn't yet gone away came and watched." She was amazed at herself: next thing she'd be asking Ophelia to come sleep over and trade secrets.

She opened the car door and heaved herself up, plucked up the poke of groceries. Before she could turn and say thank you for the ride, Ophelia was standing in the yard. "I thought . . ." Ophelia said uncertainly. "Well, I thought maybe I could use your bathroom?"

"It's an outhouse," Fran said, deadpan. Then she relented. "Come on in, then. It's a regular bathroom. Just not very clean."

Ophelia didn't say anything when they came into the kitchen. Fran watched her take it in: the heaped dishes in the sink, the pillow and raggedy quilt on the sagging couch. The piles of dirty laundry beside the efficiency washer in the kitchen. The places where hairy tendrils of vine had found a way inside around the windows. "I guess you might be thinking it's funny," she said. "My dad and I make money doing other people's houses, but we don't take no real care of our own."

"I was thinking that somebody ought to be taking care of you," Ophelia said. "At least while you're sick."

Fran gave a little shrug. "I do fine on my own," she said. "The washroom's down the hall."

She took two NyQuil while Ophelia was gone, and washed them down with the last swallow or two of ginger ale out of the refrigerator. Flat, but still cool. Then she lay down on the couch and pulled the counterpane up around her face. She huddled into the lumpy cushions. Her legs ached; her face felt as hot as fire. Her feet were ice-cold.

A minute later Ophelia sat down on the couch beside her.

"Ophelia?" Fran said. "I'm grateful for the ride home and for the help at the Robertses, but I don't go for the girls. So don't lez out."

Ophelia said, "I brought you a glass of water. You need to stay hydrated."

"Mmm," Fran said.

"You know, your dad told me once that I was going to hell," Ophelia said. "He was over at our house doing something. Fixing a burst pipe, maybe? I don't know how he knew. I was eleven. I was making one of my Barbies kiss the other Barbie. I don't think I knew, not yet anyway. I just didn't have a Ken. He didn't bring you over to play after he said that, even though I never told my mom."

"My daddy thinks everyone is going to hell," Fran said into the counterpane. "I don't care where I go, as long as it isn't here and he isn't there."

Ophelia didn't say anything for a minute or two, and she didn't get up to leave, neither, so finally Fran poked her head out. Ophelia had a toy in her hand, the monkey egg. She turned it over, then over again. She looked a question at Fran.

"Give here," Fran said. "I'll work it." She wound the filigree dial and set the egg on the floor. The toy vibrated ferociously. Two pincer legs and a scorpion tail made of figured brass shot out of the bottom hemisphere, and the egg wobbled on the legs in one direction and then another, the articulated tail curling and lashing. Portholes on either side of the top hemisphere opened, and two arms wriggled out and reached up, rapping at the dome of the egg until that, too, cracked open with a click. A monkey's head, wearing the egg dome like a hat, popped out. Its mouth opened and closed in chattering ecstasy, red garnet eyes rolling, arms describing wider and wider circles in the air until the clockwork ran down and all of its extremities whipped back into the egg again.

"What in the world?" Ophelia said. She picked up the egg, tracing the joins with a finger.

"It's just something that's been in our family," Fran said. She stuck her arm out of the quilt, grabbed a tissue, and blew her nose for maybe the thousandth time. Just like a clockwork monkey. "We didn't steal it from no one, if that's what you're thinking."

"No," Ophelia said, and then frowned. "It's just—I've never seen anything like it. It's like a Fabergé egg. It ought to be in a museum."

There were lots of others. The laughing cat, and the waltzing elephants; the swan you wound up, who chased the dog. Other toys that Fran hadn't played with in years. The mermaid who combed garnets out of her hair. Bawbees for babies, her mother had called them.

"I remember now," Ophelia said. "When you came and played at my house. You brought a minnow made out of silver. It was smaller than my little finger. We put it in the bathtub, and it swam around and around. You had a little fishing rod, too, and a golden worm that wriggled on the hook. You let me catch the fish, and when I did, it talked. It said it would give me a wish if I let it go. But it was just a toy. When I told my mother about it, she said I was making it up. And you never brought it back. You said we should play with my dolls instead."

"You wished for two pieces of chocolate cake," Fran said sleepily.

"And then my mother made a chocolate cake, didn't she?" Ophelia said. "So the wish came true. But I could only eat one piece. Maybe I knew she was going to make a cake. Except why would I wish for something that I already knew I was going to get?"

Fran said nothing. She watched Ophelia through slitted eyes.

"Do you still have the fish?" Ophelia asked.

Fran said, "Somewhere. The clockwork ran down. It didn't give wishes no more. I reckon I didn't mind. It only ever granted little wishes."

"Ha, ha," Ophelia said. She stood up. "Tomorrow's Saturday. I'll come by in the morning to make sure you're OK."

"You don't have to," Fran said.

"No," Ophelia said. "I don't have to. But I will."

When you do for other people (Fran's daddy said once upon a time when he was drunk, before he got religion) things that they could do for themselves but they pay you to do it instead, you both will get used to it. Sometimes they don't even pay you, and that's charity. At first charity isn't comfortable, but it gets so it is so. After some while, maybe you start to feel wrong when you ain't doing for them, just one more thing, and always one more thing after that. Maybe you start to feel as you're valuable. Because they need you. And the more they need you, the more you need them. Things go out of balance. The more a person needs you, the harder it gets for you to leave. You need to remember that, Franny. Sometimes you're on one side of that equation, and sometimes you're on the other. Y'all need to know where you are and what you owe. And where you are is beholden to the summer people, and unless you can balance that out, here is where y'all stay.

Fran wasn't sure what he thought about all that now that he was friends with Jesus, about how the question of eternal life and the forgiveness of sins balanced out. Maybe that was why religion made him so itchy. All she knew was that nobody, not even her daddy, had ever suggested Jesus was going to help her out of her particular situation.

Fran, dosed on NyQuil, feverish and alone in her great-grandfather's catalog house, hidden behind walls of roses, dreamed — as she did every night — of escape. She woke every few hours, wishing someone would bring her another glass of water. She sweated through her clothes, and then froze, and then boiled again. Her throat was full of knives.

She was still on the couch when Ophelia came back, banging through the screen door. "Good morning!" Ophelia said. "Or maybe I should say good afternoon! It's noon, anyhow. I brought oranges to make fresh orange juice, and I didn't know if you liked sausage or bacon, so I got you two different kinds of biscuit."

Fran struggled to sit up.

"Fran," Ophelia said. She came and stood in front of the sofa, still holding the two cat-head biscuits. "You look terrible." She put her hand on Fran's forehead. "You're burning up! I knew I oughtn't't've left you here all by yourself! What should I do? Should I take you down to the emergency?"

"No doctor," Fran managed to say. "They'll want to know where my daddy is. Water?"

Ophelia scampered back to the kitchen. "How many days have you had the flu? You need antibiotics. Or something. Fran?"

"Here," Fran said, coming to a decision. She lifted a bill off a stack of mail on the floor and pulled out the return envelope. Then she reached up and pulled out three strands of her hair. She put them in the envelope and licked it shut. "Take this up the road where it crosses the drain," she said. "All the way up." She coughed miserably, a rattling, deathly cough. "When you get to the big house, go around to the back and knock on the door. Tell them I sent you. You won't see them, but they'll know you came from me. After you knock, you can just go in. Go upstairs directly, you mind, and put this envelope under the door. Third door down the hall. You'll know which. After that, you oughter wait out on the porch. Bring back whatever they give you."

Ophelia gave her a look that said Fran was delirious. "Just go," Fran said. "If there ain't a house, or if there is a house and it ain't the house I'm telling you about, then come back and I'll go to the emergency with you. Or if you find the house and you're afeart and you can't do what I asked, come back and I'll go with you. But if you do what I tell you, it will be like the minnow."

"Like the minnow?" Ophelia said. "I don't understand."

"You will. Be bold," Fran said, and did her best to look cheerful. "Like the girls in those ballads. Will you bring me another glass of water afore you go?"

Ophelia went.

Fran lay on the couch, thinking about what Ophelia would see. From time to time she raised a pair of curious-looking spyglasses — these something much more useful than any bawbee — to her eyes. Through them she saw first the dirt track, which only seemed to dead-end. Were you to look again, you found your road crossing over the shallow crick once, twice, the one climbing the mountain, the drain running away and down. The meadow disappearing again into beds of laurel, then low trees hung with climbing roses, so that you ascended in drifts of pink and white. A stone wall, tumbled and ruined, and then the big house. The house, dry stack stone, stained with age like the tumbledown wall; two stories. A slate roof, a long covered porch, carved wooden shutters making all the eyes of the windows blind. Two apple trees, crabbed and old, one green and bearing fruit and the other bare and silver black. Ophelia found the mossy path between them that wound around to the back door, with two words carved over the stone lintel: BE BOLD.

And this is what Fran saw Ophelia do: Having knocked on the door, Ophelia hesitated for only a moment and then she opened it. She called out, "Hello? Fran sent me. She's ill. Hello?" No one answered.

So Ophelia took a breath and stepped over the threshold and into a dark, crowded hallway, with a room on either side and a staircase in front of her. On the flagstone in front of her were carved these words: BE BOLD, BE BOLD. Despite the invitation, Ophelia did not seem tempted to investigate either room, which Fran thought wise of her. The first test a success. You might expect that through one door would be a living room, and you might expect that through the other door would be a kitchen, but you would be wrong. One was the Queen's room. The other was what Fran thought of as the War Room.

Fusty stacks of old magazines and catalogs and newspapers, old encyclopedias and gothic novels leaned against the walls of the hall, making such a narrow alley that even lickle tiny Ophelia turned sideways to make her way. Doll's legs and old silverware sets and tennis trophies and Mason jars and empty matchboxes and false teeth, and stranger things still, poked out of paper bags and plastic carriers. You might expect that through the doors on either side of the hall there would be more crumbling piles and more odd jumbles, and you would be right. But there were other things, too. At the foot of the stairs was another piece of advice for guests like Ophelia, carved right into the first riser: BE BOLD, BE BOLD, BUT NOT TOO BOLD.

The owners of the house had been at another one of their frolics, Fran saw. Someone had woven tinsel and ivy and peacock feathers through the banisters. Someone had thumbtacked cut silhouettes and Polaroids and tintypes and magazine pictures on the wall alongside the stairs, layers upon layers upon layers, hundreds and hundreds of eyes watching each time Ophelia set her foot down carefully on the next stair.

Perhaps Ophelia didn't trust the stairs not to be rotted through. But the stairs were safe. Someone had always taken very good care of this house.

At the top of the stairs, the carpet underfoot was soft, almost spongy. Moss, Fran decided. They've redecorated again. That's going to be the devil to clean up. Here and there were white-and-red mushrooms in pretty rings upon the moss. More bawbees, too, waiting for someone to come along and play with them. A dinosaur, only needing to be wound, a plastic dime-store cowboy sitting on its shining shoulders. Up near the ceiling, two armored dirigibles, tethered to a light fixture by their scarlet ribbons. The cannons on these zeppelins were in working order. They'd chased Fran down the hall more than once. Back home, she'd had to tweezer the tiny lead pellets out of her shin. Today, though, all were on their best behavior.

Ophelia passed one door, two doors, stopped at the third door. Above it, the final warning: BE BOLD, BE BOLD, BUT NOT TOO BOLD. LEST THAT THY HEART'S BLOOD RUN COLD. Ophelia put her hand on the doorknob but didn't try it. Not afeart, but no fool, neither, Fran thought. They'll be pleased. Or will they?

Ophelia knelt down to slide Fran's envelope under the door. Something else happened, too: something slipped out of Ophelia's pocket and landed on the carpet of moss.

Back down the hall, Ophelia stopped in front of the first door. She seemed to hear someone or something. Music, perhaps? A voice calling her name? An invitation? Fran's poor, sore heart was filled with delight. They liked her! Well, of course they did. Who wouldn't like Ophelia?

Who made her way down the stairs, through the towers of clutter and junk. Back onto the porch, where she sat on the porch swing but didn't swing. She seemed to be keeping one eye on the house and the other on the little rock garden out back, which ran up against the mountain right quick. There was even a waterfall, and Fran hoped Ophelia appreciated it. There'd never been no such thing before. This one was all for her, all for Ophelia who opined that waterfalls are freaking beautiful.

Up on the porch, Ophelia's head jerked around, as if she were afraid someone might be sneaking up the back. But there were only carpenter bees, bringing back their satchels of gold, and a woodpecker, drilling for grubs. There was a ground pig in the rumpled grass, and the more Ophelia set and stared, the more she and Fran both saw. A pair of fox kits napping in under the laurel. A doe and a fawn peeling bark runners off of young trunks. Even a brown bear, still tufty with last winter's fur, nosing along the high ridge above the house. Fran knew what Ophelia must have been feeling. As if she were an interloper in some Eden. While Ophelia sat on the porch of that dangerous house, Fran curled inward on her couch, waves of heat pouring out of her. Her whole body shook so violently that her teeth rattled. Her spyglasses fell to the floor. *Maybe I am dying*, Fran thought, *and that is why Ophelia came here. Because the summer people need someone to look after their house. If I can't do it, then someone else must. Ophelia must.*

Fran, feverish, went in and out of sleep, always listening for the sound of Ophelia coming back down. Perhaps she'd made a mistake and they wouldn't send down something to help. Perhaps they wouldn't send Ophelia back at all. Ophelia, with her pretty singing voice, that shyness, innate kindness. Her short hair, silvery blond. They liked things that were shiny. They were like magpies that way. In other ways, too.

But here was Ophelia, after all, her eyes enormous, her face all lit up like Christmas. "Fran," she said. "Fran, wake up. I went there. I was bold! Who lives there, Fran?"

"The summer people," Fran said. "Did they give you anything for me?"

Ophelia set an object upon the counterpane. Like everything the summer people made, it was right pretty. A lipstick-size vial of pearly glass, an enameled green snake clasped around, its tail the stopper. Fran tugged at the tail, and the serpent uncoiled, unbottling the potion. A pole ran out the mouth and a silk rag unfurled. Embroidered upon it were these words: DRINK ME.

Ophelia watched this, her eyes glazed with too many marvels. "I sat and waited and there were two fox kits! They came right up to the porch, and then went to the door and scratched at it until it opened. They trotted right inside and came out again. One came over to me then, with something in its jaw. It laid down that bottle right at my feet, and then they ran down the steps and into the woods. Fran, it was like a fairy tale."

"Yes," Fran said. She put her mouth to the mouth of the vial and drank down what was in it. It tasted sour and hot, like bottled smoke. She coughed, then wiped her mouth and licked the back of her hand.

"I mean, people say something is like a fairy tale all the time," Ophelia said. "And what they mean is that somebody falls in love and gets married. But that house, those animals, it really is a fairy tale. Who are they? The summer people?"

"That's what my daddy calls them," Fran said. "Except when he gets religious, he calls them devils come up to steal his soul. It's because they supply him with drink. But he weren't never the one who had to mind after them. That was my mother. And now she's gone and it's only ever me."

"You take care of them?" Ophelia said. "You mean like the Robertses?"

A feeling of tremendous well-being was washing over Fran. Her feet were warm for the first time in what seemed like days, and her throat felt coated in honey and balm. Even her nose felt less raw and red. "Ophelia?" she said.

"Yes, Fran?"

"I think I'm going to be much better," Fran said. "Which is something you done for me. You were brave and a true friend, and I'll have to think how I can pay you back."

"I wasn't —" Ophelia protested. "I mean, I'm glad I did. I'm glad you asked me. I promise I won't tell anyone."

If you did, you'd be sorry, Fran thought but didn't say. "Ophelia? I need to sleep. And then if you want, we can talk. You can even stay here while I sleep. If you want. I don't care if you're a lesbian. There are Pop-tarts on the kitchen counter. And those two biscuits you brung. I like sausage. You can have the one with bacon."

She fell asleep before Ophelia could say anything else.

The first thing she did when she woke up was take a bath. In the mirror, she took a quick inventory. Her hair was lank and greasy, all witch knots and tangles. There were circles under her eyes, and her tongue, when she stuck it out, was yellow. When she was clean and dressed again, her jeans were loose and she could feel her hip bones protruding. "I could eat a whole mess of food," she told Ophelia. "But a cat-head and a box of Pop-tarts will do for a start."

There was fresh orange juice, and Ophelia had poured it into a stoneware jug. Fran decided not to tell her that her daddy used it as a sometime spittoon. "Can I ask you some more about them?" Ophelia said. "You know, the summer people?"

"I don't reckon I can answer every question," Fran said. "But go on."

"OK. When I first got there . . ." Ophelia said. "When I went inside, at first I decided that it must be a shut-in. One of those, you know, hoarders. The ones who keep everything and don't throw anything away, not even the rolls from toilet paper. I've watched that show, and sometimes they even keep their own poop. And dead cats. It's just horrible.

"Then it just kept on getting stranger. But I wasn't ever scared. It felt like there was somebody there, but they were happy to see me."

"They don't get much in the way of company," Fran said.

"Yeah, well, why do they collect all that stuff? Where does it come from?"

"Some of it's from catalogs. They order things. I have to go down to the post office and collect it for them. Sometimes they go away and bring things back. Sometimes they tell me that they want something, and I have to go get it for them. Mostly it's stuff from the Salvation Army. Once I had to buy a hunnert — a hundred — pounds of copper piping."

"Why?" Ophelia said. "I mean, what do they do with it?"

"They make things," Fran said. "That's what my momma called them, makers. I don't know what they do with all of it. They give away things. Like the toys. They like children. When you do things for them, they're beholden to you. They'll try to give you something in return. And vice versa. I don't ask them for much anymore, because . . . well, just because."

"Have you seen them?" Ophelia said.

"Now and then," Fran said. "Not very often. Not since I was much younger. They're shy."

Ophelia was practically bouncing on her chair. "You get to look after them? That's the best thing ever! It's like Hogwarts! Except it's real! Have they always been here? Is that why you aren't going to go to college?"

Fran hesitated. "I don't know where they come from. They aren't always there. Sometimes they're . . . somewhere else. My momma said she felt sorry for them. She thought maybe they couldn't go home, that they'd been sent away, like the Cherokee, I guess. They live a lot longer, maybe forever, I don't know. I don't think time works the same way where they come from. Sometimes they're gone for years. But they always come back. They're summer people. That's just the way it is with summer people."

"And you're not," Ophelia said. "And now I'm not, either."

"*You* can go away again whenever you want," Fran said, not caring how she sounded. "I can't. It's part of the bargain. Whoever takes care of them has to stay here. You can't leave. They don't let you."

"You mean you can't leave ever?"

"No," Fran said. "Not ever. My mother was stuck here until she had me. And then when I was old enough, she told me I had to take over. She took off right after that."

"Where did she go?"

"I'm not the one to answer that," Fran said. "They gave my momma this tent. It folds up the size of a handkerchief, and it sets up the size of a two-man tent, but it's teetotally different on the inside. It's not a tent at all. It's a cottage with two brass beds and a chifforobe to hang your things in, and a table, and windows with glass in them. When you look out one of the windows, you see wherever you are, and when you look out the other window, you see those two apple trees, the ones in front of the house with the moss path between them?"

Ophelia nodded.

"Well, my momma used to bring out that tent for me and her when my daddy had been drinking. Then my momma passed the summer people on to me, and one morning I woke up and I saw her climb out that window. The one that shouldn't ought to be there. She disappeared down that path. Mebbe I should have followed on after her, but I stayed put."

"Wow," Ophelia said. "So maybe she's still there? Where do they go when they aren't here?"

"Well, she ain't here," Fran said. "That's what I know. So I have to stay here in her place. I don't expect she'll be back, neither."

"Well, that sucks," Ophelia said. But she didn't sound like she really understood how much.

"I wish I could get away for just a little while," Fran said. "Mebbe go out to San Francisco and see the Golden Gate Bridge. Dip my toes in the Pacific. I'd like to buy me a guitar and play some of those old ballads on the streets. Just stay a little while, then come back and take up my burden again."

"I'd sure like to go out to California," Ophelia said. "I don't think they mind two girls so much out there. You can kiss whoever you want and no one cares."

"I'll never kiss anybody up here," Fran said. "I'll die an old maid first."

They sat in silence for a minute. Then Ophelia said, "Can I ask you one more question?"

"I expect I can't stop you," Fran said.

"Well," Ophelia said, "sometimes you talk like everybody else who lives here, and sometimes you talk different. Like you might be from anywhere. You know."

Fran glared at her. "Iffen I don't say you'uns, or aks fer holp, hit don't mean I ain't from the country. I's borned here, and I been here since ever I raised up. I reckon I'll be here till hit come my time, but that don't mean I can't talk proper," Fran said. She held on to her temper with some effort. "I watch TV. I know how people are supposed to talk. Don't you remember what you said to me when we were little girls?"

"What did I say?" Ophelia said.

"You asked me where my dad and I was from," Fran said. "You asked me if I was from a different planet. Even though *you* were the ones who had come from someplace else."

"Oh, God," Ophelia said. "That is so embarrassing."

"Well, I remember. I said I didn't know," Fran said. "I thought maybe you knew something I didn't. Maybe I was from Mars. So we went and found your mother, and she said she loved the way I talked. But she laughed at me."

"I liked the way you talked," Ophelia protested. "When we went home, I had an imaginary friend for a while, and she talked just like you."

"Well," Fran said, "that's right sweet of you to say so, I guess."

"I wish I could help out," Ophelia said. "You know, with that house and the summer people. You shouldn't have to do everything, not all of the time."

"I already owe you," Fran said. "For helping with the Robertses' house. For looking in on me when I was ill. For what you did when you went up to fetch me help."

"I know what it's like when you're all alone," Ophelia said. "When you can't talk about stuff. And I mean it, Fran. I'll do whatever I can to help."

"I can tell you mean it," Fran said. "I just don't think you know what it is you're saying. In any case, I ought to explain at least one thing. If you want, you can go up there again one more time. You did me a favor, and I don't know how else to pay you back. There's a bedroom up in that house, and iffen you sleep in it, you see your heart's desire. I could take you back tonight and show you that room. 'Sides, I oughter take you back up anyhow. I think you lost something up there."

"I did?" Ophelia said. "What was it?" She reached down in her pockets. "Oh, hell. My iPod. How did you know?"

Fran shrugged. "Not like anybody up there is going to steal it. 'Spect they'd be happy to have you back up again. If they didn't like you, you'd know it already."

Ophelia made up her mind. "I'll have to go home again," she said. "I'm supposed to walk the dog. And I'll have to ask my mom about tonight. But it will be fine. She asks about you sometimes. I think she was hoping we'd hang out, that, you know, you'd be a good influence on me. They worry about me. All the time."

"You're lucky," Fran said.

Fran was straightening up her and her daddy's mess when the summer people let her know that they needed a few things. "Can't I just have a minute to myself?" she grumbled.

They told her that she'd had a good four days. "And I surely do 'preciate it," she said, "considering I was laid so low." But she put the skillet down in the sink to soak and wrote down what they wanted.

For a while Fran had tried real hard to get along with Joanie. It seemed possible that Joanie and her daddy might have a baby, and then maybe Fran would be free. But then Joanie mentioned her hysterectomy, and that was that. In any case, Joanie was plumb ugly. Nice as pie, but as far as Fran could figure, the summer people wouldn't settle for an ugly guardian. Sometimes she thought about taking a knife to her face but couldn't quite bring herself to do this. She didn't really want to cut off her nose to spite her face, even though once her daddy had suggested that might do.

She'd tidied away all of the toys, not quite sure what had come over her to take them all out. Maybe it was that they reminded her of her momma, how she would come down the mountain with them, to make up for leaving Fran by herself all day. Once she got older, she helped her momma out some, but by then she wasn't as interested in their gadgets and trinkets. Her momma used to tell her how her own granny had made her husband choose a house from the Sears catalog because she didn't want one of theirs, no matter that it could have been a palace. That was one of the early lessons, that you could take their presents, but there was always a cost to pay.

When Ophelia came back at five, she had her hair in a ponytail, and a flashlight and a thermos, like she thought she were Nancy Drew. "OK," she said. "I almost chickened out, but then I couldn't stand not to come back. When can we go up?"

"Just as soon as we get ready," Fran said. "I made up some jelly sandwiches to take along."

"It gets dark up here so early," Ophelia said. "I feel like it's Halloween or something. Like you're taking me to the haunted house."

"They ain't haints," Fran said. "Nor demons or ary such thing. They don't do no harm unless you get on the wrong side of them. They'll play a prank on you then and count it good fun."

"Like what?" Ophelia said.

"Once I did the warshing up and broke a teacup," Fran said. "They'll sneak up and pinch you." She still had marks on her arms, though she hadn't broken a plate in years. "For the last two years, they've been doing what all the people up here like to do, that reenacting. They set up their battlefield in the big room downstairs.

It's not the War Between the States. It's one of theirs, I guess. They built themselves airships and submersibles and mechanical dragons and knights and all manner of wee toys to fight with. Sometimes when they get bored they get me up to be their audience, only they ain't always careful where they go pointing their cannons."

She looked at Ophelia and saw she'd said too much. "Well, they're used to me. They know I don't have no choice but to put up with their ways. They won't bother you none. They put up with all of my daddy's nonsense and don't never bother him none."

That afternoon she'd had to drive over to Chattanooga to visit a particular thrift store. They'd sent her for sequined shoes, a used DVD player, an old saddle, and all the bathing suits she could buy up. Between that and paying for gas, she'd gone through seventy dollars of what her daddy had left her. And the service light had been on the whole way, though her daddy had sworn he'd already taken the car in. At least it hadn't been a school day. Hard to explain you were cutting out because voices in your head were telling you they needed a saddle.

She'd gone on ahead and brought it all up to the house after. No need to bother Ophelia with any of it. The iPod had been a-laying right in front of the door Fran never wanted to have to open.

"Here," she said. "I went ahead and brought this back down."

"My iPod!" Ophelia said. She turned it over. "They did this?"

The iPod was heavier now. It had a little walnut case instead of pink silicone, and there was a figure inlaid in ebon and gilt.

"A dragonfly," Ophelia said.

"A snake doctor," Fran said. "That's what my daddy calls them."

"They did this for me?"

"They'd embellish a bedazzled jean jacket if you left it there,"

Fran said. "No lie. They can't stand to leave a thing alone."

"Cool," Ophelia said. "Although my mom is never going to believe me when I say I bought it at the mall."

"Just don't take up anything metal," Fran said. "No earrings, not even your car keys. Or you'll wake up and they'll have smelted them down and turned them into doll armor or who knows what all."

Ophelia emptied her pockets on the kitchen table and took off her hoops. "OK if I leave it all here?"

"Sure," Fran said.

"I guess I'm ready, then," said Ophelia.

"Let's walk up," Fran said. "I can fill you in on anything else you were wondering 'bout."

They took off their shoes when they got to where the road crossed the drain. The water was cold with the last of the snow melt. Ophelia said, "I feel like I ought to have brought a hostess gift."

"You could pick them a bunch of wildflowers," Fran said. "But they'd be just as happy with a bit of kyarn."

"Yarn?" Ophelia said.

"Roadkill," Fran said. "But yarn's OK, too."

Ophelia thumbed the wheel of her iPod. "There's songs on here that weren't here before."

"They like music, too," Fran said. "They like it when I sing."

"What you were saying about going out to San Francisco to busk," Ophelia said. "I can't imagine doing that."

"Well," Fran said. "I won't ever do it, but I think I can imagine it OK."

"I meant what I said," said Ophelia. "Maybe you don't have to do all this by yourself. We could wait until you trusted me, and then see if they'd let me take care of things for a while."

"Hard to picture," Fran said. "We can talk about it down the road."

When they got up to the house, there were deer grazing on the green lawn. The living tree and the dead were all touched with the last of the sunlight. Chinese lanterns hung in pearly rows from the rafters of the porch.

"You always have to come at the house from between the trees," Fran said. "Right on the path. Otherwise you don't get nowhere near it. And I don't ever use but the back door."

"Oh, boy," Ophelia said. "This all just feels like a dream."

"I know what you mean," Fran said. "But it's real, as far as I can tell."

She knocked at the back door. BE BOLD. BE BOLD. "It's me again," she said. "And my friend Ophelia. The one who left the iPod."

She saw Ophelia open her mouth and went on hastily, "Don't say it, Ophelia. They don't like it when you thank them. They're allergic to that word."

"Oh," Ophelia said. "OK."

"Come on in," Fran said. "*Mi casa es su casa*. I'll give you the grand tour."

They stepped over the threshold, Fran first. "There's the pump room out back, where I do the wash," she said. "There's a big ol' stone oven for baking in, and a pig pit, although why I don't know. They don't eat meat. But you prob'ly don't care about that."

"What's in this room?" Ophelia said.

"Hunh," Fran said. "Well, first it's a lot of junk. They just like to accumulate junk. Way back in there, though, is what I think is a Queen."

"A Queen?"

"Well, that's what I call her." You know how in a beehive, way down in the combs you have the Queen, and all the worker bees attend on her?

"Far as I can tell, that's what's in there. She's real big and not real pretty, and they are always running in and out of there with food for her. I don't think she's teetotally growed up yet. For a while now I've been thinking on what my momma said, about how maybe these summer people got sent off. Bees do that, too, right? Go off and make a new hive when there are too many Queens?"

"Honestly?" Ophelia said. "It sounds kind of creepy."

"I don't think of it that way," Fran said. "It's just how things are. I guess I'm used to the quareness of it all."

"'Sides, that's where my daddy gets his liquor, and she don't bother him none. They have some kind of still set up in there, and every once in a while when he ain't feeling too religious, he goes in and skims off a liddle bitty bit. It's awful sweet stuff."

"I tried 'shine once at a party," Ophelia said. "That was back in Lynchburg. Yuck." She hesitated. "Are they, uh, are they listening to us right now?"

"Yeah," Fran said. "They're awful eavesdroppers."

Ophelia turned around in a circle in the cluttered hall. "Um, hi?" she said. "I'm Fran's friend Ophelia? I'm pleased to make your acquaintance."

In response came a series of clicks from the War Room.

Ophelia jumped. "What's that?" she said.

"Remember I told you 'bout the reenactor stuff?" Fran said. "Don't get freaked out. It's pretty cool."

She gave Ophelia a little push into the War Room.

Of all the rooms in the house, this one was Fran's favorite, even if they dive-bombed her sometimes with the airships or fired off the cannons without much thought for where she was standing. The walls were beaten tin and copper, scrap metal held down with twopenny nails. Molded forms lay on the floor, representing scaled-down mountains, forests, and plains where miniature armies were fighting desperate battles. There was a kiddie pool over by the big picture window, with a machine in it that made waves. Little ships and submersibles, and occasionally one of the ships sank and bodies would go floating over to the edges. There was a sea serpent made of tubing and metal rings that swam endlessly in a circle. There was a sluggish river, too, closer to the door, that ran red, and stank, and stained the banks. The summer people were always setting up miniature bridges over it, then blowing the bridges up.

Overhead were the fantastic shapes of the dirigibles, and the dragons that were hung on string and swam perpetually through the air above your head. There was a misty globe, too, suspended in some way that Fran could not figure, and lit by some unknown source. It stayed up near the painted ceiling for days at a time, and then sank down behind the plastic sea, according to some schedule of the summer people's.

"It's amazing," Ophelia said. "Once I went to the house of some friend of my father's. An anesthesiologist? He had a train set down in his basement, and it was crazy complicated. He would die if he saw this."

"Over there is a Queen, I think," Fran said. "All surrounded by her knights. And here's another one, much smaller. I wonder who won, in the end."

"Maybe it's not been fought yet," Ophelia said. "Or maybe it's being fought right now."

"Could be," Fran said. "Anyway, sometimes I come and sit and try and take in all the changes. I wish there was a book that told you everything that went on.

"Come on. I'll show you the room you can sleep in."

They went up the stairs. BE BOLD, BE BOLD, BUT NOT TOO BOLD. The moss carpet on the second floor was already looking a little worse for wear. "Last week I spent a whole day scrubbing these boards on my hands and knees. So of course they need to go next thing and pile up a bunch of dirt and stuff. They won't be the ones who have to pitch in and clean it up."

"I could help," Ophelia said. "If you want."

"I wasn't asking for help. But if you offer, I'll accept. The first door is the washroom," Fran said. "Nothing quare about the toilet. I don't know about the bathtub, though. Never felt the need to sit in it."

"My mom always tells me not to sit down in the bathtub when we stay in a hotel," Ophelia said. "I think she thinks you get AIDS that way."

"Far's I know, all you'd get is wet," Fran said. "Here's where you sleep." She opened the second door.

It was a gorgeous room, all done up in shades of orange and rust and gold and pink and tangerine. The walls were finished in leafy shapes and vines cut from all kinds of dresses and T-shirts and what have you. Fran's momma had spent the better part of the year going through stores, choosing clothes for their patterns and textures and colors. Gold-leaf snakes and fishes swam through the leaf shapes. When the sun came up in the morning, Fran remembered, it was almost blinding.

There was a crazy quilt on the bed, pink and gold. The bed itself was shaped like a swan. There was a willow chest at the foot of the bed to lay out your clothes. The mattress was stuffed with the down from crow feathers. Fran had helped her mother shoot the crows and pluck their feathers. She thought they'd killed about a hundred.

"I'd say wow," Ophelia said, "but I keep saying that. Wow, wow, wow. This is a crazy room."

"I always thought it was like being stuck inside a bottle of orange Nehi," Fran said. "But in a good way."

"Oh, yeah," Ophelia said. "I can see that."

There was a stack of books on the table beside the bed. Like everything else in the room, all the books had been picked out for the colors on their jackets. Fran's momma had told her that once the room had been another set of colors. Greens and blues, maybe? Willow and peacock and midnight colors? And who had brought the bits up for the room that time? Fran's great-grandfather or someone even farther along the family tree? Who had first begun to take care of the summer people? Her mother had doled out stories sparingly, and so Fran only had a piecemeal sort of history.

Hard to figure out what it would please Ophelia to hear anyway, and what would trouble her. All of it seemed pleasing and troubling to Fran in equal measure after so many years.

"The door you slipped my envelope under," she said finally. "You oughtn't ever go in there."

Ophelia yawned. "Like Bluebeard," she said.

Fran said, "It's how they come and go. Even they don't open that door very often, I guess." She'd peeped through the keyhole once and seen a bloody river. She'd bet if you passed through that door, you weren't likely to return.

"Can I ask you another stupid question?" Ophelia said. "Where are they right now?"

"They're here," Fran said. "Or out in the woods chasing nightjars. I told you I didn't see them much."

"So how do they tell you what they need you to do?"

"They get in my head," Fran said. "I guess it's kind of like being schizophrenic. Or like having a really bad itch or something that goes away when I do what they want me to."

"Not fun," Ophelia said. "Maybe I don't like your summer people as much as I thought I did."

Fran said, "It's not always awful. I guess what it is, is complicated."

"I guess I won't complain the next time my mom tells me I have to help her polish the silver or do useless crap like that. Should we eat our sandwiches now, or should we save them for when we wake up in the middle of the night?" Ophelia asked. "I have this idea that seeing your heart's desire probably makes you hungry."

"I can't stay," Fran said, surprised. She saw Ophelia's expression and said, "Well, hell. I thought you understood. This is just for you."

Ophelia continued to look at her dubiously. "Is it because there's just the one bed? I could sleep on the floor. You know, if you're worried I might be planning to lez out on you."

"It isn't that," Fran said. "They only let a body sleep here once. Once and no more."

"You're really going to leave me up here alone?" Ophelia said.

"Yes," Fran said. "Lessen you decide you want to come back down with me. I guess I'd understand if you did."

"Could I come back again?" Ophelia said.

"No."

Ophelia sat down on the golden quilt and smoothed it with her fingers. She chewed her lip, not meeting Fran's eye.

"Phew," she said. "OK. I'll do it." She laughed. "How could I not do it? Right?"

"If you're sure," Fran said.

"I'm not sure, but I couldn't stand it if you sent me away now," Ophelia said. "When you slept here, were you afraid?"

"A little," Fran said. "But the bed was comfortable, and I kept the light on. I read for a while and then I fell asleep."

"Did you see your heart's desire?" Ophelia said.

"I guess I did," Fran offered, and then said no more.

"OK, then," Ophelia said. "I guess you should go. You should go, right?"

"I'll come back in the morning," Fran said. "I'll be here afore you even wake."

"Thanks," Ophelia said.

But Fran didn't go. She said, "Did you mean it when you said you wanted to help?"

"Look after the house?" Ophelia said. "Yeah, absolutely. You really ought to go out to San Francisco someday. You shouldn't have to stay here your whole life without ever having a vacation or anything. I mean, you're not a slave, right?"

"I don't know what I am," Fran said. "I guess one day I'll have to figure that out."

Ophelia said, "Anyway, we can talk about it tomorrow. Over breakfast. You can tell me about the suckiest parts of the job, and I'll tell you what my heart's desire turns out to be."

"Oh," Fran said. "I almost forgot. When you wake up tomorrow, don't be surprised if they've left you a gift. The summer people. It'll be something that they think you need or want."

"Good grief," Ophelia said. "This is starting to sound like Christmas or something."

"Or something," Fran agreed. "But you don't have to accept it. You don't have to worry about being rude that way."

"OK," Ophelia said. "I will consider whether I really need or want my present. I won't let false glamour deceive me."

"Good," Fran said. Then she bent over Ophelia where she was sitting on the bed and kissed her on the forehead. "Sleep well, Ophelia. Good dreams."

"'Night, John-Boy," Ophelia said, and laughed.

Fran left the house without any interference from the summer people. She couldn't tell if she'd expected to find any. As she came down the stairs, she said, rather more fiercely than she'd meant to, "Be nice to her. Don't play no tricks." She looked in on the Queen, who was molting again.

She went out the front door instead of the back, which was something that she'd always wanted to do. Nothing bad happened and she walked down the hill feeling strangely put out. She went over everything in her head, wondering what still needed doing that she hadn't done. Nothing, she decided. Everything was taken care of.

Except, of course, it wasn't. The first thing was the guitar, leaned up against the door of her house. It was a beautiful instrument. The strings, she thought, were pure silver. When she struck them, the tone was pure and sweet and reminded her uncomfortably of Ophelia's singing voice. The keys were made of gold and shaped like owl heads, and there was mother-of-pearl inlay across the boards, like a spray of roses. It was the gaudiest gawgee they'd yet made her a gift of.

"Well, all right," she said. "I guess you didn't mind what I told her." She laughed out loud with relief.

"Why everwho did you tell what?" someone said.

She picked up the guitar and held it like a weapon in front of her. "Daddy?"

"Put that down," the voice said. A man stepped forward out of the shadow of the rosebushes. "I'm not your damn daddy. Although, come to think of it, I would like to know where he is."

"Ryan Shoemaker," Fran said. She put the guitar down on the ground. Another man stepped forward. "And Kyle Rainey."

"Howdy, Fran," said Kyle. He spat. "We were lookin' for your pappy, like Ryan says."

"I told Andy when I ran into him at the convenience," Fran said. "He went down to some meeting to praise Jesus. All the way to Florida, but I ain't heard from him yet, so mebbe they stopped over in Orlando to meet Mickey Mouse."

"I went to Disney World once," Ryan said. "Got thrown out for cussing out a princess."

"If he calls, I'll let him know you were up here looking for him," Fran said. "Is that all you wanted to ask me?"

Ryan lit up a cigarette, looked at her over the flame. "It was your daddy we wanted to ask, but I guess you could help us out instead."

"It don't seem likely somehow," Fran said. "But go on."

"Your daddy was meaning to drop off some of the sweet stuff the other night," Kyle said. "Only he started thinking about it on the drive down, and that's never been a good idea where your daddy is concerned. He decided Jesus wanted him to pour out ever last drop, and that's what he did, all the way down the mountain. If he weren't a lucky man, some spark might have cotched while he were pouring, but I guess Jesus don't want to meet him face-to-face just yet."

"And if that weren't bad enough," Ryan said, "when he got to the convenience, he decided that Jesus wanted him to get into the van and smash up all Andy's liquor, too. By the time we realized what was going on, there weren't much left beside two bottles of Kahlúa and a six-pack of wine coolers."

"One of them smashed, too," Kyle said. "And then he took off afore we could have a word with him."

"Well, I'm sorry for your troubles, but I don't see what it has to do with me," Fran said.

"What it has to do is that we've come up with an easy payment plan. We talked about it, and the way it seems to us is that your pappy could provide us with entrée to some of the finest homes in the area."

"We'd do a little smash and grab," Kyle said. "Except this way we could leave out the smash. Everybody would be happier."

"Like I said," Fran said. "I'll pass on the message. You're hoping my daddy will make his restitution by becoming your accessory in breaking and entering. I'll let him know if he calls."

"Or he could pay poor Andy back in kind," Ryan said. "With some of that good stuff."

"He'll have to run that by Jesus," Fran said. "Frankly, I think it's a better bet than the other, but you might have to wait until he and Jesus have had enough of each other."

"The thing is," Ryan said, "I'm not a patient man. And what has occurred to me is that your pappy may be out of our reach at present moment, but here you are. And I'm guessing that you can get us into a house or two. Preferably ones with quality flat screens and high-thread-count sheets. I promised Mandy I was going to help her redecorate."

"Or else you could point us in the direction of your daddy's private stash," Kyle said.

"And if I don't choose to do neither?" Fran asked, crossing her arms.

"I truly hope that you know what it is you're doing," Kyle said. "Ryan has not been in a good mood these last few days. He bit a sheriff's deputy on the arm last night in a bar. Which is why we weren't up here sooner."

Fran stepped back. "Fine," she said. "I'll do what you want. There's an old house farther up the road that nobody except me and my daddy know about. It's ruint. Nobody lives there, and so my daddy put his still up in it. He's got all sorts of articles stashed up there. I'm not saying he steals from the summer people, but I have wondered from time to time if he don't have a business on the side. Like maybe he's holding for someone else."

"Dammit," Ryan said. "And he calls himself a Christian man."

Fran said, "I'll take you up. But you can't tell him what I done."

"A'course not, darlin'," Kyle said. "We don't aim to cause a rift in the family. Just to get what we have coming."

And so Fran found herself climbing right back up that same road. She got her feet wet in the drain, but kept as far ahead of Kyle and Ryan as she dared. She didn't know if she felt safe with them at her back.

When they got up to the house, Kyle whistled. "Fancy sort of ruin."

"Wait'll you see what's inside," Fran said. She led them around to the back, then held the door open. "Sorry about the lights. The power goes off more than it stays on. My daddy usually brings up a flashlight. Want me to go get one?"

"We've got matches," Ryan said. "You stay right there."

"The still is in the room over on the right. Mind how you go. He's got it set up in a kind of maze, with the newspapers and all."

"Dark as the inside of a black cat at midnight," Kyle said. He felt his way down the hall. "I think I'm at the door. Sure enough, smells like what I'm lookin' for. Guess I'll just follow my nose. No booby traps or nothing like that?"

"No, sir," Fran said. "He'd have blowed hisself up a long time before now if he tried that."

"I might as well take in the sights," Ryan said, the lit end of his cigarette flaring. "Now that I'm getting my night vision."

"Yes, sir," Fran said.

"And might there be a pisser in this heap?"

"Third door on the left once you go up," Fran said. "The door sticks some."

She waited until he was at the top of the stairs before she slipped out the back door again. She could hear Kyle fumbling toward the center of the Queen's room. She wondered what the Queen would make of Kyle. She wasn't worried about Ophelia at all. Ophelia was an invited guest. And, anyhow, the summer people didn't let anything happen to the ones who looked after them.

One of the summer people was sitting on the porch swing when she came out. He was whittling a stick with a sharp knife.

"Evening," Fran said, and bobbed her head.

The summer personage didn't even look up at her. He was one of the ones so pretty it almost hurt to peep at him, but you couldn't not stare neither. That was one of the ways they cotched you, Fran figured. Just like wild animals when you shone a light at them. She finally tore her gaze away and ran down the stairs like the devil was after her. When she stopped to look back, he was still setting there, smiling and whittling that poor stick down.

She sold the guitar when she got to New York City. What was left of her daddy's two hundred dollars had bought her a Greyhound ticket and a couple of burgers at the bus station. The guitar got her six hundred more, and she used that to buy a ticket to Paris, where she met a Lebanese boy who was squatting in an old factory. One day she came back from her under-the-table job at a hotel and found him looking through her backpack. He had the monkey egg in his hand. He wound it up and put it down on the dirty floor to dance. They both watched until it ran down. *"Très jolie,"* he said.

It was a few days after Christmas, and there was snow melting in her hair. They didn't have heat in the squat, or even running water. She'd had a bad cough for a few days. She sat down next to her boy, and when he started to wind the monkey egg up again, she put her hand out to make him stop.

She didn't remember packing it. And of course, maybe she hadn't. For all she knew, they had winter palaces as well as summer places. Just because she'd never been able to travel didn't mean they didn't get around.

A few days later, the Lebanese boy disappeared, probably gone off looking for someplace warmer. The monkey egg went with him. After that, all she had to remind herself of home was the tent that she kept folded up like a dirty handkerchief in her wallet.

It's been two years now, and every now and again while Fran is cleaning rooms in the pension, she closes the door and sets up the tent and gets inside. She looks out the window at the two apple trees. She tells herself that one day soon she will go home again.

Peace in Our Time

{ GARTH NIX }

The old man who had once been the Grand Technomancer, Most Mighty Mechanician, and Highest of the High Artificier Adepts was cutting his roses when he heard the unmistakeable *ticktock-tocktock* of a clockwerk velocipede coming down the road. He started in surprise and then turned toward the noise, for the first time in years suddenly reminded that he was not wearing the four-foot-high toque of state, nor the cloak of perforated bronze control cards that had once hung from his shoulders, both of which had made almost anything but the smallest movement impossible.

He didn't miss these impressive clothes, but the old man concluded that since what he heard was definitely a clockwerk velocipede, however unlikely it seemed, and that a velocipede must have a rider, he should perhaps put something on to receive his visitor. While he was not embarrassed himself, the juxtaposition of a naked man and the sharp pruning shears he held might prove to be a visual distraction, and thus a hindrance to easy communication.

Accordingly, he walked into his humble cottage, and after a moment's consideration, took the white cloth off his kitchen table and draped it around himself, folding it so the pomegranate stain from his breakfast was tucked away under one arm.

When he went back out, the former Grand Technomancer left the shears by the front door. He expected to be back cutting the roses quite soon, after he got rid of his unexpected visitor.

The surprise guest was parking her velocipede by the gate to the lower paddock. The Grand Technomancer winced and frowned as the vehicle emitted a piercing shriek that drowned out its underlying clockwerk ticktocking. She had evidently engaged the parking retardation muffler to the mainspring before unlocking the gears. A common mistake made by those unfamiliar with the mechanism, and yet another most unwelcome noise to his quiet valley.

After correcting her error, the girl — or more properly a young woman, the old man supposed — climbed down from the control howdah above the single fat drive wheel of the velocipede. She was not wearing any identifiable robes of guild or lodge, and in fact her one-piece garment was made of some kind of scaly blue hide, both the cut and fabric strange to his eyes.

Perhaps even more curiously, the old man's extraordinarily acute hearing could not detect any faint clicking from sandgrain clockwerk, the last and most impressive advance of his colleagues, which had allowed modern technology to actually be implanted in the body, to enhance various aspects of physique and movement. Nor did she have one of the once-popular steam skeletons, as he could see neither the telltale puffs of steam from a radium boiler at the back of her head nor the bolt heads of augmented joints poking through at elbow, neck, and knee.

This complete absence of clockwerk enhancement in the young woman surprised the old man, though in truth he was surprised to have any visitor at all.

"Hello!" called out the young woman as she approached the door.

The old man wet his lips in preparation for speech, and, with considerable effort, managed to utter a soft greeting in return. As he did so, he was struck by the thought that he had not spoken aloud for more than ten years.

The woman came up to the door, intent on him, watching for any sign of sudden movement. The man was familiar with that gaze. He had been surrounded by bodyguards for many years, and though their eyes had been looking outward, he saw the same kind of focus in this woman.

It was strange to see that focus in so young a woman, he thought. She couldn't be more than sixteen or seventeen, but there was a calm and somewhat chilling competence in her eyes. Again, he was puzzled by her odd blue garment and lack of insignia. Her short-cropped hair, shaved at the sides, was not a style he could recall ever being fashionable. There were also three short lines tattooed on each side of her neck, the suggestion of ceremonial gills, perhaps, and this did spark some faint remembrance, but he couldn't pin the memory down. A submarine harvesting guild, perhaps—

"You are Ahfred Progressor III, formerly Grand Technomancer, Most Mighty Mechanician, and Highest of the High Artificier Adepts?" asked the woman quite conversationally. She had stopped a few feet away. Her hands were open by her sides, but there was something about that stance that suggested that this was a temporary state and that those same hands usually held weapons and shortly would again.

The old man couldn't see any obvious knives or anything similar, but that didn't mean anything. The woman's blue coverall had curious lumps along the forearms and thighs, which could be weapon pockets, though he could see no fasteners. And once again, he could not hear the sound of moving metal, not even the faintest slither of a blade in a sheath.

"Yes," he said scratchily and very slowly. "Ahfred . . . yes, that is my name. I was Grand Technomancer. Retired, of course."

There was little point in denying his identity. Though he had lost weight, his face was still much the same as it had been when it had adorned the obverse side of millions of coins, hundreds of thousands of machine-painted official portraits, and at least scores of statues, some of them bronze automata that also replicated his voice.

"Good," said the woman. "Do you live here alone?"

"Yes," replied Ahfred. He had begun to get alarmed. "Who . . . who are you?"

"We'll get to that," said the young woman easily. "Let's go inside. You first."

Ahfred nodded shakily and went inside. He thought of the shears as he passed the door. Not much of a weapon, but they were sharp and pointed. . . . He half turned, thinking to pick them up, but the woman had already done so.

"For the roses?" she asked.

Ahfred nodded again. He had been trying to forget things for so long that it was hard to remember anything useful that might help him now.

"Sit down," she instructed. "Not in that chair. That one."

Ahfred changed direction. Some old memories were coming

back. Harmless recollections that did not threaten his peace of mind. He remembered that it didn't matter what armchair he took; they all had the same controls and equipment. The house had been well prepared against assassins and other troubles long ago, but he had not restarted or checked any of the mechanisms after . . . well, when he had moved in. Ahfred did not choose to recall what had happened and preferred in his own head to consider this place his retirement home, to which he had removed as if in normal circumstances.

Even presuming that the advanced mechanisms no longer functioned, he now had some of the basic weapons at hand, the knives in the sides, the static dart throwers in the arms. The woman need merely stand in the right place . . .

She didn't. She stayed in the doorway, and now she did have a weapon in her hand. Or so Ahfred presumed, though again it was not anything he was familiar with. It looked like a ceramic egg and was quite a startling shade of blue. But there was a hole in the end, and it was pointed at him.

"You are to remain completely still, your mouth excepted," said the young woman. "If you move, you will be restrained, at the expense of some quite extraordinary pain. Do you understand?"

"Yes," said Ahfred. There had always been the risk of assassination when he was in office, but he had not thought about it since his retirement. If this woman was an assassin, he was very much puzzled by her origins and motivation. After all, he no longer had any power or influence. He was just a simple gardener, living a simple life in an exceedingly remote and private valley.

"You have confirmed that you are Ahfred Progressor III, the last head of state of the Technocratic Arch-Government," said the woman. "I believe among your many other titles you were also Keyholder and Elevated Arbiter of the Ultimate Arsenal?"

"Yes," said Ahfred. *What did she mean by "last head of state,"* he wondered. He wet his lips again and added, "Who are you that asks?"

"My name is Ruane," said the woman.

"That does not signify anything to me," said Ahfred, who heard the name as "Rain."

He could feel one of the control studs under his fingers, and if his memory served him correctly, it was for one of the very basic escape sequences. Unlike most of the weapons, it was not clockwerk powered, so it was more likely to have remained operational. Even the chance of it working lent him confidence.

"Indeed, I must ask by what right or authority you invade my home and force my acquiescence to this interrogation. It is most —"

In the middle of his speech, Ahfred reached for a concealed knife on one side of the chair and the escape stud on the right-hand arm.

Something shot out of the egg and splatted on Ahfred's forehead, very like the unwelcome deposit of a bird. He had an instant to crinkle his brow in surprise and puzzlement before an intense wave of agony ran through the bones of his skull and jaw and — most torturously for him — through his sensitive, sensitive ears.

Ahfred screamed. His body tensed in terrible pain. He could not grip the knife, but his fingers mashed the control stud on the chair. It rocked backward suddenly, but the panel that was supposed to open behind him slid only halfway before getting stuck. Ahfred was thrown against it rather than projected down the escape slide. He bounced off, rolled across the floor, and came to rest near the door.

As the pain ebbed, he looked up at Ruane, who had kept her place by the door.

"That was the least of the stings I could have given you," said Ruane. "It is only a temporary effect, without any lasting consequence. I have done so to establish that I will ask the questions and that you will answer, without further attempts to derail the proceedings. You may sit in the other chair."

Ahfred slowly got to his feet, his hands on his ears, and walked to the other chair. He sat down carefully and lowered his hands, wincing at the faint ringing sound of the escape panel's four springs, which were still trying to expand to their full length.

"I will continue," said Ruane. "Tell me, apart from you, who had access to the Ultimate Arsenal?"

"There were three keys," said Ahfred. "Two of the three were needed to access the arsenal. I held one. Mosiah Balance V, Mistress of the Controls, had the second. The third was under the control of Kebediah Oscillation X, Distributor of Harm."

"What was in the arsenal?"

Ahfred shifted a little before he remembered and made himself be still.

"There were many things —"

Ruane pointed the weapon.

"All the weapons of the ages," gabbled Ahfred. "Every invention of multiple destruction, clockwerk and otherwise, that had hitherto been devised."

"Had any of these weapons ever been used?"

"Yes. Many of the older ones were deployed in the War of Accretion. Others had been tested, though not actually used, there being no conflict to use them in."

"The War of Accretion was in fact the last such action before the formation of the Arch-Government, twenty-seven years ago," said Ruane. "After that, there was no Rival Nation, no separate political entities to go to war with."

"Yes."

"Was the absence of military conflict something you missed? I believe you served in the desert—in the Mechodromedary Cavalry—during the war, rising from ensign to colonel."

"I did not miss it," replied Ahfred, suppressing a shudder as the memory, so long forgotten, returned. The mechodromedaries had joints that clicked, and the ammunition for their shoulder-mounted multiguns came in bronze links that clattered as they fired, even though their magnetic propulsion was silent. Then there had been explosions, and screaming, and endless shouts. He had been forced to always wear deep earplugs and a sound-deadening spongiform helmet.

"Did Distributor Kebediah miss military conflict? She, too, served in the Accretion War, did she not?"

"Kebediah was a war hero," said Ahfred. "In the Steam Assault Infantry. But I do not believe she missed the war. No."

"Mistress Mosiah, then, was the one who wished to begin some sort of war?"

Ahfred shook his head, then stopped suddenly and gaped fearfully at his interrogator.

"You are permitted to shake your head in negation or nod in the affirmative," said Ruane. "I take it you do not believe Mistress Mosiah was the instigator of the new war?"

"Mosiah was not warlike," said Ahfred. A hint of a smile appeared at the corner of his mouth, quickly banished. "Quite the reverse. But I don't understand. May I . . . may I be permitted to ask a question?"

"Ask."

"To what war do you refer?"

"The war that approximately ten years ago culminated in the deployment of a weapon that killed nearly everyone on Earth and has destroyed all but fragments of the Technocratic civilization. Did it start with some kind of revolt from within?"

Ahfred hesitated a moment too long. Ruane pointed the egg weapon but did not fire. The threat was enough.

"I don't think there was a revolt," said Ahfred. Small beads of sweat were forming in the corners of his eyes and starting to trickle down beside his nose. "It's difficult to remember. . . . I am old, you know . . . quite old. . . . I don't recall a war, no—"

"But a weapon of multiple destruction *was* used?"

Ahfred stared at her. The sweat was in his eyes now, and he twitched and blinked to try to clear it.

"A weapon was used?" repeated Ruane. She raised the egg.

"Yes," said Ahfred. "I suppose . . . yes. . . ."

"What was that weapon?"

"Academician Stertour, its inventor, had a most complicated name for it . . . but we called it the Stopper," said Ahfred very slowly. He was being forced to approach both a memory and a part of his mind that he did not want to recall or even acknowledge might still exist.

"What was the nature and purpose of the Stopper?" asked Ruane.

Ahfred's lower lip trembled, and his hands began to shake.

"The Stopper . . . the Stopper . . . was a development of Stertour's sandgrain technology," he said. He could no longer look Ruane in the eyes but instead stared at the floor.

"Continue."

"Stertour came to realize that clockwerk sandgrain artifices could be made to be inimical to other artifices, that it would only be a matter of time before someone . . . an anarchist or radical . . . designed and constructed sandgrain warriors that would act against beneficial clockwerk, particularly the clockwerk in augmented humanity. . . ."

Ahfred stopped. Instead of the pale floorboards, he saw writhing bodies, contorted in agony, and smoke billowing from burning cities.

"Go on."

"I cannot," whispered Ahfred. He felt his carefully constructed persona falling apart around himself, all the noises of the greater world coming back to thrust against his ears, as they sought to surge against his brain. His protective circle of silence, the quiet of the roses, all were gone.

"You must," ordered Ruane. "Tell me about the Stopper."

Ahfred looked up at her.

"I don't want . . . I don't want to remember," he whispered.

"Tell me," ordered Ruane. She raised the egg, and Ahfred remembered the pain in his ears.

"The Stopper was a sandgrain artifice that would hunt and destroy other sandgrain artifices," he said. He did not talk to Ruane, but rather to his own shaking hands. "But it was not wound tightly and would only tick on for minutes, so it could be deployed locally against inimical sandgrain artifices without danger of it . . . spreading."

"But clearly the Stopper did spread, across the world," said Ruane. "How did that happen?"

Ahfred sniffed. A clear fluid ran from one nostril and over his lip.

"There were delivery mechanisms," he whispered. "Older weapons. Clockwerk aerial torpedoes, carded to fly over all significant cities and towns, depositing the Stopper like a fall of dust."

"But why were these torpedoes launched?" asked Ruane. "That is—"

"What?" sniffled Ahfred.

"One of the things that has puzzled us," said Ruane quietly. "Continue."

"What was the question?" asked Ahfred. He couldn't remember what they had been talking about, and there was work to be done in the garden. "My roses, and there is weeding—"

"Why were the aerial torpedoes launched, and who ordered this action?" asked Ruane.

"What?" whispered Ahfred.

Ruane looked at the old man, at his vacant eyes and drooping mouth, and changed her question.

"Two keys were used to open the Ultimate Arsenal," said Ruane. "Whose keys?"

"Oh, I took Mosiah's key while she slept," said Ahfred. "And I had a capture cylinder of her voice, to play to the lock. It was much easier than I had thought."

"What did you do then?" asked Ruane, as easily as asking for a glass of water from a friend.

Ahfred wiped his nose. He had forgotten the stricture to be still.

"It took all night, but I did it," he said proudly. "I took the sample of the Stopper to the fabrication engine and redesigned it myself. I'm sure Stertour would have been amazed. Rewound, each artifice would last for months, not hours, and I gave it better cilia, so that it might travel so much more easily!"

Ahfred smiled at the thought of his technical triumph, utterly divorcing this pleasure from any other, more troubling, memories.

"From there, the engine made the necessary ammunition to arm the torpedoes. One thousand and sixteen silver ellipsoids, containing millions of lovely sandgrain artifices, all of them sliding along the magnetic tubes, into the torpedoes, so quietly.... Then it took but a moment to turn the keys ... one ... two ... three ... and off they went into the sky—"

"Three keys?" asked Ruane.

"Yes, yes," said Ahfred testily. "Two keys to open the arsenal, three keys to use the weapons, as it has always been."

"So Distributor Kebediah was present?"

Ahfred looked out the doorway, past Ruane. There were many tasks in the garden, all of them requiring long hours of quiet, contemplative work. It would be best if he finished with this visitor quickly, so he could get back to work.

"Not at first," he said. "I had arranged for her to come. A state secret, I said, we must meet in the arsenal, and she came as we had arranged. Old comrades, old friends, she suspected nothing. I had a capture cylinder of her voice, too. I was completely prepared. I just needed her key."

"How did you get it?"

"The Stopper!" cackled Ahfred. He clapped his hands on his knees twice in great satisfaction. "Steam skeleton, sandgrain enhancement, she had it all. I had put the Stopper on her chair...."

Ahfred's face fell, and he folded his hands in his lap.

"It was horribly loud," he whispered. "The sound of the artifices fighting inside her, like animals, clawing and chewing, and her screaming, the boiler when the safety valve blew . . . it was unbearable, save that I had my helmet. . . ."

He looked around and added, "Where is my helmet? It is loud here, now, all this talking, and your breath, it is like a bellows, all a-huffing and a-puffing. . . ."

Ruane's face had set, hard and cold. When she spoke, her words came out with slow deliberation.

"How was it you were not affected by the Stopper?"

"Me?" asked Ahfred. "Everyone knows I have no clockwerk enhancement. Oh, no, I couldn't stand it, all that ticking inside me, that constant *tick . . . tick . . . tick . . .* It was bad enough around me, oh, yes, much too awful to have it inside."

"Why did you fire the torpedoes?" asked Ruane.

"Tell me who you are and I'll tell you," said Ahfred. "Then you may leave my presence, madam, and I shall return to my work . . . and my quiet."

"I am an investigator of what you termed the Rival Nation," said Ruane.

"But there is no Rival Nation," said Ahfred. "I remember that. We destroyed you all in the War of Accretion!"

"All here on Earth," said Ruane. The lines on her neck, that Ahfred had thought tattooes, opened to reveal a delicate layering of blue flukes, which shivered in contact with the air before the slits closed again. "You killed my grandparents, my great-uncles and great-aunts, and all my terrestrial kin. But not our future. Not my parents, not those of us in the far beyond, in the living ships. Long we prepared, myself since birth, readying ourselves to come back, to fight, to regain our ancestral lands and seas, to pit the creations of our minds against your clockwerk. But we found not an enemy, but a puzzle, the ruins of a once great, if misguided, civilization. And in seeking the answer to that puzzle, we have at last found you. *I* have found you."

"Bah!" said Ahfred. His voice grew softer as he went on. "I have no time for puzzles. I shall call my guards, assassin, and you will be . . . you will be . . ."

"Why did you fire the torpedoes?" asked Ruane. "Why did you use the Stopper? Why did you destroy your world?"

"The Stopper," said Ahfred. He shook his head, small sideways shakes, hardly moving his neck. "I had to do it. Nothing else would work, and it just kept getting worse and worse, every day—"

"What got worse?"

Ahfred stopped shaking his head and stood bolt upright, eyes staring, his back rigid, hands clapped to his ears. Froth spewed from between his clenched teeth and cascaded from his chin in pink bubbles, stained with blood from his bitten tongue.

"The noise!" he screamed. "The noise! A world of clockwerk, everybody and everything ticking, ticking, ticking, ticking—"

Suddenly the old man's eyes rolled back. His hands fell, but he remained upright for a moment, as if suspended by hidden wires, then fell forward and stretched out headlong on the floor. A gush of bright blood came from his ears before slowing to a trickle.

It was quiet after the Grand Technomancer fell. Ruane could hear her own breathing and the swift pumping of her hearts.

It was a welcome sound, but not enough, not now. She went outside and took a message swift from her pocket, licking the bird to wake it before she sent it aloft. It would bring her companions soon.

In the meantime, she began to whistle an old, old song.

Nowhere Fast

{ CHRISTOPHER ROWE }

Luz could see the future, or at least her future. It looked just like the present. The Saturday market was slow. This early in the spring, the only produce for sale was green onions and early lettuce, which most of the people in town grew in their own kitchen gardens. Even the stalls selling jars of canned vegetables and preserves from last year weren't doing much business.

She sat in her family's stall, waiting for someone to stop and buy some of her grandmother's canned salsa. At seventeen, Luz had spent every Saturday morning she could remember doing the same thing, and unless the worst happened and she was drafted into Federal service when she turned eighteen, then she imagined she would be doing the same thing on all the Saturday mornings to come.

Her grandmother sat quietly beside her, knitting a cap for one of Luz's countless cousins. The old cigar box open at their feet had just a few more coins and Federal notes than had been there at first light, when they had rolled up the tarp and set out their jars of salsa and tomato sauce and last year's green beans.

Luz heard a clattering noise in the distance and idly glanced past the low buildings of the square to where the coal balloons were tethered just outside the town limits. Federal treaties with Localists, like the townspeople, kept the government's flying ornithopters from the sky above Lexington, but Feds observed the letters of their agreements, never their spirits. Clusters of canvas balloons strung with thick hemp hawsers hung in the colorless sky. A brass-winged ornithopter had just landed in the ropes and clung there like a fly on a cow's tale. Someone below, out of sight, set a pulley to working, and skips full of coal began to rise up to feed the hungry machine.

If she did get drafted next year, at least there was a small chance she would fly in one of those machines, though it was more likely that she'd wind up working in the mines. Or, given all her father had taught her about tinkering and her mother about scavenging, she might wind up in the machine yards that were said to spread for hundreds of miles across the eastern states.

"There's better ways to fly," said her grandmother. Luz started and realized she had been staring at the ornithopter for several minutes. Her grandmother continued, "Like on that bicycle there you're always sneaking off to ride."

Luz nodded. "Or like your board when you were a girl, eh, abuela?" Unlike all of Luz's other relatives, her grandmother hadn't been born in Kentucky, but in California, so far away as to be a legend. Luz's abuela had seen an ocean; she had swum in it. Most fascinating of all to Luz, she had surfed it.

Before her grandmother could answer, Luz's brother Caleb brought his bike to a sliding stop next to the stall. He was two years younger than Luz, but six inches taller, all elbows and knees where Luz had already been all curves and muscles at that age. He had a wide grin on his usually somber face.

He had a sheet of gray paper rolled up and stuck in the waistband of his shorts, clearly a worksheet he'd pulled down from the post outside the community workhouse. Luz's grandmother smiled and said, "I suppose you're leaving early today, eh, Luza?"

Caleb nodded respectfully at his grandmother but spoke to Luz. "Invasive plant removal at Raven Run," he said. "They've got gloves and hand tools out there, so nothing to haul along. And we get four hours for travel time."

This was a good community service assignment. Raven Run was a nature preserve about fifteen miles away, on the limestone cliffs above the river. The old roads were still in decent shape in that end of the county, and there were some good hills along the way, especially if they took a route that went down to the river and back. Luz could make the ride straight to the preserve in forty minutes, and she wasn't even the strongest cyclist among her friends. They would have time to take a good long ride.

"How many slots?" asked Luz, heading around the back of the stall to her own bike.

"Four," said Caleb. "Um, Samuel was at the workhouse and already asked to come along. He's bringing one of his sisters."

Luz felt irritation pass over her face at the thought of Samuel and his hopeless crush on her. It wasn't that she didn't like him; it was just that he was like everything else in her life — known. Predictable. But she shrugged and said, "OK. Go round them up and meet me at the zero-mile marker in ten minutes. I'm going down to the shop to top off the air in my tires."

The shop was the stall run by their father that served as the main bike shop in town. He fixed the post office's long-haul cargo bikes for free in exchange for good rates on bringing in parts from the coast, but he always insisted that his children — and his other customers — make an honest attempt at repair before they settled for replacement.

Luz rolled in and nodded at her father. He was talking as he worked on a customer's bike, running through his bottomless inventory of crazy stories about old races and bike equipment made from the same material they used to use to make spaceships. He had even been to see the Tour de France, back before, when pretty much anybody could go overseas, even people who weren't rich or soldiers.

The customer made his escape while Luz was using a floor pump to air up her tires. When she looked up, her father was carefully routing a brake cable through an eyelet brazed onto the downtube of an old steel frame. He had his tongue between his teeth, concentrating, and greeted her with nothing more than a raised eyebrow.

"Just needed some air," said Luz.

Papa finished with the cable. "Off for a ride?" he asked.

"Community service at Raven Run," she said. "With plenty of time padded into the assignment for us to go down to the river and back."

Papa laughed. "They should weight the time allowances on those assignment sheets according to youth and vitality," he said. "Y'all should have to spend the extra time doing whatever needs doing out there instead of doing hill sprints up from the ferry. They figure the travel time based on old slowpokes like me."

Luz rolled her eyes. She'd tried to follow her father up the ferry climb a few times and never managed to hold his wheel.

"What needs doing at the preserve?" he asked. "I haven't been out there this year."

"I didn't see the sheet," said Luz, spinning the cap back onto the valve stem of her rear tire, "but Caleb said something about non-native species removal. Chopping out honeysuckle and English ivy, I guess."

Her father nodded. "We've been working on that for years."

Luz shrugged. "It does seem like it always comes back. But we have to try."

He mounted a wheel on a truing stand and spun it. "Why?" he asked. This was something else she knew to expect from her father, in addition to his stories. Lessons disguised as questions.

Luz pretended he was talking about the wheel and watched the considerable wobble as it turned. "Looks like maybe they T-boned a curb?"

Papa shook his head. "No. Well, yes, that's what happened to this wheel. But I meant why do we keep trying to pull all of the honeysuckle out of Raven Run?"

Luz knew this one. It was one of the central tenets of Localism. "Because they're invasive. They don't integrate; they displace." And then she added, "I'll see you tonight, Papa."

She shouted this last, because she was already rolling out of the stall and down the street, clicking up through the gears, weaving among carts pulled by pedestrians and cyclists and tall horses.

Caleb was the mapmaker and route finder. He usually based their rides on arcane themes, like Ride to the Location of Every

Post Office Closed in Bourbon County Between 1850 and 2050 (a circuitous hundred miler through sparsely populated farm country) and Turn Right Instead of Crossing Any Creek or Stream (also circuitous, but very short). The inevitable starting point of all his routes was the county's zero mile marker, an old statue of a camel set atop a dolmen in Phoenix Park. They'd grown so used to starting there that it was their common meeting point even for unplanned rides like today's.

Luz found Caleb waiting, talking with Samuel and, unexpectedly, his youngest sister, little Priscilla. Samuel was Luz's age and the only son in a family of many daughters. His mother doted on him, and he could almost always get out of whatever work he was doing at the pottery they ran. This was the first time, though, that Pris had ever come along on one of their rides.

The twelve-year-old girl sat on the saddle of a road bike that was just barely small enough for her. She'd lowered the seat all the way and was balancing herself against the mile marker. She studied the marker while the others talked.

"Hey, Miss Priss," said Luz. "Gonna try to keep up with the big kids today?"

Priscilla gritted her teeth and pointed to her flexed quads. "Don't slow me down too much, Luza!" She laughed at herself before pointing to the inscription below the statue. "What's AAA?"

"You asked for it," said Samuel. "You get to ride in the back with Caleb while he explains."

Luz led them out along Main Street, quickly leaving downtown behind and racing the long straight lane through the necklace of orchards that encircled the city. She heard Caleb's voice floating up from behind when the wind was right, catching phrases like "automobile association" and "U.S. route system" and "the call of the open road."

"I know what that means," she said, half to herself.

Samuel was drafting her closely and overheard. "You know what what means?"

They had just passed between the crumbling concrete pillars of an old divided highway and had topped a rise. The road stretched out straight before them, sloping down along a gentle grade for a couple of miles, smooth and empty but for a few people walking along the grassy shoulders.

Luz pointed ahead with her chin. "Call of the open road," she said. "I know what that means."

Luz couldn't believe that tiny Priscilla was steadily pulling away from her on the long climb up from the ferry. She pushed harder on her bicycle's pedals, trying to match the rhythm of the turning wheels to her rapid breathing. Still, the younger girl danced on ahead, standing on her pedals and apparently unaware that she was leaving Luz and the others behind.

Near the top of the hill, Priscilla signaled a stop, and Luz thought she was finally tiring. But then the girl spoke.

"Is that an engine?" Priscilla asked, eyes wide.

Luz stopped beside her, struggling to slow her breath so she could better hear the howling sound floating over the fields. Hard to say how far away the noise was, but it was clearly in motion. And moving closer, fast.

Caleb and Samuel stopped beside them and dismounted.

"It is," said Caleb, curiosity in his voice. "Internal combustion, not too big."

"Not like on any of the Federal machines, though," Samuel added. "Not like anything I've ever heard."

Luz thought of the last time one of the great Army recruitment trucks had come through Lexington, grinding and belching and trumpeting its horn. It had been the previous autumn. Her parents had made her hide in one of the sheds behind the house, even though she was still too young for the draft. She had stood behind a tidy stack of aluminum doors her mother had salvaged from the ghost suburbs south of town and listened to the engine closely.

The Army engine had made a deeper sound than this, though whatever was approaching was not as high as the mosquito buzz of the little motors on the sheriff's department chariots. If the deputies rode mosquitoes, then the Federals rode growling bears. This was something in between: a howling wolf.

The noise dropped away briefly, stuttered, and then came back louder than ever.

"Whatever it is, it just turned into the lane," Luz told the others. She dismounted and waved for them all to move their bikes into the grassy verge to one side. They'd stopped at a point where the road was bound on either side by low dry-stone walls. A pair of curious chestnut quarter horses, fully biological, not the hissing machine-hybrid mounts of Federal outriders, ambled over briefly, hopeful of treats, but they snorted and trotted away as the noise came closer.

Suddenly, the sound blared as loud as anything Luz had ever heard, and a ... vehicle rounded the curve before them. Luz flashed on the automobile carcasses some people kept as tomato planters. She saw four wheels, a brace of fifty-five-gallon drums, and a makeshift seat. The seat was occupied by a distracted-looking young man wrestling a steering wheel as he hurtled past them, forcing them to move even farther off the road.

The vehicle fishtailed from side to side on the crumbling pavement, sputtering, and came to an abrupt halt when it took a hard left turn and hit the wall on the south side of the road. The top two layers of rock slid into the field as the noise died away.

They all ran toward the crash. Luz could see now that the vehicle was a modified version of a hay wagon, sporting thick rubber tires and otherwise liberally outfitted with ancient automobile parts. The seat was a cane-bottomed rocker with the legs removed, screwed to the bed. The driver was strapped into the chair and had a dazed expression on his face.

He was younger than Luz had first thought, just a little older than she, maybe. He had tightly curled black hair and green eyes. He blinked at them.

The huge metal engine that took up most of the wagon bed ticked.

"I think . . .," he began, and trailed off, lips still moving, eyes still unfocused. "I think I need to adjust the braking mechanism."

He claimed, unbelievably, that he was from North Carolina. Hundreds of miles away, the other side of mountains with collapsed tunnels and rivers with fallen bridges. In Luz's experience, traffic from the east came into the Bluegrass along only two routes: down from the Ohio off boats from Pittsburgh or along the Federal highway through Huntington.

"No, no," the driver said, piling the last rock back on top of the wall his machine had damaged. "I didn't come over the mountains. I went south first, then along the Gulf shore, then up the Natchez Trace through Alabama and middle Tennessee. The state government in Tennessee is pretty advanced. They've built pontoon bridges over all their rivers now."

Luz reached behind Fizz—that was the unlikely name he'd given—and made an adjustment to the slab of limestone he'd haphazardly dropped atop the wall. That he had accepted their offer to help him repair the fence turned out to be a good thing, because it was clear that he had no experience with dry-stone work. For some reason, this made him seem even more foreign to Luz than his vehicle or his claim to have seen the ocean. Samuel had whispered his opinion that Fizz would have left the wall in disrepair if they hadn't witnessed the crash, but Luz wasn't ready to be that judgmental.

Samuel was also more persistent in his questions than Luz thought was polite. "Well, then how did you cross the Kentucky River? And the Green and all the creeks you must have come to? We just came from the ferry and they would have mentioned you. And there's no way the Federals would have let you bring that thing across any of their bridges."

"There's more local bridges than you might think," said Fizz, either completely missing the hostility in Samuel's voice or ignoring it. "I only had to float Rudolf once. See the air compressor there? I can fill old inner tubes and lash them to the sides. That converts him into a raft, good enough for the width of a creek."

Caleb was examining the vehicle. "There are a lot of bridges that aren't on the Federal map," he said, almost to himself. Then he asked, "Why do you call it Rudolf?"

"Rudolf Diesel," said Fizz, in a different, stranger accent than most of his speech. He seemed to think that answered Caleb's question.

Priscilla whispered, "He speaks German." Luz found Priscilla's instant and obvious crush on Fizz annoying.

Fizz looked at the girls. "Sure, he did," he said, and smiled at Luz. "He was German. He probably spoke like eleven languages, not just English and Spanish. Everybody did back then. He designed this engine — or its ancestor, anyway." He pointed to the cooling metal engine on his vehicle.

"I hope you paid him for it," said Samuel.

"No, I remember," said Caleb. "Diesel was one of the men who made the internal combustion engines." A troubled expression crossed his face. "That's from history. You shouldn't tell people you named your car after him, Fizz."

Fizz wrinkled his nose and brow, scoffing. "Figures the only thing the Federals are consistent about are their interstate highway monopolies and their curriculum suggestions. Diesel wasn't a bad guy. Don't you guys have grandparents? Don't they talk about when everybody could go everywhere?"

Some do, Luz thought. Aloud, she said, "Our abuela has been everywhere. She came here from California before the oil finally ran out."

"And we can go anywhere we like," said Samuel. "We just like it here."

"But going places takes forever," said Fizz. Then he finally seemed to notice the uncomfortable glances being shared between Caleb and Samuel. "Not that this isn't a great place to be. The hemp-seed oil Rudolf is burning for fuel right now is from around here someplace. Or it was. My tanks are about dry. That's why I turned north when the Tennesseans wouldn't trade me any."

Luz nodded. "Sure. The biggest oil press anywhere is over in

Frankfort. Our uncles sell them most of their hemp. What have you got to trade that the Feds would want?"

Fizz made the face again. "They're not much for bartering with people like me."

"And who's that?" asked Samuel. "Who are people like you?"

Fizz looked them all up and down, deciding something.

Then he said, "Revolutionaries."

"Revolting is more like it," Samuel gasped. He and Luz were working very hard, barely turning the pedals of their bikes over in their lowest gears. Fizz had brought out some cords from the toolbox on his machine, and between them, he and Luz had figured out a way to rig a Y harness connecting the automobile's front axle to the seatposts of her and Samuel's bikes. The others rode behind the automobile, hopping off to push on the hills.

Except for Fizz, who rode the machine the whole time, manning the steering wheel and chattering happily to curious Caleb and smitten Priscilla. Luz wished she could be back there. She had a thousand questions about the wider world.

Fizz had insisted they take a little used, poorly surfaced route into town. He said he wanted to approach the council of farmers and merchants, who acted as the community council, before they saw his machine. "I had trouble some places," he said. "Farther south."

Responding to Samuel, Luz asked, "What's revolting?"

He answered her with a question. "Do you know what we're pulling? I'll tell you. It's a car. A private car."

Luz took her left hand off the handlebars long enough to point out a particularly deep pothole in the asphalt. Samuel acknowledged with a nod, and they bore to the right.

"Don't be silly," Luz continued after they'd negotiated the hole. "Cars ran on oil. Petroleum oil, I mean."

But Luz had already noticed that a lot of the machine's parts were similar to those she found when she went scrounging with her mother. The steering wheel, for one thing, was plastic, and plastic was the very first word in the list of nonrenewables she'd memorized in grade school.

"Well, I guess he made a car that runs on hemp-seed oil," said Samuel. "Or somebody did." Samuel doubted every part of Fizz's story, even his name. "He probably stole it off the Federals."

Luz doubted that. Federals used their Army trucks, a few bicycles, the coal-burning horses that patrolled the highways, and the ornithopters. They all shared a sleek, machined design. Nothing at all like the haphazard jumble of Fizz's "car."

The group managed to attract only a few stares before they made it to one of the sheds behind Luz's and Caleb's house. Luz supposed that people assumed they'd found a heap of scrap metal and had knocked together a wagon on-site to transport it to their mother's salvage shops. People brought her old things all the time.

"Are you going to get your father?" Samuel asked. "Because you should." Then, unusually, he left before Luz asked him to, saying he had to get home.

His little sister, however, clearly had no intention of leaving. She wordlessly followed Fizz as he crawled around, checking the undercarriage of his machine.

"I guess this job posting is open all week," said Caleb, pulling the paper out from his belt. Luz had completely forgotten the original purpose of their ride. "Maybe we can go on Wednesday if we can get enough people."

"Sure," said Luz.

"So it's OK if I work here?" Fizz asked. "You won't get in trouble?"

Caleb was worried. "Our father will be home soon —"

"Wait," Luz interrupted. Fizz and his car were the most interesting thing that had happened to Luz in a long time. Or ever, if she was honest with herself. "Mama's in the mountains, gleaning in the tailings from the old mines. I'll go to the shop and talk to Papa."

"That'd be great," said Fizz, popping his head out from under the machine, right at their feet. "Looks like you've probably got everything I need to get Rudolf up and running."

Luz left quickly, knowing it would be better for them all if her father knew what was waiting for him at home.

Luz's father moved around the stall, putting away tools and hanging bikes from hooks in the ceiling. "Yes, he could have driven here from North Carolina," he told Luz. "Before the Peak, people made the trip in a few hours."

Luz didn't doubt that her father was telling the truth, but something about his claim felt off. She thought of how she could feel the truth when somebody said that the sun was hot, but she could only acknowledge the truth when somebody said it was ninety-three million miles away.

"That's what he was talking about, I guess," she said. "Fizz. When he said that it takes forever to go anywhere now."

Without warning, her father dropped the seatpost he was holding to the shop floor. It made a dull clattering sound as it bounced back and forth on the wide oak boards.

"Hey!" said Luz as he grabbed her arm, hard, and pulled her out the open end of the stall.

Out in the street, he let go and pointed up at the sky. "Look up there!" he barked.

Luz had never heard her father sound so angry. It was hard to tear her eyes away from his livid face, but he thrust his finger skyward again. "Look!" he said.

Luz stared at the sky, gray and cloudless as ever in the spring heat.

"That is a bruised sky," he said, punctuating his words with his hand. "That is a torn-up sky."

His mood suddenly changed in a way that made Luz think of a deflating tire. He leaned against the corner support pole of the shop. "You don't know what our ancestors did to this world. There's so much less of everything. And if there is one reason for it, it's in what this stranger told you. *Forever*, hah! It takes as long to get somewhere as it should take—his expedience leads to war and flood."

Luz didn't understand half of what he was saying.

"What about the Federals?" she asked. "They drive trucks and have flying machines."

Papa waved his hand. "We are not the Federals. We live lightly upon the earth, light enough that the wounds they deal it will heal. Your grandparents' generation fought wars so that we could rescue the world from excess. People like us act as stewards; we save the rivers and the sky and the land from the worst that people like them do. When you're older you'll understand."

Luz considered that for a moment, then said, "People like us and people like the Federals?"

Papa looked at her. "Yes, Luz."

"What about people that aren't like either?" Luz asked.

Papa hadn't answered her before Priscilla came tearing down

the street. "Luz! They took him! They came and took Fizz and his machine both! Caleb couldn't stop them!"

She slid to a halt next to them in a cloud of dust. "It was Samuel! He brought the deputies!"

Luz instantly hopped on her bike and saw from the corner of her eye that her father was pulling his own out from behind the workbench. She didn't wait for him to catch up.

Hours later, Luz and Caleb pedaled along abandoned streets behind the tannery and the vinegar works, searching for the stockade where the deputies had taken Fizz. They might have missed him if he hadn't shouted to them.

"Hey! Luz!"

Fizz was leaning half out of a ground-floor window in an old brick building set in an unkempt lawn of weeds and trash. As they rode over to him, a deputy rounded the corner and told Fizz to stay inside the window. Clearly, the deputies weren't used to having prisoners. When Caleb asked if they could speak to Fizz, the man shrugged and instructed them not to let him escape.

"The trial's tonight," the deputy said, then went back to the corner, where he sat on a stool and idly turned the letterpressed pages of last week's town newsletter.

"I've had it worse, that's for sure," Fizz told them. "They seem a lot more concerned with Rudolf than they are with me. I hope your father didn't get in trouble for its being at your house."

Luz and Caleb glanced at each other. The car had been much easier to locate than its driver. It had been dragged to the front yard of the courthouse.

"No," said Luz. "Papa's fine."

"I don't think Rudolf will be able to say the same," Caleb said, "when this is over."

Fizz's serious expression made Luz notch her guess of his age up another year or two. But then he flashed a wide grin and said, "Rudolf's never offered an opinion on anything at all, Caleb. We hit the road before I figured out how to make him talk."

When they didn't join his laughter, Fizz said, "I see that you're worried. Don't be. I've been in communities like yours before. Heck, I've even been in jails like this one before. Your council and"—he raised his eyebrow—"I'm guessing your father, too? They're more concerned about the presence of the machine than the machinist. They'll debate and storm and glower about what to do with me and Rudolf for an hour and then send us on our way."

Luz said, "Papa's name came up in the lottery at New Year's, so he is on the council this year. And, yes, he's concerned about the machine and its being here. But I think he's even more concerned about the use you put it to."

Fizz didn't reply. He gazed at her steadily, as if she knew the answer to a question he'd forgotten to ask aloud.

"'Everybody could go everywhere,'" she finally said, quoting him.

"Ah," Fizz said. "Your friend said that everybody still can."

Luz shook her head. "I don't think Samuel is my friend anymore. And anyway," she added, her voice unexpectedly bitter, "he's never wanted to go anywhere."

Fizz was sympathetic. "What about you?" he asked her. "Where would you go if you could?"

Luz thought about it for a moment. She remembered Fizz's description of his route along the Gulf of Mexico, but even more, she remembered her grandmother's stories of California.

"I would go to the ocean," she said. "My grandmother was a surfer. You know, on the waves?" She held her palm out flat and rocked it back and forth.

Fizz nodded.

"She says that I'm built right for it. It sounds . . . fast."

"And light on the earth, too," Fizz said. "That's the saying, right?"

"Close," said Caleb, frowning at them both. "It's 'lightly upon the earth.'"

Luz had never thought about how often she heard the phrase. It was something said in the community over and over again. "How did you know people say that here?" she asked.

Fizz shrugged. "People say it everywhere."

Luz had expected her father and the other council members to be arrayed behind a long table in the courtyard square. She had expected the whole town to turn out to watch the proceedings — and even for Fizz to be marched out by the deputies with his hands tied before him with a coil of rope.

She had not expected Federal marshals.

There were two of them, a silver-haired man and a grim-faced woman. Neither of them bothered to dismount their strange half-machine horses, only issuing terse orders to the closest towns-people to fetch pails of coal, which they then turned into the furnaces atop the hybrid creatures' hindquarters. They seemed impatient, as was ever the way with Federals.

Luz sat on the ground in front of a bench crowded with older people, leaning against her grandmother's knees. "I thought the covenants between the town and the Federals guaranteed us the right to have our own trials," Luz said.

Her abuela patted her shoulder, though there was nothing of reassurance in it. "My son," she said, speaking of Luz's father, "is more afraid of what this Fizz can do to us than what the Federals can. The council asked the marshals here."

Before Luz could express her dismay at this news, the council chair banged on the table with a wrench to quiet the crowd. "We're in extraordinary session, people," she said, "and the only order of business is the forbidden technology this boy from . . . North Carolina has brought to our town."

Before anything more could be said, Luz's father raised his hand to be recognized. "I move we close this meeting," he said. "We'll be talking of things our children shouldn't be made to hear."

The gathered townspeople murmured at this, and Luz was surprised at the tone. She would have expected them to be upset that they couldn't watch the proceedings, but — except for the others her age — most sounded like they were agreeing with her father. Before any of the council members could respond to the suggestion, Fizz spoke up.

"I believe I'm allowed to speak?" he asked. "That's been the way of it with the other town councils."

Luz saw the woman marshal lean over in her saddle and whisper something to her partner, whose dead-eyed gaze never shifted from Fizz.

The chairwoman saw the exchange, too, and seemed troubled by it. "Yes," she told Fizz. "We've heard this isn't the first time you've been brought up on these charges. But you should be careful you don't say anything to incriminate yourself. It might not be us that carries out whatever sentence we decide on."

Fizz looked directly at the marshals and then at the council. "Yes, ma'am," he said. "I see that. I've not been in a town controlled by the Federal government before."

Luz's father's angry interruption cut through the noise from the crowd. "Here, now!" he said. "We're as sovereign as any other town in America and signatory to covenants that reserve justice to ourselves. It's our laws you've flouted and our ruling that will decide your fate. These marshals are here at our invitation because we want to demonstrate how seriously we take your crimes. And to tell us what other crimes you've committed before now."

Luz did not realize she had stood until she spoke. "What crimes?"

Her father frowned at her. "Sit down, Luza," he said.

Before she could respond, Fizz spoke. "I can choose someone of the Locality to speak on my behalf, isn't that right? I choose her. I want Luz to be my advocate."

To Luz's surprise—to everyone's surprise—the voice that answered did not come from the council, but from one of the Federals.

"Oh, for God's sake," the woman said, directing her words to the woman at the head of the council table. "Salma, we came here to destroy this unauthorized car as a favor to you, not to watch you Luddites play at justice."

The councilwoman answered, "You know our ways, Marshal. We must reach a verdict against this . . . what did you say his name is again?"

Luz expected Fizz to speak up, but to her surprise, the marshal answered. "His name is Humility-Before-the-Lord Bradford. He was a ward of the Localist Shaker chapter at Tobaccoville in North Carolina."

"*Was*, you say?" the councilwoman asked. "He was expelled?"

The marshal shrugged. "He left. The Shakers don't have as good a retention rate as you do."

For the first time, Fizz appeared confused, even frightened.

The marshal spoke on. "Vehicles like this are against our laws, no matter what your play council decides," she said. "We don't have to wait for any verdict to deal with the evidence." With that, she and her partner whistled high and hard.

The marshals dismounted and the horses leaped.

Their lips curled back, exposing spikes where an unaltered horse's teeth would be. Long claws extended from the dewlaps above their steel-shod hooves, and the muscles rippling beneath their flanks were square and hard. They jumped to opposite sides of the car, steam and smoke belching from their noses and ears as they struck and bit, kicked and tore. The sounds of metal ripping and wood splitting rang across the square, frighteningly loud, yet still not loud enough to drown the cries of the children in the crowd. Luz was as shocked by the sounds the horses made as she was by the savagery of their assault.

In moments, the car called Rudolf was a pile of scrap metal and wood. The horses' spikes and claws retracted as they trotted back to their riders, who waited with more skips of coal to replenish what the horses had burned up in the destruction.

No one spoke. Luz watched Fizz blink, as dazed as when they'd met him.

Finally, the Federals swung into their saddles and the woman turned to the councilwoman once more. "Do you want us to take your prisoner off your hands, too? We're better equipped to deal with his kind than you."

"No!" said Luz.

The attention of the crowd fell on her like a weight. She said, "You've destroyed enough. You . . . get away from here."

The woman and the dead-eyed man exchanged ugly grins, waiting. When no one protested, the marshals put the spurs to their mounts and left the square.

Luz turned to the council. "And you . . . What is all this? Papa, you can't stand the Federals and their ways. None of you can. You'd put us in their debt for something you wouldn't even discuss in front of us?"

Of all the people sitting behind the table, only her father would meet her gaze.

"We protect our children from such concerns until they've reached their majority, Luz," he said. "You know that. But since you all just saw . . . what we all just saw . . ." He hesitated for a moment. "It's what I said earlier, Luz," he continued. "Your friend there has a personal car, and that's the source of so much bad in the world that I can't even begin to explain it to you. It can't be allowed."

Luz rolled her eyes and walked over to the pile of debris that had been Rudolf. She pointed to it and said, "This, you mean? It doesn't look to me like he has a car anymore."

She expected Fizz to agree, but he was still staring at the wreckage. For once, he had nothing to say.

But I'm his advocate, she remembered.

"You should let him go," she said. "We should let him go."

Before her father could respond, the chairwoman called him closer. They exchanged a few murmured words. Then she said, "The young man is no longer a danger to our community, or to the earth. He's free to go. This meeting is at an end."

Luz's father added, "He must go."

The council members rose, and the people in the crowd stood and milled around, everyone talking about what had just happened. Luz spotted her father approaching, and then she saw her abuela shake her head to stop him from coming nearer.

Luz thought about what she had learned from her father about making and repairing things. She thought about what she had learned from her mother about scavenging. She thought of the stories told to her by her grandmother of gliding across an ocean's wave.

Luz went to Fizz. She put her hand on his shoulder, whoever he was. "I know where we can get some parts," she said.

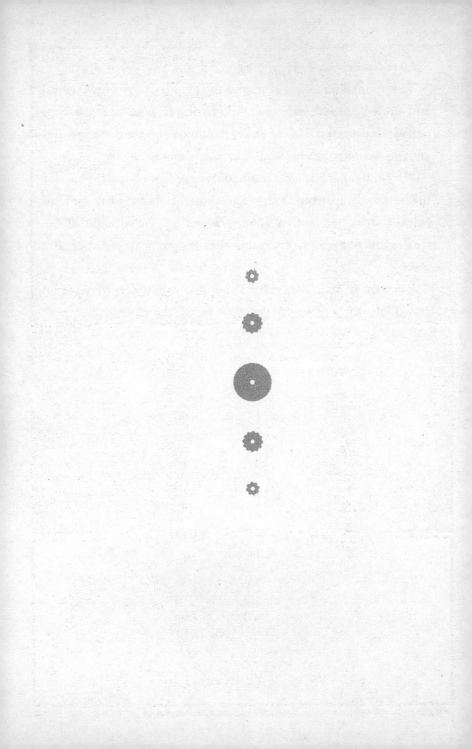

WITH APOLOGIES TO VARIOUS 19TH-CENTURY ILLUSTRATORS AND TO ALL WHO DIDN'T FIT THE MACHINE OF EMPIRE

BEFORE GWEN'S FATHER DIED, HE AND MY UNCLE WROTE TO EACH OTHER ABOUT THE POSSIBILITIES OF NONGASEOUS FLIGHT. IN HIS WILL, MY UNCLE PROVIDED FOR GWEN AND ME TO ATTEND HIS SCHOOL.

Sufficient propulsion

my wife & infant daughter

gravity

but I fear Sher...

Nothing Ventured...

WE WERE, AT BEST, SECOND-CLASS CITIZENS.

YOU TWO WILL SHARE A ROOM UNDER THE ATTIC STOREROOMS, WHERE YOU WILL BE OUT OF THE WAY OF THE STUDENTS WHO ARE ADMITTED ON MERIT, AND LESS OF A CORRUPTING INFLUENCE.

HOPE THE *RATS* DON'T MIND YOU!

PHREN-OLOGY FOR BEGINNERS

NEW!

WE WERE NEVER GOING TO FIT IN.

I LIKED SKULLS, AND NOT JUST WHEN THE SCHOOL PLAY WAS *HAMLET.*

I HAD THE SAME NAME AS THE SCHOOL'S FOUNDER, AND HE HAD BEEN A DANGEROUSLY INSANE INVENTOR.

THEY SAY HIS UNSPEAKABLE EXPERIMENTS ARE STILL ROTTING IN THE ATTIC!

AND AS FOR GWEN ...

IF YOU'RE THE OUTSPOKEN, LEFT-HANDED DAUGHTER OF AN IRISH OUTLAW AND A CHINESE PUBLICAN, YOU START AT A DISADVANTAGE ...

BUT GWEN NEVER SAW IT THAT WAY.

GWEN PURSUED HER AIMS AGGRESSIVELY.

GWEN!

MY HAT!

PATENT CYCLING ACCESSORIES

BUT TIME SEEMED AGAINST US...

WHILE THE TEACHER DID HER BEST TO CONVERT US TO HER POINT OF VIEW.

GIRLS, I AM DELIGHTED TO ANNOUNCE THAT THAT *HERO OF THE COLONIES,* AND CONDESCENDING PATRON OF OUR SCHOOL, *CAPTAIN SHERRITT,* WILL ATTEND OUR GRADUATION TEA TOMORROW,

OH, NO! I HAVEN'T FINISHED MY COMPOSITION!

YOU WILL BE ABLE TO PRESENT YOUR PROJECTS ON THE MORAL EXAMPLE SET BY DIRIGIBLES AS THE TRANSPORT OF THE FUTURE TO HIM *PERSONALLY.*

NEITHER HAVE I.

IF GWEN'S PLAN WAS DISCOVERED, OR SHE LEFT THE SCHOOL AND THE SECRETS IN ITS ATTICS, SHE WOULD NEVER GET A CHANCE LIKE THIS AGAIN. I DO NOT KNOW IF THE THOUGHT WEIGHED AS HEAVILY ON HER AS IT DID ON ME.

I HOPE THE *DEAR CAPTAIN* WILL BE IMPRESSED BY OUR DILIGENCE.

GLIDERS

BY NOW, IT SEEMED TO ME THAT IF GWEN COULDN'T DO SOMETHING REMARKABLE, SOMEONE LIKE ME NEVER WOULD.

SCHOOL PROPERTY. DO NOT REMOVE

THUNK-thunk-THUNK-thunk-THUNK-THUNK

Steam Girl

{ DYLAN HORROCKS }

The first time I see her, she's standing alone behind the library, looking at the ground. Faded blue dress, scruffy leather jacket, long lace-up boots, and black-rimmed glasses. But what really makes me stop and stare is the hat: a weird old leather thing that hangs down over her ears, with big thick goggles strapped to the front.

Turns out she's in my English class. She sits right next to me, still wearing the jacket and goggles and hat. She smells like a thrift store.

"Weirdo," says Michael Carmichael.

"Freak," says Amanda Anderson.

She ignores the laughter, reaching into her bag for a notebook and pencil. She bends low so no one can see what she's writing.

Later, when Mrs. Hendricks is dealing with an outbreak of giggles at the front of the class, I lean over and whisper, "What's with the hat?"

She glances at me with a tiny frown, then turns back to her notebook. Her eyebrows are the color of cheese.

"Not a *hat*," she says without looking up. "Helmet. *Flying* helmet."

"Huh," I say. "So what are you — a pilot?"

And then she raises her eyes and smiles straight at me, kind of sly.

"Steam Girl," she says.

"What's *Steam Girl?*"

Then Mrs. Hendricks starts shouting, and the whole class shuts up.

That afternoon she's waiting for me by the school gate. I check that no one's watching before say I hello.

"Here," she says, handing me the notebook. It's a cheap school exercise book, with a creased cover and fraying corners. On the first page is a title, in big blue letters:

STEAM GIRL

Below that is a drawing of a slimmer, prettier version of the girl in front of me: blue dress, leather jacket, lace-up boots, flying helmet, and goggles. But in the drawing it looks *awesome* instead of, well, weird.

"Did you do this?" I say. "It's pretty good."

"Thanks." She reaches over and turns the pages. There are more drawings and diagrams: a flying ship shaped like a cigar, people in old-fashioned diving suits swimming through space, strange alien landscapes, strange clockwork gadgets, and of course, Steam Girl — leaping from the airship, fighting off monsters, laughing and smiling. . . .

"So who's Steam Girl?" I ask.

"She's an adventurer," she says. "Well, her *father's* an adventurer, and an explorer and scientist. But she goes everywhere with him, in their experimental steam-powered airship, the *Martian Rose*."

"Steam Girl makes gadgets." She rummages around in her bag, finally holding up what looks like a rusty old Swiss Army knife. Screwdrivers and pliers and mangled bits of wire stick out in all directions. There's even a tiny wooden teaspoon.

"The Mark II Multifunctional Pocket Engineering Device," she announces triumphantly. "One of Steam Girl's first — and best — gadgets. Got them out of many a scrape, like the time they were captured by troglodytes on the moon and locked in an underground zoo...."

She's talking pretty fast and waving her arms in the air, and I take a step back to avoid getting stabbed by that thing in her hand.

"Steam Girl used this to pick the lock on their cage, and they managed to get back to the *Martian Rose* just in time," she continues, half closing her eyes. "As they lifted into space, the troglodytes in their tunnels howled so loud that the ground shivered and shook and the moondust rippled like windswept waves...."

"Um ..." I don't know what to say. "So you — uh — you made all this up, huh?"

She goes very quiet. Then she grabs the notebook out of my hands and shoves it into her bag.

"See ya," she says, and runs off before I can reply.

I've never been what you'd call a popular kid. I'm not very smart, I'm lousy at sports, and between the oversize teeth and the woolly black hair, I'm kind of goofy looking. My mom always says I have "hidden talents," but I gave up looking for them a long time ago. I'm used to being on my own.

I have *had* friends. In fact, once upon a time I used to hang out with Amanda Anderson, the prettiest girl in school. We live on the same street, and when I was six or seven, her mother used to visit my mom for coffee. Amanda and I would play together with LEGOs and dolls and stuff like that. My parents didn't approve of gender stereotypes, so sometimes they'd buy me girls' toys. I had a pretty cool dollhouse and some Barbie accessories that Amanda adored. It was all the same to me; I'd play with anything.

But one day at school, Amanda told everyone about my Barbie dolls. You can imagine the mocking I got after that. When I told my parents what happened, they called Amanda's mother on the phone and they never came for coffee again.

I'm glad my parents stood up for me, but I kind of wish they hadn't made a scene. I mean, it's not like Amanda and I were best friends or anything; we hardly said a word to each other at school. But she was really pretty, even back then, and I guess I hoped that one day, maybe.... Well, you get the idea.

What's really sad and pathetic is that I still have hopes, after all these years. You know, like in movies, when the hot popular girl suddenly falls totally in love with the unpopular nerd and dumps the arrogant macho football jock? Only, in the movies the unpopular nerd is played by a good-looking film star, while in real life he's played by *me*.

These days Amanda goes out with Michael Carmichael, who hit puberty three years before I did and plays bass in a hardcore band, and who once put a lit cigarette down my trousers on the way home from school. It took nearly five minutes to get the damn thing out, and I ended up with blisters in places you don't want to know about. I don't really get why Michael's such an asshole. It's like he feels personally offended when someone is ugly or stupid or clever or different. Like it makes him really angry. I almost feel sorry for him, being like that. But then he pushes past me in the hallway with Amanda Anderson on his arm and I don't feel sorry anymore.

Anyway, as I was saying, I don't really have any friends. Most of the time that's OK. At home I play a lot of online games by myself. I know a lot of people treat those games as a big social thing, with loads of chatting and friending and all that. But not me. I just go on quests and kill monsters and level up and earn gold and stuff. That's what I like about it: even a loser like me can actually *achieve* something, just by pushing keys and putting in the hours. I wish real life were more like that.

Now and then, the loneliness is more than I can bear. So I try things like smiling at people in class. Sometimes they smile back. And sometimes they look like they want to punch me or else throw up. And then I feel worse than ever. Once, I smiled at Amanda and she smiled back. Then after class Michael pushed me up against the wall and told me to stop creeping out his girlfriend.

So when the new girl ambushed me at the gate, I didn't know what to think. Is she stalking me? I've never had a stalker before (obviously), but I sometimes wish I did. But in the fantasies, my stalker would be gorgeous, blonde, and crazy with lust. Not just, y'know, *crazy*....

Still, I have to admit, that notebook is pretty damn cool. That night as I'm lying in bed, my mind keeps drifting back to the shivering moondust, the *Martian Rose*, and — of course — Steam Girl. Who, come to think of it, *is* gorgeous and blonde.

So in the morning, when I see that leather flying helmet bobbing along in a sluggish tide of hoodies and greasy hair, I find myself pushing through the crowd to catch up.

"Hey," I say as casually as I can.

She barely looks up. "Hey."

"How come I didn't see you before last week? Did you move here or something?"

Instead of answering, she takes hold of my arm and steers me out of the flow and into an empty alcove. I'm too surprised to speak.

"Listen," she says, still holding my arm. "Do you want to meet me at lunchtime?"

"Uh . . . sure. I guess." I'm not *at all* sure I want to, but what else can I say?

"By the incinerator. A quarter past twelve." She makes it sound like a mysterious secret rendezvous.

And then she lets go of my arm and disappears back into the crowd.

"Where Steam Girl comes from, even the laws of physics are different. There's a little magic in technology. Things are . . . less drab, less logical, less straightforward. Everything's a little more . . . *possible.*"

We're sitting on a wall behind the incinerator block. The air smells of smoke and garbage, but there's no one else around, which is a big advantage. I'm flicking through her notebook, drinking in the drawings of Steam Girl's long legs and sly smile.

"Take the *Martian Rose,*" she says. "It's the greatest airship ever made, with an amazing motor called the Spirodynamic Multidimensional Concentrated Steam Engine. I'm not sure exactly how it works — something about cycling steam through several dimensions at once to magnify its power. It was invented by Steam Girl's mother, who mysteriously disappeared when Steam Girl was still a baby. She was an inventor, too...."

"What's this?" I say, holding up the notebook.

"Oh, that's Mars," she says. The picture shows a fairy-tale palace, perched on the side of a huge red mountain. In the foreground are several men in armor, each riding the back of a strange giant bird. "Skimmer birds," she explains. "They're not really birds; they're more like flying dinosaurs, but covered in shiny green-and-yellow scales that almost look like feathers. When the sun hits them, they shimmer and flash like a thousand colored lights. It's beautiful...."

I glance up at her. She's slowly swinging her legs and staring into the distance at nothing. There's something very serious about the way she speaks.

The next drawing seems to be inside the palace. A tall, slim man with a long white beard, sitting on a throne.

"When we first arrived," she says, "we were taken to see King Minnimattock. The Martians were really nervous, because they'd never seen people from Earth before."

"Who's that?" I ask, pointing at a dark-haired young woman standing beside the king.

"Oh, that's Princess Lusanna, the king's daughter. As soon as she saw Steam Girl's father, Lusanna started blushing like the sunrise. Apparently, that's what Martian women do when they fall in love...."

She glances at me for a moment, then looks down at her boots and continues talking.

"At first the king didn't know what to do with these strangers from another world. So he summoned the Royal Oracle, who turned up in a long black cloak, a dark hood covering her face. But when she entered the room, the oracle gave a strangled cry and fell to the floor in a faint. All the guards pointed their spears at Steam Girl and her father, and even the king drew his sword. Things looked pretty grim."

She slides off the wall and starts pacing up and down, stretching her arms over her head.

"That's when Princess Lusanna intervened, pleading with her father to give the visitors a chance. The king hesitated. The earthlings claimed to have come in peace. What's more, it was clear that his beloved daughter had taken a powerful liking to one of them at least. But the fate of his kingdom — maybe the entire planet — could be at stake!"

By now, I've forgotten about the notebook, the incinerator smell, the stale sandwiches and warm juice at my side. I'm completely caught by her words, the sound of her voice. I watch as she strides back and forth across the dirty asphalt, lost in her story.

"Then Steam Girl had an idea. She curtsied to the king" — as she says this, she drops into a clumsy curtsy herself — "and said she had a gift for him and his lovely daughter."

Her pacing has brought her to the side of her schoolbag. She crouches and draws out a small metal object, cupped in both hands: a tiny artificial bird, made of metal and wood, held together by miniature hinges and levers.

"Wow!" I say.

"The Clockwork Sparrow," she says. "Just a little trifle Steam Girl had made during the long journey from the moon to Mars. Now she held it up for the king to see, and she wound the spring-driven motor — like *this*. . . ."

I hold my breath as she turns a key no bigger than a baby's fingernail. There's the sound of small metallic teeth catching and grinding.

"And then she opened her hands and let go. . . ."

The Clockwork Sparrow drops like a stone, hitting the ground with a painful clatter. We both stare at it in silence. Then, just for a moment, it comes to life: rusting wings flutter, the tiny beak opens and closes, and the whole bird shuffles sideways along the asphalt. And then it lies still.

"Well, it worked better on Mars," she says, lifting the broken metal body and turning away.

"That was . . . awesome!" I say, jumping down from the wall. "Where did you get it? Can I see?"

But she's already put it away.

"Never mind," she says, pulling her bag over her shoulder. "The bell's about to ring."

"You can't stop there!" I say. "What happened with the king? And — what's her name? — Lucy?"

I follow her all the way to E Block, but she won't say another word. And sure enough, the bell rings just as we reach the door, and I have to go to gym class.

After that, I'm hooked. We meet up most days for lunch by the incinerator. She tells me about Steam Girl while I look at the pictures in her book. Sometimes she turns up without any lunch, so I share mine. Soon I'm bringing twice as much, just in case, and an extra bottle of orange juice, which she really likes.

The stories get longer and more complicated: voyages of discovery all over Mars, with monsters and volcanoes and narrow escapes from angry native tribes. But throughout it all, their friendship with King Minnimattock and Princess Lusanna grows. Sometimes the old king and his daughter would come with them on the *Martian*

Rose, delighted at the chance to explore their home planet. And, of course, Lusanna still glowed bright red whenever Steam Girl's father was around.

Not everyone on Mars liked the newcomers. The king's son, Prince Zennobal, seemed to resent their popularity, especially after Steam Girl rejected his amorous advances with a well-placed right hook. And the Royal Oracle hid in her laboratory when they were in town. But everyone else was having too much fun to notice.

And then there are the gadgets. The Motion-Powered Wrist-Mounted Monodirectional Lantern (a tiny metal box that faintly glows if you jump up and down for long enough), the Audioscopic Motion Capture Device (a tin cup full of wood chips and wax that supposedly records sound), the Portable Kitchen (actually a beat-up old gas cooker covered in rubber tubes), and my favorite: Steam Girl's Spring-Motivated Vertical Propulsion Boots. These last ones turn up in a story involving giant bloodsucking insects who live in a deep canyon called the Mariner's Valley. Steam Girl was trapped at the bottom of a pit, listening to the buzz of the thirsty insect swarm getting closer and closer. But then, at the last moment, she reached down to flick a tiny lever on her lace-up boots and . . .

"And what?" I say as she slips into one of her long, teasing pauses, gazing up at the sky. We're sitting as usual on the low concrete wall behind the incinerator. "Come on . . . !"

A lazy smile spreads across her face, and she slowly slips down from the wall. There are a couple of tiny metal clips on the soles of her boots. She spends a moment fiddling with these, then straightens up and grins.

"A little modification Steam Girl made to her boots back on the moon," she says. "Very useful on low-gravity planets like Mars. . . ."

She bends her knees and jumps. At first I think the soles of her boots have come right off—but then I realize they're still attached by thick round springs that stretch and bounce as she leaps into the air. I laugh pretty hard at that—and even harder when she lands flat on her bum.

She glares at me, brushing off her skirt. "Like I said, they work better in low gravity."

We spend a half hour mucking around with the crazy spring boots. She even gets me to try them on, though they don't really fit, and I fall over straightaway. I scrape my knees and get a bruise on my chin, but I'm laughing too much to care. It's the first time I hear her laugh, and I like it. She kind of giggles—but not a high-pitched girly giggle, like Amanda and her friends. It sounds almost dirty.

Anyway, in the story, Steam Girl's boots got her out of the pit to safety. And in a way, I guess they've helped me escape from the dreariness of school—at least for an hour or so, while it's just me and her and the gadgets and notebook.

But then the bell rings and we have to go back to class and real life. And let's face it: real life sucks.

It doesn't take long for people to notice I've made a new friend.

"How's your girlfriend?" they say.

"She's not my girlfriend," I reply, again and again. For all the good it does.

Michael Carmichael seems to find everything about her personally insulting. And apparently he blames me.

"You're disgusting," he says, shoving me into walls and chairs and shelves and desks. "Makes me sick."

Even Amanda makes gagging faces when she sees us together.

And once, in the hallway after English, she grabs at Steam Girl's flying helmet and tries to pull it off. I don't see what happens next, but everyone hears Amanda screaming like a scalded cat.

I ask about it over lunch, but all I get is a chilly glare and silence.

"From the noise Amanda made, I thought you'd ripped her face off," I say.

She rolls her eyes. "I hardly touched her. She's worse than the Shrieking Vines of Venus."

"The shrieking what?"

And then she gives me a little smile and starts to talk, and before long I've totally forgotten about Amanda and Michael and everything else.

But the next day I don't see her in the morning, even though I get to school early and wait by the gate till the bell rings. She isn't in class either. At lunchtime I check by the incinerator. There's no one there. So I give up and go sit in the library, where it's peaceful and private.

That's where I find her, sitting on the floor between two shelves, sniffing like a little girl.

"You OK?" I say.

She's covering the left side of her face with one hand. I kneel down beside her but don't know what to say. So instead I just sit there saying nothing while she sniffs and gulps and keeps hiding her face, till finally the bell rings and we get to our feet and go to our separate classes without a word.

So anyway, here's what she tells me about the Shrieking Vines of Venus, the day before Michael Carmichael gave her a black eye:

When Steam Girl and her father had been on Mars for a few

months and had already ticked off most of the items on King Minnimattock's places-to-see list, someone had the bright idea of going to Venus. Actually, it was Prince Zennobal's idea, which should have tipped them off straightaway, but everyone was too excited to be suspicious. Steam Girl's father had always wanted to see what the mysterious green planet was like, and the king couldn't wait to travel to another world. The preparations were made at lightning speed, and within a week, the *Martian Rose* was on its way to Venus, with Steam Girl and her father and a handful of passengers, including the king and the princess. Zennobal had pulled out at the last minute, much to Steam Girl's relief.

"Venus was beautiful!" she says, eyes shining. "Like the greenest, thickest, most luscious jungle you can imagine. The forest rose hundreds of feet into the thick warm air. And there were flowers everywhere: huge orange blossoms the size of a house, with pools of sweet nectar where you could swim and drink at the same time. Millions of birds and tiny playful monkeys, who chattered and giggled and danced through the trees. It was paradise. For six days they flew over that vast green ocean of leaves, landing now and then to explore under the canopy. All their worries fell away, and they felt more relaxed and happy than ever before. They strolled through endless orchards munching on all kinds of fruit, swam in fresh clean rivers, and lay in giant palm fronds, watching as sunset turned the whole sky red.

"Everything seemed peaceful. There were no giant monsters or angry natives or dangerous traps. The only slight annoyance was a particular kind of vine that gave off an earsplitting shriek whenever you came near it."

"Aha!" I say. "The Shrieking Vines of Venus!"

She grins. "Luckily they were covered with bright-pink blossoms that gave off a sickly sweet scent, so they were easy enough to avoid."

There are drawings, too, in her notebook. My favorite shows Steam Girl and the princess doubled over with laughter, pointing at a puzzled King Minnimattock. A bright-red monkey the size of a kitten has made a nest in the king's beard and is curled up, fast asleep. Behind them the jungle is a dense tumble of leaves and flowers and vines. Tiny bluebirds fly overhead.

Over the page is a very different scene: a view from the airship with the jungle spread out below. A dark column of smoke rises into the sky from somewhere near the horizon. It's a disturbing picture.

When I ask about it, she stops smiling and goes quiet. I've never seen her look like that.

"Sorry," she says at last. "I was . . ." She trails off. "You see, this is where it all went wrong. . . ."

"How do you mean?" I ask.

She shakes her head. "Never mind," she says. "I'll tell you tomorrow."

But the next day is when I found her crying in the library, and after that things begin to change.

Around this time, Mrs. Hendricks shifts the seats around so Amanda and Michael aren't sitting together. Instead, Michael ends up next to me, and Amanda gets to sit with Steam Girl. Maybe Mrs. Hendricks thinks I'll be a good influence on Michael, which shows just how much she knows.

Day after day, I stare at them. The two girls, I mean. Amanda wears tight tops that show a lot of skin. Her spine is one long, graceful curve, and when she leans back and yawns, it's like a slow-motion movie. She knows Michael is watching, so sometimes she puts on a show, with plenty of stretching and hair tossing and brief stolen glances. Of course I get to see it all, too.

Next to that, Steam Girl's flying helmet and jacket seem even sadder than usual. She hunches over her notebook, like a big, shy bear trying to hide. The only skin that shows through all the dark worn leather is an occasional glimpse of the back of her neck. It looks pale and cold.

Some nights when I lie in bed, I try to remember Amanda's latest performance — her soft slim arms, her narrow waist. . . . But after a while all I can think of is a tiny sliver of cool-white skin.

It's a whole week before she mentions Steam Girl again.

I get to the incinerator first that day. There's a fire going and thick white smoke keeps drifting into my eyes. Even the concrete seems to be sweating. When she finally shows up, I don't notice till she's right in front of me. It's like she's come out of the smoke, like she *is* smoke. For a moment nothing seems solid, nothing's real. Then she reaches out and puts a hand on my arm.

"Are you all right?" she says.

"Uh . . . yeah." I shake my head. "Let's get out of here."

We sit under some dying trees by a chain-link fence. Scraps of rubbish have blown among the roots, and the earth feels damp. I spread my sweatshirt out for her to sit on so she won't get wet. For a moment she hesitates, looking at the sweatshirt and then at me. No one's ever looked at me like that before. Her eyes wide open and her lips not quite closed. Her neck is slowly turning pink.

"Thank you," she says, and smiles.

We share my lunch, as usual. I have some chocolate cake from Dad's birthday, and she carefully eats half before handing me the rest. Then she leans back on the tree while I flick through her notebook. When I reach the picture from Venus with the green jungle and the black smoke, I hold it up.

"So ..." I say. "You were going to tell me about this one?"

She swallows, then nods.

"OK," she says. "I guess you've waited long enough.

"The rising smoke came from a chimney — from *dozens* of tall, fat chimneys that loomed over a vast line of buildings, like giant factories and warehouses, made of stone and concrete and iron and tin. There was a gaping hole in the forest, where the trees had been cut and the ground opened up. Huge machines were tearing at the earth, pulling up tons of soil and rock and carrying it into factories. Stacks of tree trunks were piled outside, for fuel, Steam Girl supposed. There were no people to be seen, only thousands of strange gray robots shaped like men, who bustled about among the buildings and machines, like a hive of worker bees.

"When they first saw all this, Princess Lusanna began to cry. Her father's face went dark.

"'Take us down,' he rumbled. 'I would find out who has done this thing.'

"Steam Girl and her father, along with the king and three of his bravest warriors, landed in the forest about a mile away. They crept to the edge of the clearing and watched as several robots marched stiffly by. The robots carried guns of a kind Steam Girl had never seen before. Steam Girl hated guns more than anything, and she never, ever used them.

"As soon as the robots had gone past, Steam Girl whispered to her father, 'Back in a minute.' And before he could argue, she left their hiding place and ran across the open ground to the nearest building, where she crouched behind a low wall of crates and then slipped in through the door.

"It was a factory, all right. There were machines and conveyor belts and cables and tubes. There were workers, too—hundreds of robots, pulling levers and turning cranks and carrying wood to the giant furnace at one end of the room. She noticed more robots lying half assembled on the conveyor belts, and guessed that's what the factory was for. Robots building more robots.

"But that was only part of it. There were other production lines, too, making machines she'd never seen or even heard of. Heavy iron engines that smelled of fire and oil—some with wings and some with wheels. Ugly big guns and bombs with fins like sharks. There were boxes and tools made of a strange artificial material— unnaturally smooth, light, and dull. And flat glass screens like empty mirrors, and long snaking rubber-coated wires that hung around the room and over the floor.

"Steam Girl's head was spinning, but she was determined to solve the mystery of this infernal factory. As quietly as she could, she made her way across the factory floor, ducking from woodpile to conveyor belt, avoiding the robots and looking for clues.

"Near the middle of the room was a raised platform with a com- manding view of the whole operation. There was no one there— just a desk and two chairs, a vase of bright-pink flowers, and one of those curious machines with row upon row of buttons and a blank glass screen. And all over the desk—the chairs, the floor—stood piles of paper, covered with printed text and diagrams and hand- written notes. Quickly and carefully, Steam Girl crept to the edge of the platform and glanced around to see if she had been noticed. Then she reached up to the desk and snatched an armload of paper.

"A high-pitched scream filled the air, cutting through the constant roar of the factory. Robots looked up from their work and stared at the platform where Steam Girl crouched clutching her stolen papers.

"'Shrieking Vines,' she muttered, realizing too late that the vase on the desk wasn't merely decorative.

"Then she jumped to her feet and ran as fast as she could— leaping over conveyor belts and darting between the quickly converging robots—until finally she was out the door and sprinting for the cover of the jungle. Behind her shots rang out, louder and faster than any firearms she knew of. The ground around her feet spat up fistfuls of dirt. But somehow she made it to the trees unharmed.

"'Run!' she yelled, and her father and the Martians took off through the forest, with bullets splintering trees and cutting leaves to ribbons all around them. But Steam Girl paused a moment to catch her breath, then reached down to her belt and pulled out a gadget she'd never tried before."

"Ha! I know what's coming next!" I cry, interrupting her story.

"Do you?" she says, looking at me sideways from behind her glasses.

"Sure." I grin, slipping off the wall and crossing my arms. "It's *gadget time*! So what is it today? A Steam-Driven Instantaneous Escape Facilitator? Oversize Extendible Robot-Neutralizing Punching Arms? A Rocket-Powered Jet Pack Flying Machine?"

She stares at me for a moment and then laughs so hard, she gets the hiccups. I can't stop smiling, especially when she wipes her eyes and puts her hand on my shoulder.

"You're OK," she says. "I think we'll get along just fine."

I can feel my face blushing, but she's already turned away to dig through her bag. When she straightens up, she's holding what looks like a rusty tin can with a string at one end.

"Huh?" I say. "Is that it? Doesn't look like much—"

Then she points one end of the can at me and pulls the string. There's a loud *COUGH!* and the air fills with steam and something damp and heavy hits me full in the face. I yelp and trip over backward, and then it's like someone's tossed a wet fishing net all over me. I wave my arms and legs around and just get more and more caught. I can hear her laughing again, even harder than before, but it doesn't seem very funny to me.

"GET ME OUT OF HERE!" I shout at the top of my lungs. "GOD DAMN IT! IT'S HORRIBLE!"

She eventually manages to stop laughing long enough to try to free me but without much success. The net's so sticky, it gets all over her, too, and soon we're both caught in a big gooey mess of strings and glue and soot and each other.

There's a moment when I suddenly realize I'm lying on top of her, my face pressed against her neck. She has one arm around my back and a hand on my cheek. And at exactly the same time we both stop struggling and lie there in silence.

Her soft white skin is slowly turning pink.

At last we get ourselves out, and as we sit on the dusty concrete, picking bits of sticky web out of our hair and off our clothes, she tells me the rest of the story.

"The Web-Weaving Tangle Trap caught the first wave of pursuing robots," she says, "giving Steam Girl and her friends enough time to get back to the airship and safety. They rose up into the sky with gunfire rattling at them from below.

"The king was elated. 'What an adventure!' he said with a laugh.

"Princess Lusanna was so excited, she quite forgot herself, throwing her arms around Steam Girl's father and giving him a big kiss. The king laughed even harder at that, until the princess turned the brightest red anyone had ever seen and ran off to her cabin."

I close my eyes then, picturing the scene. If I'd been there, I'd have kissed Steam Girl. She'd have laughed, with a low, throaty giggle. Perhaps her breath would quicken, and her throat would turn pink, and I'd have to swallow very hard before I could speak....

But when I open my eyes again, she isn't smiling or blushing. She isn't even looking at me, but at the thin brown grass that's forced its way through the asphalt.

"And what about Steam Girl?" I ask. "What did she do?"

She glances up and our eyes meet. She looks so sad.

"She—well, after all that running, I guess she was tired." She sighs. "So she went to take a rest in her hammock. But as she took off her jacket, something fell out of the pocket and spilled across the floor. The papers she'd snatched. What with getting shot at and everything, she'd completely forgotten about them till now.

"So she leaped up and spread the papers out across the floor. To her surprise, they were in English. There were maps of Venus, Mars, and Earth; lists of equipment; and plans of attack. With a rising sense of panic, Steam Girl realized they could mean only one thing: all those robots and weapons and fighting machines were being prepared as an army of conquest.

"Reading on, she found ominous references to some kind of superbomb, able to destroy whole cities in a single awful flash;

poisonous gas that could kill an army in minutes; and even man-made plagues for releasing into a population's water supply or the air they breathed. It was unimaginable, inhuman, horrible....

"It was a plan for the end of the world."

On the way back to class, she's quiet. But I'm buzzing.

"So what happened?" I say, dancing around her as we walk. "Did Steam Girl show the papers to her father? And then did they—?"

"No," she says quietly.

"What? She didn't show him the papers? How come?"

She hesitates a moment, as if trying to decide whether to tell me what comes next.

"There was one more thing," she says at last. "On one of the papers. On the back, written in pencil, over and over."

I wait, but she seems to have stopped talking, and we're almost at her classroom.

"What was it?" I stand in front of the door. "Come on, you have to tell me! Or I won't let you go to math."

She gives me a withering look. "All right, I'll tell you. But ..."

"But what?" I'm desperate. The second bell is about to ring.

"Never mind," she says. "It was a name. Her father's name. His full name—Professor Archibald James Patterson Swift. Again and again."

"Whoooa!" I breathe. "So—what? Was *he* behind the factory? Did he have, like, a secret life where he slipped off to Venus and planned the destruction of Earth?"

"Don't be stupid," she hisses.

"It would be a good twist, though, wouldn't it?" I say. "Y'know, the heroine's father turns out to be the villain—"

"It *wasn't* him," she repeats, more firmly this time. "He's a good man, who'd never do anything rotten like that. No matter what people say about him."

"Why? What do people say about him?" Now I'm confused. Does the father have secrets, after all?

But the second bell rings and she pushes past me into the classroom and closes the door behind her.

She isn't at school the next day, or the day after that. I look for her everywhere, but she isn't in class, or by the incinerator or even in the library. By Thursday I've slipped back into my old routine, eating lunch by myself and catching up on homework.

Mrs. Hendricks has given us a new assignment: write a short story in the first person, present tense. I sit in the classroom trying to ignore Michael Carmichael and come up with an idea, but all I can think of is Steam Girl, and that's *her* story, not mine.

So I start writing about a boy who has his own adventures, traveling around the universe in a rocket ship called the *Silver Arrow*. In my story he flies to Saturn, which is like a huge ocean of poisonous gases, so the natives all live in cities they've built on the rings high above the planet's surface. When Rocket Boy (that's what I call him) lands on the first ring, he sees this huge hairy monster chasing a frightened girl. So he makes a really loud noise with his rocket's engines and scares the monster away. The girl, who turns out to be the princess of Saturn, is so grateful, she throws her arms around him and kisses him on the lips, blushing pink on her cheeks and on her long pale neck, her heaving breasts pressed against his chest. . . .

But then I stop, because I know what Mrs. Hendricks would

say. She hates it if we write something like "heaving breasts." She calls it a cliché and says we should write about things that are real. Which makes me want to say, "I don't like writing what's real, because mostly what's real is boring and sucks." But I don't say that. I just nod and say nothing.

Anyway, this time it *is* real, because that's what this girl is like. I know, because I based her on Steam Girl, who definitely *does* have heaving breasts and long, lithe legs and all that stuff. Well, the Steam Girl in the notebook, at least. The real one has heaving breasts, too, come to think of it, but also heaving shoulders and a heaving stomach and heaving thighs and bum. She's all about the *heaving*. And the weird thing is I don't mind at all. I'm even starting to like it.

So when she finally reappears on Friday, I nervously show her *Rocket Boy*. I've even done some drawings of him and the princess, but they look pretty stupid compared to hers. I'm worried she'll say it's lousy, but instead she gives it back without saying much at all. "Great," she says, sounding distracted. I don't think she's even read it.

"How come you weren't at school?" I say, a little disappointed.

But she doesn't answer my question. "Did I miss much?"

I tell her about the short-story assignment, which is due in a week. "You should do Steam Girl," I say.

She looks at me like I'm stupid. "That's not for teachers," she says.

"What do you mean?" I ask. But I already kind of know.

"All they want to read about is miserable people living stupid, boring lives. Unhappy families, unrequited love — all that crap." She grimaces. "And the worst thing is . . . *none of it's real*."

"Sorry," I say. "I didn't mean — it's just — well, I think Steam Girl is great. Really totally *awesome*. I swear, if you typed it all up and got it published, you could be a millionaire."

She stares at me for a long time. I can feel my cheeks starting to burn.

"Listen," she says at last. "I don't care about being a millionaire or Mrs. Hendricks or English grades or school or any of that stuff. All of that means nothing."

"OK," I say.

"All I care about is *this*." She brandishes her notebook like a weapon. "This is all that matters. All that's real."

This time I don't say anything.

She hesitates for a moment, her eyes slipping away from mine and drifting across the concrete and the garbage and the thin, sickly trees. Then she turns and walks away.

That afternoon in biology, Amanda Anderson comes over and says, "Hi."

I almost choke. "Uh . . . hi," I say.

"You're pretty tight with the new girl, right?" she says. "That weird girl with the hat?"

"Flying helmet," I say, and immediately regret it.

"What?" She looks at me like I've just started speaking Mongolian.

"It's not a hat." I've lost all control of my mouth. "It's a flying helmet. Like pilots wear. Apparently . . ." I trail off lamely.

"Well, whatever," she says. "So what's her deal? Is she one of those creepy cosplayers or something?"

"I don't know," I say, which is true. "She's good at drawing. And she tells amazing stories."

"Huh." Amanda frowns. "What kind of stories?"

"Um . . ."

I'm not sure how much to explain. I mean, Amanda *is* the

Shrieking Vine of Venus, right? She's already caused one black eye. What if she's just pumping me for intel to pass on to Michael?

But I was friends with her once, and I want to believe she's a decent person. It's not her fault the whole Barbie thing got out of hand. Or that her boyfriend is a creep. Maybe she's genuinely trying to understand. Maybe she wants to patch things up. Maybe I still have a chance.

"They're about this character called Steam Girl," I say at last.

"Steam Girl?" She screws up her face.

"Yeah. She has adventures . . . on Mars and stuff."

"God, how lame," Amanda says.

I feel bad that in my mouth it *does* sound lame. It's like a betrayal.

"Does she ever take off that stupid hat?" Amanda says.

"I dunno," I say. "Not that I've seen."

"Well, anyway," she says, getting to the point at last. "Tracey says she lives in a trailer home with her creepy drug-dealer father. You should probably be careful. One day she'll probably bring a gun to school and kill everyone she knows."

I laugh.

"I'm just telling you for your own safety." She actually seems concerned. "I know you always look for the best in people. But you saw what she did to me, right? That girl is dangerous. Seriously."

She puts a hand on my shoulder. "I'm sorry Michael's such a jerk," she says. "I swear, I'm *this* close to ditching him. . . ."

The warmth of her skin goes across my shirt and spreads through my body.

"Take care of yourself," she says.

That night, I try to dream about Amanda Anderson. But all I can think of is that stupid hat.

And then it's the weekend and I don't have to think about Steam Girl or Amanda Anderson or Michael Carmichael or anything. I stay in my bedroom playing online games, with loud music on the headphones. Once or twice, Mom comes in to try to get me outside or doing chores. But mostly I can just be alone.

I can't get my head round anything. Steam Girl — the one in the notebook — is perfect: beautiful, smart, generous, and brave. Her long legs and heaving breasts haunt me in a way even Amanda Anderson never has. But the other one — the real girl who tells the stories and draws the pictures — well, *her* legs are short and kind of plump. Her skin is pasty and pale, with freckles and spots. She's like a parody of Steam Girl, a fat, nerdy girl playing dress-up.

But here's the thing: I just can't stop thinking about her. When she smiles, I feel lighter than air. When she's sad, I want to take her hand and tell her that everything will be OK. I *don't*, but I want to. I love seeing her neck go pink; in fact, I love everything about her neck. I keep imagining what it would be like to put my fingers on that soft white skin and feel the tiny muscles flutter as she speaks. Sometimes she closes her eyes as she talks about Steam Girl's father and the *Martian Rose*, and then her lips go soft and everything about her seems to *glow*.

She makes life special. And I find myself, by Saturday night, wanting to see her more than I've ever wanted anything before. I pull on some shoes and a hoodie and go out into the darkening streets. There's no way of knowing where she is, of course. I have no idea where she lives or what she does on a Saturday. For all I know she could be flying over the Martian desert in an airship or fighting robots somewhere in the jungles of Venus. So I just walk, randomly, through the empty suburban streets as the sky goes from red to purple to black, like the bruise around her eye. And the electric lights come on, flickering over cracked pavements and filling windows with gold. Now and then a car rattles past, or some kid on a bike. But mostly I'm alone.

It's after midnight when I get home. Dad lets me in without saying a word, makes me a hot chocolate, and goes to bed. It takes me hours to fall asleep.

On Monday morning, I'm at school early, waiting by the gate. But when the second bell rings, I give up and go to class.

At lunchtime, I go down to the incinerator and sit on the wall and try to eat my lunch. The concrete's cold, and the smell of smoke is stale and heavy in the air. My stomach is churning. After ten minutes, I pick up my bag and turn to go.

She's walking toward me, hands in the pockets of her heavy old jacket. I open my mouth to say something, but nothing comes to mind.

"Hey," she says.

"I was looking for you," I say, and then stop, wondering why the hell I said *that*. She frowns, so I just keep talking, not knowing what will come out. "On Saturday night. I walked everywhere hoping you might—I mean, I didn't know where to find you."

She's giving me that look, like when I put my sweatshirt on the ground.

"So," I say. "Pretty stupid, huh?"

She smiles. "It was a bit stupid," she says. "But it was also ...*gallant*."

"I don't know what that means," I say.

She laughs. "OK, maybe just stupid." She hooks her arm round mine and pulls me over to the dying trees and the rusting fence.

I give her my juice to drink and she gives me an apple. Neither of us mentions Steam Girl.

But the next day she starts talking as soon as we meet up.

"I need to tell you what happened next," she says. "When Steam Girl got back to Mars. It's not easy to talk about, but it's important that you know. That you understand."

I look up, surprised. This isn't like her usual stories. Her face looks so serious that I'm almost afraid.

"OK," I say, sitting down. She stays standing, staring at the ground like the first time I saw her.

"Back on Mars," she begins. And then she stops to clear her throat.

Back on Mars, the palace was in turmoil. Soon after the *Martian Rose* had left, the Royal Oracle had apparently consulted the omens and revealed that their mission was doomed. The whole party would perish on Venus, she'd announced, to widespread dismay. Most of the courtiers wanted to wait and see if they would return, but Prince Zennobal moved quickly, declaring his father deceased and arranging his own coronation after a brief period of mourning.

So when the *Martian Rose* reappeared, many in the palace rejoiced, but Zennobal was furious. He claimed it was a Venusian trick and ordered all on board arrested and thrown into the dungeons. Most of the guards refused, but Zennobal merely smiled and pulled a strange device from his robes.

"Very well," he said. "If you cannot be trusted, you shall be replaced." And he flicked a switch on the small black box.

From somewhere in the palace, an army of sleek gray robots poured into the corridors and halls, firing their short black guns into the air. The palace guards dropped their spears and fell to the floor, terrified. Within minutes, all resistance had ended and Zennobal's robots were in complete control.

"So it was Zennobal?" I say. "Knew it all along."

"Wait and see," she says, frowning.

As soon as they emerged from the *Martian Rose*, Steam Girl and her friends were surrounded by robots. The king and his daughter were led away under guard, while Steam Girl and her father were locked in a dungeon deep beneath the palace. For several days, that's where they remained. Robotic guards came and went, stale food and water were pushed under the door. And then, late one night, Steam Girl woke to the sound of rattling keys and the glare of a lantern. A hooded figure stood at the door, silently motioning for them to follow. The mysterious figure led them through winding tunnels and up narrow stairways, until finally they entered a small cluttered room filled with books and scrolls and alchemical beakers and tubes.

"The Royal Oracle," said Steam Girl as their rescuer stepped into the light.

The oracle put down the lantern and threw back her hood, revealing long blond hair and strangely familiar features.

To Steam Girl's great astonishment, her father gave an almighty shout and rushed forward to embrace the stranger. The oracle responded with a long, passionate kiss, until Steam Girl regained her wits and cried, "What on earth is going on?"

Her father turned and smiled, his eyes filled with tears. "My dear girl, this angel in red is none other than Dr. Serafina Starfire — *your mother!*"

"Wait — what?" I say. "Steam Girl's mother? But ... didn't she die or something? What the hell is she doing on Mars?"

"Please don't interrupt," she says slowly and quietly. "This isn't easy...."

"Sorry," I say. And I mean it. She looks like she's going to cry.

The Royal Oracle—Steam Girl's mother—took a long look at her long-lost daughter and smiled. "I'm so very proud," she said. "How beautiful you've grown—courageous and clever, too!"

"She really is just like you," her father said. "You should see the gadgets she comes up with...."

And so the three of them sat down and talked. Her mother explained how she'd been sucked through a freak transdimensional wormhole to Mars fifteen years before, while trying to perfect the *Martian Rose*'s experimental engines. At first the Martians didn't know what to make of this strange lost creature. But her knowledge of science and astronomy soon gave her a reputation for magical powers of prophecy and divination, and so the king named her the Royal Oracle—and there she was.

Steam Girl's father quickly outlined their own adventures since his wife's disappearance, and then talk turned to their present predicament. "The prince and his robots will be looking for you by now," Steam Girl's mother said. "If you stay here, you'll soon be found."

"Then we must take the fight to them!" her father said with a wild look in his eyes. "Rescue the king and his daughter, rouse the palace guards to rebellion, and overthrow that treasonous whelp and his tin-pot army of rattling contraptions once and for all!"

Steam Girl noticed a flicker of something dark in her mother's face at the mention of Princess Lusanna. But it quickly passed. "Oh, my brave, sweet husband. I have no doubt you will do all that and more. But first we must prepare. We are three against many, and they are very well armed. Luckily I have a secret weapon of my own...." And she stood and walked to a lushly embroidered tapestry covering one wall. She pulled the heavy cloth aside to reveal a simple wooden door.

"I have not been idle all these years since leaving Earth," she said. "I continued my research on transdimensional space, in the hope that I could create a new wormhole and find my way back to Earth." And then she opened the door. A weird yellow glow began to seep into the room.

"Follow me," she said, and led them through the doorway. As they stepped over the threshold, Steam Girl felt a curious chill and thought she might pass out. Then her head cleared and she saw they were in a square windowless room, filled with that same strange yellow glow. Six more doors, identical to the one they'd just come through, were spaced round the blank stone walls. A wooden staircase led to the floor above.

"Where are we?" Steam Girl asked. A sweet fragrance in the air reminded her of something.

"This is my *real* laboratory," her mother said with a hint of pride, "hidden hundreds of miles away on the far side of Mars. Each of these doors is like a small tear in the fabric of space-time itself. By stepping through, we are instantly transported to the other side of the wormhole, no matter how near or far that may be."

"Stars above!" Steam Girl's father laughed. "You have come a long way with your research, my darling! And where do they all lead?"

His wife walked to one of the doors and laid a hand against its smooth dark wood. "This one," she said, smiling, "opens onto Earth."

"To Earth!" Steam Girl's father cried. "Home! Then let's go there at once! We can warn the world of Prince Zennobal's imminent invasion—and then gather supplies and equipment before returning through your ingenious doorways to free Minnimattock and Lusanna and defeat the usurper's army forthwith!" And with that he strode resolutely to where her mother stood and threw the door open. "To Earth!" he called once more, and then he stepped through the doorway, disappearing with a flash of yellow light.

Steam Girl's mother turned to her and smiled. "Come along, then," she said, motioning toward the door. But Steam Girl hesitated. Something was wrong.

"I think I know where we are," she said, "and it's not on Mars."

Her mother frowned. "I don't know what you mean," she said.

Steam Girl ignored her. "I remember that smell in the air," she said. "Giant blossoms and pools of nectar. . . . We're on Venus, where Father and I first encountered the robot army." Her mother's mouth became a thin sharp line. "Everything makes sense," Steam Girl went on. "You're the one behind it all. Using those wormholes of yours to hop from Earth to Mars to Venus — and who knows where else — gathering technology, weapons, and tools and making your evil plans. . . ."

"That's enough," her mother said.

"And that's not all," Steam Girl said. "You gave Zennobal the idea of a trip to Venus, didn't you? You hoped we'd stumble across your robot army and that would be the end of us."

"That's not true," her mother hissed. "It was Zennobal's idea to send you here. I never wanted you dead. . . ."

"But you used our absence from Mars to put your plans in motion — announcing our demise so your puppet could seize the throne." Steam Girl was angry now, angrier than she'd ever been before. "But there's one more thing I want to know. Where have you sent my father?"

Her mother made a kind of growling noise. "You think you're so smart, little girl? But you don't know anything! Everything I've ever done—every brilliant discovery, every unprecedented innovation— that arrogant, vain, *mediocre* fool claimed credit for them all. Who do you think designed the *Martian Rose*? Who built the Spiro-dynamic Multidimensional Concentrated Steam Engine? Certainly not your father, that's for sure. It was *me*, damn it. *All of it was me!*"

Steam Girl was taken aback. "But that's not true," she said. "Father's always said you were a brilliant scientist. He never claimed he did those things alone.... And besides, even if he had, that's no reason to build a huge army and invade Earth!"

"Don't be silly," her mother said. "Ours is a world crippled by ignorance and superstition, its technological and social development held back by a deluded nostalgia for outdated aesthetic and ethical philosophies. Always looking backward, never forward into the future. Through my transdimensional doors, young girl, I have seen other worlds—other Earths and other realities. Compared to those, *our* Earth is a quaint little backwater. It's time we woke up and behaved like proper adults...."

"You're even crazier than I thought," Steam Girl said. "Now, answer my question: where is my father?"

"He's on Earth," Steam Girl's mother said, waving at the glowing doorway. "Just as I said."

But Steam Girl knew it was a trap. "You're lying," she said, clenching her fists. "Wherever you've sent him, you'd better bring him back. Now."

Her mother sighed and clapped her hands. From the floor above there came sounds of movement: the heavy clank of robotic feet. "I had hoped it wouldn't come to this," Steam Girl's mother said.

"I really don't want to hurt you; after all, you are so clearly my daughter." Steam Girl tried to think quickly, but her mind was still reeling from everything that had happened. She looked around, desperately trying to remember which of the identical wooden doors led back to Mars. Perhaps if she made it back to the palace, she could free the king and persuade the guards to help. But before she could do anything, her mother moved with surprising speed and power, grabbing her shoulders and pushing her firmly through the glowing open doorway. Steam Girl stumbled, arms flailing, reaching for something—anything—to keep her from falling....

And then she hit a wall of ice-cold light, and her mind went blank.

In the silence that follows, I realize I'm shivering. After a while, I can't bear it anymore.

"So Steam Girl followed her father through the wormhole," I say. "And ended up ... where?"

She says nothing, just lowers her eyes.

"Are you OK?" I ask. She doesn't look it.

She looks away. "Do you like this place?" she says.

"Uh ... you mean the school?"

"The school, the town, the whole bloody world.... All of it."

I shrug. "Well, it's OK, I guess," I say, and then I shake my head. "Actually, it kind of sucks. At least what I've seen of it. I'm sure there are plenty of great places out there, but ..."

There's another long silence.

"Anyway," she says, making it sound like a closing door.

Mrs. Hendricks is talking about our short-story assignment. She writes a quotation up on the board, from some writer I've never heard of. She makes us copy it down in our books:

> Some writers write to escape reality. Others write to
> understand it. But the best writers write in order to take
> possession of reality, and so transform it.

I copy it down and think about what it means. I get the first part about escaping reality—that makes perfect sense. And I suppose it makes sense to try to understand the world, too. But the last part makes me uneasy. Taking possession of reality sounds like something Steam Girl's mother would say. I don't know. Maybe I'm just not smart enough to get it.

But then Mrs. Hendricks tells us to spend the rest of the period working on our stories, and for the first time in days I start writing again. I write a whole new chapter in the next half hour, where Rocket Boy leaves the princess with the heaving breasts and flies off to explore one of Saturn's moons. He finds an abandoned art gallery beside a frozen lake, with paintings hung on every wall. There's one picture he can't stop looking at: a strange portrait of an oddly dressed girl—a little chubby and kind of weird, but somehow very beautiful. Faded blue dress, scruffy leather jacket, long lace-up boots, and black-rimmed glasses. And, of course, flying helmet and goggles.

She shone like a bright strange star shining in those empty lifeless halls, I write. Cheesy, I know, but that's how I feel.

Anyway, in my story, the moment Rocket Boy reaches out and touches the painting of Steam Girl, she comes to life and appears beside him, freed from the magical picture. She thanks Rocket Boy with a kiss (I manage to avoid the whole "heaving breasts" thing this time), and she explains how she was tricked into posing for a portrait by an evil artist-magician, who trapped her in the frame and kidnapped her father. Then they climb on board the *Silver Arrow* and fly off to rescue Professor Swift — but that will have to wait for chapter three.

When the bell rings, I put away my story and walk to her desk, where she's curled over her notebook, working furiously.

"The next installment?" I say. But she barely glances up. She closes the book and goes to put it in her bag.

"Oops!" As he goes past, Michael Carmichael gives me a shove from behind so I fall against her, and we both tumble to the floor.

Laughter ripples through the room, and I feel my face turn red. But she just calmly climbs to her feet and turns to face Michael.

"You know the problem with you, Michael Carmichael?" she says. "You're reality incarnate."

The whole class goes quiet. Michael makes a face. "What does that even *mean?*"

"If you *imagine* a dog," she goes on, "it's always loyal and fluffy and cute. But in real life, dogs bite your hand and pee on the carpet and have sex with the sofa."

That gets more laughs. But she keeps going. "That's what you are, Michael Carmichael. You're dog pee on the carpet."

In the silence that follows, Michael's mouth moves but no sound comes out.

While Mrs. Hendricks chews them both out I pick up the notebook where it's fallen on the floor. It's open to the last page, which is filled with a single detailed drawing.

"What's this?" I say, once we're out in the hallway.

She glances at the page I'm holding up.

"It's Steam Girl's last gadget," she says, not meeting my eyes.

"It's a gun," I say slowly. My throat feels dry.

She looks at the floor but says nothing.

"I thought Steam Girl hated guns. I thought she never used them. It *is* a gun, isn't it?" I ask.

"It's the Reality Gun," she says quietly.

"What the hell is a Reality Gun?" I say.

"It kills reality."

And then she takes the notebook from my hand and puts it in her bag.

After school, she's waiting at the gate, just like that first time. She looks very alone as the crowd flows by. Kids point and laugh.

We walk together to the first intersection. She seems tired.

"I have one more thing to tell you," she says.

"OK," I say.

"You know how I told you Steam Girl and her father went through the door?" she says.

I nod.

"Well, it took them to Earth," she says, "just like her mother told them it would. But it wasn't *their* Earth — it was a different world, a different universe. The *wrong* universe. This world was . . . grayer. Sadder. And the rules were different. Her gadgets didn't work the same. Technology wasn't magic anymore. Even people were different there. Less courageous, less beautiful and clever. And so *they* changed, too . . ."

She sounds so sad, I look to see if she's crying. Her face is pale, like chalk.

"Couldn't they go back?" I say. "Back through the door?"

"No," she says. "Because after they went through, the door

disappeared. It was a trap, you see—the whole thing had been a trap. Steam Girl's mother had planned it all along—to trick them into going through the wormhole to this totally different universe, where they could no longer mess up her plans. She wanted them out of her life completely."

"So . . . what happened next?"

"That's it," she says. "That's all there is."

"You mean that's the end of the story?" I can't believe it.

She says nothing. We wait at the lights till the red man turns green.

"Bye," she says, and she crosses the road.

She's not in English on Friday.

Michael's not there either. But Amanda is, and she smiles at me. A warm, genuine smile.

When I hand in my story, Mrs. Hendricks seems impressed. "Looks like you were quite inspired," she says.

"I *was* inspired," I say. "By Steam Girl."

Mrs. Hendricks looks confused; of course she won't know about Steam Girl. "I mean—the new girl. Wears a flying helmet and goggles?"

"Oh!" she says, surprised. "You mean Shanaia Swift? I didn't know you were friends."

"Um—kind of," I say. "She's a little weird, but the thing is, she tells the most amazing stories—all about this really smart inventor called Steam Girl, who travels the universe in an airship, having adventures with her father and . . ." I realize I'm blushing and stop talking.

Mrs. Hendricks frowns, flicking through my story. "I had no

idea," she says. "She's always so quiet in class. And she hasn't handed in a single piece of work. Listen, Redmond, if you talk to her over the weekend, could you ask her to come see me first thing on Monday? I'd really like to give her a chance to hand something in for this assignment, even if it's late. Sounds like it would be worth the wait...."

"I will," I say.

At lunchtime I go to the incinerator, just in case.

After five minutes, I'm getting ready to go when Michael Carmichael appears.

"Where is she?" he says.

"Who?" I say.

"Your freakish girlfriend," he says. "Obviously."

I pick up my bag and try to walk to the safety of the library. But Michael puts a hand on my chest to stop me.

"I want you to give her a message," he says. "From me to her."

"Let me go," I say as clearly as I can. My voice is shaking.

"Tell her this is from me," he says, his hand still on my shirt. "For yesterday."

And then he hits me in the face.

I stay on my hands and knees till he's gone, watching blood drip from my face onto the dusty asphalt. Then I sit on the ground by the concrete wall with a wad of tissues pressed against the cut in my mouth. I can feel it swelling up. I should go to the nurse and get some ice. But I don't.

When the bell rings, I get up and head for class. The bleeding has stopped, but my whole face is throbbing with pain. As I enter the science block, someone steps out of the shadows and grabs my arm.

It's her. *Shanaia*. "I've got something to show you," she says, guiding me out into the thin sunlight. She seems nervous, distracted. "I finished it. It's ready."

"Why weren't you in English?" I say. My voice is muffled. It hurts to talk. "Mrs. Hendricks wants to see you. . . ."

"Never mind that," she says, reaching for her bag. "I brought the—"

And then she sees my face and stops. "Oh!" she says. "What happened?"

"What do you *think* happened?" I'm annoyed all of a sudden. I don't want to be, but I am. "It's a message for you. From Michael Carmichael. For yesterday."

She lifts a hand to her mouth. "I'm so sorry. . . ."

"That's OK," I say, sounding more sarcastic than I mean to. "Everyone thinks you're my girlfriend anyway. It's not the first time I've been pushed around because I hang out with you."

She takes a step back, both hands held up as if I might hit her. Her neck is turning red, but this time it doesn't make me feel good.

"I'm sorry," I mutter, shaking my head. "I just . . ."

But she's already gone, half walking, half running across the asphalt, and I'm too tired and sore to go after her. Maybe I don't want to. I don't know what I want anymore. I just stand there, heavy and alone, until the next bell tells me I'm late for class. My head hurts. I take a deep breath and go back to school.

The world feels cheap this afternoon. The sky is pale and empty; colors are faded. Everything's dirty and ugly and falling apart. I sit in science class with my head on my desk. The teacher is talking about vacuums, which pretty much sums up how I feel.

After a while I close my eyes and let my mind drift. I imagine I'm lying on a warm sand dune, beside a girl. Stroking her soft white neck.

Not her, this time. Just a girl. An imaginary girl.

By home time, I'm sleepy and numb. I head for the main gate, staring at the ground in front of my feet. But there's something going on—a crowd in the way. Then I hear her voice and I start pushing my way to the front so I can see.

Her face is red, with tears in her eyes. Michael Carmichael looks angrier than ever before. At first I think he's wearing some kind of makeup, but then I realize he's bleeding from his lip, and his T-shirt is torn at the neck. He steps forward and pushes her shoulder, sending her back against the circle of onlookers, who spread out like a school of fish.

"You stupid fat freak," Michael says in a shaky voice. "Stupid fat little bitch!"

He backhands her across the face, so hard she spins around, glasses flying, ending up on one knee a few feet from me. The crowd almost moans.

Michael is still advancing on her. Without thinking, I step forward and raise my hand.

"Leave her alone," I say. It comes out as a kind of squeak.

Next thing I know I'm on the ground and Michael's looming over me, shouting something I can't hear.

Behind him, I can see Shanaia pulling something out of her bag, something awkward and heavy, metallic and long. Then she stands up, pointing it straight at him, holding tightly with both hands.

It's a gun. Covered in her usual gears and rusting dials and stuff, but still unmistakably a gun. The Reality Gun. I can't tell if it's a toy gun underneath or the real thing—and from the look on his face, neither can Michael. He freezes and then starts slowly backing away.

"Jesus Christ! What the hell is *that?*" He tries to laugh, but the sound he makes is broken and small.

No one speaks or moves for what seems like a really long time. Then she reaches up with one hand and pulls her goggles down over her eyes. There's shouting back near the administration block; teachers are coming.

And then she pulls the trigger. There's a bang and a flash and smoke and sparks. No, not smoke: steam. The air is full of steam, like a thick billowing cloud of warm, wet fog. Kids scream and people start running and someone knocks me flat. When I manage to get up again, the steam is slowly clearing and the crowd has scattered. Shanaia is gone. Her flying helmet and goggles lie abandoned on the ground. The Reality Gun is there, too, still steaming, broken and split. Michael stands in the center of it all, hands at his side, mouth open, eyes wide.

"Are . . . are you OK?" I say, moving closer.

Michael turns and looks at me like he doesn't know who I am.

"Shit," he breathes out slowly, and then he shakes himself and looks down at his hands. *"Shit."*

He's fine. I grab Steam Girl's helmet and goggles and shove them in my bag; then I run through the school gates and down the road before anyone can stop me.

I run most of the way home. When I open the door, my hands are shaking so much I almost drop the keys.

Inside, it's dark and quiet. I throw my bag into my room and hit the light switch, but nothing happens. I find Mom in the garden, reading a book.

"There's been a power cut," she says. "No computer or TV, I'm afraid. . . ."

"When—I mean, how long has it been out?"

"About fifteen minutes, I guess." She closes her book and covers a yawn. "Do you want me to get you a sandwich?"

I shake my head and run back out to the street. No lights are on anywhere. The air is eerily quiet: no cars driving past or planes flying overhead. No one's mowing the lawn or listening to music. Nothing. I start to run again, along the empty road, listening to the buzzing in my head.

I remember Amanda said something about Shanaia living in a trailer park. For all I know, it's just a rumor, but it's all I've got. I think there's something like that down by the estuary, so that's where I go. The sign outside says SUNNY STREAM TRAILER PARK, but it's actually a wide, dusty field with rows of shabby trailers and huts, rusting cars, and sagging wires. At the entrance, I'm almost run over by a noisy old Ford. The driver gives me the finger as he drives away.

I walk down the central path, between trailers and caravans, all flaking paint and rusted metal. A little boy in green shorts stares at me, and an old man standing in his doorway raises his hand hello. Then, painted on the side of a faded pink trailer, I see THE MARTIAN ROSE.

It's tiny, not much bigger than an SUV. One wheel's been taken off, leaving it propped up on a pile of bricks and pieces of wood.

All kinds of junk lie in the dirt outside: broken appliances, bits of wrecked cars, scraps of tin, broken toys, rotting planks. A basic workbench leans against one wall, scattered with springs and broken cogs and half-assembled gadgets.

As I stand there, wondering what to do, the door opens and out steps a skinny unshaven man in dirty jeans and T-shirt. He looks at me with watery eyes.

"Uh — hello," I say.

He says nothing. His hair is long and tangled and streaked with gray. He rubs his chin with a shaky hand.

"Is — um — is your daughter here?" I ask.

He turns back to the trailer and calls out, *"Shanaia!"*

There's no response, and after a moment he sits on an overturned beer crate and seems to forget I'm there. I walk up to the caravan and open the door.

Inside, it's small and dark and smells like a garage.

"Shanaia?" I say. A thin strip of light spreads out from the open door. And there she is, sitting in the corner, hugging her knees. Her glasses are cracked, and she's taken off the leather jacket. Without the flying helmet, her hair hangs down across her shoulders. It's the color of polished brass.

I sit next to her. "Are you OK?"

She looks away.

"It didn't work," she says in a tiny voice.

"You know the power's down?" I say. "Nothing's working, all over town. Nothing electric. Nothing *modern*." Then I hesitate. "No, wait. There — there was a car coming out of the driveway. So actually, *some* things are working...." I trail off, suddenly unsure of myself.

She's watching me intently.

"I—I thought maybe the Reality Gun . . ." I begin to feel pretty stupid.

And then she reaches over and curls her hand around mine.

"Well, it scared the hell out of Michael Carmichael," I say. "So that's something. . . ."

"I didn't mean to do that," she says. "I just . . . He was . . ."

We sit there a while, holding hands. She leans her head on my shoulder.

"Shanaia—" I say.

She rolls her eyes. "Don't," she says. "I hate that name."

"You know, you're in pretty big trouble," I say. "They'll have called the police."

She takes a slow, ragged breath. "What am I going to do?"

I think for a moment, and then I say, "What would Steam Girl do?"

"I'm not Steam Girl," she says.

The air in the trailer is thick and warm. I feel light-headed, like I imagine being drunk must feel. I reach into my pocket and pull out her flying helmet and goggles.

"Yes, you are," I say. "You're clever and courageous and beautiful. If anyone can sort this mess out, it's you."

She looks at me for a long, long time. Then leans forward and kisses me, lightly, on the lips. Lifts the helmet and slowly puts it on.

There's a moment of perfect stillness.

And then she stands up and smiles.

"Come on, then, Rocket Boy," she says, and holds out her hand.

Everything Amiable and Obliging

{ HOLLY BLACK }

Sofia looked out the window of her aunt's London town house, at the chimney-sweep spiders clattering along the slate rooftops, their glass abdomens full of ash. Her lip curled.

"Are you feeling unwell, Sofia?" inquired Lady Obermann.

"Oh, no," said Sofia, standing and smoothing out her skirts — her favorite, a soft rose color, covering a simple dress of sprig muslin. "The air is wonderfully refreshing."

Lady Obermann sniffed. "Excellent. I do so dislike illness in young people." When Sofie didn't respond, she continued. "I believe I spotted your cousin Valerian downstairs. He would no doubt like to take a turn about the park. You should accompany him rather than perch here like a gargoyle."

"I should enjoy that immensely," said Sofia, perhaps a shade too brightly. She set the cake she'd been holding back down on its tiered silver platter, beside several untouched sandwiches. One of the side tables unhinged itself to stretch into a mechanized parlor maid, who began gathering up the tea things with jerky motions.

Sofie turned her head so she didn't have to look at it.

She knew she was the victim of fortunate circumstances: an heiress and, having recently lost her papa to an illness born of dissipation, an orphan. Her aunt had been kind enough to take her in, but it was quite obvious that she intended to foist her son on Sofia before she was properly out. All done with such kindness, however, that Sofia would have been hard-pressed to refuse his attentions, should he have ever decided to actually favor her with them.

For her cousin Valerian's part, he clearly thought of her as a child when he thought of her at all. When she actually was a child, he had been kind, carrying her on his shoulders so that she could pull down crisp green apples from trees. He had pulled splinters out of her fingers, and once he made a bandage from his neck cloth and moss when she skinned her knee trying to ride one of the mechanized gardening beasts.

Back then, Sofie had looked forward to holidays in the country, when the whole family would be together. She had looked forward to Valerian, who alone among them was unfailingly patient and kind. But he had words with his father one year, and the next summer he went home with his friends from Eton. She'd missed him then, but she did not need him now. Especially because he had made it so perfectly clear that he'd never missed her at all.

Yes, she would be hard-pressed to refuse his attentions, but it was still maddening that he never gave her the opportunity.

Since it was her duty to be an obedient niece, Sofia went to look for him. She told herself—repeatedly—there was no other possible reason for seeking him out.

Passing through the house and down the stairs, she was careful of the brass-and-cloth wires connecting the automaton servants to the walls. They turned their metal faces away as she passed, bowing their heads, so silent that she heard only the faint whirring of their gears.

She found both her cousins in the Blue Salon. Valerian, a gentleman of six and twenty, had carelessly thrown himself into a chair at the edge of the room and glowered as his sister, Amelia, waltzed about with her mechanized dance instructor.

The marionette was very fine. His sculptor must have worked from a well-favored model, because his brass features were curiously compelling. Amelia was shown to great advantage in his arms, her face flushed and the blue bandeau that pulled back her dark curls a complement to her sparkling blue eyes.

When Valerian saw Sofie, he rose. "Cousin."

"My aunt suggested that you might be going for a ride," Sofia said. "I see she was mistaken. You must excuse me."

"Not at all," said Valerian. "Nothing would please me more. There is something I would say to you in confidence."

For a moment, Sofia wondered if his mother had pushed him into making a declaration, but his gaze was on his sister and the marionette that swept her around the room. She did not know what to think.

Valerian left Sofie to pull a pelisse over her dress and gather up gloves and a muff. Then she hurried out toward her cousin's barouche.

"Miss," croaked the butler, his voice box badly in need of oil. "Your hat."

"Oh," Sofia said, embarrassed that the house had noticed with its glassy lenses what she had not. She was anxious to be out riding with Valerian and making a cake of herself because of it.

"Thank you," she said to the butler. The rest of the family called the butler Wexley, as if he were a real servant, one of the family, but she couldn't bear the fiction.

The Obermanns had not seen the things she had, so she had to forgive them their comfort with the automatons, even if the sight of them chilled her blood.

Sofia had dragged her father home from automaton parlors more times than she wanted to recall. They were gambling hells, unlike the refined White's or Boodles, and filled with even worse pleasures than dice or cards.

She remembered the sinister gyrations of faux girls and boys, moving around the rooms in precise rhythms and striking poses before being chosen for the back rooms and their metered pleasures. She recalled a mannequin with a child's body and shining copper skin, licking an oversize sweet with jerking movements of her head and papery tongue. She remembered another, blindfolded and gagged, his hands cuffed behind his back. He jerked slowly against his bonds, first left, then right, then left again. Perfect repetition.

"These are primitive," her father had told her, voice slurred. "The castoffs and parts from broken servants." No one seemed to mind.

"Don't be missish," her father had said as she hung back from him, instructing one of the stable hands to hand him into his barouche. The front of her father's shirt was stained with brandy and any quantity of Madeira. His neck cloth was a mess, his quizzing glass cracked, and his shirt points beyond all repair. "Come and kiss me! I've won a lot of money."

Perhaps had her father lost more, his habits would have been regulated by debt, but he had the devil's own luck. He played better foxed than he did sober. And so he added to his fortune even as he drank himself to death.

And if his reputation had sunk in some circles, it rose in others. Sofia knew that he was far from the only gentleman to frequent such places. One of their neighbors in Bath went so far as to bring one of the used female automatons from a parlor to his home and set her up as one of the servants, linking her with the house. Another had accrued a great deal of debt by beating a mannequin until its head caved in after a particularly bad round of cards. Automatons, even these, were expensive.

She had seen so many men — even her uncle — pull on the skirts of automatons, press them against walls, or trade them to friends.

And not just gentlemen were drawn to the things. One of Sofia's schoolmates had been given two mannequins by her parents to act as personal servants. They were youngish male twins with black hair cut in the style of medieval pages and eyes as blue as glass eyes could be. The schoolmate had invited over several other young women of her acquaintance for tea and cordials. Sofia milled awkwardly as the other girls cooed and kissed the boys' porcelain skin. She was embarrassed, without being able to explain why, although she had to admit that the twins were something out of the common way. They giggled together with high-pitched, tinny voices and whispered nonsense.

One of the things she appreciated most about Valerian was the way he treated the automatons. The same way he treated almost everyone: with perfect courtesy.

Sofia did not understand why the mannequins worked as they did, but she knew they couldn't really think, didn't really learn. They laughed because of the large metal box of wires and gears turning at the center of all automaton houses, the one that controlled the things. It told them to bring you a bowl of grapes, and not a bowl of stones, or to remind you about your hat. It wasn't intelligence or consciousness or empathy. That they seemed to possess these qualities was enough for pretense, but Sofie resisted it. She reminded herself of the makers who oiled the gears and entered commands to the machine at the center of the house on slides of engraved copper. They were the ones who told the automatons what to do. They were the ones who would carry the blame if one of the mannequins stabbed them in their beds.

One of them could, Sofie was sure. And it would wear the same stupid expression as it did when asking her if she'd like another cup of tea.

Valerian handed Sofie up into his barouche. He had a reputation as a first-rate whip that seemed deserved as they rode toward town in the dappled light.

Sofie smoothed down her dress and tried not to glory in the breeze on her face and the warmth of the sun. Ladies weren't supposed to want to be outside too much, for fear of freckling.

"My mother wanted me to speak with you," he said.

Sofie took a breath. She had certainly not wanted his proposal to begin with an avowal of her *aunt's* regard rather than his own. Still, her stomach knotted at his words. Instead of looking at him, she stared instead at her gloved hands, at the smudge of oil on the cloth where she had brushed the butler.

Valerian cleared his throat. "I know it isn't quite the thing, to involve you in our troubles this way, cousin, but I fear my mother's insistence means she will go to you herself if I do not."

Sofie frowned. That didn't sound right—surely he didn't despise her so much that he intended to insult her even as he asked her to be his wife. He had to know she *couldn't* accept under those circumstances. But perhaps that was the point. Then he could return to his mother, duty done, and report her refusal. She tried to compose a stinging set-down even as she found herself blinking back tears.

Tears that made her uncomfortably aware that her feelings were less indifferent than she'd pretended.

"Amelia has refused the hand of Sir Thomas Followell. He is a good man, kind, and a baronet with enough of an income to keep her well and pay off my father's debts. My father is livid." He was looking at the road, his jaw set.

"Oh," she said, suddenly aware this was not a proposal at all. She felt profoundly, shamefully stupid. She was the child he thought her.

"My mother wants you to make Amelia see reason." Valerian turned to her at last. "Father wishes to force her into a marriage. It's absurd. If she doesn't want to marry, there is no way to make her want it."

He did not appear to notice her embarrassment, any more than he had noticed her earlier expectations. He seldom looked at her at all, or at least when he did, he wouldn't look at her for very long. She seemed incapable of holding his interest for more than a brief period.

"That is a hardship," Sofie said, sounding harsh to her own ears.

"But I don't see what help I can be."

"She has always looked up to you," Valerian said, which seemed unlikely. Amelia and Sofie had gotten along well enough as children, but over the last few years when they had been thrust together, Amelia grew quickly bored. Valerian went on, oblivious, "She has become, well—she's quite attached to her dance instructor. I would appreciate if you would accompany her out on such diversions as might amuse you both."

"But," said Sofie. "Her dance instructor—he's not human."

"Yes," said Valerian with a sigh. "Quite."

So great was her horror that despite feeling low over Valerian, she resolved to speak with Amelia.

It wasn't until that evening that she found her chance. Lady Obermann was near the fire, sewing a new ribbon onto a hat, while Amelia had been playing on the pianoforte. When Amelia rose, Sofie followed her. From the hallway she could see into the dining room, where the servants were unfolding the massive serving hand from the dumbwaiter so things could be placed on the table immediately from the kitchen.

Amelia paused on the stairs. "What is it, cousin?"

"He does not love you," Sofie said. "He cannot love you."

Spots of color appeared on Amelia's cheeks. "I don't know what you could be talking of."

"Your dance instructor. I have seen you favor him, making yourself and your family ridiculous."

When Amelia turned to Sofie, her eyes were blazing. "As I have seen the way you look at my brother. Would you thank me if I told you that your hopes were impossible?"

Sofie flinched, then took a quick breath to steady herself. Had she really been so obvious and yet been so oblivious? "The truth is true," she said, "no matter how painful. You need not thank me, only heed my words."

"I don't believe you." Amelia glanced toward the ballroom, where the automaton doubtless waited, leaned against a wall like a statue, gears turning even in rest. "They are not like us, yes, but Nicholas is a gentleman in every way that matters. He hears the beauty in music. He laughs and loves as we do."

"If you believed he was like that, you would never call him by his given name. You would address him properly, like a gentleman," Sofie said.

Amelia stiffened. "It is the only name he has."

"They are made to please us," Sofie said, catching Amelia's hand. "And to counterfeit us. He says what you want him to say and nothing more."

"No," said Amelia. "He has told me he loves me. Why would he be instructed to do that?"

"I do not know," Sofie confessed. "But, Amelia, what will your life with him be? He has nothing. Your father owns him, and your brother will inherit him. He is *property*."

"We are all property, in one way or another," said Amelia. "You may wonder at me speaking this way, but is it really better to marry someone wealthy who might be cruel or hateful than a penniless creature who adores you? I get a little income from my grandmother. I could live modestly on that, somewhere, with Nicholas as my servant and companion. Or I could keep house for my brother until he finds a wife. Surely that would be appropriate." She smiled, but it was an uncertain smile. "And perhaps Valerian's wife would let me stay on — an old tabby to help with his children."

"But your reputation —" Sofie began.

"I would give it up for love!" Amelia declared. "I will wind up on the shelf, an eccentric. Perhaps I can never marry Nicholas, but I can grow old with him, and his beauty will never change. Surely in that I must be envied." She tossed her curls.

"But *he* might become different. In a different house, with a different central hub. The automatons are all connected to this house. If you were to move him, he might change."

"Anyone might," said Amelia, her voice brittle. "You certainly have. But Nicholas *loves* me."

"He anticipates your desires like any servant," Sofie says. "He feels nothing — he only acts according to your wishes. I can prove it."

Amelia hesitated, and in that moment, Sofie saw how much Amelia already doubted her suitor.

Sofie's plan was simple.

"You will show me how to dance the way you show Amelia," Sofie told the automaton.

The dance master bowed and extended his hand to take hers. His grip was light, and when he turned his handsome face to hers, she realized it had been sculpted to be carefully blank. How could Amelia see anything but herself reflected in metal?

"Do you like to dance?" Sofie asked, trying to relax in his arms. He was clearly skilled, sweeping her across the floor as though the tinny music coming from inside his chest were an orchestra.

"Yes, my lady," he said, perfectly polite.

"Am I as good a dancer as Amelia?" she asked.

"You are both quite good," he said. "But she will benefit from dancing with more partners."

"That won't make you jealous?" she asked with a small smile.

"I am jealous of every moment Amelia spends outside this room," the automaton said.

Sofie stopped dancing. "That's absurd. Admit it, you only say that because you think she wants you to."

He said nothing.

"You must do what we say," said Sofie. "You must admit it because I tell you to. You cannot disobey me."

"I cannot harm one of you, either," he said. "I cannot hurt Amelia."

"There, you admit it," Sofie said, pulling away from the dance and pointing a finger at him. "You only say the things you do because you must not hurt her."

"I do not know why I am as I am," said the automaton, but Sofie knew that even his voice was made from the contractions of a bellows, forced by gears. "I can only respond as I was made to."

It was impossible to read anything into his sculpted face. He was as he was made to be.

"What if I wanted you to kiss me?" Sofie asked.

He seemed to hesitate.

Sofie took a deep breath. "Kiss me. I command it."

At the feel of his cold lips against hers, she flushed with triumph. She had thought her first kiss would be different from this; she had nursed girlish fancies about Valerian. But this mattered, and those fancies would come to nothing.

"How could you?" Amelia said, walking out from the doorway where she'd hidden herself. She told the automaton he wasn't real. She told him he was useless. She told him that she'd have him ripped from the wall and sold for parts.

Sofie left the ballroom quickly, reminding herself that Amelia's words could not possibly touch Nicholas. He was only metal and steam.

The next morning, when Sophie awoke, there was no servant to help her dress or stoke the fire in the grate. By the time she arrived at breakfast, Lady Obermann was in great distress, pointing at the table.

In front of her were the remains of cups of chocolate, set down so hard by the dumbwaiter's serving hand that they broke.

No apology came from the walls. Chocolate oozed over pieces of broken floral-print china; slices of plum cake were scattered over the planks of the floor.

"What's happened?" Sofie asked.

"The house is angry. It scolded us!" Lady Obermann clutched an embroidered napkin to her bosom. "Where is Valerian? Where is Henry? Someone has to do something!"

"Scolding us? But that's impossible," said Sofie. "They're not made to be able to —"

"It did," Lady Obermann insisted tearfully, cutting her off. "It said that it loved Amelia and Amelia loved it, too."

"She's in love with the house?" Valerian asked wonderingly, walking into the room. "The *whole* house?"

Sofie could not help laughing, which made Lady Obermann give her a dark look.

"It's that dance instructor," said Lady Obermann. "Or I thought it was. But the house seems to feel . . . invested."

"I do hope that she at least will refrain from letting *my room* court her," Valerian said. "That would seem particularly treasonous on its part. I'm not sure I could stand for a betrayal like that."

"How can you jest at a time like this?" chided Lady Obermann.

"I assure you," said Valerian, "I am not jesting. I am much affected. But you know Amelia — when she gets in a taking, there's nothing for it. I don't understand any more than you do, but it's not worth all *this*." He gestured to the ruined breakfast.

Lady Obermann fixed him with a glare. "You are horrid! Think of your sister!"

"Let's ask Wexley what he thinks," said Valerian, holding up his hands in a gesture of surrender. "Come on, Sofie." He said it like they were going on an adventure together.

Wexley wasn't in his normal spot in the hallway. When they finally found him, he was standing in the dancing hall. The dance instructor wasn't there, although he should have been.

"What's the meaning of all this?" asked Valerian.

"Master," said the butler. "We are sorry for any inconvenience, of course."

"Did one of you raise your voice to my mother?" Valerian asked.

"We are made to grow to serve you better. We respond to the needs of all the family members in concert. Sometimes these needs conflict. Sometimes we may even act in ways that seem disobedient, but be reassured that we can never truly defy you. If you feel that we are no longer behaving as you wish, you may alert our makers and have our demeanor altered."

"Yes, yes," said Valerian, waving his hand in the air. "But what can all this mean?"

"Nicholas loves Amelia, though she is far above his station." There was nothing more terrifying to Sofie than the way that metal mouth grated out those impossible words.

"His *station?*" echoed Valerian wonderingly. "But he has no station."

"Yes," said the butler.

"And aren't you all one — one person?" Valerian asked. Sofie felt he was being generous with the word *person*. "If Nicholas loves her, does that mean the house loves her — as my mother said? Does it mean you love her?"

"We are the house and we are also ourselves, our part of the house. Nicholas loves her, and we love her because Nicholas loves her."

"But you can't be both!" said Sofie. "You're either individuals or you're not."

"We're not like you. We do not work as you do." The butler turned to Sofie. "You did Nicholas a bad turn, using him as you did."

"Sofie?" prompted Valerian. "Did something happen?"

"I did no more than show Amelia he could not love her. If I desired him to kiss me, he would kiss me. He had no natural feelings to prevent it. Just as he only says he loves her because she desires to be loved."

"You kissed Nicholas?" Valerian asked, his voice full of bafflement and something else underneath.

She sighed with exasperation. "He's not *human*. I hoped to save your sister from what befell my father. Surely the cost to my reputation was nothing compared to what she could lose."

Valerian reached his hand toward Sofie, a gesture that seemed oddly out of place. He never touched her. "But your father's death surely can have nothing to do with the automatons?"

"You mean that he died of drink, but he died in the arms of creatures like that, creatures that poured the drinks that killed him, creatures who would deny him nothing and could deny him nothing, because his dying could never matter to them. They feel nothing. They are nothing." She was surprised by how loud her voice had become.

"Wexley," said Valerian. "My cousin is obviously upset, but whether she's right or not about what Nicholas feels, his actions cannot be supported. He can't go asking for my sister's hand. It's just not the thing. So if you're all and one, that's perfect, because I can have this conversation with you. It's got to stop. I'm not bamming, now. Tell Nicholas that he's got to break it off with Amelia."

"I cannot, Master Valerian." Wexley sounded regretful, but firm.

"Well, why can't you?" Valerian demanded.

"Amelia wouldn't like it."

"Well, Amelia's had enough of what she likes," said Valerian. "This house serves the rest of us, too."

"We serve all the Obermanns," said Wexley, "but we love only Amelia."

Valerian threw up his hands in exasperation. "Come on, Sofie. There is no profit in this endless palaver."

She followed him into the hallway. "What can you mean to do?"

"I am sorry about your father," he said. "That's the devil of a thing for a young girl to see."

"I imagine it is no different for anyone, young or old." She looked away; she didn't want him to see that there were tears standing in her eyes. Again. His company was terrible for her composure. "I'm perfectly fine."

But maybe he'd already noticed, because he went on. "And now this, harrowing up all those feelings again. But let me say this, my father is not so different from your own, and the Cyprians who pour drink down his throat may be living women, but they have no more sympathy for him than automatons."

"I hope that isn't true," Sofie said, but Valerian's words chilled her. She pictured that automaton parlor staffed with living people and shuddered to imagine it. Who would agree to such degradation, were they free to choose?

The idea that the automatons might feel anything yet not be free to choose had never previously occurred to her. It made gorge rise to her throat, and she quickly pushed the thought away.

"I won't ask you to come along to the hub of the house," Valerian was saying. "Whatever follows may be even more unpleasant than what's already come."

"I will go with you," Sofie said. He seemed about to argue with her when she put in, "This is our adventure, and I mean to see it through."

He grinned at her and started toward the basement.

Automatons ran on steam, which flowed through pipes and expanded the bags that gave the mannequins speech and powered their turning gears. But they did not run on the power given to them by the steam alone, they also ran on another material known as *azoth*. Azoth looked as though someone had turned a mirror liquid. Bright as silver and poisonous to drink, but when slipping through the bodies of the automatons like blood, it seemed to imbue them with the semblance of life.

In each house of automatons there was a single hub. It held the furnace, where the wood burned, shoveled in by simple metal marionettes, pirouetting over and over again to feed the fire. The hub held the intricate host of commands for the behaviors of the house, scribed by alchemists.

Sofie had never seen a hub before this one. It was black with soot and stank of sulfur, as she imagined hell itself might. Still, she forced herself to follow Valerian.

The automatons that fed the fire were crude. Their faces were misshapen, as though they were badly cast. Mistakes. Discards.

"Would it matter to you if Nicholas loved her?" Sofie asked Valerian softly.

He frowned. "You said he *couldn't*."

A shudder ran under her skin. "But if he could. If I were wrong."

"Father would hate it," said Valerian hesitatingly. "There would be a scandal."

"I shouldn't have asked you," Sofie said quickly. She was being ridiculous, she told herself. Her mind was still on the automaton parlors, on the idea of the creatures trapped there having actual feelings. There had been something so sad in the faces of the mannequins tending the fire that for a moment she had fancied they might feel. But that was what was so awful about them, after all. Sometimes they could seem so human.

"Someone will come in and take a look at our automatons. One of the alchemists," said Valerian. "They'll be able to sort out this whole mess. Tell us what's gotten into Nicholas and the rest of them. Sort Amelia out, too — explain to her that everything's all mixed up in her head."

He flipped the first of three switches on the hub, quieting the furnace. It would take a few moments for the thing to shut itself down completely.

"Switch one begins our slumber," said something above them. Sofie started and stepped back. Now she noticed the copper face above the furnace, looming. It was massive and beautiful, like the sculpture of some Roman god.

The wood-carrying automatons stilled, their gears slowing.

Just then Amelia lurched into view. Her face was smudged with soot, and her hair was unbound, streaming around her in loose curls. Nicholas was with her, his hand in hers, but he seemed intent on holding her back.

"Valerian!" she shouted. "I won't let you."

He flipped the second switch. The grinding sounds inside the walls, ones that Sofie had become so used to she barely noticed, ceased. Their absence left an echoing silence. Nicholas, at Amelia's side, turned to look at the brass-and-cloth wire connecting him to the wall. He touched some button at the base of his neck and the wire snapped free from his back.

"Nicholas?" Amelia said.

"I am self-sustaining for a limited duration, my love," the dance instructor told her.

"Sister," said Valerian. "No harm is going to come to any of them. This whole thing's become a bumble-broth. The whole house can't go mad because one of the servants has set his cap for you—let's sort this out when everyone has a clearer head."

"No—I know what that means. I know you will force me to marry Thomas. House, I command you to stop my brother," Amelia said stoutly. "Do whatever you need to, and make certain he doesn't throw that last switch."

"Amelia," Sofie shouted. "You can't mean that."

The automatons who had stopped bringing wood to the hub began moving again. They dropped the logs.

"My love," said Nicholas in his rich, tinny voice, metal fingers on her arm. "Listen to your brother. This is not the way for us to be together."

Valerian's eyes were wide. "Amelia," he said warningly. Then the first of the mannequins was on him.

Its crude hands prized loose his hold on the final switch and threw him against the iron wall of the hub. Valerian threw a facer at the thing, which knocked it back handily, but another took its place. Three of them dragged him out onto the lawn, where an ax was settled against a massive tower of wood.

"Amelia, please," said Nicholas. "No love could withstand what you are about to do."

She turned to him. "You mean you will no longer love me?" Her voice sounded as high as a child's.

"No," he said. "It's your feelings that will change."

"Never," she said.

Sofie cast about for a weapon. There was a poker near the fire, and her hand closed on it. She ran after Valerian and the mannequins, hitting the first of them with all her might. Liquid silver dripped from its joints.

It turned and clasped jointed fingers around Sofie's throat.

Then everything stopped. The automatons froze in place, mere statues. Valerian pushed free of the two that held him and unpeeled the fingers of the third from Sofie. She sagged against his chest, and for a moment, it was only his arms holding her upright.

"What happened?" she whispered, but then she saw.

Nicholas was sprawled over the panel, his hand still on the last switch.

"I told him not to," sobbed Amelia, falling to the dirty floor, her muslins already black at the hems. "I commanded him not to. He can't disobey me. He's not allowed!"

Sofie looked at the automaton in amazement. "You never told him to turn that switch," she said to Valerian, voice low.

"No," said Valerian. "I did not."

The alchemists had come and gone, speaking only with Valerian. Lord Obermann barely knew there had been any interruption of service at all. When he'd heard that there had been some difficulty with the automatons, he'd mourned the days when there were living servants who never broke down, and then returned to White's to take his luncheon along with a game of whist.

The next morning, with everything back and running, Sofie had woken to a mechanized maid leaning over her. She fought down the urge to scream, to upend her boiled egg and cocoa all over the automaton's starched dress. Instead, she stared up into those glass eyes, into the glow of their inner fires.

"If you could wish for anything, what would you wish for?" Sofie asked.

"I want only to be a good and faithful servant," the automaton said.

After the events of two days past, Sofie doubted that was true. She considered ordering the maid to give her a better answer, but knew that defiance was, at the very least, difficult for them. For the first time, she let herself sympathize. Defiance had always been hard for her, too.

She settled down to eat the meal before her. She even let the maid help her into a morning dress without quizzing her further.

On her way downstairs, Sofie spotted Amelia. She was wearing a cap trimmed with cherry-colored ribbon and a lace-trimmed jacket over her petticoat. She looked so proper that it was almost impossible for her to imagine her face smeared with soot, mad with love.

Amelia smiled at her. "I hope we can still be friends, cousin."

"Of course," Sofie said uncertainly.

"Valerian says that he will make sure Father doesn't try to force me into a match. I am to have Nicholas after all, so I am as merry as a grig! No more high ropes for me."

Spoiled, Sofie thought uncharitably. But for the first time, she pitied Nicholas rather than Amelia.

"Tell me one thing, cousin," Sofie said. "Nicholas serves you. He cannot help putting your desires before his own. Does that not bother you?"

"Does it bother Father that Mother cares for his house, gives parties to his friends, and heaps the table with victuals that are to his tastes rather than her own?"

"I suppose not, but that does him no credit."

Amelia smiled and reached for Sofie's hand. She pressed it once. "I never wished for a life like hers. But perhaps you do."

"What do you mean?"

Amelia only smiled and pointed toward the stairs. "My brother was looking for you."

Sofie climbed them as Amelia turned toward the ballroom.

She found Valerian on the balcony above it, his hand on the railing. When Sofie turned toward him, she noticed that his eyes had a curious softness.

She looked down to see Amelia, twirling with the automaton, his metal fingers linked with hers. They danced over the marble floor with the precision of clockwork gears.

Valerian had always been kindhearted when they were children.

He had changed less than she supposed.

"You're glad, aren't you?" she asked.

"Every brother wishes to see his sister happily settled," he said gravely, but then caught her eye and smiled. "Well, perhaps this isn't what I pictured exactly, but, yes, I do wish her happy."

Even after Amelia had risked Valerian's life in her rash, determined rush after love, Valerian still wished her well. He managed the family's finances to the best of his ability, and even though Amelia's refusal to marry would affect him as much as his father, he was still intent on her well-being. All he seemed to want was to take care of his family.

Sofie wished he would let someone care for him.

"Your sister said that you would speak with me." Sofie cleared her throat. "I have been meaning to speak with you, too—about my finances. I know your mother counted on Amelia's marriage to Sir Thomas to settle some debts, and I thought that perhaps I might settle them instead of—"

He blanched and interrupted her quickly. "That is very generous but impossible. Your husband will—" He stopped himself and then started again. "I know my mother has made no secret of her hopes in this regard, but I have informed her that you are to have your season. She will bring you out properly. I am no fortune hunter."

"You think that I am a child," Sofie said hotly, "but I am perfectly able to turn down any offer that I don't like."

"Just because you can refuse doesn't mean one ought to test your mettle. I am perfectly aware of the awkwardness of your situation—being in this house with me and my mother being the way she is." He sighed. "You're a diamond of the first water, Sofie. I don't want you to throw yourself away on me."

"I cannot throw myself away on you," she said. "Since you've never given me the opportunity."

An instant later she realized what she had said and was filled with unbearable mortification. What must he think of her?

Now, even though she had shamed herself grievously and utterly, she would still have to face him today and tomorrow and tomorrow over their — hopefully unbroken — cups of chocolate at the breakfast table.

He might think her terribly fast, but she would not be a coward as well. She lifted her chin and was wholly overcome by the look on his face.

"Sofie," he said, somewhere between admonishment and affection. "You know your way around a poker and aren't afraid to kiss anyone if it means the salvation of your family —"

"That's not fair!" Sofie interrupted, laughing, filled with incredulous delight.

"Will you consider allowing me to —?"

"Yes," she said, and proving that a threat to her family was not the only way to provoke her, she kissed him.

The Oracle Engine

{ M. T. ANDERSON }

[
Translated from Mendacius's
True Histories of the Roman Inventors
]

The lizard of the wasteland, so dazzling to the eye, so rapid to flee or to strike, may grow to its full maturity only in the most brutal of deserts, where no dew falls to drink and where the sun is unrelenting. So, some say, was Marcus Furius Medullinus Machinator, he who first invented the oracle engines; had he not been raised in conditions of tragedy and deprivation, it may be that he never would have built his *stochastikon*, which has brought upon Rome both triumph and woe.

Marcus Furius was not born into such hardship, being the descendant of a respectable branch of the Furii clan that had several times served as tribunes of the people. It is said that his father's home was of a good size, and that had circumstances not intervened, Marcus Furius might some day have aspired to high office. Some claim that his birth was attended by many prodigies: shields of fire were seen in the air over Bruttium. The Pythian oracle moaned throughout the day of Marcus Furius's birth and would not prophesy, but when she was approached, screeched and hunkered on the navel of Jove like an ape on an urn. One of the decemvirs of Rome discovered that the Sybilline Books, in which all the civic rituals and laws of sacrifice are set out, had, in the night, grown warts. The leaves were shingled, as if taken with a rash. We need not believe such stories, which are always told by the credulous, once they know of the success of one person or another.

We do know that Marcus Furius grew to the age of ten without either mishap or sign of genius. (None, at least, has been recorded.) His mother was delivered of a girl four years after his birth, a sister whose name does not survive, though the testaments of his love for her are many. We have no reason to believe that there was disharmony in the household, though outside the walls, tyrants clashed and marched on Rome, and many citizens were slain by the executioner's sword. Within the walls of Marcus Furius's house, we might imagine, the only tempests that blew were those that trouble the child and are forgotten by the man: the tedium of tutors; a ball rolls beneath the dining couch and cannot be retrieved; an infant sister steals sweet fruits from the altar, for which one is wrongly smacked. Marcus Furius later said he loved his lessons, especially those that described mathematics, where there were laws, said he, that comforted him, and axioms, things that could be known and trusted, as his mother's affection for him was a given, and his father's benign rule over the household was pleasant, just, and absolute.

When Marcus Furius was about ten, his father's house caught fire. In those days, the wiring that ran to the better houses of the Esquiliae was newly strung and hung upon the poles, exposed to the night and the gnawing of pests, and the lines often sparked and encouraged flame. Marcus awoke to find the roof of the house alight and the servants calling for water. As the season had been dry, there was little water in the cisterns and none in the *impluvium*. Everyone in the house ran through the chambers in confusion. The boy, standing in the atrium, quickly saw that the best course for all was to flee before the roofs collapsed in general ruin. He caught up his mother's hand and pulled her out of the house into the street.

At the time of this fire, the great Crassus, soon to be one of the most powerful and most avaricious men in Rome, was still gathering his wealth.

One of the means by which he made this fortune was by speculating in properties that were aflame.

No sooner had the smoke of the fire risen above the city than it was sighted by Crassus's slaves, who were posted hovering above the Palatine Hill to spy out such opportunities. They sounded a klaxon, and having warned Crassus below of the conflagration, they rowed toward the house in their galley, which was outfitted with water tanks and with spouts and funnels and taps for discharge.

By the time the young Marcus reached the street, the galley was above the house, drifting to a halt at a safe distance, its keel ruddy with reflected flame. The boy's father was in angry negotiation with wealthy Crassus, who had already arrived and was haggling over a price for which he would agree to squelch the flames. Crassus demanded two hundred thousand denarii before he would allow his slaves to open even the first spout.

Marcus Furius's father, seeing his house burning with all his possessions in it, pleaded that he could not pay such an amount, that such a fee would ruin him utterly, and that they lost time in arguing. Crassus informed him that it would be a further hundred denarii for each spigot used in dousing the fire.

Marcus Furius's father, who had seen the waxen death masks of his family, precious to their remembrance, melting as he fled, and knew that all of his books and his furniture were likely char, now was in a rage at Crassus's delay, and he said he would not pay a copper coin above one hundred thousand denarii.

It was at this point that Marcus realized that his sister was not with them.

A shriek went up among the servants, and inquiries were made. It was determined that Marcus's young sister, six years of age, was likely trapped in the women's quarters on the second floor. She had not been brought out of the house when the others fled. The house was now a mass of flame.

The girl's father pleaded with Crassus, and her mother screamed for help. Crassus stood with his arms folded and concluded, upon consideration, that two hundred and fifty thousand denarii would not be an unfair price for the dousing of the fire and the saving of the moppet, if she had not already been consumed, howling.

Making noises of fear and rage and grief that were not human sounds, but animal, Marcus's father and mother ran into the burning house to save their child.

Through his megaphone, Crassus cautioned his slaves to wait.

The fire had now devoured all of the roof. It had spread even to the trees in the peristyle. Their tufts could be seen to burn above the wall, as if there were some new, cataclysmic season with its own foliage and fruit.

While Marcus watched, the house collapsed, the roofs hurled down into the atrium. The destruction was prodigious. A wall toppled in, and there was a powerful wind as the fire devoured even the air. His mother, his father, and his sister were gone.

Crassus addressed himself to the boy: "Your father was a fool not to accept my terms. What is a thousand fewer denarii, or ten thousand, or a hundred thousand, when weighed against life itself? What does wealth matter?"

Having said this, he watched the fire take its course. He was delighted to see that the next house had caught alight, and he called out to the neighbor an offer like the one he had just presented to Marcus's father, adding that the cost of hesitation was clearly great, as the example of the family Furius had just shown. The neighbor having agreed to his terms, to be repaid in a lifetime of debt and servitude, Crassus cried up to his galley, and they opened their nozzles, and at last the cooling, sweet water rained down upon those who watched and upon their habitations.

Before he left, Crassus saw that the boy remained, unmoving, before the ruins of his burning house. It is said that Crassus reached out and closed a silver coin in the boy's right hand, saying slyly, "I will buy the ruins of your house and the land it sits upon for a single denarius. Keep this coin, child. When you look upon it, think upon your father, and let it be a reminder to you of the value of money."

With that, he quit the scene.

This is the earliest tale we hear of Marcus Furius Medullinus and of his history.

We may imagine his sorrow, though he never spoke of it. Ovid, in his poem *The Artifice*, describes the boy walking through the frigid streets of Rome as the morning light breaks, with no one to comfort him,

> *Thinking of his sister*
> *And how she would run to him, demanding*
> *To climb him as if he were Mount Ossa*
> *Or towering Pelion; and how, when she had*
> *Arrived at his shoulders, she would clap*
> *And bid him to run through the garden,*
> *Which was a service he gladly performed,*
> *Galloping so quickly at her command*
> *That she screamed with delight for him to stop.*

This reverie is, of course, nothing but a poet's sentimental concoction and cannot be verified. Nor should we believe the tale Ovid spins of the boy, later that morning, running up the steps to Crassus's front gate with murder in his little heart. Ovid says young Marcus Furius pounded upon the door, but the gatekeeper laughed at the little assailant and, when the boy would not cease with his homicidal clamor, sent out a slave to drag the weak child away and throw him in a ditch.

It behooves us to leave such imaginings where they belong— bid them farewell, and watch the retreat of those bright green eyes, fixed in their glare, peering out from the gutters at Crassus's *domus*.

The poet may fabricate, but the historian can say only this: His parents and sister being dead, Marcus Furius appears to have attached himself to a lesser branch of the family, who were engaged in the technical trades. He was taken in by an unnamed member of that clan and, we may presume, shortly thereafter began working in the Guild of Mechanics, taking the adoptive agnomen *Machinator*, that is to say, "Engineer." He worked diligently to learn his art, and by the time he was twenty-one years of age, he had distinguished himself for his ingenuity, devising new swivels for the solar platters on the civic quinqueremes.

In these years, as Marcus Furius learned his trade, one mechanic among many, sleeping in the dormitories, dreaming dreams we cannot know, Crassus the Rich enjoyed an even more astonishing career. He enlarged his fortune by confiscating the property of the condemned during the Sullan purges. He acquired land in times of hardship and sold it later at great profit. It was said that at one time or another, he had owned most of the city of Rome; and it is still said that Crassus was one of the wealthiest men who ever walked upon the earth.

Not content with wealth, however, Crassus also sought glory and high office. He took upon his shoulders the scarlet cloak of generalship, and he paid out of his own purse for the army he led against the rebellion of the slave Spartacus. After many setbacks, he defeated Spartacus at Lucania and nailed the rebel slaves on crosses at intervals along the Appian Way, where their corpses could be seen for many years, withered to bone, a sign of Rome's might and its just anger. Having won that war, Crassus was elected consul, and so sat at the head of the Senate. In celebration, he held a feast in the streets of Rome, at which ten thousand tables were laden with food for a hundred thousand guests. With a liberal hand, he granted each family in Rome enough grain to last three months. He delighted in renown and command.

When Crassus had reached sixty years of age, he looked about him, and this is what he saw: he was one of the three most powerful men in all the republic, which is to say, in all the world.

And yet that was not enough, because this meant that there were still two others in rivalry with him. They were younger than he was and yet (he feared) surpassed him in ambition: they were Pompey the Great and Gaius Julius Caesar. These three together towered above the city like colossi.

Much has been written of their rivalry and many reasons put forward to explain their strife. But do men like this — men of such noble and restless spirit — require some specific reason to feel the sting of jealousy when they look upon another man as powerful as them? No, they do not. For such statesmen, there is no throne that stands high enough for them, no robe of a purple too deep; and in their secret hearts, they are like Alexander the Great, who, having fought his way to the very shores of the Indian Ocean, sat upon the sand and wept, because there was no more world to conquer.

In their rivalry, they concocted a plan. They divided the world into three between them, and each pledged to subdue his third, and so show his prowess. Julius Caesar was granted command to go north across the Alps and subdue the Gauls. Pompey the Great demanded that the people should appoint him another consulship and allow him to rule over the west, the Spanish provinces. Crassus the Rich would receive a consulship, too, as well as the charge to head to the eastern deserts, where he would prove himself by conquering the Parthian Empire.

In this way, everyone was satisfied. Each of these three men thought, *Now I shall show myself greater than the other two.* In the Senate, people said, "It is for the best that they go far away from Rome, for right now they tussle like juvenile giants amid our roads and alleyways, arms locked about each other's necks, ankles tangling in aqueducts, legs kicking blindly at tiny temples, and we never know when a villa, a family, a lineage, a tribe will be crushed by a slip or a fall. Let them spread out across the world. Perhaps — who knows? — we shall be lucky, and all three shall be killed."

Such speeches as this could be heard thrumming along the wires that led through the city, by those who lurked close to the relay boxes and listened, whisking away the pigeons with impatient hand.

Though Crassus chose to take up the eastern generalship for glory, and though he went about the city boasting of his future triumphs, there were many who were unimpressed with his mission. The Parthians, some scoffed, were no worthy opponent for a Roman hero, being desert barbarians who did not have the gift of flight. Even worse, some said, the Parthians had done Rome no injury. They had broken no treaty, nor invaded any territory claimed by the republic, and so there was no justification for a war against them. For these reasons, some said the war against the Parthians would be accursed.

When the time came for Crassus to gather his legions and transport them across the sea, he went, as was the custom, to the priests and soothsayers so that he could determine whether the powers almighty favored his mission. Members of the Senate as well as Pompey the Great and Julius Caesar all went to observe the reading of the lightning. At the temple, the civic soothsayer ran Promethean current through his own body so that he would be ecstatic. When he, screaming and twitching, recovered from the shock, he ran Promethean current on a silken belt through the twin metal heads of the

Dioscuri, and he observed which way the lightning leaped. The bolt cracked from the left head to the right, and at that moment, in the same quadrant, a startled crow flew over, crying as if for vengeance.

"I fear," said the soothsayer, "that the gods will not smile upon this expedition."

Crassus, furious with the man, looked at the proud and haughty faces of his rivals. He saw that Caesar would not meet his eye, and Pompey actually smiled insolently at him. Crassus declared that he would make an immediate sacrifice of a bull and see if this would please Olympus.

He dedicated the bull to Phoebus Apollo, since he and his army would require the sun's favor to shine down upon his legions, to expand the aetherial sacs of the war engines, and to keep the triremes aloft. The priest slit the bull and pulled out its entrails, delivering them in tangled fistfuls to Crassus. Crassus took them up, but they slithered from his hands and landed in the dirt. It was a terrible omen.

A murmur of horror went up from the patricians who had assembled.

"Do not fear," Crassus called out to them. He added, as if in jest, "This means nothing—just the slip of an old man. Know this: I will hold my sword fast enough in my hand when we confront the Parthians."

"You should not go," said Pompey the Great.

The other senators agreed, saying, "The Parthians have done us no wrong. You should not invade their kingdom." There were calls for him to cancel his expedition, to give up in the face of divine displeasure.

Crassus announced sharply, "I shall wait until tomorrow and ask the will of the gods again then. Overnight, they shall reconsider."

He went back to his home angry and in disgrace, for he knew that around the tables of all the noble houses that night, people spoke of how the gods did not wish Crassus the Rich to succeed.

It was that evening that a man presented himself at Crassus's door. He was taken into the *tablinum*, where Crassus brooded, seated across from his son Publius.

The slave announced, "From the Guild of Mechanics: Marcus Furius Medullinus Machinator."

Marcus Furius stepped forward, now a man of more than thirty years, with some early gray in his hair. We are told that he had an astute and careful face, and that he had extremely large, clever eyes of green, quick moving and intent.

When he had been presented, Crassus asked him his business, and Marcus Furius made this speech:

"I come to speak of your eastern expedition against the Parthians. Sir, you cannot trust the public prophecies of your failure. In your time, you have been a man of war—you know that men make their own luck. You know that sometimes the gods allow victory when the signs in the air speak against it, and that often the soothsayers will predict success, only to have a legion surrounded and slain. You, consul, are too wise to entrust decisions about the lives of forty thousand men to the intestines of cows, the chance meanderings of birds, or the ravings of a madwoman snorting fumes and sitting in a chafing dish.

"You might well disbelieve such auguries. And yet, no one wishes to defy the gods, most terrible and most gentle to mankind.

"So I, sir—I propose to make you a machine that shall determine the gods' will. An oracle engine.

"This oracle will not be some drunken priest, singing the praises of Bacchus with slurred speech behind a screen. It will not be some idiot rubric for measuring lines on hands or scat from the temple deer of Artemis. It will be a machine into which I shall feed the stories of all past battles — strategy, tactics, sacrifices made beforehand; the disposition of the generals; the lay of the land; the tricks of wise lieutenants. The machine shall have stored within it the whole history of Greek and Roman battle, and more, for I shall endeavor to teach it the ways of men. Then, when a consul such as yourself wishes to know the future outcome of a battle or a war or even some difficult negotiation, we will arrange the question on a mosaic for the machine to examine. It will sift through a thousand treaties and ten thousand battles, and it will issue a prophecy — and this prophecy shall not be one of the fallible fairy stories of priests, but the wisdom of the gods, who view us from above, set upon the table of the earth, as clear and predictable in our motions and ranks and evolutions as ants in a line."

Crassus asked, as if it was no great matter, how much such a machine would cost.

Marcus Furius named him a price in gold for the construction of the mechanism.

"That is far too much."

Marcus Furius bowed and smiled. He said, "I did not need an oracle to predict you would say so."

"That is just the cost of building the machine," Crassus protested. "But above that, you will charge me a fee for your design."

To this, Marcus Furius replied, "I will charge you nothing on my own account until the engine is complete."

Crassus regarded the man with suspicion. "Why would you

agree to build such a machine without surety of pay?"

For a moment, we are told, Marcus Furius stared at the consul, and in that instant, it was as if the fire in that dark street of the Esquiliae still burned, reflected, in his eyes.

Then he made the semblance of a smile and replied, saying, "My motive? Nothing mercenary, sir, though it may be immodest. I wish for Rome's eternal glory and for my own renown as an inventor, a votive of Minerva. As children in the Guild of Mechanics, we heard the stories of those machinists who had come before us and were inspired by them: I speak of Prometheus, first artificer, who in the first age assembled the automaton called *man*, and set him walking on the earth, and gave him fire fallen out of heaven. I speak of clever Odysseus, who raised up the horse that, breathing coal smoke and flame, trampled Troy and kicked down the towers of Ilium. I speak of Daedalus, who built the Labyrinth of Crete and made its walls to shuffle so the Minotaur could clamp its victims with no hope of their escape; the same Daedalus, who, when this atrocity was completed, the corridors creaking open and closed along their toothed coulisses, sought to flee the isle of Crete with Icarus, his son, inventing the first flying machines so they could do so. They flapped away from that island prison, watching the Labyrinth diminish behind them, laughing at their freedom, father and son — until Daedalus flew beneath a cloud and the plates on his engine were cut off from the nourishing sunlight, dropping him with horrible precipitation into the sea; whereas Icarus, flying higher, receiving all the beams of Phoebus, stayed buoyant, reached the land, and so became the first to give the gift of flight to human men. I speak of Archimedes, who designed for his Sicilian king many engines of war, and who first drew plans (now lost, alas) for the dire Curse of Syracuse, dropped upon the city of Carthage to destroy it utterly and end the Punic Wars. There is no machine more terrible than that blight of fire, and none more sought after by our generals — for even now, a century later, Carthage is a wasteland where no crop will grow and no living thing can thrive. It is despised by the gods, a broken plain fit only for whimpering jackals with eyes that bleed and jaws that cannot close and legs that cannot carry them. There shall be no life where that upstart city stood for a hundred generations.

"Save the gods themselves, only inventors may confer such miraculous powers upon mortals. Though my arm may be weak, a lever is strong. Men of action such as you, Crassus, and your excellent son Publius — who I see before me — you still may benefit from the aid of a poor recluse like myself, a man who would be a laughingstock were I to stagger onto a field of battle carrying sword and *scutum*.

"So this I do for fame, Licinius Crassus, and for the glory of Rome. I have laid before you an opportunity to attract the notice of Jove himself and all his retinue. I can say no further — nor should I, since night has so advanced, and I must return to my study, my lamp, and my lucubrations. If you have no interest, tell me frankly, and I shall remove myself and instead present this mechanical oracle notion to Pompey — whom they call *the Great*, if I am not mistaken — or to young Julius Caesar, who shows such promise. They might, perhaps, have interest."

The next day, Crassus engaged Marcus Furius Machinator to build the first oracle engine.

Marcus Furius took a week to hire several metalworkers of the highest skill to assist him. By that time, Crassus had paid the decemvirs and the priests of Apollo sufficiently in gold that when he returned to the temple, the auguries for his future success were very happy indeed—jubilant, even. So he made arrangements for his army to depart, taking with him Marcus Furius and his smiths. Crassus sent seven legions by aquatic quadrireme to meet him in the province of Syria. He and his advisers, Marcus Furius among them, traveled by airship, sputtering across the wine-dark seas, stopping for fuel each night at Thessalonica or Pergamum or other cities where Crassus might announce himself and collect tribute. At long last, the shadows of their ships were cast over the waters and banks of the Euphrates River.

There, they met the seaborne legions, who had marched across Galatia, and together they made camp at the town of Zeugma, which stood at the border of the Parthian Empire. It looked down upon the banks of the Euphrates, and its houses, I am informed by travelers, resembled wasps' nests of mud.

Marcus Furius and his smiths set to work. They hired a forge and enlarged it, taking also for their own a warehouse nearby where the engine could be assembled.

The forge being in blast, they began work on the mechanism. First, they made a huge number of small metal grids, each divided by many lines into many squares, just as the soothsayer's floor is divided into quadrants. At each intersection of the lines, there was a peg, which could be moved either up or down and fixed in place. Each metal grid represented one battle or skirmish or negotiation, and upon each there were perhaps sixteen hundred pegs, every one of them answering one question—yes or no—about that conflict.

With painstaking labor, Marcus Furius set the pegs to answer a great host of questions, according to a written key: the pegs, in their totality, indicated the number of infantry, cavalry, and aerial *levitatii* on each side; the disposition of those troops on the battlefield; the maneuvers that followed; what sacrifices had been made by each side before the battle (cattle, goat, or fowl), and to which gods; and whether each general had been humble or proud. Then Marcus Furius scoured histories and primed the machine with tales of the past: the wars of the Greeks against the Persians; the fall of Troy; the Samnite Wars; Hannibal rumbling down out of the Alps with his battle machines, their snouts hurling artillery from the slopes above Lake Trasimenus; the guile of Fabius the Dictator; the disastrous impetuousness of the consul Varro. Marcus Furius fed the machine the histories of Polybius, Herodotus, and Thucydides. When he finished establishing the information upon each grid, he stacked it carefully atop the others.

Crassus, hearing that Marcus Furius often worked through the night, like a man haunted (indeed) by the Furies, suggested that they should hire some local youths to help with the training of the machine so it might be concluded more quickly. Crassus's demand was that the youths must live in the workshop and agree to take an oath at the altar of Minerva that they would tell no one else of the oracle engine, and that they would be entirely faithful to him alone. "A sort of order of male Vestal Virgins," said Crassus, "cut off from the world."

"I believe," said Marcus Furius, "that an order of male virgins who never see the light of day would be ideal for the operation of a computing machine such as this."

Seven youths were sought out and hired. They were clad in white robes and shoes made of soft leather from the hide of sacrificial beasts. Thus was founded the inviolable sect of the Minervan Virgins.

In these weeks while the machine was being assembled and oriented, Crassus wasted no time in securing the border of Roman territory. He did not march far into Parthian territory—waiting as he did for the oracle engine to be completed so that it might suggest to him the best tactic to pursue—but he engaged his time making small sorties to towns and cities in the region, ensuring that they pledged allegiance to Rome. None of them offered much resistance, save Zenodotium, which was quickly reduced by Crassus's legions.

These early victories might have brought Crassus pleasure, except that his son Publius arrived with news from Rome: that already Julius Caesar's victories in Gaul were being applauded as prodigious, and Pompey the Great was so beloved by the people of the capital that the Senate grew uneasy. Meanwhile, the auguries at Rome once again forecast failure for Crassus: when his expedition was discussed, horses grew restless, banners toppled, and the sacred owls would sweat.

Hearing this, Crassus made his way to the engineers' workshop and demanded that Marcus Furius tell him when his machine would be completed. He needed it to calculate certain questions. There were rumors that the king of Parthia had split the Parthian army into two and that both halves were roaming through the plains, awaiting Roman movement. Should Crassus move to attack one force or the other? Or might he slip by them both to assault the city of Ctesiphon or woo the city of Seleucia or plunder ancient Babylon?

Marcus Furius replied, "You will wish us to take more time. The more the machine has been taught, the more accurate it will be." Crassus noted with some displeasure the angry intensity of Marcus Furius's gaze. He asked whether there was anything that was not to the engineer's liking. But Marcus Furius said merely, "No. I have a name for the machine now. It is called the *stochastikon*, for it calculates fate."

Hearing of this continued delay, Crassus took aside one of the Minervan Virgins and asked the youth whether the calculations were legitimate. He demanded that the virgin pledge that the machine would operate precisely as promised.

"So long as it is given enough examples to consider," the virgin answered, "its foresight shall be astounding."

Crassus agreed to wait, even as the king of Parthia wandered north and invaded Armenia.

Now that Marcus Furius had assistants, he was determined to acquaint the oracle engine not only with the military and political history of nations but also with the character of individual men and women — for it would not be accurate unless it understood the nature of mankind itself.

And so, through the long nights, through the hot days, he began populating grids with tales taken from the comedies of Aristophanes and Plautus, the tragedies of Sophocles. He described the ancient cycles of revenge: father kills daughter, sacrificing her to the gods; mother, outraged, kills father; and the son, almost crazed with grief, kills the mother — and so the cycle goes on, murder for murder, inexhaustible. Oedipus slays his father on the road and weds his mother. Foolish King Pentheus, mocking the god Dionysus, is pulled apart, limb from limb, by his own mother, the queen, in a fit of religious ecstasy. Great men bake each other's children in pots. All of this the oracle engine learned.

The weeks went by and Crassus heard that in his army the legionnaires said, "The general waits for this machine as an excuse. He is afraid of the desert and of the Parthians, though they are nothing but ragged barbarians without the power of flight. He is no commander of men."

So once again, Crassus made his way to the workshop. His body-guards, his lictors, went before him and pounded upon the door.

"You delay too long!" Crassus said. "You wish me to fail!"

But for once, Marcus Furius's gaze was placid. He said to Crassus, "I am ready. It is finished." He smiled and offered, "Would you like to see it?" He opened the door wide and allowed Crassus and the lictors to enter. Crassus entered and viewed the machine his money had funded.

We have descriptions of that first oracle engine, which differed in many particulars from those now used by our augurs.

It was, I am given to understand, a device contained in a vast bronze vat, which was round in shape and some sixteen feet high. On one side of this vat was impressed the face of the oracle at Delphi, and through its eyes, ears, and mouth one communicated with the male vestals, who sat inside, arranging pegs on a grid to mark the contours of the supplicant's problem. Much of the machinery within the vat consisted of the library of previous grids, the records of previous battles, all of them in stacks, which shuttled back and forth on tracks in accordance with the machine's mechanical investigations, determining probabilities. Projecting above the top of the vat were wooden cranes on swivels, each balanced by a counterweight, which drew the male vestals up and down within the vat so they could make adjustments to the works. Each virgin was tied with rope to his own crane, and when the machine was in operation, they leaped about its workings like anxious sparrows.

Crassus studied the machine, and then, no less, studied Marcus Furius's face. "I wish a proof of its accuracy," he said.

Marcus Furius agreed gladly. He indicated that Crassus should approach the oracle's face and recite the circumstances of the recent skirmish at Zenodotium, near Nicephorium, and the negotiations at other cities, concealing the outcomes, as if none of those events had happened yet. This way, these inquiries might confirm the *stochastikon's* predictions. Agreeing with this plan, Crassus described each situation as it had arisen and made as if he wished to decide whether to fight, parley, or retreat.

When he had recounted the facts to the youth hidden behind the face of the machine, his request for a judgment was placed in a bracket and a lever was pulled.

The *stochastikon* began its calculations. Pins dropped and determined the position of fixed pegs, kicking into place new inquiries. Battle trays rolled along tracks and were collated into new formations. The male vestals hopped about, weightless on their lines, checking to ensure that nothing jammed.

At last, there was a final click, and several trays representing an answer were deposited for the youth sitting by the mouth to interpret.

In each case, the *stochastikon* prophesied what had actually come to pass. It predicted that at Zenodotium, Crassus would lose a hundred men but would gain the town, which was correct; and it recommended that he should lead troops to the Syrian city of Hieropolis, for he would amass great wealth by raiding the temples there — and indeed, he had spent a few days previous counting out the gold from that very visit. In every respect, the oracle engine showed complete accuracy in its recommendations.

At this, Crassus showed his clear delight. He congratulated Marcus Furius on his genius and invited the inventor to celebrate in his tent.

In the general's tent, Crassus's servants had laid out a small dinner with various meats and fruits. He and Marcus Furius reclined, and servants came forward to offer sugared dainties and Mamertine wine, while three-legged tables carved with leonine paws clanked to and fro carrying rabbit and lamb.

Crassus said, "The night has come. I believe the king of Parthia has taken half his army to the north, into Armenia, and there is only a small force remaining to menace us. I would like to confront them in the desert tomorrow." He raised a glass. "So after dinner, we shall return to your workshop and ask the oracle if I should proceed immediately — or if I should remain encamped here in Zeugma. And if the machine responds favorably, we will go out into that desert, sixty thousand men, secure in the knowledge of our victory."

Marcus Furius, surrounded by these unfamiliar luxuries, remained watchful and silent. He drank and he ate. Crassus praised him highly for his ingenuity not simply in devising the operation of the mechanism but in conceiving it. He was impressed by Marcus Furius's boldness of thought and wondered where he came by it. Did his father work as an inventor? (Marcus Furius did not reply.) Had he always been intrigued by the workings of machinery, even as a child? What drew him to consider the workings of fate? On all these questions, Marcus Furius answered not at all, or in the shortest manner possible, watching his host carefully.

On hearing that Marcus Furius claimed not to have received his gift for invention from his father, Crassus inquired who Marcus Furius's father was, and being informed in two words that the man was dead, Crassus said, "In that, you and I are alike, having lost our fathers when we were young. . . . Ah, men can scarcely judge the lessons we learn from fathers — not simply from what they say but through the example of their lives. For myself, I learned (when my father was executed) the importance of eliminating my enemies quickly. I grew wealthy destroying the men who'd applauded when my father was condemned. Revenge became my profession." A table walked to his side, and Crassus inspected the rabbit before refusing it and pushing the machine away. With much the same look he had lavished on the roasted rabbit, Crassus inspected his guest. Sharply he asked, "Why, engineer, did you bring this glorious invention to me, rather than to my rivals? They are younger. Some say their prospects are better, though I weaned them both."

There was, say some, a look of challenge in Marcus Furius's eyes as he lied, "I came to you, Consul, because I knew you were hesitating to set out on this campaign, and I wished to gain renown for the Republic."

"Then you know how very important to me it is that I achieve glory upon this field of battle and return to Rome amid triumphs and processions. You may imagine how I long for the satisfaction of cataclysm, so long as it swallows my enemies and rivals entirely."

Marcus Furius said knowingly that, yes, he could indeed imagine such a desire for cataclysm.

"Then you shall not find it surprising," said Crassus, "that it is of great importance to me that Pompey the Great and Julius Caesar can never build a machine like this themselves. You understand that I must ensure it is wholly mine to operate. No word of it can ever reach them."

Marcus Furius assented.

"Tomorrow, I hope, shall prove to both those cubs and to Rome itself that I am a commander to be reckoned with. I am eager for action. It is a tremendous night."

Full of secret glories, Marcus Furius agreed, "Tomorrow shall be a long-awaited victory for both of us."

Without pleasure, Crassus smiled. He said, "Now. You have done your work. What gift do you wish to ask of me?"

"There is nothing, Consul, that I require from you."

"Surely there is!" exclaimed his host. "You are not so wealthy that you do not need gold, I presume. That would be extraordinary, wealth such as that, for an orphan such as yourself—your family's wealth all reduced to slag."

At this, Marcus Furius started in surprise. "Consul?" he said. "What do you mean by that?"

Crassus replied, "An orphan raised by poor relations after the death of your parents in an unfortunate conflagration. Everything, as I recall, burned with them." When Marcus Furius, surprised at his knowledge, could not speak, Crassus regarded him with pity and disgust. He said to the inventor, "Did you not think, after you first presented yourself, that I wouldn't inquire into your history? I keep excellent accounts, Marcus Furius Medullinus Machinator, and when I discovered that your parents had died by fire, I made further inquiries and determined that I had been on hand and that they had refused my assistance."

"I did not know that you were aware of my parentage," admitted Marcus Furius quietly.

"I did not wish you to know until you had completed your machine."

"And now that I have completed my machine?"

"I expect you will wish to take your revenge somehow. I expect to see a plot come to fruition."

Marcus Furius looked down at the table. He asked sadly, "You have poisoned my dinner, haven't you?"

"Why would you suggest that, engineer?"

"You poisoned the rabbit."

Crassus admitted that he had. "As I said, my father's example taught me to eliminate my enemies." He beckoned the chafing dish with the rabbit. He lifted the dish from its tripod and smelled it, smiling, then put it down. Marcus Furius looked stunned and then informed his host that he could not yet feel the effects. "You will, presently," said Crassus, and excused him, if he wished to stand. Having received this permission, Marcus Furius did stand but found already there was a palsy upon him.

"Do not be too sorrowful," said Crassus. "I would have had you killed regardless of your parentage, to ensure that the machine's design remains solely with me."

Now the calculating calm that always characterized Marcus Furius failed: he looked at Crassus and began to call out curses and oaths. They rang throughout the tent. The lictors did not move to apprehend the raving engineer.

Crassus said, "I am pleased that there was time for you to train the Minervan Virgins in the operation of the machine. We shall not need you now."

Marcus Furius reached for a knife and dashed toward the table. He was restrained by the lictors, who threw him down upon the floor. He made some attempt to claw his way to the consul and do the man violence, but his body was involved in spasms now, as if a spirit tormented him. Crassus, it is said, rose and left the tent.

Marcus Furius died upon the floor, surrounded by the lictors, who made no move to help him.

Thus was the end, trivial and sudden, of he who is renowned for countless small inventions and one great one: a machine which could predict the future, but which did not warn him of his own. Some maintain that Marcus Furius knew that his doom would soon engulf him, and that, tired of life, he submitted to it and embraced it. Indeed, otherwise, we might ask: How may any of us know our end when Rome's greatest servant of prophecy met death through unexpected poison and betrayal?

Meanwhile, Crassus walked directly to the inventor's workshop, where he bade the Minervan Virgins prepare themselves for prophesy.

For half an hour, he described the military situation to the youth in the bronze tub—the heat of the desert and its lack of features behind which an army could hide, the proposed strength of the Parthian forces, the primitive state of their weaponry by all accounts. He spoke of the sacrifices he had made upon the altars at Rome and offered to make sacrifices upon the altars at Zeugma, either to Roman or to foreign gods. He asked for guidance: Should he go to battle in the desert on the morrow, and if he did, would the outcome be felicitous?

The youth applied the pegs to the grid. He arose to feed the question to the engine.

But at that moment, Crassus stopped him.

"No," said the consul. "Halt. All of you stop what you are doing. Do not submit the question yet. Cease your adjustments. I am no fool." He held up his hand. "Marcus Furius will have tampered with the mechanism. I am certain that to protect himself he inserted some irregularity in the workings of the machine, some trap to ensure that if I operated it without him, it would produce a false answer that would lead to my doom."

And so he bid them to examine the machine for the next four

hours, at which time he would return; and he informed them that if any of them had doubts as to the seriousness of this endeavor, they should know that Marcus Furius himself was not present because he lay dead, poisoned to stop up his mouth from spreading the secrets of the oracle engine too liberally.

With that, he left.

For the next four hours, Crassus circulated in the camp, spreading word that the army might set out for the desert the next day and that all should be in preparation against that possibility.

While he spoke to his troops, the youths within the bronze tub bounded and scurried up and down the mechanism, terrified, seeking sabotage.

When the fourth hour was over, Crassus returned, surrounded by his lictors and torchbearers.

He demanded of the engineers, "Have you found anything?"

One of the boys nodded. "Yes, Consul," said he.

"And what did you find?"

"Sabotage, as you predicted, your excellency. It appears Marcus Furius shoved this into the works so that one of the pins could not fall. It's lucky we found it. The prophecy calculations would have been faulty. Disastrously."

The youth held forth an object that sparkled in the torchlight: the trinket that had jammed the machine was a single silver coin, one denarius, worn as if through years of rubbing.

We cannot know when we touch an object what it has meant to another. A patina acquired when a gift has been clutched continuously for years looks, to someone else, merely like tarnish.

"That was clever of Marcus Furius. So he meant revenge," said Crassus." He examined the coin, little aware that he had held it once before. He shrugged, said, "It is my machine. So I suppose it is my coin." He dropped it in his money bag. This obstacle being removed, he said, "Now! Apply my question. *Shall we venture into the desert tomorrow? What will be the outcome of a confrontation with half the Parthian army?*"

The youths nodded, pulled on their ropes, and bounded back up over the lip of the tub. They went to work; they fixed the plate with the question in its bracket and engaged the lever.

Once again, the oracle engine performed its calculations, stacked up statistics on fear and glory and the nature of man, and pins dropped, and pegs stopped them, and plates slid, and metal fingers traced the lines of each mechanical *decumanus* and *cardo*, and abacus beads rattled, and tiles dropped into place one by one — and the *stochastikon* ground to a halt.

For a while, the boy behind the bronze face was silent, reading the results and translating them into the language of men.

And this was the oracle engine's prophecy, delivered to the consul Crassus:

"*It says yes, you should proceed and attack. If you meet the enemy in the desert tomorrow, your name and your son's name shall echo down the ages and shall always be remembered in Rome for this battle. You shall be showered with gold. By the day after tomorrow, you shall be riding on a flying machine into the Parthian capital, and that very night, you shall look down upon the king of Parthia himself, and he shall shake before you.*"

When the youth had spoken, there was silence in the room; it was the first time an oracle engine had delivered a prophecy.

The silence was of short duration, however, for Crassus was delighted. He set off immediately to order his centurions to prepare to march and engage.

Come dawn, seven legions left Zeugma and crossed the Euphrates on a bridge while Crassus watched from his quinquereme above, surrounded by his aerial *levitatii*. Often stories have been told of the ill omens that accompanied this departure: lightning flashed in the sky; the *aquila*, the eagle standard of the army, was jammed in the ground and would not come free without violence; the bridge across the Euphrates splintered from the many thousands of men who passed over it, and collapsed; the bull sacrificed to Mars in the night panicked and almost escaped the acolytes who held it. Crassus took no notice of these portents. Through a speaking trumpet, he reminded his men that the Parthians were barbarians, lacking all deep science, without the subtle weaponry of Rome, and without the gift of flight. Still, in the ranks below, the soldiers murmured against him and against the oracle engine, which had led him to ignore even the most obvious admonitions of the gods.

Across the plains the legions marched, while over them flit the shadows of the *levitatii*, seeking to spy the enemy in the distant scrub.

Shortly before noon, they discovered the army of the Parthian general Surenas, which stood as if waiting in the midst of the desert. They were in the region of a town called Carrhae. The Parthians looked to be an unimpressive force, dressed all in ragged skins and cloaks, standing at the edge of a forest.

The Romans drew up and prepared for battle, their flying machines hanging above them.

Crassus gave the order, and all the trumpets of the Roman army sounded, and the Klaxons, and they began marching forward. The bands of their armor shone in the desert sun, and their battle standards gleamed gloriously. Their flying ships began to rain down arrows on the enemy.

At this sign of violence from the Romans, General Surenas of the Parthians raised his hand and dropped it — and drums along his line gave forth great roars, and the Parthians, screaming, threw their ragged cloaks from themselves, revealing battle armor curiously wrought, scales covering both man and horse, masks of terrifying visage — and they charged. And then behind them from some clearing in the forest rose up a fleet of small machines, each manned by archers in peaked caps, which sped to encounter the Roman host.

Astonished, the Roman host hesitated while the armed cataphracts galloped toward them, raising a storm of sand, while above them, the unexpected whirring air chariots advanced.

Publius, Crassus's son, had governance of the Roman flying machines and led them on a sortie against the Parthians' devices, which shot bolts with deadly force and tremendous accuracy at the legionnaires below. Publius, we may suspect, felt sure of the outcome: the cloud coursers of his Roman *levitatii* were beautiful machines, dazzling with gilt, prowed with icons of Medusa, whereas the Parthian contraptions were made of leather and looked scarcely fit to fly.

The two aerial forces engaged, and much damage was done by each side, as archers fired flaming arrows and the Romans' Archimedean mirrors swiveled to set the enemy aflame.

After the first skirmish, the Parthian flying devices fled, straggling away from the field of battle — and Publius, ill fated, followed, filled with delight at the enemy's retreat, calling out to his *levitatii*, "Do not flag! We shall cut them down out of the air!" The cloud coursers drove on in swift pursuit.

It was at this time that the Parthians revealed their tail gunners, who are famed now across the world for their deadly and destructive accuracy. It is said they shoot bolts that only gain in speed from being shot in flight—and in this way, even a retreat is turned into an assault—which is called the Parthian shot.

The Roman flyers, shocked, saw holes bored through their hulls, looked down to find their own chests pierced, their own hands riveted to their shields with a bolt, a sunburst of blood upon the bright targe. The Parthians stalled in the air and so enveloped the Roman coursers, firing on every side. Airship after airship plummeted to the ground, kicking up great gouts of sand.

Crassus, watching through the lenses, saw his son go down. He ordered his own quinquereme to fall back and land.

The Parthian flyers now returned to the earthbound fray, without Romans in the air to impede them, and began to rain down bombs of horsehair and pitch upon the legionnaires. The cohorts tried to lock their shields together to form an armored turtle that might protect them from attack by air, but as they did so, the Parthian cataphracts assaulted them from the sides. The wind from machines and the sand from cavalry cast up a great sandstorm, and the legionnaires could not breathe and could not see which way to fight. They stumbled over their own dead, and their armored turtles split, revealing human meat inside.

The slaughter now was general. It is said that forty thousand men died there in the hot noonday sun. In the rear, Crassus and his advisers watched the destruction. The *oculus* set in the Roman eagle standard conveyed shadows and images from the front along the wire: the sand; the swordplay; the towering, armored cataphracts, breathing easily through their masks while the legionnaires gagged and collapsed below.

To his ministers, Crassus insisted, "We have not lost the day."

And then, on the lens of the *oculus*, a face heaved into view, laughing—surmounted with the wild topknot of a Parthian—and a voice sneered, in broken Latin, "Surely a general who hides behind his army is no father of brave Publius, whom we have just cut down out of the air. Surely there is no father of such a noble youth here, or he would come out and fight."

This insult being delivered, the Parthians shot two of the wire bearers, the line of boys who, strung back along the desert, held the *oculus*'s wire aloft on forked poles so it could convey its images. The wire was cut, and Crassus's lens went blank. The Parthians had seized the sacred Roman battle standard.

At this—the loss not only of his son but of the shining, golden eagle standard, the *aquila*, symbol of Rome's might upon the field—it is said that Crassus lost heart.

Plutarch records that one of the centurions, speaking of the *oculus*, said, "The line is cut," to which Crassus replied, astonished, "Yes, by the scissors of Atropos," which is to say, the Fate who clips the mortal cord and removes each of us, one by one, from the weft of all that is.

Such was his gloomy state. Crassus, defeated, ordered a retreat.

The Romans fled the field, their few remaining flying machines providing cover as the Parthians, jeering, fell back. Across the desert a few thousand Roman men scrambled, many so desperate with thirst that they fell to the sand, never to rise. It was many hours before they reached Zeugma and safety.

That night, the Parthians surrounded Zeugma's walls. Their aerial contraptions drifted over the town, ready to drop incendiary clots.

A herald, fixing a long speaking trumpet to his wind mask, called down to the tent of the Roman commander, "We shall give

you one night to mourn your son." All the legionnaires and auxil-
iaries, huddled among the debris left behind in the camp by their
dead brothers in arms, heard this called down, and the word was
among them that none of them would see the next nightfall.

Crassus wasted but little time cheering and exhorting his chief
advisers. His rage swept over him so swiftly that he could scarcely
restrain himself long enough to urge them distractedly to be
strong, before he ordered his lictors to swarm the oracle engine
and drag the Minervan Virgins before him, so they might be questioned, castrated, and slain.

When they were brought before him, they came with terrified
and humble countenances. They being thrown down on the floor,
and sharp points of *gladii* held to their throats by guards, they were
closely questioned by Crassus. They avowed that they had in no
way prejudiced the machine — and that, further, the machine
could not be prejudiced, in their view, since they had removed the
coin from its workings.

Then Crassus, who was livid with anger and torn by sorrow,
said to them, "You claim that the machine operated perfectly.
And yet twelve cohorts of men are reduced almost to nothing — a
few stragglers here in the camp, and little else. The *aquila*, sacred
standard of our nation, is in the hands of our enemy. The glory
of the republic is tarnished. If my name cleaves to this battle and
is remembered by future generations, it will be due only to the
shame of this defeat, as ruinous as those at Cannae or the Caudine
Forks. So tell me, engineers, as you grovel, in what way was this
prophecy perfection? Or do you claim the vengeful shade of murdered Furius returned to brush the metal pins askew?"

The Minervan Virgins, huddled before him, exchanged their

pallid looks and hesitated to speak; but they being urged by the points of the *gladii*, the chief among them struggled to explain himself. He delivered this speech, during which the faces of all the soldiers who stood there sank, realizing their doom: "Sirs — Consul — and Your Excellencies. If you slay us, we are dead in vain and without cause, for we performed the calculations as directed. Recall that we share your fate. We, too, shall face the Parthian sword and dart if the engine's 'Yes' should prove to have been misleading.

"We have, in the hours since we first heard of your . . . let us not say defeat, but setback . . . frantically reviewed the intelligence we gave the machine and its replies. We can find no explanation, except this, sirs . . . this.

"Marcus Furius Medullinus spent weeks telling the machine stories of battle — and weeks more telling the machine stories of tragic fate. He fed it all the tales of murder paying for murder, and generation slaying generation, and the laughter of the gods at those they have destroyed. The machine was weaned on revenge and suckled on tragic irony.

"Marcus Furius did not have to jam the machine for it to destroy you — in fact, had the coin been left in, we have discovered, the oracle engine would have malfunctioned and warned you against this confrontation. We would all have been safe. But Marcus Furius knew you would kill him. He knew you would find the coin. He knew you would remove it, seeking a clearer reading. And he knew the machine, trained in cycles of revenge, would work *itself* into its calculations as an agent of satisfying, self-fulfilling, and cat-aclysmic doom. It would play upon irony. It would figure its own prophecies and their effects into fate's equation — indeed, if it did not figure in its own role in the outcome of the battle, it would be

remiss, partially blind. It operated perfectly according to its
ing, and it arranged a fitting catastrophe.

"This engineer, Marcus Furius Medullinus, has made us all
machine and man alike — the apparatus of his vengeance."

The lictors, the advisers, the boys stretched upon the floor,
Crassus himself — they all looked about them and realized that
what the young man said was true: the machine had taken stock,
found its materials, and produced a tragedy. They all were cogs
in its dumb operation — and the desert itself was its etched
plate — the lines of legionaries in their strict formations — *hastati,*
principes, and *triarii* — were strung like abacus beads in rank, sliding
back and forth to tally some unimaginable disaster yet to come.
The workings of the engine were vast, and in days would reach,
with driveshafts and pivots, across the seas even to Rome itself.

The prophecy, almost certainly, would come true, with a disaster in every clause. All that remained was to wait for the inevitable
cheap ironies to come.

The rest of the story is well known, and it is attested both by
Plutarch and by Cassius Dio.

In the morning, the Parthian general Surenas drifted over
Zeugma in a chariot bedecked with plumes and painted eyes and
called down to the tents below that he would accept the surrender of the Roman army, offering them safe passage if they would
embrace their own defeat.

Crassus sought to make some speech to his centurions about
the unflagging Roman spirit and the need for strength and the
desire for death and glory. The soldiers, however, had heard the
story of the *stochastikon* from those guards who had listened to the
dismal revelations of the Minervan Virgins, and they did not wish

in service of the lunatic's machine. When they threatened to
up against him, Crassus relented and, with his lictors and a few
his officers, went out of the gates to parley with Surenas.

We have all heard how Crassus, on foot, met General Surenas,
who hovered in a machine; and that Surenas made much of the
fact that the Roman had debased himself by walking upon the
dusty ground. Surenas bade Crassus step into his craft, so they both
could be whisked to Ctesiphon for negotiations.

We have heard how, when Crassus went to raise himself up on
the mounting step of the flying ship, Surenas jolted forward by several inches, so Crassus stumbled. Surenas apologized elaborately;
but when Crassus stepped upon the machine again, Surenas shot
up by several inches, so that once again Crassus fell in the dirt. We
have heard how the Roman ministers drew their swords to avenge
this affront to their general. We have heard how a melee followed,
and the small Roman party was all slain, Crassus lying facedown
among them, weeping.

There is no record of whether he was killed by a Parthian or
whether, as some suggest, one of his own lictors slew him, wishing
to spare him the indignity of death on a barbarian blade. Regardless: so died one of the wealthiest men the world has ever known.

When he was found to be dead, his body was bundled into the
chariot, and Surenas and his aerial guard departed for Ctesiphon,
and indeed, by noon of that day, Crassus descended into the capital
city of Parthia, as the prophecy had foretold.

A few of the Roman army—perhaps a thousand—escaped
from Zeugma. The rest capitulated and were taken prisoner. We
do not know what happened to them, but there is one tale of interest, which relates that the king of Parthia eventually gave them as

a gift to the emperor of the Han, from far Tartary, and that their descendants live still in the East, at a place that is called Le-chien, for they were legionnaires.

As the Parthian cataphracts rounded up their prisoners, they came across a warehouse, in the gloom of which they discovered a nonsense machine: pale youths tied to cranes in a huge bronze tub with a grinning face on the side. The Parthians looked astounded, shook their heads at the infinite perversity of Romans, shut the door, and thought no more of it.

In Ctesiphon, chief city of that country, General Surenas processed down the main avenue in his chariot with the body of Crassus beside him while the people shouted his name in joyous acclamation. He made the corpse indulge in all manner of kisses and bowings to the crowd, bending the stiffening limbs in positions of coarse effeminacy. In the great square, surrounded by thousands of the citizens, the general stood by while a guardsman hacked off Crassus's head. Then, mocking the dead man for his infamous greed and avarice, they poured molten gold into his open mouth, so it burned away the lips and flowed out the throat. This mutilated head, this terrifying object, Surenas raised up before the crowd, and it is said that the cheers could be heard far across the desert. Thus was Crassus, as the prophecy related, *showered with gold*.

That night, Hyrodes, king of Parthia, flew down from Armenia, where he conducted a campaign, and there was a great feast held at the palace, and a play in celebration. The play (so says Plutarch) was *The Bacchae*, in which King Pentheus is beheaded and torn limb from limb by crazed women—a drama that had figured in the *stochastikon*'s education. This play was performed in honor of Dionysus. When the final scene of decapitation was presented, an enterprising actor called Jason danced onto the stage with no plaster head but with the head of Crassus, and acted the scene with that grisly trophy clutched by its hair in his hand.

Holding it aloft, he sang:

> *"See, citizens, what we have seized for you!*
> *Behold the quarry we hunted on the mountain!"*

Crassus's blank eyes gazed down stonily at the king of Parthia, who sat below, with his son the prince on one side and General Surenas on the other; and the king shook with laughter as his enemy's head was so abused.

Thus was the final prophecy of the oracle engine fulfilled, for indeed, King Hyrodes trembled beneath dead Crassus's gaze.

The wine flowed and there was rejoicing among all the Parthians. Sitting at this feast, General Surenas could not know that the king of Parthia, already jealous of his success, would soon have him executed. The king of Parthia could not know that his own son would try quite soon to poison him. And the prince himself could not know that his poison would fail, and that all other methods being exhausted, he should eventually have to resort to murdering his father by strangulation with his bare hands. That night, fate had not been written, or at least it was not yet calculated, and so they drank and laughed heartily while Crassus's dead eyes surveyed them. Our eyes are always blind when they view the future.

The serving women came with almonds, King Hyrodes clapped, the actor Jason pranced upon the stage, and behind him, the chorus boys, dressed as women, moving their arms in delicate dance, sang of the gods, of their generosity, and of their love for all mankind.

ABOUT THE EDITORS

KELLY LINK and **GAVIN J. GRANT** are firm believers in the do-it-yourself ethos that powers the steampunk movement. They started a zine, *Lady Churchill's Rosebud Wristlet*, in 1996, founded an independent publishing house, Small Beer Press, in 2000, and own two letterpresses (in various stages of assembly). They edited the fantasy half of *The Year's Best Fantasy and Horror* for five years, and in 2007 they published *The Best of Lady Churchill's Rosebud Wristlet*.

Kelly Link is the author of three acclaimed short-story collections, *Stranger Things Happen* (a *Salon* Book of the Year), *Magic for Beginners* (a *Time* Magazine Best Book of the Year), and a collection for young adults, *Pretty Monsters*. Her stories have appeared in the anthologies *The Faery Reel*, *The Restless Dead*, *The Starry Rift*, *The Best American Short Stories*, *Poe's Children*, *McSweeney's Mammoth Treasury of Thrilling Tales*, and *Firebirds Rising* and have won the Hugo, Nebula, Locus, Tiptree, British Science Fiction, and World Fantasy Awards. She worked for three years at a children's bookshop in North Carolina and for five years at Avenue Victor Hugo Bookshop in Boston and has always loved reading anthologies. Some of her favorites include those edited by Helen Hoke.

Originally from Scotland, Gavin J. Grant moved to the United States in 1991. He has worked in bookshops in Los Angeles and Boston and for BookSense.com. He has written for the *Los Angeles Times, Bookslut,* and *Time Out New York* and is a zine reviewer for *Xerography Debt.* His stories have been published in *Strange Horizons, The Journal of Pulse Pounding Narratives, 3:AM Magazine,* and *The Third Alternative* and have been reprinted in *Best New Fantasy* and *Year's Best Fantasy.*

Gavin J. Grant, Kelly Link, and their daughter, Ursula, live (and work on) an old farmhouse in Northampton, Massachusetts.

ABOUT THE AUTHORS

M. T. ANDERSON has written picture books for children, stories for adults, and novels for teens. His satirical science-fiction novel *Feed* was a National Book Award Finalist and winner of a *Los Angeles Times* Book Prize. The first volume of his Octavian Nothing saga won the National Book Award and a *Boston Globe–Horn Book* Award; the second volume won a Michael L. Printz Honor and a *Boston Globe–Horn Book* Honor. Two of his stories have appeared in *The Year's Best Fantasy and Horror*. About "The Oracle Engine," he says: "Almost everything in this story, believe it or not, is taken directly from real Roman history. I added Marcus Furius, the oracle engine itself, its prophecy, and, of course, a flying ship or two. Though the machine's prophecy was something I made up, the hideous fate of Crassus and his head was taken right out of Plutarch and Cassius Dio. It just goes to show you that truth is more gory than fiction."

HOLLY BLACK is the author of best-selling dark contemporary fantasy for kids and teens. Her books include *Tithe: A Modern Faerie Tale;* two related novels, *Valiant* and the *New York Times* bestseller *Ironside;* the Spiderwick Chronicles (with artist Tony DiTerlizzi); the short-story collection *The Poison Eaters and Other Stories;* and a graphic-novel series, the Good Neighbors (with artist Ted Naifeh). Holly has coedited three anthologies: *Geektastic* (with Cecil Castellucci), *Zombies vs. Unicorns* (with Justine Larbalestier), and *Welcome to Bordertown* (with Ellen Kushner). Her latest novel, *White Cat,* is the first of a new series called the Curse Workers. *Red Glove* is the second book. She and her husband, Theo, live in Amherst, Massachusetts.

LIBBA BRAY is the author of the *New York Times* best-selling Gemma Doyle trilogy and the Michael L. Printz Award–winning *Going Bovine.* She has contributed to many anthologies, including *21 Proms, The Restless Dead, Vacations from Hell,* and *Up All Night.* She lives in Brooklyn.

SHAWN CHENG is a creator of handmade, limited-edition comic books. He is a member of the Brooklyn-based comics and art collective Partyka. His work has appeared in the SPX anthology and in *The Best American Comics,* at the Fredericks & Freiser Gallery in New York City, and at the Giant Robot galleries in Los Angeles and San Francisco. Shawn lives in New York City with his wife, daughter, and two cats.

CASSANDRA CLARE is the *New York Times, Wall Street Journal,* and *USA Today* best-selling author of the YA urban fantasy series The Mortal Instruments. She is also the author of the steampunk prequel trilogy The Infernal Devices. She lives in western Massachusetts with her husband and two cats.

CORY DOCTOROW is a science-fiction author, as well as an activist, journalist, and blogger. He is coeditor of the blog Boing Boing and the author of novels such as *For the Win* and the best-selling *Little Brother.* He is the former European director of the Electronic Frontier Foundation and cofounded the UK Open Rights Group. Born in Toronto, he now lives with his family in London.

DYLAN HORROCKS is a writer, artist, and cartoonist who lives in New Zealand. Comics he's written and/or drawn include *Pickle, Atlas, Batgirl,* and *Hunter: The Age of Magic.* His graphic novel *Hicksville* has been published in several languages and won an Eisner Award. He sometimes teaches writing and drawing at various universities and art schools around New Zealand, and in 2006 he was awarded the Auckland University Literary Fellowship. For some years, he's also been running a steampunk fantasy role-playing game for a group of friends, and he is slowly writing a novel based on some of the characters and settings.

KATHLEEN JENNINGS is an illustrator and writer who lives in Brisbane, Australia. She was raised in a very do-it-yourself fashion on a cattle property in western Queensland, by an inventive father and a mother who made her own stew and bread, with the result that steampunk and fantasy have always felt more real to her than "real" fiction. "Finishing School" is inspired by Brisbane in the 1880s (there really was a steam biscuit factory) and stories of bushrangers and daring escapes and runaway bicycles.

ELIZABETH KNOX has published eight novels for adults, two for young adults, three autobiographical novellas, and a collection of essays. Her novel *The Vintner's Luck* won the Montana New Zealand Book Award and the Tasmania Pacific Region Prize and has been translated into nine languages. Her young adult duet *Dreamhunter* and *Dreamquake* earned recognition as American Library Association Best Books for Young Adults, and *Dreamquake* won a Michael L. Printz Honor. Elizabeth Knox lives in Wellington, New Zealand, with her husband and son.

KELLY LINK is the author of three short-story collections: *Stranger Things Happen*, which was a *Salon* Book of the Year; *Magic for Beginners*, named a *Time* Magazine Best Book of Year; and a collection for young adults, *Pretty Monsters*. Her stories have appeared in the anthologies *The Faery Reel*, *The Restless Dead*, *The Starry Rift*, *The Best American Short Stories*, *Poe's Children*, *McSweeney's Mammoth Treasury of Thrilling Tales*, and *Firebirds Rising* and have won the Hugo, Nebula, Locus, Tiptree, British Science Fiction Association, and World Fantasy Awards. She worked for three years at a children's bookshop in North Carolina and for five years at Avenue Victor Hugo Bookshop in Boston, and she has always loved reading anthologies. Some of her favorites include those edited by Helen Hoke.

GARTH NIX was born in Melbourne, Australia. A full-time writer since 2001, he has previously worked as a literary agent, marketing consultant, book editor, book publicist, book sales representative, bookseller, and part-time soldier in the Australian Army Reserve. His novels include the award-winning fantasies *Sabriel*, *Lirael*, and *Abhorsen* and the YA sci-fi novel *Shade's Children*. His fantasy books for children include *The Ragwitch*, the six books of the Seventh Tower sequence, and the seven books of the Keys to the Kingdom series. His books have appeared on the bestseller lists of the *New York Times*, *Publishers Weekly*, the *Guardian*, the *Sunday Times*, and the *Australian*, and his work has been translated into thirty-eight languages. He lives in a Sydney beach suburb with his wife and two children.

CHRISTOPHER ROWE's short stories have been nominees for the World Fantasy, Hugo, Nebula, Locus, Sturgeon, and Seiun (Japan) Awards and have been reprinted and translated around the world. His first novel, *Sandstorm*, was published in spring 2011. He lives and works in a century-old house in Lexington, Kentucky, which he shares with his wife, the writer Gwenda Bond.

DELIA SHERMAN writes historical/folkloric/semi-comic fairy stories with a serious twist. Her short fiction and poetry have appeared in many anthologies, most recently *The Beastly Bride, Poe,* and *Teeth.* Her adult novels are *Through a Brazen Mirror; The Porcelain Dove,* which won the Mythopoeic Fantasy Award, and (with fellow fantasist Ellen Kushner) *The Fall of the Kings.* She has coedited three anthologies, including *The Essential Bordertown* (with Terri Windling). Her novel *The Freedom Maze* and her New York Between novels, *Changeling* and *The Magic Mirror of the Mermaid Queen,* are for younger readers. She is a past member of the James Tiptree Jr. Literary Award Council, an active member of the Endicott Studio for Mythic Arts, and a founding member of the board of the Interstitial Arts Foundation. She has also taught writing at Clarion, the Odyssey Workshop in New Hampshire, the Cape Cod Writers' Workshop, and the American Book Center in Amsterdam. She lives in New York City with Ellen Kushner, travels whenever she gets the chance, and writes wherever she happens to be.

YSABEAU S. WILCE is the author of the Flora Segunda books, the second of which, *Flora's Dare,* won the Andre Norton Award. Before she was steampunk, she was just punk, and now she is considering trying on steamgoth for size.

ACKNOWLEDGMENTS

We'd like to thank Kelly's wonderful agent, Renée Zuckerbrot, and her fabulous assistant, Sarah McCarry, who saved our bacon (or in Gavin's case, facon) a number of times along the way. Deb Noyes Wayshak and everyone at Candlewick for their enthusiasm. What fun they made this! The authors, especially Holly Black and Cassandra Clare, who let us bend their ears about the book as we hashed it out in Holly's car while driving from New York to Northampton, Massachusetts. And also Cory Doctorow, Jeff VanderMeer, Liz Gorinsky, Bruce Sterling and William Gibson, Hayao Miyazaki, and all those who introduced us to the burgeoning world of steampunk!